DISCARD

Praise for the novels of

Dianne Blacklock

"*Call Waiting* is full of genuine warmth and gentle humor . . . the perfect example of utterly relaxing escapism."
—Cathy Kelly,
bestselling author of *Just Between Us*

"[A] bright American debut. Blacklock develops her likable characters in some depth while making wry observations on the difficulties inherent in any married or 'singlet' life. . . . Lively, always believable dialogue and vivid descriptions of Sydney and the surrounding countryside."
—*Publishers Weekly*

"*Wife for Hire* is a lively combination of personal growth, romance, and light humor . . . Great reading."
—Aussiereviews.com

"A funny, fresh, and fast-paced novel of love, friends, and the anguish of heartfelt self-examination . . . Imbued with an unusually appealing mix of gentleness and forthrightness, Blacklock's is one of those novels that friends will recommend to each other."
—*Booklist*

continued . . .

Almost Perfect

dianne blacklock

BERKLEY BOOKS, NEW YORK

THE BERKLEY PUBLISHING GROUP
Published by the Penguin Group
Penguin Group (USA) Inc.
375 Hudson Street, New York, New York 10014, USA
Penguin Group (Canada), 90 Eglinton Avenue East, Suite 700, Toronto, Ontario M4P 2Y3, Canada
(a division of Pearson Penguin Canada Inc.)
Penguin Books Ltd., 80 Strand, London WC2R 0RL, England
Penguin Group Ireland, 25 St. Stephen's Green, Dublin 2, Ireland (a division of Penguin Books Ltd.)
Penguin Group (Australia), 250 Camberwell Road, Camberwell, Victoria 3124, Australia
(a division of Pearson Australia Group Pty. Ltd.)
Penguin Books India Pvt. Ltd., 11 Community Centre, Panchsheel Park, New Delhi—110 017, India
Penguin Group (NZ), Cnr Airborne and Rosedale Roads, Albany, Auckland 1310, New Zealand
(a division of Pearson New Zealand Ltd.)
Penguin Books (South Africa) (Pty.) Ltd., 24 Sturdee Avenue, Rosebank, Johannesburg 2196,
South Africa

Penguin Books Ltd., Registered Offices: 80 Strand, London WC2R 0RL, England

This is a work of fiction. Names, characters, places, and incidents either are the product of the author's imagination or are used fictitiously, and any resemblance to actual persons, living or dead, business establishments, events, or locales is entirely coincidental. The publisher does not have any control over and does not assume any responsibility for author or third-party websites or their content.

PRINTING HISTORY
Berkley trade paperback edition / September 2006

Library of Congress Cataloging-in-Publication Data

Blacklock, Dianne.
    Almost perfect / Dianne Blacklock.—Berkley trade pbk. ed.
        p.   cm.
    ISBN 0-425-21162-2 (trade pbk.)
        1. Married people—Fiction.   2. Infertility—Fiction.   I. Title.

PR9619.4.B56A79   2006
823'.92—dc22

                                                                              2006042748

PRINTED IN THE UNITED STATES OF AMERICA

10 9 8 7 6 5 4 3 2 1

For Mum and Dad,
Jan and Peter Blacklock

Acknowledgments

In my last two books I thanked all my family and friends who have helped and nurtured me along the way. My deepest gratitude remains with all of you; you know who you are and I hope you know how much I appreciate you. But I want to take this opportunity to thank some people who specifically helped this time around.

First, thanks must go to my son Joel Naoum, and the lovely Jeska Allan, who always listened, offered feedback and ideas, and made me work harder at getting it right. And thanks, Joel, yet again for being my "test" reader. While I'm at it, I want to thank all my gorgeous sons, Dane, Patrick, and Zachary, as well as Joel, for coping with a very preoccupied mother.

Thanks always to my publishing family in Australia, Pan Macmillan, for their tremendous, ongoing support.

I'm particularly pleased to have the opportunity to thank my astonishingly dedicated and attentive agent, Faye Bender. Despite being half a world away, she somehow manages to make me feel that she's always close at hand. I really lucked out.

A very special mention must go to my editor, Leona Nevler, who sadly passed away before this book made it onto the shelves. But it would not be here without her; she shaped and styled it with consummate care and a diligent attention to detail. From all reports, the publishing world has lost a legend, and I'm so sorry that I never got the chance to thank her.

I'd like also to thank Leona's assistant, Tova Sacks, and editor Kate Seaver for taking over and seeing *Almost Perfect* through to publication.

Georgie

"You did it again, didn't you?"

Louise was perched on a stool at the counter checking invoices when Georgie skulked out of the Tuesday morning book club meeting.

"I just don't know why they always have to choose something so dull and worthy to read," Georgie said, walking around the counter. "It's like a study group in there."

"Well, it is a book club," Louise reminded her. "They need a little meat to chew on."

"Oh, sure, but a book should be readable at least, it is written to be read, after all," said Georgie. "I don't want to have to struggle through it, to feel like my high school English teacher is standing over my shoulder, waiting for a fifteen-hundred-word essay on the major themes. I want to be entertained. I want to care about the characters, to like them, to feel like I know them, that they might be someone in my family or one of my friends. And I don't want to be able to put the book down." Georgie leaned against the coffee machine, a dreamy look in her eyes. "I want to enter into its world and get lost in it, like Alice in Wonderland or somebody. And I want to be sad when I finish it, like I've had to leave a very special place."

"Earth to Alice," Louise said, getting her attention. "Like I keep telling you, not everyone has the same taste as you, Georgie. Our customers are allowed to read whatever they please. And as they buy the books from us and rent the room from us, I think they're entitled to do so in peace. Agreed?"

"Agreed."

"With a cup of coffee, if so ordered."

"Okay, okay," said Georgie, reaching for the stack of cups.

The two women had been business partners for more than a decade, sisters-in-law for even longer, and friends forever. They'd opened the bookshop out of sheer bravado, or plain ignorance, depending on which way you looked at it. *Hey, we like books, we read books, wouldn't it be fun to own a bookshop!* And with a surname like Reading, they felt it was almost their destiny. Besides they knew they could do something really cute with the name of the shop.

The first years were so lean they were almost anorexic, but Louise had an entrepreneurial spirit and decided they had to offer something the big chains didn't. Dee Why was deemed to be the perfect place: Close to where they lived and crammed with apartment buildings, it was one of the most densely populated suburbs in the Sydney metropolitan area and therefore provided a huge potential customer base. There was no bookstore in Dee Why and, as far as Georgie and Louise were concerned, no soul. They found a voluminous old shop for lease that hadn't had a revamp since it was built sometime during the suburban retail boom of the sixties. It had variously been a frock shop, a haberdashery, a caneware emporium, and finally a reconditioned white-goods outlet that went out of business because their prices really were *The Cheapest on the Northern Beaches!* But the building was too big and impersonal, the place looked sad and empty and, worst of all, uninviting.

And so Georgie's brother, Nick, was roped in to refurbish the shop. By happy coincidence Nick was also Louise's husband, as well as an architecture dropout turned enthusiastic amateur carpenter, as evidenced by the building site they called home. Little more than a quarter of the floor space of the shop was cordoned off and Georgie kept the business a barely going concern, while Nick built a new office, an enclosed meeting space for book groups, an enormous toddlers' playpen, a preschoolers' story cave, a reading loft for older children, and the centerpiece—literally—a sweeping, curved counter, painstakingly and somewhat obsessively handcrafted by Nick out of recycled timbers from an old wharf. It functioned as sales desk around one side, and café on the other, where coffee, cakes and pastries were served daily. Georgie and Louise added an "s" to the original name and The Reading Rooms reopened to a boosted clientele. A café in a bookshop was still something of a novelty then and the child-friendly attractions kept the shop busy through the normally quiet midweek. If people weren't buying books, at least they were buying coffee, and if they didn't come for coffee, they came for the storytelling sessions, or the guest authors, or the special theme days. And then, more often than not, they bought books. These days there was even a waiting list for book groups wanting to hire the meeting room.

Georgie yawned loudly. "I'm so tired."

"What did you get up to last night?"

"Trace had a few people round."

"Not again." Louise frowned. "How many's a few? More than six?"

"I didn't do a head count." Georgie shrugged, loading the espresso machine.

"More than ten?" Louise persisted.

Georgie nodded, trying unsuccessfully to stifle another yawn.

"More than twenty?"

Georgie crouched down, ostensibly to get milk from the fridge under the counter, but mostly to avoid eye contact with Louise. "Probably."

"God, she's having parties on a Monday night now?"

"Crazy, isn't it?" Georgie agreed, standing up again. "The only night there's anything worth watching on the telly and she has a party. I mean, everyone knows Monday's a three-VCR night."

"You have to do something about her, Georgie. This is what happens when you pick up strays."

She was about to say that it wasn't very kind to call Tracey a stray, but unfortunately there was a fair element of truth in it. Tracey had shown up at the shop one day asking for a job, barefoot, dressed in a sarong and a bikini top, with hair that looked as though it hadn't seen a brush or a comb in a week. Louise told Tracey they had no positions available, despite the Help Wanted notice on the front window. It was old and out-of-date, Louise had explained, they could not afford to take on extra staff at this time, she went on, all the while standing on Georgie's foot to stop her from blurting out the truth. But Tracey was not easily put off; what she lacked in presentation, she made up for in persistence. She pitched a rather flimsy "woe is me" story at them and Georgie raced forward eagerly to catch it, like some desperate single woman at a wedding as the bride tosses the bouquet. Georgie exclaimed that the thought had crossed her mind *that very morning* that it might be fun to have a flatmate. It was clearly fate! Louise had promptly dragged her into the office and pointed out that they hardly knew this girl, but what little information they did have suggested she would be a highly unsuitable flatmate as she did not meet even the most basic criteria; to wit, an ability to pay a share of the rent. Georgie's response was one of hapless resignation—there was nothing she could do about it now; she'd already asked. And it was better than advertising in the paper, where she might end up with an axe murderer, or worse. Louise had tried to use logic to dissuade her, but logic never really worked with Georgie. In the end Tracey's parents, who were obviously as keen for Tracey to move out as she was, paid her first two months' rent in advance, deposited her stuff at Georgie's the same weekend, and rather expeditiously moved to Queensland.

"Georgie, she's using you, and she'll go on using you as long as you let her," Louise persisted.

"It'll be okay," Georgie assured her as she jiggled a pitcher of milk under the steam nozzle. "She's got another interview this week, and she promised after that . . ."

But Louise wasn't listening anymore. She had chosen instead to bang her head repeatedly on the countertop.

The problem lay in the fact that Georgie had a naïve belief in the goodness of her fellow man. Because she was pathologically honest herself, she trusted everyone else at face value. This meant that she went through her life with a great big sign on her forehead that read SUCKER. Tracey was not the first stray she'd ever picked up. That habit had started when she was just a little girl and she used to bring dogs and cats home on a regular basis. Her mother discovered eventually that most of them were not strays at all, and Georgie was forbidden to bring any more animals home.

So she moved on to people. She made friends with anyone and everyone. Talked to people on buses and trains, and, yes, had been known to bring home the odd—very odd—desperate soul, who had once again cast a line into Lake Gullible and reeled Georgie in. Her father had finally put

.his foot down when he'd found a couple of homeless men camped out in their garage. No one faulted her sense of compassion, she just had to find more appropriate, and less perilous ways to express it.

So she went to work for the RSPCA during school holidays, but she couldn't bear that animals had to be put down, and as her parents did not want to turn their home into an animal shelter, she had to leave that job. Then she volunteered in the children's ward of a hospital and was so sad she cried herself to sleep every night. Clearly Georgie was overwhelmed by the plight of others up close and personal. So she took an after-school job as a waitress and never felt happier. The customers adored her. Soon she had her regulars who came in knowing they'd always get a smile from Georgie, that she would never forget how they took their coffee, that she would keep aside the type of muffin they liked or the last piece of their favorite cake.

Georgie started to dream of having her own café one day. It was not an ambitious dream, but it was a vexing one. Nick was already at university and her sister, Suzanne, was certain to be named valedictorian at school, which meant, as everyone kept saying, "Zan will be able to do anything she wants." With a successful architect as a father and two brainiacs for siblings, running a café might be considered a little ordinary. By the same token, Georgie had a suspicion that, as the youngest, not much was expected of her. In fact, she even wondered if her family would think that running a café was beyond her rather meager abilities. Not Georgie's mother, of course. She had a fervent, even myopic belief in the potential of all her children, regardless of any evidence that may have suggested otherwise.

Gillian Reading was a vibrant, quixotic, roller-coaster ride of a woman who approached motherhood like she did everything else in her life, paying as little heed to convention as she could possibly get away with. Growing up, Georgie had vivid memories of being hurried outside whenever it rained so they could cleanse their auras, at least until the three of them came down with the flu after a particularly bad storm in the middle of winter when Gillian had pulled the door shut and locked them all out accidentally. And then there were the picnics on a bluff overlooking the ocean at midnight on the full moon, including the time Nick went missing and they couldn't find him in the dark and they had to call the police, who had to call in the rescue squad, which was all pretty exciting when Nick retold it to friends as they signed his plaster cast. And then there were Gillian's "projects." Like when they spent the afternoon painting a mural on the living room wall to surprise Dad, unfortunately ruining the carpet in the process. Their father had certainly been surprised, but the most negative reaction Georgie had ever witnessed from him was a shake of the head accompanied by a resigned sigh.

Malcolm Reading had been an architect of some note. *Architectural Digest* had referred to him as "this decade's most innovative practitioner," but you'd never have guessed it looking at him. He was a tall, handsome man, but understated, even reserved. Gillian and Malcolm were like yin and yang, the perfect balance to each other. Their whole family was perfect. It was not like anyone else's family that Georgie was aware of, but it was perfectly suited to them.

That was until her sixteenth year, when her father ruined everything. When her wonderful, loving, extraordinary family disintegrated before her eyes. A year that ended with Georgie and Zan and Nick burying both of their parents on the same day.

"Oh, while I think of it," Louise said, watching Georgie arrange the cups onto a tray. "Nick wanted to know if you have any special requests for Thursday night."

"Thursday night?" Georgie frowned.

"Your thirty-third birthday, in case you'd forgotten."

"I'm not going to be thirty-three."

"Oh, yes you are, you were born the same year as me, chook. I should know."

"No, I mean, I'm just not going to *be* thirty-three this year."

Louise looked up. "What are you talking about?"

"Jesus died when he was thirty-three," Georgie explained matter-of-factly. "It's bad feng shui."

"Feng shui has to do with houses and furniture and stuff."

"Oh, you know what I mean."

"Hardly ever." Louise sighed. "Do you still want a birthday dinner?"

"Of course." Georgie lifted the tray and headed for the meeting room.

"Presents? Cake?"

She turned around. "Duh."

Mac

The lift doors opened and Mac strode confidently down the corridor leading to his office. His eleven o'clock meeting had gone exactly to plan. He'd raised the points he considered essential, the client had agreed to the concessions, decisions were made, goals were achieved. This was how he preferred to operate. He was not so much the problem solver, running around putting out fires. He'd rather assess all possible outcomes and risks, plot his approach with meticulous attention to detail and then stick to it rigidly. And he had an almost perfect strike rate. He felt a sense of power here at work that was deeply reassuring.

He had made it, and that was no mean feat considering where he'd come from. In the normal course of events Mac would never have even stepped foot inside a university. He could vividly remember overhearing his father talking to his cronies on more than one occasion. . . . *The boy needs a trade. Toughen him up. Get him out earning a living and paying board.* But Mac had had other ideas.

He was the eldest of nine children from a working-class Catholic family who, despite being many generations Australian, still clung to their distant Irish heritage. In particular, his father diligently applied himself to the role of Irish Catholic alcoholic head of the household. But, unfortunately, he had never been a happy, ditty-singing Irish drunk, though he curbed his violent temper and kept to verbal abuse once a couple of his sons had grown taller than him. Mac's mother had all but sacrificed herself for her family. Moira MacMullen was a wonderful woman who loved all of her children, and it was no secret that she idolized her firstborn.

Mac was intensely aware of this. He had always been made to feel special, a cut above the rest of his siblings. He watched his mother, knee-deep in babies, unable to give him the attention he had been led to believe he deserved. Still only a child, he had a keen understanding of their impoverished circumstances and of the path his life would probably take unless he did something about it. With his mother's help, he applied for scholarships to elite Catholic schools and was successful. He took on two runs as a paperboy to pay for his uniform when his father threatened not to let him go, given all the extra costs involved despite the "so-called scholarship." Mac continued to work through high school in a series of menial part-time jobs, pushing pamphlets into letterboxes, washing dishes at the local Chinese takeaway or pumping petrol at the service station. He didn't care, as long as it provided him with money and an excuse to be out of the house. At university he worked up to three jobs at a time, but his fellow students had no idea. By then he was living on his own, and he allowed people to believe his family was on the land. He never actually lied. He just found creative ways of getting around the truth. He always had the books and equipment he needed, and he always dressed well. His greatest moment was when someone suggested he'd been born with a silver spoon in his mouth. And when he met Anna.

Stella jumped to her feet when Mac arrived in the outer office. Bright, outspoken and from a big, loud Italian family, she had been Mac's assistant since he'd moved from the Melbourne office to Sydney and he'd taken her with him as he scaled the ranks to director. She had exceptional organizational skills and she was highly intuitive: She knew what Mac needed before he did, when to hold his calls, what he had to take to a meeting. He'd be lost without her, though he never let her know that. He didn't need to, she was quite well aware of it herself.

"Any calls?" Mac asked automatically as Stella followed him into his office. She hesitated, watching while he walked around the desk and set his briefcase down, flicking the catches open. He looked up at her expectantly.

She swallowed. "Anna."

Mac frowned, tapping the lid of his briefcase, looking away. "How did she sound?"

"She was crying."

Stella saw his shoulders drop as he breathed out heavily. He reached for the phone and she stepped noiselessly from the room, closing the door behind her.

Mac listened to the buzz in the earpiece as the phone rang, pictured in his mind where Anna would take the call, steeled himself. She was probably in bed. She'd have kicked off her shoes, perhaps let her jacket drop to the floor.

"Hello." Anna's voice, barely.

"Hi, it's me."

He heard the shallow gasp as she let go of whatever composure she had mustered to answer the phone. "Mac . . ."

"What happened?"

"It's negative."

He wasn't surprised. It had never been any different. Except for that one time—when was it? Probably three years ago now—their first and only positive result, prefaced however by a po-faced warning that her hormone levels were really not high enough to sustain a pregnancy. Eight days later that prediction was fulfilled, taunting them. *Fooled you! Made you dream, made you hope!*

"We have to try again, straightaway," Anna was saying.

"Didn't the doctor mention taking a break?"

"Only if we wanted to, and I don't want a break, I want to keep going . . ." Her voice was strangled by a sob.

"But, Anna, you know that was the last of the frozen embryos. That means you'll have to start a full drug cycle." The whole fucking nightmare all over again. "You need to give your body a rest."

"But Mac—"

"We'll talk about it when I get home."

"When will that be?"

"As soon as I can get away, Anna."

"Promise?"

"I promise."

Stella let an hour pass. Mac had not buzzed her, had not reappeared. The phone call to Anna had lasted only a minute and he hadn't made another, not on the main office line anyway. It was time. She knocked lightly on his door, opening it and stepping inside without waiting for a response. Mac was sitting low in his chair, turned sideways toward the window, staring out.

Stella cleared her throat. "I canceled your two o'clock, and I let Bob know you won't make the directors' meeting." She paused. "You can go home."

Mac swiveled around slowly in his chair and looked squarely at Stella. "Maybe I'd rather keep my two o'clock and go to the directors' meeting."

"Go home, Mac. And buy her something nice on the way."

Liam

"Everyone in the whole world is having sex except for me," Georgie announced, strutting into the office.

"What, right now?" said Louise.

"It wouldn't surprise me," she grumbled, plonking herself on a chair.

"Are you having sex right now, Adam?" Louise asked as he appeared in the doorway.

He looked momentarily confused, glancing furtively around himself until he realized they were having another one of their inexplicable conversations. It was best to give straightforward answers that could not be misconstrued.

"No, I'm not having sex right now," Adam stated categorically. "Though I would like it noted for the record that I am open to all reasonable offers—"

Simultaneously Georgie and Louise picked up the nearest object and threw it at him. A roll of masking tape and a box of tissues hit the doorjamb but Adam had already ducked away. He'd forgotten what he had gone in there for, and he didn't want to hang around and be drawn into their strange little clique.

Over the years, Louise and Georgie had assembled a cohort of trusty shop assistants, mostly students who were willing to work weekends and the odd shift through the week. But eventually they had needed another full-time staff member, particularly after Louise got pregnant with Molly. Enter Adam Bevan, shop assistant extraordinaire-cum-computer whiz, and also coffee-machine, photocopier, fax and just-about-everything-else whiz. Adam was indispensable, which was a relief considering the basis on which Georgie and Louise had hired him. He was no more qualified than the four women they had interviewed for the position; in fact he had virtually no relevant sales experience, but he did have a degree in contemporary literature and the most gorgeous azure blue eyes, a devastating smile and impressive biceps straining through the shirt he had worn on the day of the interview. And a cute bum. Georgie and Louise figured they had a right to hire him for those reasons alone. Men did it all the time. Why shouldn't they have some eye candy at the workplace as well? There had to be some perks to owning a business. It was all very innocent; Louise was married and Adam was too young for either of them anyway—he'd barely graduated when they first hired him. He was just nice to look at. Fortunately he turned out to be the consummate employee and they could keep their sordid secret to themselves.

"So, clearly, Georgie, not everyone in the world is having sex right now," Louise resumed. "There's a couple of people out in the shop who appear to be keeping their hands to themselves. And," she continued, getting up from her desk and peering out to the street, "there are more people going past, some in cars, I don't see how they could be having sex—"

"Alright," Georgie relented, "not everybody is having sex. It just seems like it."

"Did you finish the romance section?"

"I did. It's been emptied, dusted, culled, sorted, repacked and restocked."

"Well, there's your problem," said Louise drily. "You've been absorbing the stuff through osmosis. I bet you got to reading the covers, didn't you?"

Georgie shrugged despondently.

"Speaking of sex . . ." Louise murmured, gazing out into the shop.

"What? Who's there?" Georgie stood and came to lean against the doorjamb, peering out. She spotted him straightaway. Not bad looking at all, nice height, great haircut, snappy suit.

"Mm, cute. But he's not single," Georgie decided.

"What makes you say that?"

"His shirt's too white."

"Good point," said Louise dubiously.

"He could be gay."

"He could be divorced."

"He could be a gay divorcé!" Georgie quipped.

Louise winced, shaking her head.

"Anyway," Georgie continued. "He doesn't have that wounded divorced look."

"No, he just has that 'does anybody even work in this place' look," Louise said pointedly.

"Okay, okay, I'm going." Georgie walked out and along the row of shelves parallel to where the man was standing. "I bet I know what you're after," she said.

He looked startled as he lifted his gaze to meet hers. "Pardon?"

"You're after a book. Am I right?"

She noticed a smile flicker across his eyes. Blue-grey eyes. Matched his tie.

"Well, this is a bookshop. . . ." he was saying.

"Hmm, I bet someone has to get up early in the morning to fool you."

He was staring at her in a strange way. Not that Georgie wasn't used to that, being stared at. In a strange way. Usually people were checking out the color of the streaks in her hair, or the fact that quite often her earrings didn't match, or for that matter, the rest of her outfit. Everyone assumed Georgie was arty like her mother and Nick, but that wasn't it at all. Long before she first dragged on a pair of floral shorts over purple tights and topped it all off with a striped pajama shirt, her mother's philosophy had been that children should be allowed to make their own choices, especially about what to wear. Which was all well and good if one was born with a modicum of taste, some sense of color, some kind of aesthetic. Sadly Georgie was not. Gillian insisted she always looked gorgeous, but she didn't, she looked as though she'd been dressed by a blind person. She tried to copy Zan for a while, but she couldn't carry off the classy, pared-down look her older sister achieved so effortlessly, aided in no small way by the fact that she was tall and statuesque, with sleek, dark hair that did exactly as it was told. She and Nick could have been clones of their father, while Georgie was smaller, not short, but finer, skinny as a kid. Everyone said she was just like Gillian, but Georgie knew she was nowhere near as beautiful as her mother. It was just the hair. Gillian had a glorious mane of tumbling russet curls which had somehow genetically mutated one generation down into the frizzy mess Georgie inherited. Oh, sure, subtle, coppery streaks could occasionally be detected in a certain light, but in most lights her hair was dilute brown. Until she discovered hair dye.

"So, are you looking for something for yourself, or for a gift?" Georgie asked the man whose blue-grey eyes were still regarding her curiously.

"Um, a gift. For my mother."

Georgie considered him. "Birthday?"

"That's right." He nodded.

"When?"

"Oh." He cleared his throat. "Tomorrow."

"Hmm, don't put off today what you can leave till the last moment," she muttered. What were the chances of that—sharing a birthday with this guy's mother? Georgie didn't know if it was a good or a bad omen. "So that makes her a Libran?"

He shrugged. "If you say so."

She started to peruse the shelves. "Mm, that means she would favor love stories spiked with a little intrigue, murder, espionage perhaps, set around the nineteen-thirties or forties, preferably in warmer climates. She likes her heroines to be strong and willful and her heroes to be tall and somewhat mysterious." Georgie selected a book from the shelf and passed it to him.

"You can tell all that from a person's star sign?"

"No, I just made it up." Georgie grinned broadly and this time he laughed. Just a gentle chuckle really, half of a laugh if there was a way to measure such things. But it brought his face to life and made his eyes crinkle at the corners. She leaned on the shelf in front of her, watching him as he scanned the book cover. He had nice hair, nut-brown, cut quite short and painstakingly arranged to give it that ruffled, natural, unstyled look when in fact it had been styled to within an inch of its life. Georgie reckoned he'd need to have it cut every few weeks to keep it looking that perfect. She couldn't imagine him letting the hair grow over his collar, he wasn't the three-day growth type.

"So you'd recommend this?" he was asking, turning the book over in his hand.

"Mm, depends what your mother likes. What does she read?"

He scratched the back of his neck. "I don't really know."

Georgie smiled. "Maybe you should have got your wife to do this."

He looked at her. "What makes you think I'm married?"

She shrugged. "You're too well groomed to be single."

"You can't be well groomed and single?"

"Well, you can, of course. But it all comes down to laundry. You see, women separate darks and lights, it keeps whites whiter. I've never met a straight man who will separate his darks and lights willingly—he has a partner or a wife doing it for him or telling him to do it. Now, look at your shirt."

He glanced down at it.

"Positively glowing," Georgie remarked sagely.

"So that means I must be married?"

"Or gay."

"You thought I was gay?"

"No, I thought you were married."

He considered her for a moment. "It's a brand-new shirt," he said. "First time I've worn it."

"Oh."

"Kind of blows a hole in your theory, doesn't it?"

"Or it could be the exception that proves the rule," she suggested.

He leaned against the shelf, opposite her. "Do you subject all your customers to this kind of scrutiny?"

Georgie shrugged. "Only when I'm trying to suss out if they're available," she said bluntly. "Are you going to take that?"

He looked perplexed for a moment, till he glanced down at the book he was still holding. "Sure, thanks."

Georgie walked over to the register and he followed, handing her the book and his credit card. She swiped it through the machine and glanced at the card, "William?"

He seemed surprised. "How did you know my name?"

Georgie held up his credit card. "Because it says so right here."

"Oh, sure, of course."

He looked a little like he didn't recognize his own name. Great, he was using a stolen card. To buy a single book. He was a pretty poor excuse for a criminal.

"It's just that I don't really go by that name," he explained.

Uh-oh, he must use an alias. Billy the Hood, Will the Wayward . . .

"It's a family name, you know, a tradition," he explained. "But nobody calls me William."

"So what do they call you? Junior?" Georgie asked, handing him a pen to sign the receipt.

"No, not Junior." He hesitated. "My mother only ever called me Liam," he explained. "It comes from William, you know. It's the way the Irish shorten it."

"I didn't know that," said Georgie, slipping the book into a bag. "Trust the Irish to do it back to front."

The man, aka Liam, smiled and his eyes crinkled up again. He couldn't possibly be a criminal.

"So what's the name on your credit card?" he asked.

"I don't have a credit card."

"How do you get by without a credit card?"

"A lot better than I get by with one, let me tell you." She passed him the bag.

"Are you going to make me ask again?" he said.

"Hmm?"

"What name do you go by?" he persisted.

"Oh." She hesitated, fingering her necklace. It was one of those plastic ones with letters on squared-off beads strung together to spell out a name. The kind of jewelry you ended up with when you had time to fill with a precocious niece. She slipped her thumb under the necklace to hold it up as she leaned forward across the counter. Liam bent to read it, his face close to hers.

"Georgie," he said slowly, his eyes meeting hers directly. He smiled. "It's nice to meet you."

"So, married or gay?" Louise asked when Georgie wandered back out to the office.

"Neither apparently. It was a new shirt."

Louise grinned. "What do you know?"

"Shut up."

"Hey, Ad, did you see Georgie and the suit in a clinch before?" Louise asked him as he walked in the door.

"He was just checking out my necklace," insisted Georgie.

"I bet that's not all he was checking out," Adam muttered.

"And I bet he comes back before the week's over," predicted Louise.

Adam narrowed his eyes, considering. "Do you want to make it interesting? I'll stick my neck out, ten says he's back tomorrow."

Georgie rolled her eyes.

"Ooh, high roller. Nuh, I'll give him till Friday," Louise decided.

"Oh, look at that out there," said Georgie, interrupting them.

"What?"

"It's the real world. Excuse me, I have to get back to it." She walked out to the shop, removing herself from the target range.

Besides, she needed a moment. A very unsettling thing had occurred when Liam had leaned across the counter to read her name. The words *I'm going to spend the rest of my life with him* had popped into her brain, uninvited and out of nowhere. Like some giant cartoonist in the sky had drawn a bubble above her head, imposing the thought on her against her will. It was ridiculous. This was all because she'd spent the entire day in the romance section. It was probably written on one of the covers.

Charlotte knew she would spend the rest of her life in Dashiell's arms.

Lame.

Georgie took one look at the enigmatic stranger and knew she was destined to spend the rest of her life with him.

Lamer.

But try as she might to put it out of her mind, and she did try, it would not go away. Georgie had a profound respect for psychic experiences. The thought had come out of nowhere. It had to mean something.

She had been dreaming of Mr. Right since she was a little girl. He changed persona every few years but he never disappeared altogether. It had started with Ken, though that infatuation didn't last long. He was, she discovered, merely a handbag for Barbie. She went through the requisite pop-star mania as a teen, then progressed to movie stars, and movie stars were interspersed with the occasional real, flesh-and-blood man. The wedding fantasies got serious—she'd mentally sized him up for a suit, chosen her dress, flowers, cars, the venue, even invitations. But she was perennially disappointed. Real men never lived up to her expectations. Or her fantasies.

So that explained it. Mr. Liam Nice Suit Great Haircut was just the latest in a long line of fantasy dream men. She should be able to see them coming by now.

Anna

Mac pulled into the driveway and cut the engine. He sat for a minute, staring down at the bouquet of roses placed carefully across the passenger seat. Lush cream roses, their long stems wrapped in thick brown paper, tied with a raffia bow. Classy, elegant. Because that's how Anna liked things, and that's how he liked things. Stella said to get her something nice, but it always ended up being flowers. Roses usually. How could Anna still find them beautiful, find any comfort in them at all, when they were associated with so much loss?

He sighed as he climbed out of the car and walked across the lawn to the front door. It had given him an enormous sense of pride and achievement to buy this house. Sure they had sold their souls to the bank to pay for it, but they were making the mortgage payments and it was worth it to buy into Mosman. Not the eastern suburbs, they didn't appeal at all. Flashy and glitzy, all new money, very Sydney. Mosman had prestige, respect, it was like Melbourne but with harbor views. The people who lived here had grown up with privilege and they took it for granted. Now Mac was living as one of them.

He turned his key in the lock, but as the front door swung open his heart sank. The maudlin music drifting from the back of the house meant only one thing. Mac had no reason to expect Anna would be anything but sad, but there were two ways she generally coped with this kind of bad news. She would go quiet, withdrawn, take to her bed and not want to talk about it. He'd worry about her, but he had to admit it was easier to deal with than this, which had lately become her preferred mode. Getting smashed every time the procedure didn't take, and then the tears, and then being sick usually, later on. He couldn't blame her, but he didn't know if he could stand it again.

Mac followed the music out to the sunroom. On the real-estate blurb it had been referred to as a family room but it upset Anna to call it that. In her less rational moments, her hormone-driven, hysterical, defeated moments, she talked about tearing it down. *We don't need a family room, we're never going to need a family room. It's mocking me, that room.* So they called it a sunroom and pretended it was ever thus.

As he walked to the end of the hall he could see the back of her silky blond head nestled into the cushions of the sofa, a shoeless foot perched on the coffee table, and one long, slender, elegant arm stretched out across the back of the sofa. He was not surprised to see a bottle in her hand.

"Hello, hushband," she slurred, tossing her head back. "Wanna drink?" She thrust the bottle up at him and Mac took it from her, momentarily distracting her with the flowers. "Oh, they're so beautiful!" she gushed. "I have to put them in water."

She struggled to get up but Mac put his hand on her shoulder. "I'll do it." He walked into the kitchen and laid the flowers on the bench. He tried to focus on finding a vase and ignore the feeling of desolation creeping up his body, into his chest, making his breathing labored.

Anna burst through the door unsteadily, waving a cigarette in one hand. God, if she was smoking as well she was going to be sick sooner rather than later. "You took the bottle, naughty boy!" she scolded, picking it up off the bench where Mac had left it. She looked around vaguely for a few moments, frowning. "Where did I leave my glass?" she muttered, before shrugging and drinking straight from the bottle.

Mac eased it gently from her. "Anna, keep going like this and you know what's going to happen."

"I'll get pissed."

He decided not to point out that she already was. "You'll get sick," he corrected, deftly plucking the cigarette from her fingers. "Especially if you smoke."

"Oh, Mackie!" She pouted, but she didn't stop him from tossing it in the sink. Instead she looped her arms around his neck and slumped against him.

"Are you okay?"

Anna shook her head and let out a sob. She'd descended to the next level. Tears.

"Come on. Let me take you up to bed," Mac said gently.

She threw her head back to look at him. "Okay," she crooned, attempting to sound seductive. "Take me to bed." She kissed him hard on the lips. She tasted of alcohol and cigarettes and desperation. "We'll do it properly, for real, like we used to. I'll even be on top if you like."

"Let's get upstairs and we'll see."

Mac knew she would barely make it up the stairs, he was almost carrying her by the end as they staggered through the door to their bedroom and across to the bed. Anna fell back like a dead weight, closing her eyes and sighing loudly. Mac loosened his tie and removed his jacket, arranging it carefully across the back of a chair nearby. He stared down at her. She was still so beautiful, as beautiful as the day he first laid eyes on her. They'd met at one of those murder-mystery parties that were all the rage. Anna was close to completing her degree before starting an internship as a clinical psychologist. Mac had finished university and was celebrating being accepted into the graduate intake of an international firm of management consultants. It was a dream come true. And so was Anna. She was dressed as a 1920s flapper in an authentic hired costume, not the makeshift outfits the rest of them had put together. She'd taken his breath away. All in white and silver, fair and fragile, like a porcelain doll. She was perfect, and he had to have her. Not just for the night, he had much longer term ambitions. So he didn't come on to her at the party. He was polite and attentive, even charming he hoped. He didn't drink so he was one of the last men standing at the end of the night and could offer to drive Anna and her friends home. When he saw where she lived he was even more determined. It was not simply that Toorak suggested her family had money, Mac knew he could make his own money. It was the kind of money it suggested. Old money bought respect, position, a certain status. People said Australia was a class-free society. When you came from the underclass, you knew better.

So Mac did not make a pass at Anna at all that night. The next day he sent flowers to her house, the right kind, the kind that cost him what he'd make in an eight-hour shift at the pub where he was still working until he took up his graduate position. He let another day pass and then he phoned. He said he would feel honored if she would consider going out for dinner with him sometime. Whenever Anna told the story she said that his formal, old-fashioned manner was quaint, it had intrigued her and impressed her parents.

Mac rested one knee on the bed as he leaned forward and began to unbutton her blouse. Anna roused, blinking a couple of times and rubbing her eyes. She reached out and hooked her fingers around his belt, yanking him forward.

"Anna," he chided gently, resisting. "Come on, you have to get out of these clothes."

"Can we make love then?" she murmured, raising her hand to stroke his hair. "We never make love anymore."

"Of course we do," he dismissed. But, of course, they didn't. At first they did, all the time. They had to mark it off with a cross on a chart which they presented anxiously to a nurse at the clinic. And she would assess if they were doing it at the right times, according to the right pattern. Sometimes it was important to save up his sperm for a while so that it would be a good potent hit when the conditions were right. Other times they had sex as often as they could manage. But nothing worked. So then they had sex at a time prescribed by the doctor, after which Anna would go to the clinic for a postcoital examination to determine just why his sperm and her eggs weren't hitting it off. But no one could tell them. And so they moved onto "assisted reproductive techniques" and ever since Mac had had more intimate moments with a plastic cup than he'd had with his own wife.

"We're so busy trying to make a baby, we never make love," Anna said quietly. Mac looked down into her eyes and she stared steadily back up at him. Sometimes the truth reared its ugly head when they least expected it. And then it would disappear again. Mac knew Anna would remember nothing in the morning; there was no point pursuing it now.

"Come on, you have to sit up," he said, pulling her upright. He peeled the shirt off her shoulders and she obediently lifted her arms out of the sleeves. He walked across to her chest of drawers to find her a nightgown.

When he turned back Anna was standing. She had removed her bra and tossed it aside, and now she was unzipping her skirt. She stood looking at him plaintively as she let it drop to the floor. Mac didn't say anything. A moment passed, followed by another. She was breathing heavily, waiting, anticipating, her eyes almost pleading. He walked back toward her, raised the nightgown over her head and pulled it down, covering her. Then she leaned against him, burying her head into his shoulder.

"Oh, God, I think I'm going to be sick," she gasped suddenly.

Anna fled to the bathroom, making it just in time. Mac followed her, and sat on a stool beside her, rubbing her back, wiping her face between bouts. Sometimes he hated everything about IVF. The scientists who had developed it, the clinics that administered it, the hope it fostered, the pain it caused. IVF had changed their lives. They had thought they were incomplete without a baby, unhappy somehow. But Mac had never been so unhappy in his whole life. And he didn't know how they could ever make it back to where they were before.

When it was over, he helped Anna to the bed. She climbed in gingerly, turning on her side and curling up. Mac leaned down and kissed the side of her head, and she reached up to grab his arm. "Please stay with me," she said in a small, fragile voice.

"Sure." He lay on the bed behind her, on top of the covers, bringing one arm around her and she laced her fingers through his.

"I'm sorry," she whimpered. "You must be disgusted."

"Don't say that."

She was quiet for a while, and Mac sensed her breathing settling into a sleeping rhythm.

"I want to try again," she said, her voice faint but clear. "As soon as we can."

His heart froze.

"Shhh . . ." he soothed. "Go to sleep."

He remembered being surprised when Anna agreed to move to Sydney so readily. Mac had been offered an irresistible promotion, but Anna had built up a solid caseload within a reputable practice and she was unusually close to her parents, which Mac completely understood; she was their only child.

But she had jumped at the chance to leave Melbourne and had set about enthusiastically updating her résumé and researching real estate. They decided to rent an apartment in the city at first, and Anna set up interviews with a number of practices. One evening after they were settled, she sat Mac down with a drink and announced she wanted to start investigations into their infertility.

That was the first he had heard anything of their apparent infertility. He knew they hadn't been using any birth control for . . . maybe a year? But Anna had corrected him—it had been almost two years. When she first suggested going off the pill she had assured him it would take her some time to get pregnant, if she was anything like her mother. He was too involved in his work to dwell on it much and Anna hadn't mentioned it again. It had more or less sunk to the back of his mind. The reality of a baby had not taken shape yet.

But it had never been far from Anna's mind. She didn't want to think the worst, so she came up with dozens of rationalizations for why she wasn't getting pregnant. She was becoming as bad as some of her clients. Then she started to track her cycle obsessively, but even if they had sex every night at the appropriate time of the month, she still didn't conceive. She read everything she could find and began to form more educated opinions to explain why she wasn't getting pregnant. Finally Anna had to face the fact that there was a problem. She didn't want to follow it up in Melbourne because it would have been impossible to keep it from her parents and she didn't need the added pressure. When the chance to go to Sydney presented itself, she grabbed it. It would be a fresh start, a change of scenery. And Mac didn't know it, but part of her enthusiastic research had included fertility clinics.

Her announcement therefore left him understandably stunned. He was reluctant at first. It caught him by surprise, and besides, he had a niggling feeling that if Anna was doing all the right things, it must be him, which was not the easiest thing for a man to face. But Anna was relentless. She convinced him he couldn't possibly be the cause, considering he was from a family of nine children, and Anna was an only child born late in life when her mother had given up any hope of ever having a baby. Mac underwent a simple test which confirmed her theory, so she insisted that, as further investigations and treatment would all be undertaken by her, he just had to agree to let her go ahead. Mac had never been able to refuse Anna a thing, and he was beginning to understand how important this was to her.

Besides, something had started to creep up on Mac that he hadn't expected. It was the picture of his child. The son he was supposed to have. He'd never really thought about it before, it was just part of the shadowy photograph album of his life, tucked away somewhere in his subconscious. The certainty that one day there would exist in the world a child of his. Suddenly not so certain.

And now, seven years later, much less certain. Despite the drugs and the hormones and the injections and the endless procedures and charts and cycles, Anna remained without child. It was destroying their lives. And he didn't know how to stop it.

Anna walked briskly into the kitchen at 7:30 sharp, fully dressed, makeup flawless, hair perfect. She knew Mac would be there, drinking his coffee, giving the paper a cursory scan. Usually he would have left for the office by now, but not this morning. He wouldn't leave until she was up, just to make sure she did get up. There had been mornings when she had been unable to. Now that he saw her dressed and ready for work, he'd leave shortly, and then she'd be able to relax.

It was no use discussing it. They had talked and talked over the years. They had explored every emotion—sadness, anger, guilt, overwhelming disappointment, blame. They had said everything that could possibly be said. Now there was only the unspeakable left to say, and Anna didn't want to hear it.

So these days she got drunk, and Mac put her to bed. Once she'd fallen asleep, he'd get up and work most of the night, because that was how he coped. He would have showered and dressed downstairs this morning so as not to disturb her. And then he'd wait for her to appear. Which she did, calm and collected, as though nothing had happened. Leaving him no opening to utter the unspeakable.

"Morning," she said casually. She could never quite muster chirpiness, it would only seem fake. Casual was better. She walked straight to him and kissed him on the cheek, in that perfunctory husband-and-wife way, like they were a normal husband and wife greeting each other on a normal morning.

"How did you sleep?" he asked as she turned to the coffeepot, neatly avoiding eye contact.

"Fine thanks," she said, pouring a cup. She busied herself with milk and sugar, as though these steps required an enormous amount of concentration. She heard him fold the paper, rinse his cup and then he was beside her, and his lips were pressed to the side of her head. For a brief moment she relaxed against him, closing her eyes. She felt his arm circling her, his hand squeezing her shoulder.

"I love you." She heard him say.

"Love you too," she said, in that same perfunctory way, without moving, without looking up at him. It wasn't fair. He didn't deserve this. But she couldn't risk anything more.

He was leaving the kitchen now. "Bye, have a good day."

"Oh, I'll be late this evening," she said, finally looking up. He was standing in the doorway and their eyes connected and, for the first time, Anna could see the sadness. And worse, the resignation. She swallowed. "I've got supervision."

He nodded. "Okay, see you later."

And then he was gone. And he never saw the tears fill her eyes, and he never heard her sobs, or heard her say, "I'm sorry, Mac."

The Reading Rooms

Louise and Georgie were eating lunch in the office when Adam walked in and stuck his hand out across the desk in front of Louise.

"Ten bucks, thank you very much."

"Why?"

"Lover boy's back."

Georgie nearly choked on her focaccia.

"Woohoo," Louise cooed suggestively, reaching for her purse. "He's keen."

"Oh, get over yourselves, you two," said Georgie after she'd managed to swallow. "Just because he's come into the shop two days in a row doesn't mean anything. You think he's the first customer who's ever done that? Did you ever imagine he might be interested in books, seeing as this is a bookshop after all?"

Adam sighed loudly. "He came straight to the counter and asked me if Georgie was in today."

Louise laughed. "You've got a live one, Georgie, go for it."

Georgie got to her feet, straightening her skirt, though she never could tell what was straight for this particular skirt. She had found the solution to her wardrobe woes when she discovered the new-age/peasant look. It added to the perception that she was bohemian and eccentric, instead of seriously style-deficient.

Liam was standing, gazing at a poster of *Duck Egg Blue* as Georgie came up behind him. "Have you read it?"

He swung around, apparently surprised, but his features softened when he saw it was Georgie.

"I know it's being touted as the next Booker prizewinner and all," she went on. "And maybe it is 'an honest and disturbing account of a woman's descent into depression,' but who wants to read about that?"

Liam looked blankly at her. "I'm sorry, I'm not following you."

Georgie indicated the poster. "*Duck Egg Blue*. Waste of good trees if you ask me. So, what brings you back so soon?"

Liam cleared his throat. "Well . . . actually, um, I'm after another gift. For my father this time."

She suppressed a smile. "What's the occasion?"

Liam hesitated. "His birthday."

Georgie lifted an eyebrow. "So your father's birthday's a day after your mother's? That's a rather huge coincidence, isn't it?"

"I'll say."

"You didn't remember this yesterday?"

"Slipped my mind." He shook his head regretfully. "So, what do you suggest?"

She folded her arms, considering him. "I suggest you buy a cup of coffee. It'll only cost a couple of dollars and you won't have to fork out thirty bucks for a book you don't want, when all you really wanted was an excuse to see me again."

Liam stared at her incredulously. For a second she thought she'd really put her foot in it. But then his face relaxed into a sheepish smile and Georgie breathed again.

"So what'll it be?" she asked tentatively.

"White with one."

She smiled at him. "Take a seat, I'll bring it over to you."

He wandered across to what they referred to as the sitting room: an area bordered by bookshelves on three sides, with comfy armchairs and sofas and a couple of coffee tables. Georgie carried two cups over and handed one to Liam as she parked herself beside him on the sofa.

"This is a pretty impressive setup," he remarked.

"Thank you."

He shifted to face her. "So, it really is your business?"

"Half of it."

"That's right, you said you were partners with your sister . . . no, sister-in-law?"

Georgie smiled. He remembered.

"How long have you owned the business?" Liam asked.

"Going on twelve years."

"You must have been a child when you started."

"And you must have been to flattery school."

He smiled. "No, come on, it's a pretty big deal, starting a business so young. And making such a success of it."

"Well, blame that on Louise. She's the brains, I just work here."

Liam considered her. "I'm sure you're being modest."

"I'm sure I'm not," Georgie insisted. "I don't have a head for business. You ask Louise, she won't even let me in the room when there are numbers about in case I manage to screw them up somehow."

"So what are you good at?" Liam asked.

Georgie eyed him. "I'm not sure I know you well enough to answer that yet." She grinned. Then she noticed his face was going darker. God, he was blushing, or whatever you called it when a guy did that. She had to put him out of his misery.

"Making coffee," she said. "I'm good at making coffee."

Liam took a sip of his. "Yes, you are." His mobile phone started to ring and he lifted it out of his breast pocket, frowning as he looked down at the screen. He turned it off before letting it drop back into his pocket. "Sorry about that," he said.

"It's okay," she said. "Work?"

He rubbed his forehead. "You'd think I'd be able to get away for half an hour without being hounded."

"So what do you do?"

"I'm a lawyer, I specialize in taxation law." He smiled, watching her reaction. "You don't have to make a face."

"There was no face," she denied. "So what exactly does a tax lawyer do?"

"Well, in a nutshell, I advise large corporations, multinationals, on how to best minimize or offset their tax liability, particularly when they're involved in mergers, that kind of thing."

Georgie was listening intently. "Wow, so how do you sleep at night?"

Liam was just taking another sip of his coffee and he nearly coughed it up. "I beg your pardon?"

"How do you sleep at night doing a job like that? I mean, I know it's bona fide and someone has to do it, yada yada." She waved her hand dismissively. "But, you know, helping the rich get richer, get out of paying their fair share . . ."

Liam was gobsmacked. "Are you always so . . . honest?"

"I'm afraid so." She nodded. "You have a problem with honesty? Oh, I suppose you would, being a lawyer."

"Being a lawyer in fact makes me acutely aware of the truth."

"Mm. You mean like how to bend it so you're not actually lying but you're not so much telling the truth either?" Georgie jumped up. "Oh, excuse me for a tick."

She hurried over to the door of the shop as an elderly gentleman was pushing against it. Georgie grabbed the door and held it open for him.

"Hi, Mr. Petrovsky," she said in a loud voice. "How are you this afternoon?"

"All the better for seeing you, Georgiana," he replied in a heavy accent.

"Guess what arrived this morning," Georgie said, her eyes wide. "Adam, can you bring Mr. Petrovsky's special order please? It's on Louise's desk."

Adam waved, heading for the office.

"You sit down," she said, pulling out a chair from a table in front of the window, "and I'll bring your espresso and your bran muffin."

"Thank you, Georgiana."

When Georgie turned around Liam was waiting at the counter. Her heart sank.

"I'll let you get back to your work," he said as she approached. "What do I owe you for the coffee?"

Georgie walked around behind the counter. "It's on the house."

He went to protest but she held up her hand. "It's a cup of coffee, Liam, it's hardly going to break us."

Adam crossed the room holding up a small hardcover book. "Here it is."

"I discovered you can order Russian language editions of a lot of books," Georgie explained to Liam. "It gives Mr. Petrovsky such a thrill to read Dostoyevsky and Solzhenitsyn in his native language."

Liam was intrigued. "Do you treat all your regular customers so well?"

"Come again and you'll find out."

He looked a little embarrassed. "Well, thanks for the coffee."

Georgie smiled weakly as he made his way to the door, then began loading the espresso machine to make Mr. Petrovsky's coffee. She put his muffin on a plate and took it over to him.

"Who was the young man?" he asked. "Not a new boyfriend?"

"I doubt it, Mr. Petrovsky." She sighed. "I doubt it very much."

North Side Counseling and Psychotherapy Clinic

Anna accepted that she was perhaps not in the best state of mind to deal with clients, but Magda was the last person she felt like seeing today. Then again, she was the last person Anna would be seeing today, so at least there was an upside.

"*Duck Egg Blue* has spoken to me like nothing else before," Magda confided, leaning forward in her chair. "You just have to read it, it will change your life."

Anna sighed inwardly. She had feared this was exactly what would happen when Magda had announced she was joining a book club. They had been through this before when she was still obsessed with films. *American Beauty* had changed her life. *Life Is Beautiful* had changed her life. *Moulin Rouge* had changed her life. At that point Anna had started to become a little concerned. But when she claimed that *Miss Congeniality* had changed her life, Anna had to insist they didn't discuss movies anymore. Then Magda had begun to obsess about a very complicated and at times rather far-fetched relationship between two people called Ross and Rachel, and it had taken Anna ages to work out that Ross and Rachel were apparently characters in an American sitcom.

Now, clearly, it was going to be books.

"The yogurt metaphor was what really got me," Magda continued. "I mean, how did she come up with the idea that life is like a fridge full of tubs of yogurt? You see, we think we have choices, but it's all so bland, so much the same. And yogurt itself, well, it's good for us, but not very tasty really, eh? We usually add something to it, or buy the flavored kind. But in the book, it's all *plain* yogurt."

Anna took a deep breath and cleared her throat. "It's wonderful to find something that speaks to you in such a profound way, and we should be open and alert to all the signs life sends us," she said on automatic pilot. "So how do you think this relates to your own life at present, Magda?"

"And what was her response?" Doug asked, clearly amused by another installment of the whimsical Magda chronicles.

"Oh, that just sent her off into a lengthy spiel about the themes in the book. I'm sure she was repeating verbatim what was said at her book club."

"Have you read *Duck Egg Blue*?"

Anna shook her head, taking a sip of her coffee.

"I wouldn't bother," Doug advised. "It's a piece of pretentious twaddle. All the reviewers are breathlessly trying to outdo each other heaping praise on it, but I think it's a case of the emperor's new book jacket." He shifted in his chair, signaling a shift in the conversation as well. Anna had learned to read Doug's body language over the years. He was the reason she had never considered leaving the practice. He and Carl had started the clinic, but Carl had always divided his time between clients and teaching. Doug was the soul of the place.

"So, how are you?" he asked eventually. People said those three words all the time, but when Doug said them he expected nothing less than a meaningful answer in return.

"Okay." Why did she even bother?

"Let's try that again," he persisted gently.

Anna sighed. "Not so good." She put her cup on the coffee table between them and brought her feet up underneath her. Supervision provided the opportunity to debrief with a more senior practitioner. Therapy was monitored, approaches discussed and treatment assessed. But it was also in itself a kind of counseling session. "I'm sure you've worked out that I failed again."

"Are you saying it was another failed cycle?"

Anna looked up at the ceiling. "Okay, it's not my failure."

"You don't believe that though, do you?"

She shook her head. "Of course not. The evidence is stacked against me, Doug. Despite a husband with an impressive sperm count, a truck-load of drugs, I can't remember how many laparoscopies, six intrauterine inseminations, seven drug cycles, nine frozen ones, and a partridge in a pear tree, I'm still not pregnant. Clearly, I'm not meant to have a baby."

Doug paused. "So what are you going to do?"

"What do you mean?"

"I'm wondering what your next step will be, now you've come to the conclusion you're not meant to have a baby. I assume you'll cease treatment?"

Anna frowned. "I haven't decided that for sure."

"Then you're not sure you're not meant to have a baby?"

"Oh, I'm sure about that."

"So why continue with the treatment?"

"Don't double-talk me like that!" Anna said, exasperated. "I'm not one of your clients."

Doug didn't say anything, so Anna had to.

"Okay, no decision has been made about anything."

"Including the decision you're not meant to have a baby?"

"Including that."

"How is Mac feeling about everything these days?" he said after a while.

Anna bit her lip. "I don't know." She took a breath. "I don't think he wants to keep going with the treatment." Hearing it out loud was excruciating.

"Did he tell you that?"

She shook her head. "He didn't have to. There's just some things you know, Doug. Intuition has its place. I've known him for more than fifteen years. I can see it in his eyes. He's had enough."

"And how does that make you feel?"

She focused on a spot on the coffee table between them. When she went to speak, she found she didn't quite have a voice. She cleared her throat. "Terrified."

"Of what?" Doug persisted gently.

Anna sighed. "I don't know how to describe it. The emptiness, I guess, the finality. The complete absence of hope."

"So, while you continue with the treatment, you at least have hope?"

"That's right, exactly."

"How long do you expect that to work?"

"Pardon?"

"I can't imagine you could continue with the treatment indefinitely. There must be a point where you need to decide."

"I guess I'm not at that point yet."

"But Mac is, is that what you're saying?"

She nodded.

"So, you want to hold on to the hope, so you don't have to face the emptiness?"

Anna stared into her cup. "Yes," she said in a small voice.

"Do you feel your life is empty now, Anna?"

"No, no, of course I don't."

"And yet you don't have a baby."

"There's still hope I may in the future."

"And that makes life bearable in the present?"

She shook her head. "No . . . I don't know, I don't think my life would be unbearable. I love my work, I love Mac. It's just, for seven years, longer, there's been the idea of a baby, a family. I don't know what it would feel like without that. . . ." Anna stared across the room. "You know what worries me lately? We used to look at our own baby photos and imagine how our baby would look. Blond, blue-eyed. It sounds clichéd but it's in the genes. Anyway, lately, I can't do it. I don't have a picture of my baby in my head anymore. And I don't know what happened to it."

Nick

"Daddy, is this enough sprinkles yet?"

Nick turned around to see his daughter upturning the whole packet onto the cake. "That ought to just about do it, Molly." He sighed. "Why don't you go see what Gracie's doing?"

"She's in the sandpit," said Molly plainly. "See, she's just right there."

Gracie was indeed playing quietly, as Gracie was wont to do, in the sandpit that was clearly visible through the kitchen window. Her older sister was not so quiet, nor easy to occupy.

"Okay, well, why don't you go and practice singing 'Happy Birthday' with her, for when Auntie Georgie gets here?"

"But I already know 'Happy Birthday.' "

"Gracie doesn't. You could teach her."

Nick watched Molly thinking that one over. "Are we going to shout 'Surprise!' as well?" she asked hopefully.

"I wasn't planning to."

"Why not?"

"Well, it's not a surprise."

"Why not?"

"Because Auntie Georgie knows we're having dinner for her birthday."

"How come?"

"Because we always have dinner together on birthdays, don't we?"

Molly nodded, thinking. "Can I shout 'Surprise!' anyway?"

"If you want to."

"Will Georgie get a surprise?"

"Probably."

"Why?"

"Because she won't be expecting you to shout 'Surprise!,' will she?"

Molly seemed satisfied with that and skipped off out of the kitchen and through the back door. Nick turned his attention to the mound of sprinkles piled on top of the cake. As he glanced out the window to check on his daughters he caught sight of his reflection in the glass, and he smiled.

Nicholas Malcolm Alexander Reading had once upon a time been meant for greater things. As a boy he had displayed a talent for drawing, so it had been a foregone conclusion he would become an architect, fulfilling his ambitious but loving father's dearest wish to have his only son follow in his footsteps. Nick didn't mind. Nick never minded anything. Everyone who knew him pronounced him to be the most easygoing person they'd ever met. He had ended up with his father's patience but not his drive, and his mother's love of life without her manic tendencies.

Which was probably how he came to be househusband while his wife was out building empires. Louise tried to tell him that a suburban bookshop was not exactly an empire, but Nick wouldn't have it. She was a star as far as he was concerned, and he was happy to be the man behind the successful woman. Nick pottered around on various projects, made furniture, surfboards sometimes, worked the odd temp job. The ambition gene had bypassed him and gone straight to Zan. And that was just fine. Nick was content. No, more than content, he was pretty bloody happy. He had a smart, attractive wife whose company he actually enjoyed; he had two beautiful daughters, and he and his sisters appeared to have survived their harsh initiation into adulthood.

Nick was twenty-two and halfway through his degree when his parents were killed in the accident. So he was well and truly old enough to assume the care of Zan and Georgie, especially considering Zan was no longer a minor. She had, of course, been named valedictorian, and while she could have chosen to do anything, she had been drawn inexorably toward architecture, despite herself. Zan hadn't wanted to follow in her father's footsteps, but she was more like him than she cared to admit. She quickly assumed their mother's maiden name, however, when the lecturers began to catch on that she was the daughter of the renowned Malcolm Reading.

Nick deferred his own studies for a year. He wanted to make sure Zan got off to a good start at university and that Georgie finished school without further disruption. He stepped into the role of surrogate father with ease and had never really stepped out again, nor had he returned to university. He was probably not built for it, he claimed some years later, shrugging it off. He didn't have the discipline; he was more artisan than architect, craftsman than draftsman.

Besides, as executor of the estate and guardian of his sisters he had more important things to attend to. They had not been left wanting, but obviously their parents had planned to be around for a long time. There was substantial equity in the family home, but a substantial mortgage along with it, and no income to service it. It would not have made good financial sense to sink the life insurance payout into the house. Fortunately their uncle Jon was an invaluable help to him at the time. Although he lived in Singapore, he traveled back and forth six times in that first year or so. He'd wanted to take them all back with him at first, as their father's brother and closest next of kin. They had never known their mother's family. Gillian had run away from home at fifteen and had refused to have any contact, despite her husband's gentle urging. They didn't even know if she was alive, he'd pointed out. They wouldn't care either way, Gillian had steadfastly maintained.

Nick felt that the family should be spared any further upheaval, and Uncle Jon reluctantly agreed. It was decided they would remain in the house for the meantime to give them space to grieve and time to heal. Jon helped Nick invest the money to defray their expenses, and when a year had passed they put the family home on the market.

Nick wanted the girls to invest their share of the proceeds back into real estate and Zan needed no encouragement. She promptly bought a dingy apartment in a rundown block on the edge of the city, much to Nick's alarm. All the more when she insisted on moving in straightaway. He had hoped to keep the family together for a little longer, but Zan was going on twenty and while she loved her brother and sister, she was also doggedly independent.

Georgie had needed a little more encouragement and guidance to spend her money wisely. Nick finally persuaded her to buy a drab but solid investment flat in Dee Why, while she lived with him in the fixer-upper he had found a couple of suburbs away in Harbord. Louise was virtually living there too and when she and Nick decided to marry, Georgie gave notice to her tenants and took up residence in her own flat. Nick had felt torn at the time. Of course he and Louise needed their own space, but he hated that Georgie was on her own. He worried about her, worried that he'd miss something, that he wouldn't notice the signs. But she worked with Louise all day and spent a lot of time with them besides, so he had to trust that would be enough. He just wanted to see her settled with someone, but she hadn't had much luck in that department. He didn't know why, but what often started off hopefully seemed to go nowhere pretty fast. Nick was well aware there were some dickheads around, but sometimes he had a disquieting feeling that Georgie was hard to please, that she was waiting for someone she was never going to find.

Nick heard a car in the driveway and when he turned around Georgie was standing in the doorway, with her feral hair and her ragamuffin clothes. She didn't look much different than when she was eleven or twelve, though she didn't have purple streaks then, as he recalled.

"Hey there, Georgie girl!" he greeted her.

"Don't you ever get sick of saying that?" she said as she sauntered over to him, tossing her bag on the couch as she passed.

"You'd think so, wouldn't you?" He gave her a hug. "Happy Birthday, though I refuse to accept that my baby sister is thirty-three years old."

"So does she," said Louise, coming through the door. "Where are the girls?"

"In the sandpit."

She sighed. "Not having their baths?"

"No."

"Why not?"

"Because they're in the sandpit."

She sighed again, more loudly this time.

"Ah," said Nick, coming toward her. "The sigh of disdain, followed by the groan of contempt." He pulled her into his arms but she didn't protest. "Yes, the girls are still in the sandpit, but dinner is in the oven, the birthday cake is baked, three loads of washing have been hung out, brought in and put away, and our two small daughters, as yet unbathed in water, have, however, been bathed in the light of paternal devotion all day. I didn't even catch *The Bold and the Beautiful*." He dipped Louise back, holding her steady. "So now, don't I deserve the kiss of unconditional love and affection?"

She smiled as he bent to kiss her. Georgie watched them enviously. Well, not really enviously, Nick was her brother after all, and Louise her lifelong friend. Growing up, Louise had spent more time at their house than she had at her own. She came over even when Georgie was out. Georgie was apparently the last one to realize that Louise and Nick's fondness for one another was much more than platonic. Meantime Zan met Jules and finally understood why she'd never enjoyed dating men. She and Jules had been together ever since and were deeply committed to each other. So Zan clung to Jules, Nick clung to Louise, and Georgie clung to them all.

Not that Georgie didn't want someone for herself. She did, with a longing so powerful at times it would engulf her in a depression that had been known to last for days. She had a series of disappointing relationships behind her, though Louise often pointed out that two weeks did not a relationship make. And so Georgie found herself, at thirty-three years of age, single, living with a spoilt, unemployed good-time girl who treated her place like it was a drop-in center for her friends. Needless to say Georgie was not living the life she had thought she would be by her age. She should have had a couple of kids and a reasonable-looking, affable husband who could make her laugh and sit beside her on the lounge at night watching telly, maybe rub her feet when she'd had a long day. It didn't seem much to ask. But as each year ticked by, Georgie knew it was getting further and further out of her reach. She'd heard the line about a woman her age having more chance of getting hit by a space shuttle than getting married, or something like that, but worse, she'd read the stats. Georgie was part of an emerging generation destined to remain single and childless. She didn't know how she'd ended up in this particular demographic, and it was becoming increasingly obvious there was no way out.

Molly and Grace burst through the doorway shouting "Surprise! Happy Birthday!" slightly out of sync. Molly boomed the words out loudly and Grace, unable to keep up, echoed them a few seconds behind, in her soft, sweet little voice. It said a lot about their relationship. Physically, they were chalk and cheese as well. Molly was tall for her age with angular features, just like Nick, while Grace was all Louise, round, cherubic and cuddly. Which was fine for a little girl, Louise bemoaned, but not so much for a thirtysomething woman.

"Were you surprised, Georgie?" Molly asked.

"Absolutely!" she declared, crouching down to hug her nieces.

"Why?"

"Because I didn't know you were going to do that."

"Champagne?" Nick interrupted from the kitchen, popping a cork.

"Is the Pope Catholic?" said Zan loudly from the front door, Jules trailing her.

They were all a little intimidated by Zan. She was the high achiever of the family, no one else even came close. After graduating with first-class honors and a job offer from one of the most prestigious architectural firms in Sydney, if not Australia, she had sold the one-time dumpy flat for a tidy profit, bought a warehouse in Surry Hills and now operated her own business from the premises, Zan Underwood Designs. She and Jules had lived there until a year ago, when they moved after completing major renovations to a five-bedroom bungalow with ocean views. The house had already been featured in *Belle* and *Domain*. Zan was on the A-list, but what made her really cool was that she could not have cared less.

"Happy Birthday, Georgie," said Zan, kissing her sister on the cheek as she handed her a large, exquisitely wrapped box. Georgie just knew it would be some fabulous objet d'art or designer widget she would absolutely adore but that would stick out like a sore thumb in the cacophonous interior of her flat. Zan's beautiful, tasteful gifts just made the rest of her place look like a junk shop.

"So how was your day, George?" Zan asked, accepting a glass of champagne and a kiss on the cheek from her brother.

"She had a visit from her new boyfriend," said Louise.

"What new boyfriend?" asked Nick. "I didn't know about any new boyfriend."

"George doesn't have boyfriends," Zan scoffed. "She has illusions that never quite survive reentry into the earth's atmosphere."

"What does that mean, Daddy?" asked Molly.

"It means Auntie Zan is being smug," Nick said, placing a consoling hand on Georgie's shoulder. "Come on, tell us, who is he?"

"He's a figment of Louise's imagination this time," Georgie said firmly.

"Uh-uh, he came into the shop the second day in a row just to see Georgie."

"Yeah, well, he won't be back," Georgie assured them. "I'm pretty sure I frightened him off."

"What did you do, Georgie?" Molly was staring up at her, wide-eyed.

Georgie grinned wickedly. "I crept up behind him . . ." She flung her arms out and swooped down on Molly. "And I grabbed him and threw him into the air . . ." she cried, picking Molly up and flying her around the room. "And then I tossed him out onto the street," she finished, skittering out through the front door while Molly squealed and Grace ran behind them, giggling wildly.

"I would have liked to have seen that," Nick muttered.

Georgie looked over her shoulder to the kitchen bench and counted the number of empty wine bottles. Three, as well as the open one on the table. Jules didn't drink at all and Louise was a Cadbury's drunk, it only took a glass and a half. Zan liked a drink but she was disciplined. On a weekday, two would be her absolute limit. Dammit. That left only her and Nick, and Georgie suspected she'd had the lion's share of the rest, which was why she couldn't quite focus all the way across to the bench. She turned back to the faces around the table and discovered she was having trouble focusing on them too. Bugger, she had to work tomorrow, and it was so much harder to ring up and fake a sickie when you were the boss.

"Great dinner, Nick, as ever," said Zan, sitting back in her chair. Zan and Georgie were in awe of their brother's ability to cook because that particular talent was beyond them both. Jules did all the cooking in their household, and Ronald McDonald, Colonel Sanders and any number of talented southeast Asian chaps did the cooking for Georgie.

"Jules and I have an announcement to make," Zan said importantly.

She reached for Jules's hand and cleared her throat. "We're going to have a baby."

There was stunned silence around the table.

"Wow." Nick was the first to speak. "Ah, which one of you . . ."

"It'll be Jules," Zan said in a matter-of-fact voice, and, strangely, Georgie could feel the collective sigh of relief. "But it hasn't happened yet. We wanted to run it by you first. We realize it's a bigger deal for a same-sex couple, it'd hardly be fair to foist it upon you once we were already pregnant."

"How are you planning to go about it?" asked Louise, refilling her glass. "Will you go to a sperm bank, or, um, will it be someone you know?" She hoped no one noticed this was her second glass of wine. But the first question that had come into her head was who the father was going to be. And then her thoughts had spiraled out of control. What if they wanted to ask Nick? It was not as perverse as it first sounded. Zan wasn't intending to carry the baby and Jules wasn't related to Nick, and if they used Nick's sperm it was a way for the baby to be genetically linked to Zan, but it would be Nick's child and Louise couldn't pretend otherwise and she certainly knew Nick couldn't either and had Zan thought about that?

"We're going to a sperm bank," said Zan.

Thank God, thought Louise, gulping down half her glass. When she looked up, Nick was regarding her quizzically. She just winked at him.

"We had been thinking about approaching a couple of gay guys we know," said Jules. They all looked at her, startled. Jules didn't say much, ever, sometimes they got a shock when they heard her voice. She was a quiet, doting woman, a few years older than Zan, a fact which did not, however, make her the dominant partner. No one dominated Zan. They had met at university, where Jules was trying to find herself after a brief but stormy marriage. Instead she found Zan.

Jules glanced lovingly at her. "But we want to be the baby's parents. We don't want to have someone else involved. Using a sperm bank keeps it anonymous."

"What's a sperm bank, Mummy?" Molly asked.

"What are you doing up, young lady?" Louise demanded, twisting around in her chair. "Daddy put you to bed more than an hour ago."

Molly sidled closer to Georgie. "I was firsty."

"Did you have a drink?"

She nodded.

"Then off you go back to bed now please, Molly."

"I'll take her," said Georgie, rousing. She didn't want to hang around for the rest of the conversation anyway. She was spectacularly unqualified to proffer any opinions about making babies, artificially or otherwise.

About half an hour later Georgie heard the door open behind her as light spilled into the room. She'd lain down next to Molly, what seemed like only moments ago. She lifted her head as Nick approached.

"Were you asleep?" he whispered.

"Nearly."

"Come on," he said, helping her up. "We're all wondering where you'd got to."

They crept out of the room, closing the door behind them. Under the light in the stairwell, Nick noticed Georgie wiping her eyes with the palms of her hands.

"Hey, what's this? You can't cry on your birthday. You know what Mum used to say, 'Tears on your birthday, tears the whole year through.'"

That was supposed to console her? A sob caught in Georgie's throat and she covered her face with her hands. Nick drew her head against his shoulder, rubbing her back to soothe her. After a while he motioned for her to sit down next to him on the stairs.

"It's the baby talk, isn't it?"

She nodded. "Even my lesbian sister is going to have a baby. I don't begrudge her, really I don't, but that's how it'll look. I didn't want them to see me getting upset."

"Zan would understand."

"Zan thinks I'm a flake."

Nick put his arm around her. "No she doesn't," he chided gently.

"You heard what she said about my pathetic love life."

"Come on, that's just Zan."

"But she's right. How did I get to this age without one decent stab at the brass ring, or the gold ring or whatever it is? Am I so ugly, or unappealing or stupid—"

"That's enough," said Nick. "You've never seen an ugly married person? Or a stupid one?"

Georgie rested her chin in her hands. "Then what's wrong with me?"

He took a deep breath. "According to my reckoning there have been plenty of chances at the brass ring. But do you ever wonder if you're a little fussy sometimes?"

Georgie thought about it. "You think my standards are too high?"

"No, I don't want you to settle for second best, that's not what I mean. I just don't know whether you give guys much of a chance. It seems to be over before it gets started."

"That's not always my fault. Remember Scott? He thought we were getting too serious when I made a booking at a restaurant two weeks in advance."

Nick regarded her dubiously. "I bet for every Scott there's three others you've dumped first."

"Prove it."

"Okay." He was thoughtful for a moment. "Matt from the Surf Club, whatever happened to him after the second date?"

"That's the point, he was absolutely and entirely 'Matt from the Surf Club.' He ate, drank and breathed the Surf Club. He didn't have any other life."

"Okay, then there was Ben the book rep."

"He drank like a fish."

"David, the Reillys introduced you at their party?"

"Well, he was just boring."

Nick cleared his throat. "Your Honor, I give you Exhibit A, Exhibit B and Exhibit C."

Georgie made a face at him.

He leaned back, resting his elbows on the step behind him. "Do you ever think that maybe what happened between Mum and Dad has made you a little, I don't know, skittish?" he asked carefully.

"You think?" She arched an eyebrow.

"Okay, so I'm stating the bleeding obvious." He sighed. "It's just, nobody's perfect, Georgie, but sometimes I think that's what you're holding out for."

She looked at him. "You're perfect."

"This is what I keep telling Louise, and yet, strangely, she remains unconvinced."

They smiled at each other.

"What about this guy that came into the shop?" Nick asked.

"What about him?"

"Well, what's he like?"

Georgie saw Liam in her mind's eye. "He seems nice, but I hardly know him."

"Promise me you'll at least try to get to know him?"

"I might never see him again. Louise is blowing this way out of proportion."

Which was something Louise never did and they both knew it. Georgie wasn't fooling anyone.

"Nick," she said, "if I tell you something, do you promise not to laugh at me?"

He smiled broadly. "Well, I can't guarantee that . . ."

She crossed her arms, frowning at him.

"Sorry, sorry, go ahead. I won't laugh at you," he assured her. "Not out loud anyway."

Georgie hesitated. "Well, yesterday, when I met Liam—"

"Who's Liam?"

"The guy, from the shop."

"Didn't picture him as a Liam. I was seeing a Justin, maybe a Jason . . ."

"Anyway," Georgie continued, dragging him back, "when I was talking to Liam, this thought came to me out of nowhere, I swear." She paused, swallowing. "Well, our eyes met and without warning, the words 'I'm going to spend the rest of my life with him' popped into my head."

Nick looked like he didn't know what to say. His mouth was open but nothing was coming out.

Georgie dropped her head in her hands. "Oh shit, I know, it sounds like something from a bad Jennifer Lopez movie. . . ."

"There are good Jennifer Lopez movies?" Nick patted her gently on the back. "Come on, there may be something to it."

She frowned at him. "You don't really think that."

"Sure, why not? But the thing is, you can't just leave it at that, you know," Nick pointed out. "You have to play your part."

"What do you mean?"

"You have to give him a chance. . . ."

To break my heart into tiny little pieces and then stomp all over it with his big size-ten shoes? Where did that come from?

"More than two dates," said Nick. "Promise?"

She smiled faintly. "Okay."

He stood up and reached for her hand. "So, Liam, eh?" he said. "Okay, Liam works. I could get used to Liam."

Georgie smiled. So could she.

Northwestern IVF

*Anna sat in the same chair she had sat in countless times before, listen-*ing to the same spiel she had listened to countless times before. Actually she could count the times. She knew exactly the number of appointments she had had with Dr. Tran. She just didn't want to dwell on it.

Dr. Tran was reviewing the last cycle of treatment, from the initial retrieval of nine eggs (very satisfactory!), fertilization resulting in six viable embryos (excellent!), allowing the (successful) implantation of three embryos and the freezing of the three remaining embryos, of which two survived thawing (an elegant sufficiency!) to be implanted (again successfully) this time around in a natural cycle. Anna was sick to death of hearing the treatment objectively rated in terms of the success of the steps along the way. It had not been a successful cycle. She wasn't pregnant. No matter how many battles medical science had won along the way, it had not won the war. Surely they could only claim success when Anna was holding a baby in her arms.

"How soon can I start the next treatment, Doctor?" Anna asked when he had finished.

"You know by now that we recommend at least one month's rest. You've also been through"—he checked his notes—"two stimulated cycles and three frozen cycles almost back to back. It may be time for a slightly longer break."

"But there isn't time."

"I beg your pardon?"

"I'll be thirty-eight next year, you know how the statistics plummet after that."

"Anna, it doesn't happen overnight. Fertility diminishes over years, a few months is not going to make a significant difference either way."

Easy for him to say, with photos of two cute little boys sitting on his desk.

"Where is Mac today?" he asked.

Anna looked away. "He's working, he couldn't make it."

"You realize it is vital for your physical and emotional health," Dr. Tran continued, "that your partner remains involved and fully supportive of the treatment?"

"Mac is fully supportive," Anna declared. "He's just incredibly busy at work at the moment. In fact, he had a few questions of his own. He wanted me to ask you if it's worth trying ICSI after all?"

Of course Mac had not asked any such question, he wasn't even aware of her appointment today. Anna wanted to come alone this time, find out exactly where she stood, arm herself. She didn't need Mac here, coming up with his own questions, hearing firsthand what the doctor had to say, drawing his own conclusions.

"As you know, Anna," Dr. Tran was saying, "ICSI is the injection of the sperm directly into the egg and is only indicated when male infertility is a factor."

And they both knew it was not. The blame lay squarely with Anna.

"What about blastocyst transfer?" she persisted. "It seems to be getting higher pregnancy rates."

Dr. Tran leaned back in his chair. "The blastocyst stage occurs about five days after fertilization," he explained. "The wisdom behind transferring at this stage is that the blastocyst is a more developed embryo, sturdier if you like, and thereby has a greater chance of survival. The impressive pregnancy rate being reported is, however, from a select group of patients. In this clinic we will not consider proceeding past day two with fewer than ten fertilized eggs."

Anna knew that ruled her out. "Why is it so strict, why can't we try with fewer fertilized eggs?"

"Not as many embryos make it to the blastocyst stage in culture, so there is the risk that no embryos will survive to be transferred, and a much reduced chance of having any excess embryos frozen. That would amount to a complete drug cycle for nothing."

"Which is the story of my life," Anna said flatly. "How do we know this won't work for me?"

"Anna," he said calmly, with a hint of condescension, she was sure, "I believe with your particular set of factors, blastocyst transfer is not the solution."

Her "set of factors." Not problems, abnormalities, flaws. Anna and Mac had laughed in the past about the medical profession's penchant for euphemisms. She wasn't laughing now.

"What about assisted hatching?" Anna clutched wildly at her last straw.

Dr. Tran removed his glasses and rubbed the bridge of his nose. "You've been doing some reading. Assisted hatching is still experimental at best, and once again I don't see any applicability in your case." He sighed, replacing his glasses and leaning forward across the desk. "You are one of the most thoroughly informed patients I have treated. Perhaps I shouldn't say that. I'm constantly amazed by the amount of knowledge my patients learn and absorb. But, Anna, you're an intelligent woman, you know we have taken into consideration every available treatment, your history and all relevant factors. We'll continue to monitor your outcomes very closely and fine-tune where appropriate. But we're confident we have developed the most suitable protocol for Anna MacMullen."

Which was doctor-speak for, We're doing the best we can, so back off. But the best was clearly not enough. Anna had arrived at this point twice before and had changed clinics both times. This was arguably the best private facility in the country, but apparently even they couldn't perform miracles.

Anna left the office more despondent than when she had arrived. She had not been told she couldn't try again straightaway. Dr. Tran had recommended a break, but ultimately it was up to her. It was always up to her. She could keep on the treatment as long as she wanted, pretty much. There was nothing to stop her, except menopause, she supposed. Or pregnancy. Or Mac. Whichever came first.

She suddenly felt an urgency to see him. She didn't know why she'd been shutting him out, he was the only person who could fully share this with her. If she talked to him and poured out all her fears and hopes, he'd understand. He always did. He couldn't stand to see her upset. He always said he could never refuse her anything.

Anna sat in the car in the parking area outside the clinic and phoned Mac on her cell. It was only eleven-thirty. Plenty of time to schedule a break for lunch.

"Hi, Mac, it's me," she said brightly when he answered the phone.

"Hello, how are you?"

Was it her imagination or did he sound guarded?

"I'm okay." She hesitated. What she said next would break the embargo and open the discussion, not right now, over the phone, but it would be the green light. Anna took a deep breath. "I've just come from Dr. Tran's office."

There was a significant pause. "I didn't know you had an appointment today."

"No, I thought I'd handle it myself this time, not bother you."

Mac didn't say anything.

"Anyhow, I'm feeling a little overwhelmed. I thought we could have lunch—"

"I can't get away right now, Anna, I'm flat out." His tone was curt. Final.

"Mac, this is important."

"Well, if it was so important you should have told me about the appointment and I would have scheduled around it and gone with you."

"You know there's always a follow-up appointment," she defended herself.

"Oh, don't do that, Anna. Don't turn this around onto me."

He was being unusually belligerent, it wasn't like him. Maybe this wasn't the best time.

"Mac, don't be cross. I know I've been shutting you out lately. But I'm ready to talk now. We should talk."

"We've got the whole weekend to talk, Anna, and I've got a lot of work to get through today."

Anna sighed inwardly. "Okay, I'll see you tonight."

"Ah, yeah," he said vaguely, "but I'll probably be late. You shouldn't wait up."

The Reading Rooms

"Hello, The Reading Rooms, how can I help you today?"

"I was wondering if I could speak to Georgie, please?"

"Well, wonder no more. You're speaking to her as we speak, so to speak." Georgie laughed. She was amusing herself at least.

"Oh, hi. It's um, well, it's Liam here."

Georgie swallowed. "Hello."

Uncomfortable Pause. One of them needed to speak before it became an Awkward Silence.

"How are you?" Liam asked, just in time.

"I'm fine, you know . . . fine."

Somebody should write this sparkling banter down. Why was she having so much trouble finding something to say? It wasn't normally a struggle, but she felt tongue-tied.

"So, whose birthday is it today?" she asked finally.

Georgie heard a faint, nervous laugh. "No, no one's birthday today," he assured her. "I was, uh, well, I was just wondering if you'd like to do lunch?"

Cringe. "Well, I'm—up for *eating* lunch. Or even *having* lunch. Don't know what *doing* lunch is, it's always seemed an odd expression to me."

That's the way, Georgie, make fun of the guy! But he was asking her to lunch and that made it a date and she'd promised Nick and sarcasm was the only protection she had.

"Okay, do you have any plans for lunch today?" he persisted.

"I was going to take something down to the beach actually." Her head was still fuzzy from the night before and she wanted to blast it with a good salty nor'easter.

"Do you mind if I join you?" Liam asked.

"Really? You don't seem the beachy type."

"Don't worry about me, I'll manage. Now, where and when?"

Liam climbed out of a sleek silver car as Georgie strolled up to the parking strip at Dee Why Beach. She considered him skeptically across the roof.

"You're going to walk along the beach wearing that suit?"

"We don't actually have to go right down onto the beach, do we?" he said. "There's all that paved area, seats and tables . . ."

"Okay then, I'll wave to you from the sand."

He looked momentarily taken aback, but Georgie could see a smile in his eyes. "I'll tell you something about this suit. You see, the jacket's fully detachable," he said, taking it off and tossing it inside the car. "So's the tie." He loosened it and undid the top button of his shirt. "Also, you'll find the shoes are easily removed," he said, disappearing from view. "As well as the socks," he called out.

Georgie walked around to the other side of the car. Liam was perched on the edge of the driver's seat, rolling up the legs of his trousers. "And look, even the pants are adjustable."

"My, my, I never realized how versatile a business suit was," Georgie remarked. "You could almost live in it."

"Sometimes I feel like I do," he muttered, standing up.

"Oh, poor overworked corporate lawyer," Georgie said, heading for the stairs. "Sounds suspiciously like yuppie angst to me."

He swung the car door shut. "Thanks for the vote of sympathy."

She shrugged. "I'd feel sympathetic if you were a factory worker struggling to feed six kids. It's not as if you don't have a choice about how much you work."

"I don't, not really," he said, catching up to her.

"Why not?"

"Well, in my position there are certain expectations, obligations."

"Are you on a contract?"

"No."

"Are you being held against your will?"

"What?"

"Well, are you some kind of a prisoner? Are they blackmailing you? Are you working off embezzled funds?" Georgie stopped at the foot of the stairs.

"Okay, okay," he surrendered. "I get your point. But I still have commitments, a mortgage, a lease on the car."

"So downsize," said Georgie as they started across the sand. "Get a smaller place, a cheaper car. I bet that one you're driving's worth a bomb."

"You get what you pay for, Georgie. It is a Saab, after all."

She raised an eyebrow. "Am I supposed to be impressed?"

"I wasn't trying—"

"Because you could say it was an ocelot and I wouldn't know the difference. I'm way out of the car loop. I don't even drive."

"You don't even drive?"

Georgie shook her head, smiling at his incredulous expression.

"Why not?" he demanded.

"I never learned how."

"I've never met an adult who can't drive."

"This must be a big day for you then."

"Why haven't you ever learned?"

She shrugged. "Never really needed to. There's these things called buses, and the drivers are very accommodating. They pick me up in the same spot every day, at roughly the same time, and deposit me a mere few steps from the shop. And then they're back to pick me up again in the evening. You should try it some time. You may find you don't need the Saab and there's one 'commitment' you're rid of."

He smiled ruefully. "It's not that simple."

"Of course it is." They arrived at the water's edge. "People behave as though they're trapped like a little mouse on a wheel, but if you have more brains than a mouse, you'd realize that all you have to do is stop and get off." Georgie loped ahead, kicking the froth of the waves splashing onto the sand.

"Okay, Ms. Business Owner," Liam called after her. "I don't see you taking your own advice."

She pirouetted around to face him. "I don't need to."

"Oh, I see," he said. "It applies to everyone but you, does it?"

"I wasn't the one complaining. I love my job." She skipped off ahead as he watched her. He hadn't met anyone like her before. Her honesty was almost brutal yet it was delivered so ingenuously, without a scrap of hubris, that he found it compelling. He found her compelling.

Georgie had plonked down cross-legged on the sand. She opened the drawstring of her backpack, glancing up at Liam. "Where's your lunch?"

"I already ate," he said, joining her on the sand. "I was hungry, I missed breakfast this morning."

"Well, that's no good for you! I never miss breakfast. This morning I had a bacon-and-egg roll with cheese and onions and barbecue sauce," she said matter-of-factly.

Liam grimaced. "That doesn't sound so good for you."

"It's my hangover breakfast."

"Big night last night?"

She nodded. "My birthday."

"Was it?"

"Uh-huh, same day as your mum's. How weird is that?" she remarked. "Did you do anything with your family?"

He was looking blankly at her. "Hmm?"

"You know, for your mum's birthday?" she prompted.

He stirred. "Ah, no, she doesn't live in Sydney."

Georgie nodded absently as she retrieved a McDonald's bag from her backpack.

Liam shuddered. "You actually eat that stuff? It tastes like plastic."

"I've never eaten plastic, so I'll have to take your word for it."

He sighed. "I mean, it all tastes the same."

"So do bananas but that doesn't seem to bother anyone," she said squarely. "You're a snob is what it is."

"I don't think an aversion to McDonald's exactly makes one a snob."

"But referring to oneself in the third person'll do it." George grinned. "Have you ever actually tried it?" she asked, thrusting a bag of fries at him.

He held up his hand to decline. "Sure, when I was a teenager."

"Oh, I get it, and now one is all growed up and one's palate is too so-phisticated?" Georgie said in a snooty voice, before taking a bite of her hamburger.

He laughed. "You don't let anything by, do you?"

She shook her head, swallowing. "It's a bit of a personal flaw actually."

"Your brutal honesty?"

"So." She sighed. "You've noticed?"

"Noticed? I think I'm being gradually beaten into submission by it."

Georgie looked contrite. "I didn't think I'd see you again."

"Oh, why's that?"

"I thought I'd offended you yesterday. I do that sometimes, and I don't mean to. Like I didn't mean to imply that you were dishonest, I don't even know you. I was just musing. Forgive me for doing it out loud."

He smiled at her. "You don't have to apologize, I find your honesty . . . refreshing. Confronting, but refreshing."

"Not used to it, eh? Honesty? In your profession?" She chuckled be-fore clearing her throat. "That really was just a joke."

A wave broke in front of them, lapping up onto the dry sand. Liam leaned back on one elbow, watching her while she ate. "You surprise me, you know."

"Good," she declared. "Why?"

"I would have thought someone like you . . ."

Georgie raised an eyebrow, waiting.

"Well, I'm surprised you're even eating meat, much less meat from a multinational conglomerate like McDonald's."

She started to laugh, shaking her head. "You took one look at me, the clothes, the hair, and labeled me 'tree-hugging vegetarian,' didn't you?"

He looked sheepish.

"Actually, I thought about becoming a vegetarian once," she said. "But then I noticed how happy butchers are. I mean really, have you ever met a grumpy butcher in your life? They're always so jolly, it has to be something in the meat."

Liam laughed, shaking his head. "I've never thought about it like that before."

"Well maybe you should try to do that more often. If you thought about things from a different perspective, maybe you wouldn't be so quick to label," said Georgie. "People have a tendency to oversimplify things, make judgments on outside appearances that have little to do with reality."

"You're talking about stereotypes."

"That's right. You looked at my hair and my clothes and decided a whole lot of things about me that may or may not be true."

"You did the same with me," he pointed out.

Georgie frowned at him.

"The first day we met you made conclusions about me based on the whiteness of my shirt."

She looked sheepish. "If I plead guilty, can you get me off with a warning?"

Liam smiled. "I'll see what I can do." He paused, staring at her intently. Georgie was beginning to feel self-conscious, and she hardly ever felt self-conscious. "You have a little . . ."—he touched her cheek lightly—". . . piece of lettuce," he finished, flicking it off his fingers.

She grimaced. "Well, now I'm embarrassed."

He smiled again, resting his hand against her cheek. "Don't be." He was still staring at her, his eyes flickering to her lips. She knew he was thinking about kissing her, unless he'd noticed another stray bit of food. But no, he was leaning closer. Georgie felt her heart beating fast and a not unpleasant tingling in her toes, of all places. When his lips touched hers it was tentative at first, they touched, pulled back, touched again. It was nice. Then his lips touched and lingered, pressing more firmly against hers, then shifting, their lips overlapping, so she could just taste the inside of his mouth. She felt his fingers lacing through her hair as his lips became more determined. Their mouths opened against each other, she felt his tongue, the edge of his teeth. Her heart started to race. . . .

A wave crashed onto the sand right beside them, spraying them with a fine salty mist. Liam was on his feet before Georgie had time to register. "I have to get back," he said abruptly.

"Okay," she murmured, watching him brush the sand off his clothes with an almost violent resolve. "You think you got all the sand off there?"

"I can't go walking half the beach through the office." He didn't look at her as he kept whacking furiously at his clothes. It was a little like self-flagellation.

They marched back to the stairs in an uneasy silence. What had got into him? Georgie wondered. Kissing her one minute and springing up like a startled rabbit the next. And what's more, why did she find it strangely appealing?

When they arrived at his car Liam opened the door and reached in for his necktie. He ignored Georgie as he set about tying it, and when he had finished, he began to roll down his left sleeve, brushing and smoothing it as he went. Two things were stopping Georgie from just walking away and leaving him to his obsessive preening. One was her promise to Nick. The other was the way he had kissed her. The way it had made her feel. She had to do something drastic, or at the very least memorable.

She stepped closer and in one swift movement she swiped a pen from his shirt pocket and grabbed his right wrist, swiveling around so that she was encircled by his arm.

"What are you doing?" He didn't sound mad, more resigned if anything.

"I'm writing my phone number on your arm," she said. "You know, so you . . . have it."

"I already have your number."

"At the shop. I don't live there, you know."

"Georgie . . ." Liam sighed heavily, and then to her surprise she felt him relax, leaning his cheek against the top of her head. "I'm sorry."

She turned around to face him. "What are you sorry for?"

He looked at her plaintively. "I'm not very good at this. I think I might . . . disappoint you."

"You'll only disappoint me if you don't call."

He breathed out. "The thing is, I told you I work long hours, and this weekend's not good for me." He hesitated. "We're having some major problems, it's the only chance I'm going to have to sort them out. . . ."

Georgie held a finger to his lips. "It's okay. It doesn't have to be this weekend." She had to stop herself from saying "We've got the rest of our lives," which, of course, would have been insane. Mad, barking insane. She barely knew him, but it had been right on the tip of her tongue. It was quite overpowering, this connection she could feel deep inside her, like his face would forever be forged on her mind. That he would always be a part of her. Georgie wondered if she was a little insane after all, but sanity had never felt this good.

She drew closer and pressed her lips against his. She let them linger there, her hand touching his cheek, just feeling the closeness of him. When she pulled back his eyes were still closed. He opened them slowly, staring at her, his eyes glassy now.

"I'll see you then," Georgie said in the softest voice, smiling at him as she turned and slowly walked away. She knew he was watching her. Should she turn back around? No, just a wave. She raised her hand above her shoulder and fluttered her fingers. She wondered how she looked to him. Appealing? Intriguing? Memorable? She wondered what he was thinking right now. She wondered if he would call.

Morgan Towers, Twenty-third Floor

"Mac?" Stella said tentatively, standing in the doorway to his office. He hadn't heard her quiet knock a moment before. He'd turned his chair to face the view and he was just sitting there, staring out. He'd been doing that a lot this week. Usually he threw himself into work. It must have hit him hard this time.

Stella stepped farther into the room. "Mac?"

He jerked round abruptly.

"Sorry," she said. "I was just going to head off, if there was nothing else you needed?"

He seemed a little out of it. He looked up at her, gradually coming back to Earth. "Stella, I didn't realize you were still here."

She nodded. "Just finished printing up those reports so they're ready for your breakfast meeting Monday."

"Thanks," he said with a weak smile.

"So, if there's nothing else—"

"Have a drink with me," he said, getting up from his desk.

"What? Now? Where?"

"Here." Mac crossed to a cabinet against the wall that housed a small bar fridge. He crouched down and opened the door. "Do you drink beer?"

"I've been known to."

He opened two bottles and passed one to her. "What shall we drink to?"

"What do you suggest?" she replied uncertainly. He was acting a little strange, artificially buoyant. Why didn't he just go home?

Mac looked at her. "I'm sorry, am I keeping you from something?"

"Just Friday-night drinks with the girls. I'll be able to catch up."

"Sounds like a regular thing," he said, lowering himself into his chair, and indicating for her to sit also.

Stella sat down opposite. "It's really a chance to get together, talk philosophy, politics, the global economy, you know the kind of thing."

"It's really about picking up guys, isn't it?"

"Absolutely," she said, taking a sip of her beer. "Unfortunately only the married ones come anywhere near us."

"Really?" he remarked, eyebrows raised.

"There's not a whole lot of half-decent thirtysomething fish in the ocean who aren't already taken. The cliché about them all being married or gay is only a cliché because it's true. Anna was lucky, she snapped you up young."

He smiled faintly, but Stella could see the sadness in his eyes. "How is she?"

"I don't know." He paused. "Not good."

Mac and Anna had decided not to tell anyone when they first embarked on IVF. Even Anna's parents didn't know after all this time. But as the process became more complicated, more clinic-centered, there had been no choice but to tell Stella, and not just so she could cover for him. He could still recall the profound relief he'd felt sharing it with her. And Stella remained his only confidante. She was discreet to a fault; most of the time she acted as though it had never been mentioned, yet she seemed to know innately when he needed to talk.

"What are you going to do?" she asked.

"I don't know," he said plainly. "We're supposed to discuss it this weekend."

"What do you want?"

Mac became thoughtful. It was such a simple question. What did he want? Foresight would be a good thing. If someone could assure him that the next cycle would result in a pregnancy that would proceed to full-term, then, of course, he would go ahead. The one after that? Sure. Five more? He didn't think he could do it. The hardest part about stopping was that it made everything they had gone through seem like a waste of time.

Seven years of their lives, half their marriage, had been consumed by the quest to have a baby. He understood Anna's reluctance to give up, but they couldn't go on forever, or at least he couldn't.

"I want it to be over," he answered finally. "One way or the other."

"Even if that means no baby?"

Mac sighed heavily. "You know, sometimes I don't even know if I want a baby anymore. I can't see how a baby will make us happy now. But what worries me more is what are we going to expect of this child after all these years, waiting, agonizing?" He paused. "It's unnatural. I just think it's gone on too long, we've lost perspective. We have to admit defeat and try to salvage a life."

"Wow," Stella said quietly. "You really are over it, aren't you?"

He nodded slowly, scratching at the label of his beer bottle. "Yeah, I think maybe I am."

"How does Anna feel about that?"

"I haven't told her."

"Oh." Stella looked uncomfortable.

"I hadn't even admitted it to myself till just then." Mac realized something huge had just occurred. A person could pretend for so long, persevere, ignore the niggling doubts, but he couldn't pretend to himself anymore. He'd said it out loud.

"So how do you think she's going to take it?" Stella said eventually.

Mac regarded her steadily. "How would you take it?"

She shook her head. "God, I dunno, Mac. I'm not Anna, I haven't been through what she's been through."

"But how would you feel if you thought you would never have a child?"

Stella stared across at him, clearly taken aback.

"Sorry, that's none of my business."

"It's not that." She shook her head. "I think about it all the time. I hear it from my parents constantly. 'You're never going to get married and have babies,'" she said with an Italian accent. "'What are we going to do with you?'"

Stella had turned thirty last year, but she didn't have a party because, as far as her family was concerned, thirty-year-old unmarried Italian women had nothing to celebrate. Career was a foreign word to them; probably French, they suspected. Whatever, it was wrong. It had taken Stella's focus away from the important business of finding a husband. If she didn't spend so much of her time at work, she might have a chance. But she was getting too old, and as her *nonna* liked to remind her more often than she cared to hear it, her eggs were shriveling up.

"I've faced the possibility of being single for the rest of my life," said Stella. "And I've decided I can cope. I mean, what's the alternative? But you know what? In the back of my mind I hold on to the fact that even if the right guy doesn't come along, I could still have a baby."

"What, on your own?"

She sighed. "Oh, I know I'd probably never go through with it. Can you imagine how that would go down at home? But the option is there, for a while yet."

"So you're more prepared to face life without a partner than a baby?"

She screwed up her face. "Not when you put it like that. I'm just saying that single doesn't have to mean childless, and that's a comforting thought at times. It's different for women, Mac. We get a pretty hard-to-ignore reminder every frigging month about exactly what we're supposed to be doing with our bodies and our lives. Is it any wonder we get tense?"

Mac smiled faintly. He looked so tired. Stella remembered the young, aspiring executive who had arrived here seven years ago, full of ambition, even a little full of himself, which was perhaps to be expected given his meteoric rise in the corporation. But over the last few years, she had watched him grow weary and worn down, as though he was gradually being sucked dry.

Stella got to her feet. "I'm leaving now so that you can go home. Want to walk down with me?"

"No, it's okay, I have a couple of things to finish up."

"Mac," she said sternly, "go home, you look terrible."

"I'm just tired. I've got the whole weekend to rest."

"Maybe what you and Anna need is a holiday."

"Maybe." If only it was as simple as that. Go away somewhere, just the two of them, erase the last seven years, rekindle what they once had, look to the future.

"Night," Stella called from the doorway, breaking his reverie.

"Goodnight, Stella."

"Don't stay too late," she warned.

A moment later he heard her leaving the outer office, and soon after, the *ping* of the elevator. He picked up his beer and swiveled his chair around to face the window. The last sliver of orange sunset had faded from the sky and darkness had officially taken over for the night shift. Mac watched the red and white trails of car lights as they snaked along the expressway, making their way home to wives, husbands, families. But he wouldn't go home, not yet. He'd stay here until he could be reasonably certain Anna would have gone to bed. He wasn't avoiding her, he was avoiding a late-night 'discussion.' They were the worst kind. The later it got, the more logic, understanding and common sense retreated from the front line—leaving only frayed nerves and raw emotion to carry on the fight. Mac knew it was going to be almost impossible, but somehow they had to try to leave emotion out of it. It was important that they rationally assess the situation and come to objective conclusions based on concrete evidence.

Who was he kidding?

Mosman

At 8:30 Mac heard Anna coming down the stairs. He closed his laptop and stood up wearily, stretching his arms up over his head. He'd only slept a few hours, but that was not unusual these days. He felt tired right through to his bones. Maybe Stella was right, maybe he did need a holiday.

When he walked into the kitchen, Anna was making coffee. He could feel the chill as he approached.

"Morning," he said, leaning over to kiss her, but she just offered her cheek.

"What time did you get home?" she asked crisply.

"Around midnight I think."

"Once you knew I'd be asleep?"

"No, once I'd finished what I had to do."

She reached into the cupboard above her head for cups. "You were up early as well, I gather. You're not getting enough sleep lately, Mac."

"Mm." He shrugged. "Stella thinks I need a holiday."

Anna turned abruptly. "Oh, does she? I suppose Stella would know, she sees more of you than anyone, certainly more than me."

Mac sighed, leaning back against the bench behind him and crossing his arms. "This is going to be a fun weekend."

Anna stared at him. He was right, she'd gone on the offensive as soon as he'd walked into the kitchen. There was no reason to treat him like the enemy. "I'm sorry," she said quietly. She put the cups down and turned around to face him. "Can we start again?"

"If you want."

She stepped tentatively toward him. "I want."

Mac uncrossed his arms and she rested her head against his chest. "Good morning," she murmured.

"How did you sleep?" he asked.

"Okay." She lifted her head to look at him. "Breakfast outside?"

The garden was beautiful at this time of the year. The azaleas were in full bloom, as well as most of the roses, and the gardenias were budding, along with the hydrangeas and agapanthus, all ready to burst into flower in the next few weeks. The lawn was lush and green, helped in no small way by the computerized watering system. The rest was courtesy of hired help. They both figured it was worth paying a gardener; they wanted to be able to enjoy the garden on weekends, not spend the little free time they had mowing and weeding. They sat at their genuine French provincial outdoor setting, sipping Italian coffee from Scandinavian china and eating bagels and Tasmanian smoked salmon.

Suddenly Mac felt ridiculous. They looked like a photograph out of a lifestyle magazine, drinking their imported coffee, sitting on imported furniture, gazing out at their impossibly perfect garden. He could almost hear Nero fiddling.

Anna followed Mac's gaze across the garden. They had landscaped with a child in mind. Wide, shallow steps led out from the back of the house, easy for a toddler to negotiate; level patches of soft grass provided somewhere for a baby to crawl, paved areas a place where he could ride his first little trike; and a jacaranda with wonderful, low-arching branches would be perfect for a swing one day.

"What are you thinking about, Mac?" she asked him.

He glanced at her. "I was just thinking you haven't told me about your clinic visit yet," he said.

She sighed inwardly. They no longer spoke of blond-headed toddlers playing in the garden. It was too painful. Now they talked of eggs and sperm and fertilization and embryos, almost as though they had nothing to do with a real baby. And sometimes Anna felt they didn't.

"It was a pretty standard visit really," she answered him. "You've heard it all before. You know, how successful the procedure was up to the moment it failed spectacularly."

Mac placed his cup back on the table. "Did Dr. Tran recommend a break?"

He watched Anna. She was squirming. *Tell the truth. There's nothing left if we don't at least tell the truth.*

"He said it was up to me," she said lightly. "Of course I have to take one month off, as usual, but he said I should just ring the clinic when I'm ready."

She hadn't answered him. She hadn't lied, but she hadn't answered him. "Anna," he said patiently, "did he recommend a break?"

She swallowed. "He suggested I might benefit from a slight delay before the next round of treatment. But he made it very clear that it's up to me."

"Up to you?" Mac raised an eyebrow.

"To us, it's up to us."

"Then I think it's a good idea."

"Well I don't," she returned squarely, a defensiveness creeping in.

"Why not?" he persisted. "What difference will a couple of months make?"

"It could make all the difference in the world, Mac!" Anna said firmly. "You know the statistics. In the next couple of years my chances of getting pregnant drop dramatically."

"But what if you get sick again? That could be dangerous this time around."

The first time Anna had suffered from OHSS, Mac had been ready to give the whole thing up there and then. Ovarian hyperstimulation syndrome was usually mild, treated with rest and light pain relief. However, in some cases it was so severe it required hospitalization, the treatment cycle had to be abandoned and the embryos frozen. The doctors had assured Mac that Anna would recover fully. Certain women were sensitive to some of the drugs and they simply needed to adjust her protocol. She'd since had a couple of much milder recurrences, but Mac was worried she was due for a more serious bout because of the number of treatment cycles she had undertaken over the last couple of years. There was probably no medical basis to his fears, but fear did not usually have its genesis in reason.

"I'm not going to get sick again," Anna insisted. "I haven't had any problems for ages."

"Then why is the doctor suggesting a rest?"

"I don't know, maybe they're overbooked."

Mac frowned at her. "Why can't we talk about this, Anna?"

"We're talking."

"We're talking around it," he said bluntly. "And you know we are. I want to talk about what's really going on here."

"Okay, Mac, then why don't you start by admitting that hyperstimulation is not your main concern?"

"Fair enough." He sat forward, resting his elbows on the table. "My main concern is us." He paused. "I'd like to see what we have together when we're not trying to have a baby."

Anna was unprepared for that. Mac was not usually so direct when it came to expressing his feelings. "What are you getting at?" she said warily.

"We've only ever approached this one way, like it's a problem that has to be fixed. We've never looked at it from another angle. We haven't even considered the possibility of not having a child, of living child-free. Can't we discuss that? Can't we stop and think about how to have a life without kids?"

Something was flooding into her chest. It felt like panic. "Clearly you don't want children as much as I do," she said tightly.

"Maybe, I don't know, I've never had a chance to consider it. The thing is, I know I don't want a child so much that I'm prepared to be this unhappy."

She stared across the table at him. "You're unhappy?"

Mac looked at her steadily. "Yeah."

"All the time?"

He shrugged. "More often than not, lately."

Anna didn't want Mac to be unhappy, she loved him . . . but was she supposed to give up everything, all of her dreams? She wanted a baby, more than anything. Was her happiness less important than his?

"What about you, Anna, are you happy?"

She jerked her head up to look at him. "I, um," she hesitated. "I don't know, but I do know I wouldn't be happier if we gave up."

"I'm not saying we give up now. I'm just asking for a little time to re-group," said Mac. "Time to think, consider other options."

Anna swallowed. Didn't he realize? There was no time. There were no other options.

Mac was watching her. "Could you at least think it over? You can't start treatment for another month anyway."

"Sure." She nodded, smiling thinly. She would think it over and arrive at the only possible answer. And Mac would come around.

The Reading Rooms

"So what did you get up to over the weekend?" Louise asked Georgie as she unlocked the front door of the shop and flipped over the Closed sign. "Nick was going to call you to come over Saturday night but I told him not to hound you."

Georgie smiled faintly. It was a rare weekend that she didn't spend at least some time at Louise and Nick's. A rare weekend that didn't include videos and pizza, a little babysitting, maybe the beach on Sunday, or just hanging out, drinking pot after pot of coffee, sharing the weekend papers. She felt more comfortable at their place than she did at her own.

"Well, don't faint, but Trace went away for the weekend," said Georgie as she slid a chair off one of the tables and set it down.

"Where'd she go, and more to the point, how did she pay for it?" asked Louise, raising a suspicious eyebrow.

"I don't know and I don't care," Georgie dismissed. "I had the place to myself for a whole weekend, so I stayed in."

Louise looked up from the cash register. "You weren't hanging around all that time waiting for him to call, were you?"

"Who?" Georgie said innocently.

"Cut it out," said Louise. "Were you waiting for Liam to call?"

"No, and I wasn't expecting him to. He told me he was working this weekend."

"What's he doing working weekends?"

"You think he only puts in a forty-hour week?" Georgie declared airily. "He sets up major international deals, he can't just work nine-to-five, five days a week."

"I don't get it. What kind of lawyer is he?"

"He's a tax law specialist. He has to minimize the taxes for companies when they're buying and selling other companies, and merging and stuff like that."

Louise lifted an eyebrow. "Doesn't exactly sound like your type."

Georgie raised her hands in exasperation. "Just what exactly *is* my type anyway? And why can't it be Liam?" She sighed. "I like him, there's something very sweet about him. I mean, you'd think being a big-shot corporate lawyer he'd be a real wanker. But he's not. He seems almost out of his depth sometimes, even a little shy."

"Somebody's smitten."

Georgie looked plainly at Louise. "It's different this time," she insisted. "There's this connection I can feel, it's almost eerie—"

"Oh, don't, Georgie!" Louise interrupted her, wincing.

"What?"

"You say that every time."

Georgie was wide-eyed. "I do not!"

Louise looked at her dubiously. "Come on, Georgie! 'This is the one, I feel it in my bones,' 'I had a dream about him,' 'I've never felt so in tune.' Doesn't any of that sound familiar?"

Georgie pushed a chair into place roughly. "I haven't said anything like that since I was fifteen, Louise. Give me a little credit."

"Remember that David guy you met at the Reillys' dinner party?" Louise persisted. "You told me that you could see yourself with him for the rest of your life. Two weeks later you wanted to know where you could buy a gun because if you had to spend another second in his suffocating company you were going to shoot yourself. That was all of four months ago."

Georgie felt an ache in the back of her throat. She knew if she tried to speak her voice would come out all broken and pathetic, and then she'd probably cry.

Louise was watching her, frowning. "Are you okay?"

She nodded, turning abruptly and walking briskly to the back of the shop.

"Georgie!"

"Just going to the loo," she called without looking around. She made it to the tiny staff bathroom, closed the door behind her and locked it. She sat down on the lid of the toilet seat and drew her knees up, hugging them, while she tried to swallow down the wretched lump in her throat. At least the "tears the rest of the year" prophecy appeared to have some truth in it. Unlike her own ridiculous predictions. She felt so stupid. Why hadn't she seen this in herself before? Obviously everyone else had. She knew she was a romantic, a dreamer, but she hadn't realized she was such a joke. Uh-oh, Georgie's met another guy, here she goes again, off with the pixies.

But even as she was staring her own foolishness in the face, she couldn't ignore the powerful attachment she felt every time she so much as thought of Liam. She barely knew him, yet she couldn't shake the idea that they were meant for each other, that he was the one, that he was perfect.

It couldn't all be in her imagination. Liam had done the pursuing so far. He'd come in the second day looking for her, he'd asked her out to lunch, he'd kissed her. He'd acted weird afterward, but then he'd held her close, and in his eyes she'd seen the same sense of this being something bigger than the both of them.

Oh, what the hell does that mean? Georgie banged her head against the wall beside her. "Ow!" That was harder than she'd expected.

"Are you alright?" Louise called from the other side of the door.

"Yep. Be out in a minute."

The cold, uncomfortable truth was that Liam hadn't called all weekend. She hadn't expected to see him, but a phone call would have told her that at least what had passed between them was real. And now she had to face the fact that it wasn't. It was just her overactive, hyperromantic imagination that knew no boundaries and couldn't tell reality from fairy tale.

Enough. She was going to stop this nonsense and act her age, thirty-... in another year she'd be thirty-four and knights in shining armor did not exist, perfect men certainly did not exist, and you did not meet someone and decide you're going to spend the rest of your life with him. That was the stuff of books and movies and ... other people's lives.

Mosman

Mac pulled into the driveway as the six o'clock news bulletin was wrapping up on the radio. They were forecasting rain and already the sky was turning black. As he got out of the car he could smell a storm in the air. Normally he wouldn't leave the office for another hour, and often much later. But Anna had phoned insisting he come home as soon as possible. She wouldn't explain, but there was a kind of restrained hysteria in her tone that Mac knew he shouldn't ignore.

As he entered the house he could see her at the end of the hall, pacing back and forth across the sunroom, a drink in one hand, a cigarette in the other. Not a good sign. Anna wasn't a smoker, it was something she reserved for her bleakest moments. Self-medication, she told Mac.

"What's going on?" he said, coming into the room.

She stopped pacing, turning to glare at him. "You think I don't know what's going on?" she retorted.

"What are you talking about?"

"You don't think I didn't see what you were doing all weekend?"

"Could you stop speaking in double negatives and get to the point, Anna?"

She groaned, exasperated. "The play Saturday night, the drive to the country Sunday?"

Mac just looked at her, mystified.

"You filled the weekend with 'child-free' activities in a very transparent attempt to prove to me how great our life would be without children."

He sighed heavily. "There wasn't any hidden agenda, Anna. Would you have been happier going to McDonald's or the zoo or somewhere you'd be surrounded by children and families? You're always telling me you can't stand that."

"And all the talk about a holiday?" she went on, ignoring him. "That's just an underhanded way of getting me to take a break from the treatment."

"Anna, did you call me home from work just to make ridiculous accusations?"

"You only stay at work so late so that you can avoid being with me," she snapped.

Mac rubbed his forehead. "Well, keep it up, Anna, and that'll become a self-fulfilling prophecy."

That seemed to stop her in her tracks. Mac walked across to the liquor cabinet, and poured himself a Scotch. He wasn't much of a spirits drinker but he could use the hit. He took a large swig and turned to face Anna again. She was standing at the open French doors, looking out into the failing light of the garden. She turned around slowly.

"You don't believe we're ever going to have a baby, do you, Mac?"

"What?"

"Admit it, you don't think it's going to happen."

"I don't know—"

"If you really believed we were going to have a baby, you wouldn't even consider giving up."

He didn't say anything.

"Well, there you have it," she said grimly. "You realize you've taken away the only thing I had left."

"What's that?" He frowned.

"Hope."

Mac tossed the rest of his drink back. "You're putting words into my mouth, Anna. I don't know if we'll ever have a baby, okay? Nobody seems to know. The best fertility specialists in the country haven't got a clue, so how do you expect me to know?"

"I expect you to have some faith, I expect you to support me."

"I have supported you, Anna, for seven fucking years all I've done is support you. Is it so much to ask just to have a break for a while?"

"What the hell do you need a break from?" she cried. "I'm the one who takes the drugs and has the injections and the blood tests and the surgery. I'm the one who gets bloated and sore and has headaches and nausea and pain!"

"Which is exactly why you need a break!" he declared, raising his voice.

Anna glared at him, breathing hard. "Well, that should be my decision."

Something snapped then. "Why?" he demanded.

She frowned. "What do you mean?"

"Why is everything your decision, Anna?"

"Because it's my body."

"But it's my life!" he exclaimed. "No, I don't take drugs or have surgery, but you don't think it affects me?"

"I didn't say that—"

"The years of watching you go though this, the time, the energy, the constant, utter, fucking misery." He paused, catching his breath. "Is this what you wanted our lives to be about?"

She'd never seen him so hostile. "I want a family. I thought that's what you wanted too."

"I would have loved to have a family of our own, Anna. But not at any price."

"What? It's the money that's bothering you?"

"Christ, Anna!"

"Sorry, I'm sorry, I shouldn't have said that. That was stupid. But you have to help me out here, Mac, I'm just trying to understand. Yes, our whole lives have been about this, it's why we bought this house, it's been behind every decision we've made for nearly a decade. This is what we both wanted, we can't just give up now."

Mac was glaring at her. There was a strange look in his eyes. "What if I asked you to?"

"What?"

"What if I asked you to give up, Anna. To do it for me."

The panic was rising in her chest again. She swallowed. "When you love somebody, you give up anything for them, that's the deal. But if they love you, they have to have a very good reason for asking."

"I have a good reason," said Mac. "I want to get our life back."

"By giving up a life?" she accused. "You're asking me to choose between you and our child. That's not fair, Mac."

"There is no child!" he cried. "I'm asking you to choose me. To choose us."

"This is ridiculous."

"Is it so ridiculous to think about a life together, just you and me?"

"That's not what I meant—"

"Can't you see that I've had enough? I can't live like this. I can't do it anymore, Anna. I swear if I have to walk into that god-awful room with the videos and the magazines one more time—"

"For Chrissakes, Mac, you wank into a cup and you think that gives you the right . . ." Anna stopped suddenly, biting her lip.

He was just staring at her. "What did you say?"

"I'm sorry, Mac," she said breathlessly.

"No, please, go on, Anna. I'd love to hear the rest of that sentence."

She swallowed. "I didn't mean it the way it came out."

"What? You didn't mean that I have no rights, that I'm pretty insignificant in the scheme of things?" His voice was deep and grim, his jaw clenched. "You're not saying I'm just a means to an end, eh, Anna?"

"Of course that's not what I'm saying, Mac, I would never say that."

"I think it's exactly what you're saying," he said bitterly. "If we can't have a child, then what's the point?"

Anna was dumbstruck, she didn't know what to say.

"See, I can stand the thought of a life without a child," he went on. "I'd be disappointed, sad, heartbroken probably. But I could move on, make a life with you. But that's not enough for you, is it, Anna?" he said resignedly. "I'm not enough."

She found her voice again. "You can't possibly understand what it's like for a woman, Mac."

The French doors swung out behind her as a gust of wind smacked them back against the house. Anna turned and stepped outside to grab both door handles, pulling them closed and securing the barrel bolts. The rain had started; it was spraying against the glass panes of the door, sweeping in sheets across the garden. Anna jumped as she heard the front door slam. She turned around. The room was empty.

"Mac?" she called as she hurried up the hall. She opened the front door but the rain swept in, forcing her to close it again. She peered through the glass, in time to see Mac's car take off up the street.

Morgan Towers

The lift door opened and Stella stepped out, holding her dripping um-
brella away from her body as she walked down the corridor. She dumped
it in the wastepaper bin beside her desk. The office was so quiet she could
hear the hum of the fluorescent lights. She liked coming into work at this
time of the morning. Mac was an early starter and she felt better if she
was here first, organized and ready for whatever he needed as soon as he
arrived. Stella derived a great deal of satisfaction from her job, from being
valued, being useful, occasionally even indispensable.

She switched on her computer and left it to start up while she went to
open Mac's office. As she unlocked the door she was surprised to find the
room in darkness, the blinds firmly closed. Mac had a superb view across
the city and the harbor and he always kept the blinds open. She walked
around behind the desk and twisted the slim rod that controlled the slats,
allowing stripes of muddied light into the room. She peered out. One
pitiful ray of sunlight had escaped through a chink in the clouds and was
reflecting off the main sail of the Opera House, illuminating it. The rest
of the city, however, was grey and dismal, the water metallic. Stella took
hold of the cord and gave it a yank, pulling the blind all the way up to the
top of the window.

"Stella?"

She screamed and dropped the cord, sending the blind hurtling back
down, knocking over a framed photo in its haste. She spun around, her
heart thumping in her chest. "Mac!"

He was lying on the couch, his forearm shielding his eyes. He lifted it,
squinting at her.

"What are you doing?" she demanded.

"I was sleeping."

"You scared me half to death!"

"I could say the same thing about you," he said, his voice still croaky. He cleared his throat. He pulled himself upright, dropping his feet onto the floor. "What time is it?" he asked, raking his fingers through his hair.

"Just after seven," said Stella. "Have you been here all night, Mac?"

He nodded, leaning his elbows on his knees as he supported his head in his hands.

"I thought you went home?" she asked carefully.

"I had some things I wanted to catch up on, so I came back again."

Stella knew something was wrong. Mac often worked late into the night, but he'd rarely ever bedded down here. "You'd better go home, get some rest."

"No, I slept alright."

"Then go home and take a shower, change your clothes."

He looked up at her. "What did you say the time was?"

"It's just after seven."

"Okay, I'll go in a little while."

"After Anna's left for work?"

Mac slumped back against the couch, tucking his hands behind his head and stretching his legs out before him. Stella dragged a chair away from the desk and sat facing him. "You told Anna what you told me the other night?"

He sighed heavily. "We talked it all through on the weekend. I thought it went alright. But it obviously didn't sink in till yesterday."

"That's why you went home when she called?"

He nodded, but he didn't say anything. Stella didn't know how much she ought to push it. He stood up suddenly and walked over to the window, taking hold of one of the blind cords and pulling it up to reveal the grey skyline. He did the same with the second blind, still not saying anything. Stella stood and turned around just as Mac noticed the frame that had been knocked over. He picked it up and stared at it. It was a picture of Anna.

"You know," he said quietly, almost to himself, "I just wanted to have a break, to see what we had left together." He replaced the frame on the shelf that ran along under the window. "Turns out—"

The phone rang suddenly, invasively. Stella reached over to pick it up. She'd blow off whoever it was, Mac didn't need to be bothered now. "Good morning, Morgan Trask," she said crisply.

"Oh, I was after Mac. . . . Is that you, Stella?"

Stella recognized the voice. "Hello, Anna." Mac jerked his head up. Stella waited for his instruction. He nodded. "I'll put him on," she said, passing the phone across the desk. "I'll get you some coffee," she whispered.

Mac gave her a wan smile as she left the room, closing the door quietly behind her. He raised the phone to his ear. "Anna."

"Mac, where have you been? Did you sleep at the office?"

"I did."

She paused a moment. "I'm so sorry, Mac, so incredibly sorry—"

"It's okay."

"No, it's not okay!" she insisted. "I said some terrible things last night. I was angry, that's all, it didn't mean anything."

He turned his chair around to face the view. "Oh, but I think it did, Anna."

"How can you say that?" she cried. "I was angry and upset, we both were."

He sighed. "Look, it doesn't matter anyway."

"Of course, it matters. Would you stop saying that, Mac?"

"I just don't want you to feel bad about this. To be honest, you've put things into perspective for me."

"What are you talking about?"

"Well, relegating me to sperm donor—"

"Mac!"

"Hear me out," he continued over the top of her. "I've thought this over very carefully, Anna, and now I realize that—how did you put it again?—'wanking in a cup' is a fairly crucial part of the whole process."

"Mac, don't . . ."

"It's all been up to you, Anna, everything. How you felt, what you wanted, what you could cope with. I've never refused you anything, I just wanted you to be happy." He sighed. "Well, it didn't work. We're both miserable. And I'm sick to death of being miserable. I want my life back. I want to be happy for a change."

"I want you to be happy."

"I don't think you could give a damn whether I'm happy or not, Anna."

She said nothing for a moment as his anger reverberated down the phone line. She couldn't let everything fall apart because of one thoughtless, stupid remark. She wouldn't let it.

"I do care about your happiness, Mac," she said firmly. "And I'll prove it to you. If you want me to take a break from the treatment, then that's what I'll do."

"Yes, Anna," he said wearily, "that's what we're going to do."

The Reading Rooms

Georgie had been trying hard to focus on work, to see her life as rich and rewarding, to be content. She wasn't succeeding. She could not pretend she hadn't met Liam, even if she had put the whole "rest of her life" mirage to bed. More or less. But erasing Liam from her consciousness was proving more difficult.

He hadn't called. And she was pretty sure he was never going to now, and that sat in her stomach like a lead weight. Of course, it confirmed what everyone thought of her. She was a sad romantic, a pathetic loser in the game of love, and really bad at metaphors as well. Liam had told her he'd disappoint her, and then gone right ahead and done just that. She had no right to expect otherwise. He'd been honest. She'd been foolish. End of story.

The phone rang and Georgie jumped, glancing at the clock on the wall. It was pouring rain, they'd barely had a customer all afternoon. "Close enough, don't you reckon?" she said to Adam.

"You're not going to do your answering machine thing?" he cautioned.

Georgie winked at him, picking up the phone. "You have reached The Reading Rooms, unfortunately the store is closed. . . ."

"I'm going to tell Louise on you," said Adam, shaking his head.

She covered the handpiece, shushing him. "If you would like to leave a message—"

"Georgie?"

She held her breath.

"Hello? Is anyone there?"

"Is that you, Liam?"

"Yes," he said uncertainly.

"Sorry, sorry . . . um, it was nearly closing . . ." She felt like a twit. "Anyway, what can I do for you?" she said, fast-forwarding past an explanation, seeing she didn't really have one.

"Well, I was ringing, well, I wanted to ask . . . but first I wanted to apologize for not calling over the weekend."

Georgie smiled. "That's okay, you told me you wouldn't be able to call."

"But I wanted to." He paused. "I thought about you. I wanted to call."

He'd thought about her, he'd wanted to call. He was calling now.

"So I was wondering if you'd like to go out for a drink?" Liam asked. He was asking her out.

"Sure . . . when did you have in mind?"

"Well, now, or soon, at least. I was thinking this afternoon."

Clearly Liam was not into planning ahead. But that was okay. Georgie could live with that. Spontaneity was good. "Okay."

"You will, you want to?"

"Sure."

"Well, great . . . that's great." He sounded relieved. "I can be there in twenty minutes, or whatever suits you."

"That's fine. Just pull up out front, I'll look out for you."

"Date with the suit?" Adam asked when she hung up the phone.

"His name's Liam."

"Who? The suit?"

She rolled her eyes. "You can leave now, I'll lock up."

"Don't you want me to hang around? In case he tries anything?"

"What makes you think that if he's going to try something, I would want you hanging around?"

Adam smiled slowly. "Okay, Boss." He collected his jacket and bike helmet from the office and headed for the door. "Don't do anything I wouldn't do," he warned.

"That should leave me with all the options I'll ever need, and then some," Georgie quipped. She locked the front door and turned over the Closed sign, before walking out to the staff bathroom to freshen up. She considered her reflection in the mirror and took a deep breath. This was the critical date, the one where she'd start to find fault.

"So don't, Georgiana Reading," she said out loud. "And don't picture him beside you in the wedding album either. You need to exercise some balance, don't expect too much of him, but then don't expect too little. Get to know him. Enjoy yourself. Just be in the moment." She sighed, staring at herself. "And most importantly of all, stop talking to yourself in the mirror."

Georgie came flying out the door as Liam's car pulled up to the curb.
"That was quick," he remarked as she climbed into the front seat.

"I saw you coming," she said, strapping up. "So where are you taking me?"

"There's supposed to be a nice place up at Newport. I've never been there, a friend recommended it."

"Ooh, a secret hideaway."

Liam turned his head sharply. "What makes you say that?"

"No reason." Georgie shrugged.

"If there's some place you'd rather go?"

"No, there isn't."

"So you're okay with this?"

"I'm fine," she assured him. She didn't know why he seemed so nervous. Though she liked the idea that it had something to do with her.

They chatted amiably as they drove along. Georgie asked Liam all the appropriate questions about his work, content just to listen to him. He took on a more confident tone when he was talking about his job. There was an authority in his voice that she hadn't heard before. With her he was a little tentative, not so sure of himself.

By the time they arrived the rain had eased and they were able to get from the car to the entrance and remain relatively dry. Liam pushed the door open for Georgie and followed her inside. The place was quiet, which was to be expected on a wet afternoon in the middle of the week. They sat at a table by the windows, looking directly out at the marina. A waiter approached to take their drink orders.

"Do you have Bacardi Breezers?" Georgie asked him.

"Seriously?" Liam frowned.

She looked across at him. "What?"

He hesitated. "It's just . . . well, you can have anything you want."

"Then I'll have a Bacardi Breezer. Anything orange-colored, thanks," she smiled at the waiter. Liam ordered some kind of imported beer, Georgie assumed, and the waiter left them.

"You know that stuff is just alcoholic soft drink?" Liam said.

"So? Beer is just fermented hops. What's your problem exactly?"

He opened his mouth to reply, but then obviously thought better of it. "Nothing," he said finally.

Georgie raised an eyebrow. "You just can't help yourself, can you?"

"Help what?"

"Being a snob."

He looked away from her out at the view. Now Georgie had made him feel uncomfortable again. It was becoming a habit. She hit herself on the forehead. "Well, that was just me and my big mouth."

"You mean you and your brutal honesty?"

She looked across at him. "No, Liam, honesty is not an excuse to be rude. I apologize."

"It's okay, you probably have a point. I don't mean to be a snob—"

"And I don't mean to be insulting. Liam, you're going to have to learn to take me with a grain of salt. Most people do, believe me."

He had a slight, tentative smile on his lips as he leaned forward, about to say something, when the waiter returned. He sat back in his chair while their drinks were set down on the table.

"Cheers," said Georgie, clinking her bottle against his after the waiter had left. She took a sip, trying to ignore the fact that he was watching her with an intensity that was a little unsettling. Now she was the one feeling uncomfortable.

Liam leaned forward again. "I'm sorry for not calling over the weekend."

"We already went through this," Georgie reminded him. "It's okay."

"But you said the other day that I'd only disappoint you if I didn't call—"

"I didn't mean—"

He held up his hand to stop her. "What I'm trying to say is that all weekend I kept thinking, I don't want to disappoint her."

Georgie felt her heart thumping. She felt her blood pulsating through her veins and she felt giddy. It was like cresting the highest peak on a roller coaster—you know what's ahead of you, ups and downs and thrills and fear and exhilaration. You wish you had never gotten on the ride, but you hope the ride will never end.

"It's just that," Liam went on, "there are things you don't know about me."

Georgie shrugged. "And there are things you don't know about me. We could have fun finding out."

"I'm sure we could." He smiled faintly, but the expression in his eyes was serious. "I just don't know if I'll be able to . . . meet your expectations."

Georgie considered him thoughtfully. "How do you know what my expectations are?" she said. "Or even if I have any, for that matter."

"What do you mean?"

"I might prefer to not have any expectations of you, Liam, then I can't be disappointed."

"Everybody has expectations," he said wryly.

"Maybe I'm not everybody."

"I can't argue with that, you're certainly not like anybody I've ever met." He paused. "And I meant that as a compliment."

"I took it as one." Georgie smiled, leaning toward him. "Look, I admit I felt a little anxious over the weekend, like you did, and it was all because we had expectations. I wondered if you would ring, you wondered if you should ring. It'd be a relief not to worry about stuff like that, don't you reckon?"

"You actually think it's possible not to have any expectations in a relationship?"

Georgie thought about it. "Well, let's not call it a relationship in the first place. The word itself is loaded with expectations."

Liam frowned. "So if it's not a relationship, and there are no expectations, what are we doing?"

"What we are doing," said Georgie calmly, "is enjoying each other's company, getting to know each other, without some preordained destination in mind. The thing is, Liam, I'm so glad you rang, and right now, right at this moment, I'm enjoying myself, just sitting here, having a drink with you. I don't want to spoil it by thinking about tomorrow, or next week, or what might happen six months from now. I have a tendency to do that. Maybe this time I'd like to do it differently."

Georgie met his gaze openly. She actually felt excited. She genuinely believed she could do this. Live in the moment as each moment presented itself, instead of becoming buried under doubts and demands, missed cues and misunderstandings.

Liam stared down at his beer bottle, scratching at the label with his thumbnail. "I can't fault what you're saying. But I just don't think people can help themselves. They always expect more, more than you can possibly give. And even after you've given yourself completely, it's not enough. That's when you realize that obviously what you had to give was never going to be enough."

Georgie wondered what he was on about. He looked up after a while. "Sorry," he said.

"What happened to you?"

"I guess I have a few battle scars."

"Yeah, I can see them from here."

He sighed. "That's why I'm a little . . ."

"Bitter?" she suggested.

Liam grinned sheepishly. "I was going to say apprehensive."

"Oh, see, the problem with being apprehensive," said Georgie, "is that you stick to the safe paths." She took a sip of her drink. "And I, for one, am sick of feeling apprehensive."

"Who broke your heart?"

She didn't want to talk about her father right now. One day she'd tell him, but not tonight. "Paul Robertson in grade two," she replied. "He was such a worm."

Liam smiled. "No one since?"

"No one I'd take seriously. My brother thinks I'm too fussy. He said I should stop waiting for Mr. Perfect."

"Oh, so that's why you agreed to come out with me tonight?"

Georgie laughed.

"So, this Mr. Perfect," Liam went on, "what's he like?"

"I don't know, he never showed."

"So, not so perfect after all?"

"You're absolutely right," agreed Georgie. "Mr. Perfect would be punctual."

"And sensitive? Women like that, don't they?"

"Hmm, but we're over the Sensitive New-Age Guy. I mean, he still has to be sensitive and completely in tune with my needs. But he should be strong as well. You know, a 'take charge' kind of SNAG, when the situation calls for it. The rest of the time he should do whatever I tell him."

Liam grinned. "Anything else?"

"Well, he'd have to be good-looking, of course, but beauty being in the eye of the beholder as it is, there's room to move there. A sense of humor, on the other hand, is essential. He'd have to be able to make me laugh. And he'd have to be able to fix leaking taps and hang pictures, that kind of thing."

"Oh?"

"I know it's sexist, but we are talking perfect, aren't we?"

"We are."

"So he'd write me poetry on Valentine's Day," she went on, "but he'd also be quite athletic, though he'd never watch a football game when he could be spending time with me. He'd be accomplished in at least one musical instrument, and fluent in a couple of languages. And he'd be a gourmet cook, who always cleaned up after himself. . . ." Georgie paused, frowning. "He'd be really insufferable, wouldn't he?"

They both laughed.

"So what about the perfect female?" said Georgie. "That's easier to define, isn't it?"

"Why do you say that?"

"Because it comes down to one thing with blokes. What's that joke, something about the perfect woman arriving naked with a six-pack of beer and turning into a pizza at midnight?"

Liam shook his head. "I can't believe you just said that."

"But it's true."

"Not for me, it isn't."

"Okay, give me your wish list," said Georgie.

"I don't have a list."

"Come on, hypothetically," she urged. "Complete the following sentence, 'My perfect woman would be . . .'"

Liam became thoughtful. "Happy," he said finally.

"That's it?"

"That's a lot."

"Define 'happy.'"

He shrugged. "Content . . . with herself, with her life, happy sharing it with me," he said simply.

Georgie looked at him. "That doesn't seem such a lot."

"You'd be surprised."

She wondered what had happened to him. Who had hurt him. And why she had the overwhelming feeling she wanted to make it all better.

"Well, you've made me sound positively greedy," said Georgie. "I'd like to revise my position."

Liam smiled. "Go right ahead."

She took a deep breath. "The perfect man . . . would only want me to be happy."

He just stared at her, and she met his gaze unblinking. Slowly his hand moved across the table until his fingers grazed against hers. "How would he go about making you happy?"

"Oh, you see, I don't expect a lot." Georgie turned her hand over and entwined her fingers through his. "It seems to me he's pretty much on the right track now."

They were still holding hands when they left the bar and meandered back to the car. It wasn't raining just then, and neither of them seemed to be in any hurry. Liam aimed the remote at his car to unlock it and went to open the door for her. Georgie stepped around, facing him as he reached for the handle. They looked at each other for a moment, and then without saying anything, Liam brought his arms around her, drawing her close, and Georgie dissolved into him, meeting his lips without hesitation. It was as though it had been choreographed, like they had rehearsed it over and over to get it perfect. Liam kissed her tenderly but firmly, there was none of the tentativeness of the other day. Georgie tucked her arms around him, under his jacket, holding him tight as they kept right on kissing, even after it started to rain again. It was only light at first, but before long it was falling steadily and she could feel it soaking into her hair, dripping down the side of her face. Reluctantly, she drew back.

"It's raining," she said.

Liam smiled down at her. "So it is."

As they drove home Georgie had a debate with herself about whether to ask him up when they got to her place. It didn't necessarily mean they had to have sex, though it was a pretty powerful nudge in that direction. They'd had enough dates, hadn't they? If she counted Liam's second visit to the shop, along with lunch on the beach, then this was their third date. That was acceptable, wasn't it? And who made the three-date rule anyway? Georgie was trying to recall if she'd heard it somewhere, or if she'd made it up herself. And if she had made it up herself, did it have anything to do with her tendency not to venture past the second date. Had she made up a stupid rule to give herself an excuse to avoid intimacy?

She gave Liam directions, while putting a firm muzzle on her inner voice. She was supposed to be living in the moment. There were no rules. If she felt like asking Liam up when they got to her place, then that's what she would do. She'd allow the moment to simply assert itself.

"You can park just over there," Georgie told him.

Liam cut the engine and shifted sideways, unbuckling his seat belt. "Which one is yours?" he asked, leaning across her to see out the window.

Georgie pointed up. "It's on the third floor, second from the back." Was that a hint? Was she supposed to say, "Come on up, I'll show you"?

He turned his head to look at her and without hesitating, without even the slightest hint of awkwardness, he drew close to kiss her again. They really did have this kissing thing down pat. In fact, she realized, bringing her hand up to hook it around his neck, they were pretty good at it. She liked the way he kissed. Kissing compatibility was very important, if you didn't have that, you were unlikely to get much further. Georgie had heard dozens of stories from women who had dropped an unsatisfactory kisser after the first date. But Liam was perfect. Not too firm or overpowering, but not inhibited either, or worst of all, sloppy. And not too forceful with the tongue. It was just there, wandering around, getting to know hers. She could imagine that tongue wandering elsewhere. . . . Okay, the moment was asserting itself loud and clear.

"Do you want to come up?" Georgie said breathlessly, against his lips.

Liam pulled back, gazing earnestly into her eyes. "I would love to." He kissed her softly, holding her face in his hands. "But I can't."

Georgie felt her heart plummet. Suddenly she wanted him more than anything. She didn't know why she'd had even a moment's pause.

"I have to get back to the office," Liam explained.

"Now? Tonight?"

He nodded. "I left early to meet you. I never leave the office that early. I have a couple of things I need to finish up."

"Sure, of course," she said, trying unsuccessfully to hide her disappointment.

"I'm sorry," he said.

Georgie could see the regret in his eyes. She put a finger to his lips. "You don't have to be sorry. No expectations, remember?"

He smiled at her. "So you'll still take my calls?"

"Of course," she said lightly. "Oh, but do you mind if we swap cell numbers?" She really didn't want to hang around the flat another weekend.

He sat back against his seat. "You want my cell number?"

"Uh-huh," she replied absently, rummaging in her bag. She drew out her cell phone and handed it to him. "Could you program it in for me? And give me your phone and I'll program my number."

Liam was contemplating her phone. "I'm not sure it's such a good idea."

Georgie's stomach lurched.

"It's just that I always turn my phone off during meetings, and I spend a lot of time in meetings, unfortunately. And then I usually turn it off after work, when I don't want to be contacted. . . ."

She looked squarely at him. "If you don't want me to have your number, Liam, just say so. I'm not trying to keep tabs on you, it's only for convenience."

He sighed. "Of course you can have my number." He took his phone out of his pocket and handed it to Georgie. "I just hope you won't be offended if I can't always answer right away."

"I'll cope." She grinned. "Besides, I'll probably text you most of the time."

"Sounds intriguing, I'll look forward to that."

After he had keyed in his number, they exchanged phones again and Georgie dropped hers into her bag. "Well, I'll let you get back to it," she said, leaning over and planting a solid kiss on his lips. "Don't work too hard."

She went to turn away but he stopped her, drawing her back into his arms and kissing her again. "I'll talk to you soon then," he said.

"Whatever," she said lightly, smiling up at him. She climbed out of the car and began up the driveway. She hadn't heard his engine start up, so she turned around and waved. He flashed his lights, but he didn't drive off till she walked into the building.

Georgie felt elated as she climbed the stairs. The sound of music coming from inside her flat couldn't even dampen her mood, though she knew what it probably meant. When she unlocked the door she saw a half dozen bodies draped across the lounge chairs and the floor. The distinctive aroma of dope hung in the air and the sound of a cat being strangled was coming from the stereo as the TV played footage of surfing without any volume.

"Hi!" Georgie said brightly.

A couple of heads turned.

"I'm Trace's flatmate," she continued. "Georgie."

A man with white-blond hair, which looked as though it had only ever been washed in salt water, pointed to the other end of the lounge where, Georgie presumed, it was Tracey's head buried under a pile of cushions. "She crashed," he grunted.

Georgie smiled at no one in particular, stepping over a body on her way to the hall. "Well, goodnight everyone," she chirped.

A couple of arms moved and she heard a communal murmur. She walked into her room and closed the door, tossing her bag on the bed just as it started to emit a ring. She picked it up again and reached inside for her cell. "Georgie speaking."

"I thought your name was Georgie Reading?"

It was Liam. She knew his voice now. "Hello, miss me already?"

"Absolutely."

She felt like a schoolgirl. "So what's up? Did I leave something in the car?"

"No, I missed you already," he said. Georgie smiled. "And I forgot to thank you for tonight."

"I should be the one thanking you," she insisted. "You invited me."

"Well, I'm glad you said yes."

"I'm glad I did too."

There was a pause.

"So I was thinking," said Liam, "I'm probably free for lunch tomorrow."

"Oh?" Georgie was smiling. "Well, if you are, come by the shop, if you like."

"Alright, I might just do that."

"Maybe I'll see you then."

"I think it's a distinct possibility."

"Okay."

"Bye."

Georgie felt a lightness she had never known before. This was what people meant when they talked about walking on air. She had a delicious sense of anticipation with none of the fear. Clearly she had been doing this all wrong before now, she realized, undressing for bed. She had always set her hopes so high there was only one way for them to go—crashing down. But this, well, it felt almost indulgent. Like she'd stumbled upon some wonderful forbidden food that no matter how much she ate she would never put on weight.

She pulled on a T-shirt and climbed into bed, lying on her back, gazing up at the ceiling and grinning like a mad thing. She was insanely happy and she was going to revel in it. And she was going to make Liam happy, delirious if she could. She was determined to be the most enjoyable thing in his life. She would not add a moment's stress, not cause him pain or angst or become a complication in any way.

And who could say where they might end up? Or what exquisite secret paths they might find along the way.

Mosman

Anna checked her watch. He couldn't be much longer, surely. She couldn't remember the last time she'd waited up for Mac, but she had assumed he'd be home by midnight. It was 12:30 now and still no sign of him. It had been weeks since they'd sat down to a meal together. Weeks since she'd made that stupid remark. Weeks since Mac had been able to look her in the eye.

Anna wished she could take it back, but she knew that was impossible. It was out there, on the record, she couldn't pretend she hadn't said it. Worse, she couldn't pretend there wasn't an element of truth in it. Not that she only saw Mac as a sperm donor, that was patently ludicrous. She loved him. She had loved him for so long she couldn't imagine her life without him. But the fact was, she couldn't imagine her life without a child either. Why couldn't Mac understand that all of a sudden? It was hardly a new idea. Did he think she'd gone through everything over the past few years just to fill the time? But now he seemed to be taking it personally, as though her longing for a baby meant he was inadequate, that their relationship was deficient.

When he walked out that night Anna had asked herself if she really could be happy with Mac but without a baby. And she'd decided yes, she could, of course she could. But why did she have to? One didn't preclude the other. She wanted to be pregnant, to give birth and mother a child . . . their child. No matter how much Mac loved her or she loved him, no matter how much fulfillment they could find in a life without children, there would always be something missing.

It wasn't as though Anna was the only woman to feel this way. And surely other men didn't think their partners' desire to have a child was because they didn't love them enough? That was clearly absurd. The problem with infertility, apart from the obvious, was that it turned a natural phenomenon into an overwrought, convoluted process involving previously unconsidered matters of ethics and morality and an unhealthy amount of soul-searching and just plain navel-gazing. Every aspect was turned inside out, debated, evaluated, deliberated upon, obsessed over. Anna wondered what it must feel like to wake up one day and find yourself pregnant. By accident even. The idea was almost unimaginable to her, yet it happened to women around the world every day. Every minute.

She heard the key in the front door. Mac was home finally. When he'd called to say he'd be late, and Anna had sat eating her meal alone for the umpteenth time, she had come to the decision that she was not going to do this anymore. One of them had to end the cold war. Mac had said that he wanted a break, that he wanted to see what they had together apart from IVF. Well, if the last couple of weeks was any indication, they had very little. But Anna didn't want to believe that. It was just a bad patch. They simply had to make an effort if they were going to reconnect.

"Hi," she said.

He had a frown on his face. "What are you doing up? Is something wrong?"

That was a loaded question. She just shrugged. "Thought I'd wait up for you."

"I told you not to bother," he said a little awkwardly.

"It was no bother." Anna opened the fridge and took out his plate of food. "Have you eaten? Do you want me to heat this up for you?"

"I'll do that," he chided, taking the plate from her. "You should go to bed, Anna, it's late for you to be up." He peeled back the plastic wrap a little and put the plate in the microwave.

"I hardly see you anymore," she said tentatively, as he programmed the oven.

He pressed Start and turned around to face her. "What are you implying? You know it's been hell at work."

"I'm not implying anything." She didn't want to put him on the defensive. "I just thought we could talk," she said. "We haven't talked for a while."

Mac opened the fridge door, looking inside rather than at her. "It's not exactly the best time to talk, Anna. I'm exhausted." He picked up a bottle of beer. "Do you want anything?" he asked her.

She shook her head. "No thanks."

He twisted the top off the bottle and swallowed down a few mouthfuls. The oven beeped and Anna turned.

"I'll get it," Mac insisted, passing her. She opened a drawer and took out a knife and a fork, then a napkin from the next drawer. She followed him over to the breakfast table and handed him the cutlery.

"Thanks," he said, taking it from her as he sat down.

She slid onto the chair opposite as he began to eat. "How is it?"

"Fine, thanks."

"Because sometimes steak reheated in the microwave—"

"It's great. Thank you."

Anna rested her hands on the table, clasping them together. "Mum rang today."

Mac nodded, chewing, his mouth full.

"She was asking when we think we'll get down there next."

He swallowed, then took a swig of his beer. "I don't know. I told you, it's crazy at work."

Anna sighed. "Maybe you need to get away. You were saying you needed a holiday."

"A weekend with your parents was not exactly what I had in mind," he muttered.

"You've never minded visiting my parents before."

"You know I like spending time with your parents. Don't make this about them, Anna."

"Then what is this about, Mac?"

He breathed out heavily. "You know what it's about."

"So how long are you going to keep punishing me?"

Mac stared down at his plate, moving food around with his fork. "I'm not punishing you," he said without looking up.

"Then why won't you talk to me?"

"Because we've talked enough, Anna. There's nothing more to say." He paused. "I want to talk about something else, anything else."

"Fine," Anna said calmly. "But at the moment we don't seem to talk at all."

Mac dropped his fork on the plate and pushed it away. "You pick your times, don't you?" he said, consulting his watch. "Nearly one o'clock on a Friday night, or should I say, Saturday morning. What kind of sense are we going to make now?"

He picked up his plate and walked over to the kitchen bin, scraping off the remainder of his dinner. He opened the dishwasher and stacked the plate, dropping his cutlery into the basket.

Anna sat staring at her hands. They were the first part of the body to show the signs of aging, someone had once told her. Her hands looked alright, though the skin was starting to feel a little crepey. This was one of her tricks, focus on something trivial to detract from the pain. Like biting on a knuckle when you had stubbed a toe.

What was happening to them? Mac seemed so angry with her, he could barely look at her. How had it all turned around so fast? He must have been bottling this up for ages. Resentment was like that, like rust. By the time it made its way to the surface where you could see it, it had already destroyed everything underneath. And by then it was almost impossible to do anything about it.

Anna cleared her throat. "What shall I tell Mum?" she said. "It's Dad's birthday in a couple of weeks. She was hoping we'd make it down." She looked across at Mac. He was standing in the middle of the kitchen, staring down at the floor, apparently deep in thought.

Finally he sighed. "E-mail a couple of dates to work so I can check them against my schedule."

Anna swallowed. She stared at her hands again. She should treat herself to a manicure, she hadn't had one in quite a while.

"I'm going to bed" she heard Mac say as he left the room.

Harbord

"Cross the road, would you? Just cross the road, Meg! You know you want to."

"Get over it, Nick. She's not going to cross the road." Louise groaned.

Louise and Georgie were watching *Sleepless in Seattle* with Nick. They should have known better.

"If she crossed the road now and they met, that would be the end of the movie," Georgie explained.

"And that's bad, how?"

"No one asked you to watch this, Nick," Louise reminded him.

"I didn't have much of a choice," he grumbled. "The odds are always against me around here. Where's your boyfriend anyway, Georgie? I need an ally."

"I told you, he's in Perth." Georgie checked her watch. "Actually, he's probably on his way back right now."

"You don't see a lot of him on the weekends, do you?" said Nick. "He hasn't got a wife and twelve kids tucked away somewhere, has he?"

"Oh yeah, that's right, I forgot to tell you." Georgie rolled her eyes. "He travels a lot," she explained. "And he works at least part of every weekend."

"Does that bother you?"

She shook her head. "I have to work part of most weekends too. And we see each other lots when he is home."

"He turns up at the shop every second day," Louise chimed in. "Always with something for her, usually flowers. The beautiful, expensive kind."

"What do you mean?"

"Nothing," Louise replied offhand. "Who wants coffee?" she said, picking up the remote to pause the video.

"You know, the bar keeps getting raised," Nick complained. "It used to be enough to remember to buy flowers once in a while. Now it has to be the right kind of flowers."

"You don't have to bring me any kind of flowers," Louise assured him, leaning over to kiss his cheek. "I love you just the same."

"She doesn't mean that," Georgie confided as Louise walked over to the kitchen.

"You think I don't realize that?" Nick sighed heavily. "I can see having Mr. Big around is not going to be so good for me."

"Who's for coffee?" Louise called.

They both raised their hands.

Nick looked across at Georgie. "So, he's making you happy?"

"He is. He's absolutely perfect." She sighed deeply. "Except for the sex."

Nick covered his ears with cushions off the sofa. "Not hearing this, do not want to know about my sister's sex life. In fact, would rather not be aware my sister has a sex life. I'm supposed to lynch men who want to sully your virtue."

"Yeah, if we were living in the Dark Ages," Louise pointed out, carrying a tray over and setting it down on the coffee table.

"Well, you don't have to worry." Georgie sighed. "We're not having sex."

Louise and Nick looked at her, wide-eyed.

"I suppose we haven't been seeing each other that long," she went on. "And he has been really busy with some huge deal at work. He always seems to have global conference calls or a late meeting or an early flight in the morning, that kind of thing." Georgie paused. "And he's a little battle-scarred from his last relationship," she added. "But I still think it's a bit odd. He's never even come up to the flat."

Louise was thoughtful. "Are you absolutely sure there's no wife and kids?"

"Don't be ridiculous," Georgie scoffed. "He's not married, I asked him the first time we met. He wouldn't lie to me barefaced."

"How do you know that?"

"I trust him, he hasn't given me any reason not to."

Louise sighed loudly, pouring herself a cup of coffee.

"I know you think I'm gullible, Louise," said Georgie, "but I don't want to go through life being suspicious of everyone's motives. I don't want to believe people are that sinister."

"She has a point," said Nick. "Women always think more is going on with guys than there really is. When a bloke says there's nothing wrong, he generally means it, whereas a woman means anything but."

"Think about it, Louise," Georgie added, "if Liam was married and having an affair with me, do you think I'd be complaining about not getting any sex?"

Louise sighed. "Good point."

"Look, I don't know why I'm even complaining," said Georgie. "He's so romantic, all the wining and dining and flowers and everything. It's nice that he's not just trying to get me into bed."

"Maybe he has performance anxiety?" Nick suggested.

"What?"

"Women think men never have any insecurities when it comes to sex, that they'll always be more experienced. We don't know as much as you think we do. It can be pretty daunting the first time."

"Are you suggesting I seduce Liam?" asked Georgie.

"Yes." He nodded, before shaking his head frantically. "What am I saying? No, definitely not!"

"What?"

"Would it be too much to ask that you give up sex, for your only brother's sake?"

"Idiot." Georgie laughed.

Nick dropped his head onto Louise's lap and covered his face with a cushion.

"Imagine what he's going to be like with the girls." Louise groaned.

He sat up again. "I'm not worried about the girls," he said calmly. "I realize that one day, when they're old enough"—he paused, taking a breath— "I'll simply have to lock them in their bedrooms and throw away the key."

Melbourne

The taxi pulled up out front of the apartment block on the banks of the Yarra River. Anna's parents had joined the migration of empty nesters, selling the family home and buying a modern city apartment after Anna and Mac moved to Sydney. Anna had been heartbroken, not that she ever said anything. But she had always pictured her own children running around playing in the garden, sleeping over in her old room. She had so wanted to give her parents a grandchild, to be able to announce it one day when they least expected it. Though she suspected that all potential grandparents lived in a permanent state of anticipation of that particular announcement. Which was why she had never wanted to tell them about her IVF treatment. Anna knew how long and hard they had waited to have her, she couldn't make them go through it again.

But now . . . well, now things had changed.

Mac jumped from the taxi to get their bags, leaving Anna to pay the driver. The trip had been an ordeal. They had barely spoken in the car on the way to the airport and as soon as they were settled in their seats on the plane, Mac had opened his laptop and started to work. She had never known him to act with such studied indifference toward her. But he wouldn't be able to ignore her for much longer.

"Darling, you're here," her mother crooned into the security intercom. Mac and Anna took the lift to the twelfth floor where her parents were waiting as the doors opened. Caroline Gilchrist held out her arms, rushing forward to greet her daughter.

"Mac," said Bernard, shaking his hand heartily. "It's been too long, Son."

Her father did love Mac like the son he'd never had, and Bernard and Caroline were like the parents Mac had always wanted. Anna was confident he wouldn't willingly hurt them or see them upset. She was counting on that.

"How's corporate life treating you?" Bernard asked him.

"Cracking the whip lately, I'm afraid, Bernard," Mac answered ruefully.

Bernard enjoyed the stimulation of the younger man. He had not taken easily to retirement. A highly regarded psychiatrist, he had served on the boards of both hospitals and universities. He still retained a couple of honorary positions, as much as he could manage really. Bernard could feel the weight of his advancing years. His mind was sharp but his body was betraying him. It was not so much retirement as old age that he despised.

He turned to Anna, smiling in that way fathers reserve for their daughters. He still saw the four-year-old, the seven-year-old, perhaps the twelve-year-old, but it was hard for him to see far past that. Anna knew her father loved her, adored her in fact, but he still treated her like his little girl, and like a little girl she was still desperate to win his approval. She had his affection, but she wanted more. When she didn't make it into medicine after school, Anna chose psychology, telling herself and anyone who would listen that it had nothing to do with her father, it was what she wanted to do. But it had everything to do with her father. And the irony of it was that he regarded psychology as pop psychiatry and had never really taken her career seriously.

"Leave the bags for now," Caroline insisted once they were inside the apartment. "I have lunch all but ready, you must be starved. Come along, Anna, give me a hand."

She followed her mother into the kitchen. In many ways Caroline had fulfilled the traditional role of wife despite a stellar career of her own as an academic. She had always been overshadowed by the formidable reputation of her husband, and it didn't appear to bother her one bit.

"You look tired, darling," Caroline said, taking hold of Anna's hands and looking into her eyes. She said it with genuine concern; it was not the kind of veiled put-down many mothers engaged in with their daughters. Caroline was not like that. They enjoyed an easy, open relationship, and

Anna knew she could tell her anything, which was going to make what she had to do all the harder.

"I'm fine, Mum." Anna smiled.

"Are you getting enough sleep?" Caroline persisted.

"Sure, I've just had a lot going on lately. I'll tell you all about it when we sit down."

"This looks wonderful, Caroline," said Mac when they brought the food to the table. There was a basket of fresh rolls and a huge antipasto platter groaning with cold meats, marinated vegetables, olives and cheeses.

"It all comes straight from the markets, Mac," Caroline dismissed.

"She lives at those Queen Victoria Markets," Bernard added, opening a bottle with a corkscrew. "Who's having wine?"

Only Anna declined, and she didn't miss the meaningful glance from her mother when she did. After everyone had filled their plates, Anna took a sip of water and leaned forward in her chair. She cleared her throat. "There's something Mac and I have to tell you."

Mac looked up abruptly. "Anna," he cautioned.

"Well, I've been waiting for this," Bernard smiled, lifting his glass.

"No, Dad, I know what you're thinking," Anna stopped him. She glanced at her mother. Caroline was looking slightly puzzled. "I'm not pregnant, though not for want of trying. You see, for a few years now we've been on the IVF program."

Mac dropped his cutlery onto his plate and sat back in his chair. His expression was grim.

"IVF . . ." Caroline said, trying to take it all in, "for *years*, did you say?"

"Yes, Mum. Please don't be offended. I haven't told you because I didn't want you to have to go through it with me, so to speak."

"Oh, darling, we're your parents. It's not your job to protect us."

"When did you start the program exactly?" Bernard asked.

"Well, it was not long after we moved to Sydney."

"But that's seven years." Anna could hear the hurt in her mother's voice.

"It hasn't been quite that long," said Anna. "There were all the investigations first, then they try you on fertility drugs, and . . ." she faltered. She didn't want to say insemination. Anna had barely spoken to anyone about the treatment in detail, and sharing it with her parents was a little embarrassing. "They try other less invasive procedures first, until eventually you're offered IVF."

"What made you decide to go ahead with it, Anna?" asked Caroline. "And Mac," she added, "how do you feel about this?"

Anna spoke before he had a chance to answer. "We had been trying to have a baby for a couple of years with no luck, so we decided to investigate."

"But you knew my history, darling."

"Yes, Mum, but it's an oxymoron to presuppose that infertility is genetic."

"But I wasn't infertile," Caroline corrected her. "I did get pregnant eventually. You didn't think of just adopting a wait-and-see attitude?"

"There was no need. They didn't have the technology years ago that they have now. There were options available to me that weren't available to you."

Caroline and Bernard exchanged a glance.

"What about side effects?" Bernard asked. He'd been wearing The Face since Anna broached the subject. The inscrutable face he had perfected as a practicing psychiatrist. It allowed him to ask questions, comment, weigh up what he was hearing without ever giving away how he felt.

"There are some side effects. . . ." Anna began.

"There are many side effects," Mac interrupted, finally taking the chance to speak. "Headaches, nausea, fatigue, pain. She's been through it all. Once she even had to be hospitalized for a serious reaction to the drugs."

"Hospitalized!" exclaimed Caroline. "Why didn't you tell us, Anna?"

"Like I said, I didn't want to worry you."

"So why are you telling us now?" Bernard asked, his expression still unreadable. Mostly. Anna could sense his disapproval, her mother's too. She felt defensive. She'd expected them to be miffed, but she hadn't expected an inquisition. It was almost as if she had to justify it to them.

"It seemed about time," she said weakly.

"We're at a bit of a stalemate," Mac explained. Anna wished he'd just shut up. "The doctor's recommending that we take a break, and I agree. Anna's . . . reluctant."

"You should listen to your doctor," said Bernard soberly.

"Your father's right," Caroline chimed in.

Anna took a deep breath, almost gritting her teeth. "It was a suggestion more than a recommendation," she asserted. "What the doctor actually said was that it was entirely up to me."

The silence that met her was icy. As was the expression in her parents' eyes, staring back at her.

"Surely," said Bernard, "what you meant to say is that it's up to you and your husband?"

"Don't blame me because your little plan backfired."

"Keep your voice down, Mac!" Anna whispered irritably. They were in the guestroom, getting ready to go out to dinner for a slightly belated celebration of her father's birthday. "I'm just saying you didn't have to be so negative," she went on, her voice hushed. "Now you have them thinking the program is somehow dangerous and my health's at risk."

"Well, it is, Anna."

"That's rubbish and you know it. Plenty of people go through IVF with no ill effects at all."

"But not you," he replied firmly. "And not for such a long time."

Anna turned away. She didn't have a comeback for that.

Mac sat down to take off his shoes. "Look, you decided to tell your parents, so deal with it. I had to deal with it all these years when I wanted to tell them, when I was worried about you, when you were in the hospital, for Chrissakes, and you wouldn't let me say a word."

"Because I didn't want to worry them," she insisted.

"But you don't mind worrying them now?"

Anna sighed heavily. "You don't understand. I just didn't want them to have to go through all the highs and lows with us. I thought I'd be able to surprise them one day. Show up and announce I was pregnant, that we were expecting their grandchild." She paused. "But that was beginning to look like it was never going to happen, so I thought it was time they were told what's been going on."

Mac was unmoved. "Be honest, Anna, you only wanted them to know so you could get them on your side." He stood up and walked over to the bed where his suitcase lay open. "But you didn't count on your parents having objections, did you? You cooked up this little game and now you're pissed off because you couldn't control all the players." He picked up his shaving bag. "I'm going to have a shower," he said, leaving the room.

"Tom, you have an IVF program running at the Royal, don't you?"

Anna's ears pricked up. Tom York was an old family friend, a medical researcher who divided his time between Monash University and the Royal Hospital for Women. If she hadn't known better, Anna might have suspected her father had invited Tom tonight simply to lecture her. But as she'd only made her revelation this afternoon, that was unreasonably paranoid of her.

"I think you'll find they pioneered IVF at the Royal, Bernard," Tom answered.

"So they did," Bernard deferred. "Tell me, is there much research being done these days into side effects?"

Anna groaned inwardly.

"What, you mean immediate side effects from the drugs?"

"No, no, I was thinking more long-term. Now that IVF has been around for a while, are they finding any causal links to cancer, for example?"

"You've hit on a contentious issue there, Bernard," Tom replied. "For years there have been concerns about the higher incidence of breast, uterine, ovarian, cervical cancers in IVF patients, but no studies have been able to prove anything conclusively. Still, IVF is relatively young. Time will tell. Why the interest?"

Bernard hesitated, glancing across the table. Anna made sure her face conveyed a mixture of anguish and pique that would stop her father in his tracks.

"Well, I for one do not wish to spend the evening talking about cancer," Caroline declared. "It's certainly not the topic for a birthday party."

Anna picked up her wineglass and proceeded slowly, though she hoped discreetly, to drain it. Edward O'Brien was sitting to her left. He and Bernard had been psych registrars together, Anna had known him forever. He noticed that her glass was empty and immediately refilled it for her. "Thank you, Ed."

"My pleasure, dear," he said, squeezing her hand.

Anna took a long, slow sip from her glass. The wine was beginning to infuse her with warmth; she was feeling that pleasant buzz, that sense of well-being that made her problems seem very small and infinitely manageable. Her eyes came to rest on Mac. He was seated across the table from her, engrossed in a conversation with Phillip Selway, who was neither an academic nor any kind of medical practitioner but an economist who worked as an adviser in the merchant banking sector. Mac and Phil tended to gravitate toward each other at these get-togethers, soul mates from the corporate sector. Anna watched her husband. He was a handsome man. Not in a movie idol kind of way, but he had strong, defined features and bottomless eyes the color of slate. His face was so familiar to her that sometimes she forgot how handsome he was, how attractive she had found him when he first came to court her. An old-fashioned term, but it was the only way to describe the way he had behaved. He was at once charming and confident, full of ambition and mature beyond his years, yet at the same time quite awestruck and boyish around her. Anna had felt it keenly, it turned a girl's head to be the object of such devotion, such single-minded determination to win her over. If only he'd known he didn't have to try so hard.

Anna sat back in her chair, her legs crossed, clutching her arms around herself as she rested the glass against her lips, drawing the wine into her mouth in a slow, steady stream. It was like honey, gliding down her throat, filling her up like a sweet elixir, soothing her soul, warming her belly. Anna wanted to go home and lie naked next to Mac. No, not next to him. She wanted to be entwined around him, she wanted to feel his skin against hers, to feel his heart beating, his lips . . .

Anna swallowed. She felt flushed and a little breathless. Her glass was empty again. She reached for a bottle on the table in front of her. Mac must have seen her out of the corner of his eye and he picked it up first. Ever the gentleman. He began to pour the wine into her glass, his head bent toward Phil, still listening to him. He glanced across at Anna, only fleetingly, but enough to make a flash assessment of her condition. He stopped pouring, the glass half full. Or half empty. A brief, disapproving cloud passed over his features before he returned his full attention to Phil. Anna picked up the glass and resumed her slow, steady pattern of emptying its contents. Ed would refill it for her soon enough. She was going to drink as much as she wanted tonight. As much as she needed.

As much as she needed turned out to be a little too much. Anna slowed down when she realized she was getting woozy, but the damage had already been done. When she went to get up from the table she felt unsteady, but before she knew it Mac was at her side, discreetly supporting her. She leaned heavily against him as they walked from the restaurant to her parents' car, and he kept hold of her while he opened the door and helped her into her seat. Bless him.

But back at the apartment, alone in their room, Mac ignored her. Anna had to put all her concentration into getting changed, preferably without falling over. She didn't want to disgust him. He'd been kind, even a little affectionate, helping her to the car. She had to get him to respond to her tonight. They had to reconnect. If he was insisting on this break, "to see what they had together," then she had to show him that what they had was fine. More than fine. And she had to do that as soon as possible so they could stop all this nonsense and get back onto the program.

She went to the bathroom to brush her teeth. Staring at her reflection in the mirror, Anna realized this wasn't only about whether or not they continued with IVF. She missed Mac. She missed the way he was gentle and tender and caring toward her. Always. He had been such a good husband, but she feared she hadn't always been the best wife. Not intentionally, but the hormones and the treatment had at times made her pretty hard to love. And throughout Mac had been steadfast and patient. She had been wrong to suggest he hadn't been through much. He deserved a medal just for putting up with her.

Anna sniffed. Tears had crept into her eyes. She knew it was the alcohol making her sentimental, but so what? That didn't make what she was feeling any less valid. She couldn't wait to get into bed and hold Mac close. She rinsed out her mouth repeatedly before drinking a large glass of water. She wasn't feeling too bad now as she switched off the light and walked back into the bedroom. It was in darkness, Mac was already in bed, turned away from her. Anna lifted the covers and climbed in, sidling over until she was snuggled against his back. He didn't move. She slid her arm around him, bringing her hand up to his chest. Still nothing. Anna was undaunted. She ran her fingertips across his skin, through the fine layer of hair covering his chest as she lifted her head to kiss his shoulder.

"Anna, I'm trying to get to sleep."

Not the reaction she was hoping for, but the one she was half-expecting. She held him tighter, drawing her thigh up against his, speaking softly into his ear.

"I was watching you in the restaurant, Mac, and all I could think about was being with you. We haven't . . . for such a long time."

He sighed heavily. "You're drunk."

"I had a little too much to drink, I know—"

"You had a lot too much."

"Mac, look at me," she said, propping herself up on one elbow. He shifted slightly, turning his head around toward her. "I'm fine, I stopped when I felt it going to my head." She couldn't see his expression in the darkness, not what was in his eyes. "Mac?"

"What do you want me to say?"

"Nothing, nothing at all," she whispered huskily, drawing closer and kissing him softly on the lips. He didn't respond.

"I'm not in the mood, okay, Anna?" he said, turning away from her again.

Anna ignored the tight feeling in her chest and bent to kiss his shoulder, inching toward his neck as she moved her hand down his chest to his abdomen. "I bet I can get you into the mood," she breathed, slipping her fingers under the edge of his shorts. But before she could get any farther, Mac grasped her wrist and pushed her hand away.

"For crying out loud, Anna!" he exclaimed, throwing the covers off and sitting up on the edge of the bed. "Can't you just take no for an answer?"

Anna lay back against the pillows, tears pricking the corners of her eyes. "But we haven't made love for ages, Mac."

She saw his shoulders drop. "Your timing is incredible, Anna. Why would you choose to wait until we're at your parents' place, for Chrissakes?"

"I didn't wait. . . . Look, I didn't plan this, okay?" Anna returned. "At home I'm always asleep by the time you come upstairs. You never get home before midnight—"

"Don't you think you're exaggerating just a little, Anna?"

She levered herself upright and leaned back against the headboard. "All I know, Mac, is that you said we had to take a break so we could see what we had together, but ever since then you've been keeping your distance from me. I don't understand what's going on with you lately."

Mac turned around to look at her. She still couldn't clearly see the expression in his eyes. "Did you expect me to forget what you said, to act like you never said it?"

"No, but I told you I was sorry. And you know I didn't mean it anyway."

"How do I know that?"

Anna groaned. "If you love me, then you'd know I could never have meant it."

"Huh," he scoffed ruefully, "that's rich. So now it becomes a test of my love for you? Very clever, Anna."

"That's not what I meant—"

"And that's becoming a habit. Saying things you don't mean."

Anna sighed. "This is an argument about words, Mac. It's ridiculous. We're not getting anywhere."

"I agree," he said, lifting the covers and lying down, turning away from her.

Anna glared at the back of his head. "So you're just going to ignore me now?"

"This is not the time, Anna."

"Well, just exactly when is the time, Mac?" she demanded. "Whenever I try to talk to you, you say it's not the right time!"

Mac breathed out audibly. "I'm not going to have the conversation you want to have, here in your parents' home, at"—he turned the bedside clock round to face him—"12:42 in the frigging morning," he finished. "I'm going to sleep."

Anna bit her lip, sinking back down under the covers. She looked across at Mac. She would have liked to cuddle into him, but she couldn't even do that now. If only she hadn't pushed it tonight. Mac was probably right, it wasn't a good time, but she was starting to wonder if there was ever going to be a good time. The vacant expanse of bed between them was like a deep chasm, they were so far away from each other. And getting farther all the time.

Next Morning

Anna rolled over, stretching, allowing her eyes to adjust to the light, and to the surroundings. She peered over at the clock. 9:23. She never slept this late, but she supposed she must have needed it. Mac was already up, which was not remarkable—she doubted he slept much at all. The memory of last night crept up on her, engulfing her in sadness again. They were in serious trouble. It made her feel sick but she couldn't ignore it anymore. She'd counseled enough couples through the death throes of tattered marriages. But they could usually recount a long and steady decline. Anna felt like a bomb had dropped on them. Unexpected, out of the blue. Though she wondered if Mac would tell it like that.

There was a light tap on the door and Anna called, "Come in," her voice husky.

The door swung open and her mother entered, carrying a cup of tea. "Did I wake you, darling?"

"No." Anna managed a smile, sitting up. "Not that I've been awake for long."

Caroline passed her the cup. "Well, that's good, you've had a nice sleep-in then." She walked around to the other side of the bed. "I might make myself comfortable, if that's alright?"

"Please," said Anna as her mother climbed over next to her, propped the pillows against the headboard and settled onto them.

Anna sipped her tea. "What are Mac and Dad up to?"

"Well, your father was thrilled to see Mac up bright and early and he dragged him off for a game of golf."

"I doubt he had to do much dragging."

"They're only going to play nine holes. Mac promised he'd have him back no later than eleven so we can have a nice relaxed brunch before you have to leave for the airport." Caroline sighed. "It feels like you've only been here five minutes."

Anna placed her cup on the bedside table and moved closer to her, linking her arm through her mother's and resting her head on her shoulder. "I miss you too, Mum."

Caroline leaned her head against her daughter's. "I wish we weren't so far away, with everything you're going through."

"That's exactly why I didn't want you to know, Mum, I don't want you worrying."

"Well, now we'll worry regardless."

"I'm sorry."

"Don't apologize. I told you yesterday, it's not your job to protect us. Frankly I was quite surprised that you kept it from us all this time. I can't help thinking there was more to it."

Anna sighed. "It's just that I always dreamed of arriving here, sometime special like Christmas maybe, and announcing we were pregnant. Make grandparents out of the two of you."

"Oh, Anna," Caroline chided, shifting to face Anna. "Giving us a grandchild should have been the least of your concerns."

"But I'm your only child. You're not going to get one from anywhere else."

"And guess what? Our lives will go on full and rich without one, just as they always have."

Anna considered her doubtfully.

"I mean it, darling," Caroline insisted. "We haven't been sweating on a grandchild. To be honest, your father and I suspected you and Mac weren't especially bothered about having children. I thought if it was going to happen it might be late in the piece, like it was for me. I was right about your age now when I had you, so it has been in the back of my mind lately. But we were pleased that you seemed to be content, getting on with your lives, building your careers. You reminded us of ourselves in some ways."

"But weren't you trying the whole time till you had me?"

"Oh no, what gave you that idea? After we were married for a few years and I hadn't fallen pregnant, we did go and see some doctors about what we could do. I was teaching, your father had just started his practice. All they could offer us were fertility drugs, and there always seemed to be reports in the paper of women having nine babies and losing them all, so we didn't want to take that route. I was a little uneasy. I was only twenty-five, but all our friends were having babies, it's what you did back then. You didn't question it. You didn't plan it either, not too rigidly anyway. By and large, women didn't think about careers because they knew they'd be interrupted. So your father turned to me and said, "Caroline, you're not going to sit around waiting to fall pregnant. What are you going to do with your life?" And you know, it was the first time I'd ever thought that way. And it was wonderful, liberating really. Suddenly I had all these choices, just like a man."

Anna sat listening to her, wide-eyed, her stomach churning. Her mother had actually been glad she couldn't have a baby?

"So I went back to university and studied for my master's degree, as you know. There weren't many women doing that, barely any who had children. And, of course, I went on and did my Ph.D. and gained tenure at the university. Your father and I traveled a lot during that time as well. We used to plan our big overseas trips for months, and other times we'd fly out at a moment's notice to catch a show in Sydney on a Saturday night." Caroline paused, smiling. "It was a wonderful time. Our lives were rich and full, we couldn't have been happier."

Anna swallowed. "So I came along and spoiled it all."

Caroline frowned at her. "Anna," she chided, "you're sounding like a child yourself now. You didn't spoil anything. When I discovered I was pregnant, well, I can't tell you the joy . . . and your father was beside himself. Yes, Anna, we loved our life, but you, you were the icing on the cake. We couldn't believe that we'd managed to have it all. That we had gone on with our lives and still we were blessed with this wonderful bonus when we least expected it."

Anna sat taking it all in. She had gone through her life believing she was precious to her parents, that they had yearned for her for a long time. But she was just a "bonus," a nice little unexpected extra.

"The thing is, Anna," Caroline continued, "we didn't wait around for a child to complete us as a couple, or as individuals for that matter. And I'm glad we didn't. We loved you with all our hearts, but we didn't have you to fill a gap in our lives. That's an enormous burden for a child to carry. We've watched enough friends do just that, investing their own happiness and fulfillment in their children's achievements." Caroline shook her head at the very thought of it. "So we just enjoyed you, dear, watched you grow, become your own person. And it was no surprise to us that a wonderful man came along who appreciated how wonderful you are. We've only ever wanted you to be happy, darling. And we thought you were. That's what's difficult to understand about all this."

"I am happy, Mum," said Anna. "It's not weird to want to have a child."

"Of course not, darling, I didn't mean to imply it was. But I wonder if you two couldn't just leave it in the lap of the gods now? Relax and enjoy your life together for a while?"

Relax and enjoy what? Holidays and trips to the theater? Maybe those things made her parents' lives "rich and full," but Anna was having a hard time imagining her and Mac . . . She had a sick feeling in her stomach. A sick, uncomfortable feeling. It wasn't anything. They had been trying for a baby for so long they had got out of the habit of holidays and the like. That was all it was. They had got out of the habit.

"You know I fell pregnant around your age without drugs or any intervention," Caroline was saying. "Maybe you have to give your body the chance to do its own thing. You never know."

"You're making it sound a little cosmic, Mum."

"Well, isn't it, to a degree? If we were dependent on technology to bring babies into the world, the human race would have died out long ago."

Anna frowned. "Do you have some kind of ethical objection to IVF?"

"No, of course not," she insisted. "Your father and I are just concerned about the long-term effects on your health, on your whole life really."

Anna started to crumble inside. Was there not one person who would support her anymore? Was she so unreasonable to want a baby?

"Come along," Caroline said, patting her on the arm. "We'd better get a wriggle on, those men will be home soon, and I bet they'll be hungry."

Dee Why

Georgie decided that kissing Liam was probably her favorite thing in the whole world. And she could only imagine if the kissing was this good, the sex would be amazing. But that was the problem, she could only imagine. They still hadn't made love and Georgie was beginning to think something was wrong. He couldn't be gay, he couldn't kiss her like this if he was gay. He wasn't married, because, as Louise had agreed, they'd have had sex long ago. Perhaps he had some physical problem, but she had been pressed up against him enough times to know that everything seemed to be in working order. Yet here they were once again, parked outside her place, necking in the front seat like two hormone-charged teenagers with nowhere else to go.

Maybe Nick was right. Maybe Liam was nervous, anxious even. But if they didn't have sex soon Georgie was quite sure she was going to burst. It was time to take matters into her own hands, for want of a better expression.

So when Liam had phoned that morning to arrange an early dinner, Georgie had mounted her assault. She told Louise she needed to take care of some errands so she'd be gone for a couple of hours. She took a bus down to Manly where she knew she'd find what she was looking for in one of the trendy, surfer-girl boutiques that littered the area. It was relatively easy buying an outfit for such a finite purpose as seduction. It simply had to reveal lots of flesh and cling to the right bits. Georgie quickly found just such a dress made of flimsy fabric in a deep shade of rust, close to red but definitely not red. A red dress would have been a little too obvious. This dress suggested red without being so brazen as to actually be red. Though it was brazen in just about every other respect. Georgie didn't have the most impressive breasts, but the dress certainly made the most of what she had, with a barely there bodice held up by threadlike straps, leaving nothing much to the imagination. The rest of the dress clung to her slender frame, finishing just above the knees. Georgie never wore clothes like this, even though she had the figure for them. They just seemed too out there; she felt exposed. But because she was dressing for Liam it didn't bother her in the least.

Her next stop was home, to attempt a brief clean-through and warn Tracey off. But Tracey wasn't there. So she wrote a note requesting the place to herself tonight. She aimed for an assertive tone, but she suspected it sounded more like a plea. Georgie swept through the flat, picking up anything of Tracey's and depositing it on her bedroom floor, where it joined the rest of her belongings. She pinned the note to her pillow and stepped back. Was it unmissable? Georgie propped the pillow vertically against the headboard and readjusted the note. That was the best she could do.

In her own room she pulled the sheets off the bed and shoved them into the laundry hamper along with every piece of clothing scattered around the room. She made the bed, and before replacing the quilt, she sprayed perfume across the sheets. She'd read about that in magazines, but she'd never actually done it. Probably because she'd never had to work so hard at seducing anyone before.

Georgie took a quick shower, dousing herself in the same perfume and rubbing her hair dry with a towel. She had considered making an appointment with the hairdresser but thought that might be overkill. Besides, she'd only had her hair cut and streaked a couple of weeks ago. Copper this time, with wide slashes of gold. She scrunched some sort of gel, wax, mousse, lard for all she knew, through her hair and hoped for the best. Georgie never wore much makeup, so mascara and lip gloss were as far as she was prepared to go. She'd already crossed the line with the perfumed sheets.

She ran naked back to her room and realized she should have bought some underwear while she was out. She didn't have anything slinky or sexy. Oh, well, if all went to plan she wouldn't be wearing them for long. She pulled on a plain pair of undies and then wriggled into her dress, but as she caught sight of her reflection in the wardrobe mirror Georgie got a bit of a shock. In the shop she could have been anyone, but here in her own bedroom she was unmistakably Georgie, in the most revealing dress she'd ever worn in her life.

And she was going to have to go back to work in it. Bugger, Adam and Louise were going to have a field day.

"Be still my beating heart, what vision do I see before me?" Adam fell to his knees holding both hands to his chest.

"Don't start," Georgie warned. She had left the bus one stop early so she could duck around the block and come into the shop by the back way. She'd slipped directly into the storeroom without anyone noticing her, and then she froze. She felt excruciatingly self-conscious. She'd been pottering around for the last ten minutes, pretending to be busy, when Adam had appeared in the doorway.

"Don't make a big deal, okay? It's just that I'm going out straight after work."

Still on his knees, Adam lurched forward, wrapping his arms around her waist. "Take me with you," he pleaded.

"Oh, for crying out loud." His head was almost buried into her breasts and Georgie had to push his forehead back with the palm of her hand. "Get a hold of yourself, Adam."

"But you're so beautiful," he cried, a twinkle in his eye.

" 'Ello, 'ello, 'ello, what do we have here then?" Louise stood watching them, bemused, her hands on her hips.

"Would you call your dog off, please?" said Georgie.

"Down Fido."

Adam released Georgie, sitting back on his haunches. "Look, honey, our little girl's all grown up."

"I reckon," said Louise.

"Please, can we just drop it? I already feel self-conscious enough."

"Why? If you've got it, flaunt it," Louise declared.

"But I never wear clothes like this, I'm always worried I look like a slut."

Adam got to his feet. "No need to worry, guys like that."

"Adam!"

He put an arm around her shoulders. "You don't look like a slut," he assured her. "You look gorgeous. I hope the suit realizes how lucky he is."

When he arrived at the shop, it was quite obvious to everybody that Liam was in fact awestruck by his good fortune. "Do you want me to pick his jaw up off the floor?" Adam muttered under his breath to Georgie when Liam first laid eyes on her.

Throughout dinner he was clearly distracted, even flustered at times, losing his train of thought, slipping into a kind of trance when Georgie was speaking. When they left the restaurant, he'd pressed her up against the car and kissed her ravenously for probably ten minutes, until Georgie suggested he should take her home. They had been getting hot and bothered parked out front now for quite long enough.

"Don't you think it's time you came up?" Georgie breathed into his ear.

Liam stopped abruptly. "I can't stay, Georgie," he croaked, clearing his throat. "I have to go back to the office."

"You always have to go back to the office," she said, before biting her lip. She didn't want to sound like a shrew, but jeez, what was a girl supposed to do?

Liam blinked, for a moment he was speechless. "That's because you're the worst thing that's ever happened to me," he said finally.

"I am?"

He nodded. "It's true. I used to be able to focus on work when I was at work, nothing distracted me. And I used to be able to follow a conversation, read a newspaper. . . . Now you come into my head and I can't think straight, I have to see you. So I leave work, and that's why I always have to go back to the office later."

Georgie melted inside as he bent to kiss her again. But she was not going to be put off this time. She responded provocatively, sliding her hand along his thigh. She felt him quiver under her touch. "Why don't you come up," she whispered, flickering her tongue across his lips, "just for a little while?"

He swallowed, breathing hard. "Maybe just for a little while then."

Georgie jumped from the car before Liam could change his mind. As they walked up the stairs to her flat, she could feel her heart hammering against her rib cage. She was sure he would stay, that this would be the night, and she could barely stop herself from leaping up the stairs two at a time. But when they got to her floor, Georgie's heart sank. There was music coming from the flat. Strangled cat music. She hesitated at the top of the stairs.

"What's the matter?" Liam asked, following her gaze to the door of her flat.

"Um, it sounds like my flatmate's home." She winced.

"Is that a problem?"

"I don't think she's alone." Then Georgie had an idea. "We could go to your place!"

"No, we're here now," he insisted, taking her by the arm. "Come on, it'll be alright."

But Georgie suspected it would not be alright at all, and any chance that this was going to be The Night evaporated into the smoky haze that enveloped them as she opened the door. This was a proper, full-scale, no-holds-barred party. Georgie and Liam had to squeeze their way through the crowd to get to the kitchen. She hadn't spotted Tracey, which was lucky because the mood Georgie was in, she was likely to strangle her. And in this crowd no one would hear her scream.

"Can I get you a drink, or something?" Georgie asked loudly.

Liam shook his head. He was obviously uncomfortable, physically re-coiling as he looked around. "It's probably better if I go," he said.

Georgie felt a lump rise into her throat. It wasn't fair. She'd finally got him up here, only to have the flatmate from hell spoil it all. She reached for his hand. "Do you have to?"

"I'm sorry, Georgie," he said, "but do you even know any of these people?"

"No, the rent-a-crowd comes courtesy of my flatmate, whose life is currently in grave danger."

"Oh?"

"I'm going to kill her when I find her."

Liam smiled faintly. "It's okay. There'll be another time."

But *WHEN?* she wanted to scream. It had taken a herculean effort to get him this far, and now she'd have to do it all over again. Georgie felt bewildered, powerless and overwhelmed with disappointment. And then she felt tears welling. She looked down at the floor.

"Hey, are you okay?" Liam said, stroking her hair back from her face.

She sniffed, smiling bravely at him. "Will you come and sit out on the balcony with me for a minute?"

"Sure."

They weaved their way through the pack to the sliding doors, finding the balcony mercifully empty save for a few dead plants and one lone banana lounge that had seen better days. Though not for some time.

"Do you want to try it?" Georgie said.

"Will it support the two of us?"

"Only one way to find out." She grinned, leading him over by the hand. He sat gingerly and then settled himself back while Georgie squeezed in beside him. He wrapped his arms around her and she rested her head against his chest. This was one of those times when she had no difficulty living in the moment.

"Look at that sky," she said, gazing up at the stars.

"Mm," Liam murmured, but he wasn't looking at the sky at all. She held his chin and turned his face upward.

"No, really look," she insisted. "I know it sounds corny, but just look at those stars. On a clear night like this you can see the Southern Cross, and the pointers, and the big saucepan."

"You mean Orion?"

"You say tomato . . . it's beautiful whatever you call it."

"You're right. It's one of the things I notice most when I'm overseas," said Liam. "How different the sky is in the northern hemisphere. It's strange, kind of unsettling, don't you think?"

"I don't know, I've only seen it from here."

Liam looked down at her. "Really?"

"Well, not just from this balcony, but from this part of the world."

"You've never been overseas?"

"Oh, it's not that I didn't want to." She hesitated. "After my parents died, a lot of plans had to change."

Liam was watching her intently. "How old were you then?"

"Sixteen."

"I didn't realize you were so young. That must have been hard."

Georgie shrugged. "Nick took care of us, we did alright."

"How come you never talk about it?"

"It was a long time ago." She looked up at the sky again. "So, how about those stars."

"Georgie?"

"Mm?"

"Why don't you like talking about it?"

She shrugged.

"Does it upset you?"

"No . . . a little. It dulls over the years."

"Do you miss them?" he persisted.

"I miss my mother."

"Oh? What about your father?"

She didn't say anything.

"Georgie?" Liam prompted. "What happened?"

"It was a car accident, I told you."

"But before the accident, was everything alright?"

Georgie sighed. It was about time she told him. "Everything was perfect. My parents had been married for twenty-five years. They seemed so happy, we were a bona fide happy family. And then one day, out of the blue, my father told my mother he was having an affair. There was no reason for it, there'd never been the slightest hint of it. He said he would end it, but it was too late. He'd already destroyed her . . ." Georgie's voice faded.

Liam was staring at her. He looked shocked.

"It's not that big of a deal, Liam," she assured him. "It happens in every second family, I just never expected it to happen in ours. I thought we were different." She paused. "I wish he'd never had the stupid affair, or that he'd kept his mouth shut at least."

Liam stirred then. "You'd rather he lied about it?"

"No! Oh, I don't know." She groaned. "I can't stand lies, but he'd already been lying for who knows how long. And he said he was going to end it, so why tell her? Mum might never have found out . . . and maybe they'd still be alive today."

"I don't understand, what did it have to do with the accident?"

Georgie gazed up at the sky. "You had to have known my mother. She was bright and bubbly, always full of life, the first to arrive at a party and the last to leave. After it all came out, she was a different person. She was depressed and short-tempered, she was so unhappy." Georgie paused. She looked back at Liam. "They were at a party the night it happened. Apparently they argued and they left early. Mum was driving, probably distraught. They should never have left the party."

"What are you saying?"

"Well, they wouldn't have been on the road at that exact moment."

"It was an accident, Georgie." Liam was looking earnestly into her eyes. "You can't blame your father for that, you can't blame anyone." He took a breath. "Sometimes things happen . . . and no one's to blame."

He looked weird. "What is it, Liam?" she asked.

"Nothing." He cleared his throat. "It's just, well, I'm sure your father never meant to hurt anybody."

"But he did," said Georgie bluntly. "I don't go in much for the 'never meant to hurt' defense. I mean, I should hope he didn't do it to hurt us. But he knew what he was doing. And he knew it was wrong. And he should have known a lot of people would get hurt."

Liam was listening, his forehead creased, apparently deep in thought. "I should go," he said suddenly, climbing out of the chair. He reached his hand down to help her up and Georgie launched herself straight into his arms, pressing up against him.

"Do you really have to go?" she murmured, nuzzling into his neck. "I could see if my room is free."

"No, Georgie," he said pulling away.

"Liam!" She groaned, frustrated. "What exactly is going on here?"

"What do you mean?"

"This is not normal! There's something you're not telling me," she persisted.

He stared at her, apparently dumbstruck.

"You're supposed to be the one who puts the hard word on me, and then I'm supposed to play a little harder to get, or not, or whatever, but this, this is all wrong."

Now he just looked confused.

"Why don't you want to have sex with me?" Georgie implored. "Is it that you're not interested, or is there something wrong with you . . . or is it me . . . ?"

"Is that what you think?" he finally managed to say, his tone incredulous. "You think I don't want to have sex with you?"

"I don't know what to think," she said lamely.

"Oh, Georgie," he breathed out, pulling her into his arms. He held her tight, laughing with obvious relief. "Believe me, it's pretty much all I think about."

"Then what's stopping you?"

He looked down at her. "Well, I guess I didn't want to assume . . . I mean, I didn't know if that was one of the 'paths' you wanted to take."

Georgie made a face. "What were you waiting for, a written invitation? I thought you were a smart guy, Liam." She looped her arms around his neck and kissed him soundly. "There's your invitation."

"Georgie, do you really want to go into your room now in the middle of all that?" he said, glancing inside. "Is that how you want our first time to be?"

She sighed. He was being reasonable and sensible and Georgie didn't feel like being reasonable and sensible. She felt like tearing his clothes off. "Well, when?"

He looked awkward now. Maybe he was nervous. Maybe whatever happened with his last girlfriend had destroyed all his confidence. And now Georgie was bullying him like some kind of sex-starved dominatrix. Or someone with unreasonable expectations, which she'd promised him she would never have.

"Hey," she said softly, "it's okay, I didn't mean to harass you."

He sighed, gazing down at her. "Don't think I'm not flattered," he said, his voice low, his arms drawing her close. "You want to know what I fantasize about?"

"Are you sure you should be telling me this?"

He smiled, pressing his forehead against hers. "I picture you and me, no worries, no work, no flatmates, no one else to think about except ourselves, like we're the only two people in the world and we can do whatever we want, for as long as we want. That's my fantasy."

The Reading Rooms

"So I told Tracey she had two weeks to move out. End of discussion."

"Wow, you really did it," said Louise. "After all this time."

"Sexual frustration is a powerful motivator," Georgie said wryly. "I want my life back, now that I've got a life." She picked up a carton of books and heaved it onto a trolley.

"Here," said Louise, coming over, "don't try and lift those on your own."

They crouched on either side of the next box and, on Georgie's count, lifted it onto the trolley.

"That party was the final straw," Georgie continued, straightening up. "You know, after Liam left I battled my way through the crowd to my room and that's when I finally found Tracey, having sex on my bed, on my perfumed sheets!"

"Perfumed sheets?"

"Oh, never mind," Georgie grumbled. "She claimed she couldn't get into her room because I had put all her stuff back in there. That was her excuse for not seeing the note I left. She'd been at the pub and just decided to ask anyone within cooee back to the flat. Which left Liam and I huddled out on the balcony like a couple of vagrants."

"Why didn't you go to his place?" Louise asked. "Or doesn't he have a home, does he actually live at the office?"

"He does almost live at the office, poor thing," Georgie lamented.

"So," Louise was waiting, "why didn't you go back to his place?"

"Oh, he's got this crazy housemate," Georgie said, scanning the labels on the remaining boxes.

"Crazy how?"

"She doesn't cope with strangers and—"

"He lives with a woman?"

Georgie nodded absently. "He's known her since university, they have a bit of a history together apparently."

"What? They used to go out or something?"

"I don't know." She shrugged. "He didn't go into details. This one's next," she added, crouching beside a large carton.

"It doesn't make you uncomfortable that Liam is living with a woman he may have been involved with in the past?"

Georgie gave her a blank look. "Why should it make me uncomfortable?"

Louise frowned. "I don't know if this is old gullible Georgie or new savvy Georgie."

"Well, would you mind helping one of us lift this box at least?" she asked.

Louise crouched down and they barely managed to heave the largest carton onto the trolley, almost upsetting the whole thing.

"I hate it when Adam's away." Georgie groaned.

Louise supported the faltering boxes as Georgie attempted to negotiate the trolley into the main part of the shop. "So why doesn't Liam get his own place?" Louise asked. "Surely he can afford it."

"It is his place," Georgie said simply.

Louise frowned. "Then why does this woman get to dictate who comes over?"

"Like I said, she's a little unstable. Apparently she's on medication and the whole bit."

"What's he doing sharing his house with her? Why would he do that? Unless . . ." She paused, thinking. "Unless he was married to her once."

"What?"

"Maybe that's the 'history,'" Louise exclaimed triumphantly, as though she'd solved a mystery. "He was married to her, in fact, maybe he still is, but she went round the twist and he keeps her locked up in the attic—"

"And his last name's Rochester!" Georgie cried, interrupting her monologue.

Louise blinked at her.

"That comes straight out of *Jane Eyre*, Louise!"

"So it does," she said thoughtfully.

"And you reckon I have a dodgy grip on reality."

Louise looked chastened. "Sorry, you must be rubbing off on me."

"Look, the woman living in his house is just an old friend who's going through a hard time," Georgie explained. "He can't turf her out the minute he'd like the place to himself. What kind of person would do that? I think it's sweet he feels responsible for her."

Louise sighed. "Sounds like you two are as bad as each other. Did he bring home strays as well when he was a kid?"

North Side Clinic

"It's funny, I'd always thought my parents had pined for a baby their whole lives," Anna mused. "It was a bit of a shock to learn that they had quite happily come to terms with being childless."

Doug gave one of his customary pauses. "Does that make you feel less loved, less wanted in some way?" he asked after a while.

Anna shrugged, sipping her coffee. She suspected these supervision meetings were becoming therapy sessions. And whereas supervision used to occur only once every few weeks, she was meeting with Doug weekly now. It didn't seem to bother Doug, and there was certainly no reason for Anna to rush home. She had no more clients for the rest of the afternoon, while Doug had to wait around regardless, with evening appointments scheduled.

"Imagine being worried about whether my parents wanted me, at my age." Anna shook her head. "It's a little egocentric, isn't it?"

"Is it?"

"I mean, it's not as though people often planned their pregnancies in that era."

"So is that what makes a child wanted or valued—whether they were planned?"

Anna inclined her head to one side. "I suppose I think that way because of my experience. I feel resentful sometimes when I hear about people who fall pregnant accidentally, especially when they're ambivalent about it. It doesn't seem fair."

Doug sat quietly. Which usually meant he was waiting for her to work out something for herself.

"So I guess we're all the same, never satisfied?" she said.

"You suggested your parents were satisfied before they had you."

"Apparently so," said Anna. "They were happy just the two of them, together. I think I envy them that."

"Why do you envy them? You can't see yourself happy with Mac?"

Anna frowned. The idea had been plaguing her ever since their visit to her parents. "I used to. I thought we had a very strong relationship. He's my best friend, we've been through so much together."

"But you were reluctant to consider postponing treatment," Doug reminded her. "You feared the emptiness."

"It's just that we'd been on this journey so long, it was hard to imagine giving up," Anna tried to explain. "And now . . . Well, Mac wanted the break, but he's become so withdrawn, I don't know what's going on with him. I always hear these amazing stories about couples who are so close, going through IVF has drawn them together. It seems to have torn us apart."

"Different stressors have different effects on different people. That's what makes psychology such an inexact science," said Doug. "Some marriages are strengthened by tragedy and hardship, others fall apart because of it."

"Are you saying we didn't have a good marriage to begin with?"

"No, I'm saying everybody's different. Perhaps the ones who stick together have dependency issues, who's to say? As for the others, there could be many contributing factors. IVF may have provided a distraction from some fundamental problems in your relationship, or it may have unearthed them."

Anna's eyes widened. "Is that what you think?"

"I have no idea, Anna. Only you can answer that," said Doug. "IVF has been the focus around which you've related for a large part of your marriage. It's the same for couples with children who find it difficult to work on their relationship when they're so busy juggling work and family. Then when the kids are gone and they have their lives back, they've forgotten how to talk to each other. How many couples have you counseled in that situation?"

"I take your point," said Anna.

"In the end, I would suggest it's quite normal for you and Mac to be going through a period of adjustment. It's what you do about that, how you handle it from here, that will make the difference."

Anna drove home deep in thought. She realized she hadn't taken this whole "break" concept to heart, if she was being completely honest with herself. She'd paid lip service so that they could get back into the treatment as soon as possible, which wasn't exactly in the right spirit. She hadn't made a genuine effort to reconnect with Mac. Little wonder he had withdrawn, burying himself in his work where he felt control and order, where solutions were possible, where there were black and white answers. He wasn't able to solve their problems, or he surely would have a long time ago. Mac would have given her a baby if he could have, Anna knew that. He would have gone along with anything she wanted. And all he'd asked for was some time out. Why did she find that so difficult? She didn't really like to think about it. It was exactly the kind of question she asked clients all the time. The confronting question. The clincher. The one that made them face their own part in their problems.

So, what would she tell herself if she were her own client?

Don't look at what you're getting out of the relationship but at what you can put in. Work at it. It's not going to improve all on its own.

Anna stopped the car at a red light. They had to start spending more time together. It was the only way. That meant Mac had to start coming home earlier. And she had to make it so that he wanted to come home earlier. Anna tapped her fingers on the steering wheel. She could call him right now, suggest dinner together tonight. But she wouldn't get sullen or demanding if he couldn't make it. It was coming out of the blue, so he wouldn't be prepared. The light turned green and she pulled onto the next side street and took out her phone, speed-dialing his direct number. The ring tone sounded odd. She must have pressed the button for his cell.

"MacMullen," he answered briskly.

"Hi," she returned, her voice uncharacteristically chirpy.

"Hi to you too. I was just about to phone you."

"You were?" Anna was surprised. He actually sounded pleased to hear her voice. "What were you going to call me about?"

He didn't answer. Anna wondered if one of them had dropped out. Damned cellular networks. "Are you still there, Mac?"

"Yeah, sorry, um, I was only ringing to say I'd be late tonight."

Anna's heart dropped into her stomach. "Oh, that's a shame," she said as lightly as she could manage. "I was hoping I could talk you into coming home a little earlier."

"Oh, is everything okay?"

"Everything's great," she assured him. "I was just going to pick up something nice to cook for dinner. But it's okay, never mind." She tried to keep her tone positive.

He sighed. "I'll see what I can do."

"It's okay, Mac," she insisted. "Really, I don't want to interrupt your work, I know how busy you are. We can do it another night."

There was a moment of silence.

"Look," he said, "I might be able to make it by about eight thirty."

"Are you sure, Mac? Because, honestly, it doesn't matter."

"As long as nothing comes up between now and then, it should be okay. I'll call you if I'm going to be late."

"Well, great!" she said brightly. "I best go and do some shopping."

"Don't go to any trouble—"

"It's no trouble, you know how I love to cook. I'll see you around eight thirty if I don't hear from you."

iWan2cu:)(:L8R

"Hi, Georgie."

She wondered if she'd ever be able to hear Liam's voice on the phone without it sending her pulse racing. She hoped not.

"Hello," she replied warmly. "Did you get my message?"

"That's why I'm calling," he said.

"Well, what do you think?"

"I would tell you if I only knew what it meant."

"Oh, Liam, you never understand my text messages, and they're so straightforward."

He laughed gently. "Honey, 'straightforward' would be recognizable words in complete sentences with punctuation."

"I'm not writing a novel."

"No, you're writing some kind of indecipherable code."

"Listen, it's only a tiny little screen, you have to be succinct to get your message across."

"But you don't get your message across. I have to ring you every time to find out what it means."

"Well, then maybe it works after all," she suggested. "Do you want me to tell you what the message said?"

"Please."

"I want to see you, let's meet later."

"Well, why didn't you just say that?" he said. "Pick you up at the shop?"

* * *

When Georgie opened the door just after five thirty, Liam was standing there holding his cell phone, smiling broadly.

"I'm very proud of you," he said.

"Oh?"

"Look at that." He showed her the screen of his phone.

LEFT WORK
EARLY, MEET AT
MY PLACE

"I know what it says, I sent it," she said, drawing him inside and closing the door. Georgie had planned for Liam to come here all along, and she had no intention of leaving this flat tonight. Or of allowing him to leave.

"See, you can write messages I can understand," Liam went on. "These are sentence fragments, granted, but they are grammatically correct, and what's more important, they make sense. We'll have to talk about the whole upper- and lowercase thing, but this is effective communication, Georgie."

"So's this," she said, looping her arms around his neck and giving him an effective kiss on the mouth. He took a moment to catch up, but soon she felt his arms close around her.

Eventually they came up for air.

"Hello," said Liam, smiling at her. "You're wearing that dress."

"I am." She figured it deserved a repeat appearance, seeing as they didn't even get to the second act last time. "I wondered when you were going to notice."

He glanced around. "What's going on here?"

It was still light outside, so to create atmosphere Georgie had drawn all the blinds and lit candles around the room. The place looked better in the dim light anyway. And there was soft, slow, slinky jazz playing on the stereo. No animals had been harmed in the recording of that music.

"I thought we'd celebrate," Georgie said, watching the bemusement on his face as he looked around the flat.

"Oh, what are we celebrating?"

"I am officially the sole occupant of this dwelling. My flatmate is no longer. I mean, she didn't die or anything, but she has moved on."

On Saturday afternoon Tracey had climbed into a friend's Kombi and disappeared off into the sunset. It was like the end of a Clint Eastwood movie. No fanfare, no fuss. She just left. Georgie had tried to feel sad for a while, she thought it was the polite response, but she couldn't sustain it. Truth was, she was over the moon.

"So that means we have the place to ourselves," she went on. "We have the whole night—"

"Except that we don't." Liam's tone was almost curt. "I have a late meeting."

Georgie considered him calmly. "What time's your meeting?"

He frowned at her. "Well, it's . . ." he said, flustered, "later on."

"Then, you've got time for a drink," she said lightly, taking him by the hand and leading him over to the kitchen. She opened the fridge door. "Look, I have beer, the foreign kind you drink. Or," she said, turning around to the bench, "I know you like red wine, so I asked the man at the bottle shop to help me choose a good one."

Liam saw the bottle sitting on the bench. "You're letting it breathe," he said quietly. He brought her hand to his lips and held it there for a moment. "You're sweet, you know that?" he said as he drew her close and kissed her tenderly. Georgie knew she had melted the polar ice cap. Now she just had to keep the heat on.

"Are you going to have a drink with me?" Liam asked eventually.

"Mm," she mused. "I always get a headache when I drink red wine."

"I'm just guessing, but does the red wine you drink normally come out of a box?"

She nodded. "Or sometimes from a glass carafe at the pizza place down the road."

He smiled indulgently at her before turning to examine the bottle. "Well, this won't give you a headache, Georgie. This is expensive wine, you shouldn't have."

She shrugged.

"At least let me teach you how to drink it properly," he said, pouring the wine into glasses Georgie had left out on the bench.

"There's something more to it than putting the glass to your lips and knocking it back?"

He laughed gently, handing her one of the glasses. "You should never gulp red wine, you're missing the best part if you guzzle it."

"Okay, so what do I do?"

"Sip it slowly, take a small amount back onto your tongue and hold it there."

Georgie followed his directions. "Now what?" she gurgled.

He smiled at her. "Try not to talk, for one thing. See if you can discern the different flavors. You should be able to taste raspberry, mulberry . . ." He waved the glass under his nose. "Perhaps a little mint."

Georgie frowned, swallowing.

"So what did it taste like?"

"Red wine," she said bluntly.

He shook his head. "This is a superb wine, Georgie, you're not enjoying it to its full potential."

"Oh, I'm enjoying it alright. It's much smoother than the red wines I've tasted."

"That's because it has a low level of tannin."

"That's good?"

"Absolutely. Tannin comes from grape skins and stalks mostly," he explained, warming to the topic. "You must have tannin to preserve the wine so that it ages gracefully, but if it's not balanced against the fruit and other flavors it can overpower, leaving that bitter, mouth-puckering aftertaste. A good wine is at its peak when the tannins have mellowed enough to release . . ." Liam paused. "Okay, I'll shut up now."

"No, it's very interesting," Georgie protested.

"Your eyes were glazing over."

"See, it is a good wine."

He smiled and leaned back against the kitchen bench, taking a sip from his glass. Georgie stood there too, not sure what to do next. She felt as though a stopwatch was ticking away in her chest. No, that was her heart beating. She didn't know when Liam's meeting was, but she figured she must have at least an hour or so before he had to leave. There was no time to waste.

"Do you want to sit down?" she asked.

"Ah, no," he said. "I'm alright."

"Don't you want to take off your jacket at least?"

"No, no. I'm fine."

Georgie looked at him directly. "Relax, Liam, I'm not going to bite."

He lifted an eyebrow. "I'm not so sure about that."

She took a slurp of her wine and put her glass down on the bench. Her heart was pounding so hard now she almost felt sick. He must realize what she was expecting. If he rejected her advances this time, what would that mean? Maybe he had second thoughts about taking this "path" after all. But that was ridiculous. They were two consenting adults, they couldn't keep necking in the car forever. Georgie had to take charge.

"So this is your place," said Liam. He was using the small-talk shield. It would be no match when she pulled out the big guns. "Couldn't really see much the other night."

"Have a look around," she said, turning back into the main room. It was a fairly standard L-shaped living area, with a couple of sofas grouped in one arm and a dining table and chairs grouped in the other. Various cabinets and bookshelves filled the available wall space; and books, framed photos and knickknacks filled the available shelf space therein. Georgie was an incorrigible hoarder, a trait she had picked up from her mother.

Liam wandered over to one of the bookshelves. "You have a lot of books," he commented.

"Hazard of the profession."

"Of course." He nodded. "Is this your family?" he asked, stooping a little to look more closely at a grouping of photographs.

Georgie came up beside him. "That's my brother, Nick, and my sister, Suzanne."

"And these must be the nieces I keep hearing about?"

Georgie nodded. "Louise and Nick's girls. That's Molly and that's Grace."

Liam smiled, considering them. "Cute." His eyes scanned further along the photos.

"Hey," said Georgie, "I love this song, dance with me?" She didn't give him much choice, looping her arms around his neck and swaying to the music. But he was obviously uncomfortable. Georgie reached to kiss him, tentatively at first, taking it slowly till she could feel Liam relaxing.

She was well aware of their time constraints, but she wasn't going to rush this. Pretty soon they were going to make love for the first time. Georgie wasn't going to rush any of it.

After a while she slid her hands under his jacket, easing it over his shoulders.

"What are you doing?"

"It's getting a little hot, don't you think?" She tossed the jacket across a nearby chair and turned back to face him. He was watching her, breathing hard. She could feel the energy sparking between them. Time to strike. She backed him toward the sofa, not breaking eye contact. As he lowered himself to sit, she climbed onto his lap, facing him, her legs straddling his.

He swallowed. "What are you doing?"

"You keep asking that. Haven't you worked it out yet?"

"Like this?"

"You don't like it like this?"

"I . . ." But he couldn't speak, he seemed overwhelmed. Georgie held his face and tilted his head, bringing her mouth down hard onto his. She could feel him responding, gradually letting go. His arms slid around her, his hands stroked her back, her shoulders, moving aside one strap of her dress, caressing her breast. Georgie pressed her pelvis against him and he moaned. They were both becoming more urgent, but when his mouth left hers and found its way to her breast, Georgie really started to lose it. She knew she had to hang on to the last shred of self-control she had for a little longer.

"Liam," she murmured into his ear, "have you got anything with you?"

He stopped, looking up at her, an almost bewildered expression in his eyes. "What?" he said vaguely.

Georgie smiled at him. "Protection?"

Blank.

"Prophylactics?"

Now he was frowning.

"Condoms?"

Third time lucky, though he was clearly gobsmacked. "No, I'm sorry. I wasn't expecting . . ."

"It's okay."

He sighed. "It's been a long time since I've had to think about that."

"I figured as much," Georgie said, flicking the strap of her dress back over her shoulder as she climbed off him.

"Where are you going?"

"I'll only be a sec." She disappeared into her room and grabbed a packet from her bedside drawer. She supposed she could have suggested they move into the bedroom, but she didn't want to break the momentum. She had Liam now, right where she wanted him. Besides, it was a little exciting out there in the middle of the living room.

She virtually ran back out to him, resumed position and handed him the packet. He regarded it vaguely for a moment. She saw the slightest hint of hesitation, of uncertainty, in his eyes.

"So where were we?" she said, claiming his attention. Georgie held his gaze while she slid both straps off her shoulders and let the soft triangles of fabric fall away from her breasts. She slipped her arms out of the straps and the dress dropped into folds around her waist. She watched Liam watching her, taking short, shallow breaths, swallowing as though his mouth was dry. Georgie leaned forward, kissing him while she unraveled his tie and pulled it out from under his collar. As she dropped it over the side of the sofa, she felt his hands circling her ribs, then sliding up, slowly, to cup her breasts. She was trembling, but she focused on unbuttoning his shirt, conscious of his eyes, his hands on her. She spread his shirt open and eased herself closer, pressing her torso against his chest and wrapping her arms around his neck. He held her tight while they kissed voraciously, as though they couldn't get enough of each other. This was the most exquisite, excruciating feeling. Wanting him so bad it ached, but it ached in a such a delicious way. Georgie couldn't hold out any longer. She felt for Liam's belt buckle. He leaned back, watching her as she undid the buckle, pulling the belt up slowly, till it was free. She tossed it behind her and then started on the button of his trousers. Liam brought his hands to her thighs, sliding them up under her dress.

"You're not wearing any . . ."

"No," she breathed.

And that was it. Any control either of them had, any restraint, any idea of taking it slowly was abandoned. They fumbled a little with the condom and finally Georgie lowered herself onto him, staring into his eyes. Their bodies began to move together in a hypnotic rhythm, faster as they rocked against each other. Georgie went with it, losing herself to the sensation till it was all she was conscious of. And then the rush came, thundering throughout her entire body as the blood coursed through her veins. Liam grasped her hips firmly and thrust once, and again, and then slumped back against the sofa, catching his breath. Georgie draped herself across him like a rag doll. They stayed that way, she was not sure for how long, but her breathing had calmed when eventually he moved, touching her softly on the cheek. "Where's the bathroom?" he asked, his voice husky.

Georgie shifted off him. "Just through there."

Liam zipped up his trousers and got to his feet. She watched him walk into the hall and then she heard the bathroom door close. She sighed deeply and curled up against the back of the sofa. She felt a profound sense of contentment, and more than that, an enormous surge of love for him. They were bonded now, and nothing could break the bond. Georgie had never been more certain of anything.

In the bathroom, Liam ran cold water into the sink and splashed it repeatedly onto his face. He picked up a towel and held it against his face. He could smell Georgie's perfume on it. He put it back on the rail and stared at himself in the mirror. He wondered if he looked different.

Georgie had readjusted her dress and refilled their glasses. She was sitting on the sofa, sipping her wine when Liam walked back into the room. He stood for a moment, contemplating her. Georgie thought he was going to say something, but then he turned abruptly began to gather up his things.

"What are you doing?" she asked in a small voice.

"I have to go," he said thickly. "You know, I've got that meeting."

Georgie slowly got to her feet, watching him as he replaced his belt and jacket without saying a word, without even looking at her. He considered his tie briefly before shoving it into his pocket.

"Is everything alright?" she asked tentatively. She felt sick; there was an ache in the back of her throat. He couldn't leave like this. He wouldn't.

But then he was saying "Everything's fine" and kissing her lightly on the forehead and then "Bye, I'll call you" and walking out the door and closing it behind him.

Georgie started to shake. They had finally made love, wonderful, sublime, breathtaking love. How could he walk out like that? She turned back to the coffee table, picked up her glass and gulped down the whole thing. Fuck sipping it. Fuck the strawberries or raspberries or whatever fucking berries it was supposed to taste like. She'd chug down car polish right now if it would get her drunk. She didn't want to feel what she was feeling. She didn't want to feel at all. She picked up Liam's glass and started to empty it as well. She didn't hear the phone ringing at first, and when she did, her first impulse was to leave it. It rang out. But then it started again. It was her cell. Georgie walked unsteadily over to the kitchen bench where it was plugged into the recharger.

She looked at the screen. It was Liam. She hesitated. It kept ringing. She picked it up. "What?" she said, her voice flat.

"I'm sorry."

Georgie pressed her fingers to her eyelids to stem the oncoming tears. She felt like shit. He'd treated her like shit.

"Georgie?"

She couldn't speak.

"Georgie, please talk to me."

She swallowed. "I don't know what you want me to say. I don't understand what just happened here."

She heard him sigh. "I just . . . I had to go, Georgie, I told you that. You should have let me know what you were planning."

"I wanted to surprise you."

"It wasn't a surprise," he exclaimed, "it was an ambush!"

"What? Why are you talking like that, Liam?"

"I'm sorry." His tone softened. "I didn't mean to get angry, I'm just frustrated . . . I didn't want to do that to you but I have obligations, people counting on me—"

"What is so important that you couldn't stay for half an hour even?" Georgie cried. She'd had enough. "You screwed me and walked out the door not five minutes later! God, Liam, it's a wonder you didn't leave money on the table on your way out." A huge sob escaped from her throat, she couldn't help herself.

"Georgie, don't cry."

But the avalanche had started and Georgie couldn't stop it.

"Honey, I didn't want to hurt you. I never meant to hurt you," he continued over her sobs. "Please don't cry. I can't come back now, I'm expected. I need you to understand. Please stop crying, sweetheart."

She sniffed, reaching for a tissue and dabbing her eyes.

"I promise you I'm telling you the truth. I can't come back right now or else I would." He paused. "Do you believe me?"

She hesitated for a moment. "I suppose."

"Can I see you tomorrow?"

She didn't say anything.

"Georgie?" He waited. "Please?"

She cleared her throat. "Okay."

"When?"

"After work, I guess."

"Do you want me to pick you up?"

Georgie thought about it. "No, come here . . . to the flat."

"If that's what you want."

"I do."

"Then I'll be there."

Mosman

Anna was sure that was the sound of Mac's car pulling into the drive. It wasn't even seven thirty. This was unbelievable. She hurried up the hall and opened the front door in time to see him getting out of the car.

"Hi!" she exclaimed.

He gave her a wan smile as he walked across the lawn toward her.

"I can't believe you're here already," Anna went on. So this was all it had taken? One tiny nudge from her and Mac was home even earlier than he said he would be. Maybe he was as keen as she was to put all this bad feeling behind them. She could only hope.

He stopped in front of her. Anna was standing on the threshold and their faces were level. She had to keep the effort up. She looped her arms around his neck and kissed him. He almost pulled back, not quite, but she felt his resistance. He was probably not expecting it, that was all. She stepped back out of his way as he walked inside.

"It's cooler in here," he remarked.

"Mm, you look hot," said Anna. "Is the air-conditioning working in your car?"

Mac set his briefcase down outside the study. "Maybe it needs servicing, I'll have to get it checked." He paused. "Is there time for me to grab a quick shower before dinner?"

"Of course, go ahead. Take your time. I've got salmon and asparagus . . . I'll put it on right away and we can eat at a civilized time."

He hesitated, one foot on the first step. "Really, don't go to any trouble, Anna."

"It's no trouble," she insisted.

Anna walked down the hall into the kitchen, feeling positive. She could tell Mac was a little uncomfortable, but it didn't matter. He would come around, she just had to give him time. The main thing was that he was here.

When he came down the stairs half an hour later everything was ready. Anna had set the table in the dining room and she was placing the platter of salmon in the center as Mac appeared at the door.

"Anna, this is too much."

"Nonsense," she chided. "I cooked it in the time it's taken you to have a shower."

Mac surveyed the table. The food, the best dinnerware, wine, candles. "Have I missed an anniversary or something?"

Anna smiled. "We don't need a special occasion to have a nice dinner together, do we, Mac?" she said, indicating for him to sit. "Wine?" she offered.

"Just a little, I'm not feeling all that great." He grimaced faintly.

"Oh?" Anna frowned at him. "You are looking a little flushed," she said, touching the back of her hand to his cheek.

"I thought it was just the heat, but now I'm not so sure," he said.

"Do you want to go and lie down?"

He shook his head. "No, I'll be fine, let's eat."

Anna served up the salmon, trying not to feel annoyed. It wasn't Mac's fault, he really didn't look very well. "You work too hard, you know," she remarked as she sat down. She hoped that didn't sound critical. She'd been aiming for loving concern.

Mac shrugged, scooping up a forkful from his plate. "This is good, Anna," he said eventually. "Really good."

"Thanks." They ate in silence for a while, until eventually Anna cleared her throat. "So Mum and Dad have finally decided to come up for Christmas," she began. "They thought it would make a nice change for us not to have to travel, and they're going to Noosa, so we're on the way. . . ."

Anna was watching Mac. He was pushing his food around on his plate, only taking very small amounts onto his fork at a time.

"Have you given any more thought to us joining them in Noosa?" Anna resumed. "Mum asked again."

He looked at her through glazed eyes that were slightly bloodshot.

Anna could see a light film of perspiration on his upper lip and across his forehead.

"Are you alright?" she asked.

Mac sighed, resting one elbow on the table and rubbing his forehead. "I've got a rotten headache."

"Anything else?"

"My stomach . . ."

"Okay," said Anna, standing up. "Enough, Mac." She lifted his plate away from him. "You need to go up and—"

"No, Anna," he protested. "You went to so much trouble."

"Mac, it's nice that you care about that, I appreciate it. But you're obviously coming down with something. Now go upstairs and get into bed."

He pushed his chair back and stood up wearily. "What are you going to do with all this?"

"I'll wrap it up and you can eat it tomorrow when you're feeling better."

He nodded faintly. "Sorry I ruined dinner."

Anna put down the plates she was holding and reached her hand up to his face. "I'll take a raincheck," she said as she leaned closer to kiss his cheek. But he stopped her, taking a step back.

"You better keep your distance, Anna. You don't want to get sick as well."

Her hand slid away from his face and she smiled up at him bravely. "Go to bed," she insisted. "I'll come and check on you in a while."

Anna cleared the table, blew out the candles and bundled up the tablecloth, leaving it in the laundry. She packed the salmon and vegetables into separate airtight containers and stored them away in the fridge. She stacked the dishwasher, wiped down the benches and sat down to have a cup of tea. Only then did she let herself feel the full weight of her disappointment. The one night when it felt as though she was breaking through, when Mac seemed to have his defenses down. But maybe that was only because he was ill. She sniffed, tears pricking her eyes. She mustn't let herself think negatively. Mac had agreed to come home before he'd started feeling sick, and he seemed genuinely sorry that dinner was spoiled. She had to focus on the positive. Doug said it was all about how they handled it from here on in.

Anna pushed her cup of tea aside and went to the fridge. She picked up the bottle of wine she'd opened for dinner, poured herself a glass and walked into the sunroom. She took a cigarette from a drawer in the liquor cabinet and stepped out through the French doors. She lit the cigarette and drew back deeply, looking up at the sky. But Anna didn't see the stars. She only saw black nothingness stretching off into infinity.

Friday

Mac stood hunched over his desk, pushing files and papers around. He couldn't function in chaos, he was going to have to get Stella to sort this mess out. He would never find the Montano file at this rate. He reached toward the phone to buzz her and a stack of files fell onto the floor.

"Fuck!" he breathed. "Stella!" He watched the closed door of his office expectantly. *"Stella!"*

After a moment the door opened and Stella appeared. "Yes, Stanley?"

Mac frowned. "What did you call me?"

"Stanley, as in Kowalski."

He looked blankly at her.

"A Streetcar Named Desire."

"What are you talking about?"

"For a smart guy you're not very literate, Mac," she said drily, walking into the office. "I'm referring to the play written by Tennessee Williams and famously made into a film starring Marlon Brando as the aforementioned Stanley Kowalski."

"This is going to start having a point sometime soon?"

"You were shouting my name just like Marlon Brando did in the movie."

"I wasn't shouting. I was just calling . . . in a loud voice."

Stella folded her arms, unimpressed.

"I had to shout because you didn't come," Mac reasoned.

"And I didn't come because you were shouting. You have an intercom, Mac. What if there was an important client in the outer office and they heard you bellowing like that?"

"You're right," he surrendered.

"I know. Now what was it that you wanted?"

Mac sighed, rubbing his forehead. "I have to do something about this mess."

"When you say 'I,' I assume you mean me?"

"Well, before anything, I have to find the Montano file."

Stella frowned at him. "Mac, you gave me the Montano file yesterday afternoon. You asked me to type up that memo and I needed to check details, remember?"

He looked up at her, perplexed.

"What's up, Mac?" Stella said plainly.

"What do you mean?"

She pulled a chair closer and sat down. "You're distracted, on edge, you're missing appointments, meetings, and then you sit here half the night catching up. People are noticing."

"Who's noticing?"

"Bob was down here the other day asking questions. Don't worry, you're still his golden-haired boy. He's concerned about you, that's all." Stella paused. "What's going on, Mac?"

He slumped back in his chair. "Have you ever had the feeling you're living the wrong life?"

She laughed. "Only every other day."

Mac looked at her, intrigued.

"I'm quite certain I was supposed to be Angelina Jolie," Stella explained. "I was supposed to have her looks, her body, her men, her career . . . her men. Angelina Jolie stole my life, and I ended up with the ordinary one she was supposed to have." Stella regarded Mac. "Look at that, you're smiling, I hardly recognize you."

"Have I been that bad?"

She shrugged. "I have been starting to miss the dynamic young exec who walked into this place seven years ago like he was going to own it one day."

Mac twirled a pen between his fingers. "It's just not doing it for me anymore."

She sat back in her chair. "What do you mean?"

He breathed out heavily. "Ever since I was a kid, this is all I ever wanted. Status, respect, to be an important person doing an important job. But this job isn't important. What good am I really doing? If Morgan Trask folded tomorrow, would it make one iota of difference in the scheme of things?"

Stella was frowning. "Well, I'd be out of a job, along with a few thousand others around the world."

"Sorry, I didn't mean to imply . . ."

She waved it aside. "Where's all this coming from, Mac?"

"Maybe it's not coming from anywhere, maybe it's always been here, inside me, but I ignored it, pushed it out of the way so I could keep climbing the ladder." He paused. "But you know, Stella, when you get to the top of the ladder, there's nothing to hold on to anymore, and it's such a long way down, you realize you've lost perspective. . . ." He stared across the room.

"This sounds serious," Stella muttered. "I believe you may be coming down with a bad bout of social conscience," she went on. "And I don't know if that's entirely compatible with your role here."

"This is what I'm thinking."

Stella leaned forward. "You know, Mac, sometimes when things are going, um, badly, in one area of our lives," she suggested carefully, "well, it can make everything look bad."

He looked at her directly. "Or perhaps it makes everything suddenly clearer."

She lifted her eyebrows. "So what are you going to do?"

"That I don't know," he said plainly.

"Well, it seems to me that if you think you're living the wrong life, you've got a few changes to make."

"Easier said."

"Oh, don't make excuses," Stella chastised him.

He blinked at her.

"Do you really want to look back in twenty years, nursing a truckload of regrets because once upon a time you knew you were unhappy but you did nothing about it because it was too hard?"

Mac was staring at her, as though he were in a trance.

"Mac?"

Still nothing. Stella was about to wave her hand in front of him when he jumped up.

"You're absolutely right," he said, picking up his briefcase. Then he reconsidered. "I'm not going to need this," he muttered to himself, dropping it down beside the desk again.

"What are you doing?" Stella asked gingerly.

"Making some changes," he announced. "Starting with knocking off early on a Friday," he added as he strode to the door. "And you should do the same, Stella."

"But what about all this?" she asked, pointing to the chaos on his desk.

Mac shrugged. "It'll still be here Monday. Have a good weekend, Stella." He paused, tapping the door frame. "And thanks," he said before he walked out the door.

Dee Why

Georgie had spent the day trying to avoid conversation, eye contact, anything that engaged her with other people. It wasn't an easy thing to do. Everyone kept asking her if something was wrong. She would have been better off trying to fake it all day but she didn't have the energy. Her mind was clogged with thoughts of Liam; confused, futile, crazy thoughts that kept going around and around in her head and getting nowhere. She was frightened of what lay ahead this afternoon, but she couldn't stand the suspense either. She finally announced she wasn't feeling well and went home early.

The only problem with going home early was that she had longer to wait for Liam. It was a clammy day, it looked as though there might even be a storm later on. Georgie shed her clothes and took a shower to cool off. She didn't bother with makeup or perfume or fussing over her hair, she just threw on a T-shirt and tied an old sarong around her hips. Then she waited. And waited.

She tried to feel angry, but she couldn't sustain it. She just felt hurt and confused. And the only reason she was hurting was because she was in love with Liam. That much had become painfully obvious to her in the last twenty-four hours. Pain and love were a double act. If you wanted one, you had to be prepared to sit through the other. It was like some cruel joke.

Georgie was startled by a knock at the door. She glanced at the clock, it was only just past four, it couldn't be Liam.

"Georgie, are you there?" It was Liam. He knocked a couple more times.

"You're early," she said as she opened the door. It was a good, mean-ingless deflector. A statement of the bleeding obvious to mask the embar-rassment of the moment when she had to look at him again. Only she couldn't look at him. Not yet.

"I rang the shop to see if you could get away earlier and they said you'd already left." He paused. "I came straight over."

She shrugged, stepping out of his way. "Come on in."

Liam walked inside and Georgie turned around, leaning back against the door as she closed it. She still couldn't look him in the eye, but she saw he was wearing jeans and a loose shirt. This was only one of a handful of times she'd seen him in anything other than a suit. It made him seem younger, more vulnerable somehow.

"Do you want a drink . . . or something?"

He shook his head. "No thanks." He looked at her, concerned. "Why did you leave work early?"

Georgie dragged her hand through her hair. "I felt like shit."

"I'm sorry."

"It's okay."

"No, it's not."

She met his gaze then. "No, it's not." And then she couldn't hold it in any longer. Her chest had been seized into a painful cramp all day and now the muscles were giving up, releasing a flood of repressed tears. Georgie covered her face with her hands and sobbed, and as she did, she felt Liam draw her gently away from the door.

"I'm just going to hold you, that's all," he murmured into her ear.

She cried a day's worth of tears, and then some. And Liam didn't move except to stroke her hair and rub her back gently. Finally the sob-bing subsided and Georgie wiped her face with her hands.

"It's just, Liam," she started, not able to actually meet his eyes again, "I know I was the one who suggested the whole thing about no expecta-tions." She sighed tremulously. "But I don't think it's working anymore."

"No, it isn't," he said calmly.

"The thing is, I think I've fallen in love with you." She sniffed. "And I don't think you can't have expectations when you love somebody."

"I know that."

She looked up at him then.

"We have to talk, Georgie. Can we sit down?"

She avoided the sofa of yesterday's debacle and sat instead on its twin, drawing her knees up in front of herself and hugging them. Liam sat next to her, facing her. He seemed very calm and resolved.

"I told you once there were things you didn't know about me," he began, looking steadily at her.

She nodded faintly. She didn't know where he was heading with this.

"The thing is, I wasn't looking for a relationship. It wasn't the right time, I wasn't . . . it wasn't fair to you. I tried to tell you that, I was worried I'd let you down. And then you said all that stuff about no expectations, and I thought I could do that." He paused. "But I can't."

He was breaking up with her. It was actually happening. Georgie had tried to prepare herself for this all day, but obviously she had failed. Miserably. She felt sick, and her chest was cramping up again, the muscles clenching into a ball of pain so tight it was making it hard to breathe.

"Georgie, what's the matter?" Liam was saying.

She shook her head, unable to speak. She stood up, trying to catch her breath. The pain traveled from her chest across her shoulders and down her arms. She could feel it in her hands and she started to shake them, biting her lip to stop another onslaught of tears.

"Georgie." Liam grabbed her by the shoulders and turned her to face him. "Honey, what's wrong?"

"Don't call me honey!" she cried.

He just stared at her.

"I know I have to take this on the chin and there were no expectations and it was all my idea after all and you could have done this anytime, but if you're going to break up with me then DON'T CALL ME HONEY WHILE YOU'RE AT IT!" she shouted. She stood there trembling, clenching her hands, breathing hard.

"I don't want to break up with you," Liam said quietly. "I'm in love with you, Georgie."

"What?" She mouthed the word, it didn't quite make it out of her throat.

"I love you," he repeated. "When we made love yesterday, I knew it for sure. I've been kidding myself that I wasn't getting emotionally involved, that I was just having fun, that it was all innocent. . . ." He paused, sighing heavily. "I didn't expect this to happen. I've never felt like this before, or maybe I did, but it was a very long time ago." He was still holding her by the shoulders and he let his hands slide down to grasp hers. "I love you, Georgie. I want to be with you and I want to make you happy, I think I can make you happy." He gazed at her, his eyes full of tenderness. "You seem like you would be a very easy person to make happy."

Georgie felt tears rising again, but this time she felt no pain. They came bubbling out of her like champagne out of a bottle. Liam drew her close and they stood together, holding each other tight. He loved her. He actually said he loved her. She knew it, she knew it all along. He was never going to leave her. He said he wanted to make her happy. Well, he only had to be here.

After a while he leaned back to look at her. "Are you okay?"

She nodded, sniffing. Of course she was okay. She was much more than okay, she was thrilled, elated, overjoyed. Except for a tiny little niggle, like a pebble in your shoe that you try to ignore but you know won't go away till you take the shoe off and shake the cursed thing out.

"Um, Liam," said Georgie, "can I ask you something?"

"Sure, anything."

"I still don't understand," she began. "What was going on yesterday? Is everything alright?"

He took a breath. "Everything's going to be alright, I promise you. I need a little time, that's all."

Georgie was still lost. He seemed to speak in riddles sometimes.

"Let's sit down again," he suggested.

This time she didn't hug her knees defensively. They sat turned toward each other and Liam took hold of her hand, bringing it to his lips and kissing it firmly.

"I do love you, Georgie, and I want us to be together. You believe me, don't you?"

She nodded, listening.

"But like I told you, I wasn't prepared for a relationship, and my life is . . . how can I put it"—he hesitated—"a little complicated at the moment."

Georgie frowned. "Why?"

"Well," he began, "there's my job. I've filled my life up with work, for a lot of reasons, but I don't need to do that anymore, I don't want to do that anymore. But now I've got myself into this position, this level of responsibility, I can't suddenly bail on them."

"I wouldn't expect you to, Liam," said Georgie. "And to be honest, I don't see what's so hard about juggling a job and a relationship. Most people seem to manage."

"I know that," he said, squeezing her hand. "But I'm juggling a little too much right now. Can you be patient with me while I sort myself out?"

Georgie looked into his blue-grey eyes and saw the man who had just told her he loved her, that all he wanted was to make her happy. The man she was going to spend the rest of her life with. And she couldn't feel the pebble anymore.

She smiled. "I think I can manage that."

They leaned toward each other, slowly, and a little shyly. Their lips met at a space between them, a space their bodies weren't inhabiting. A neutral space. And then his arms closed around her, and she brought her arms up to wrap them around his neck. She moved her leg up over his thigh as he leaned into her, pressing her back into a pile of cushions. Their bodies melted into each other, no neutral territory now. Georgie could feel Liam's urgency building, but she knew she was holding back. She wanted to make love to him again, of course, but what if he got up and left like he did yesterday? He wouldn't do that, surely, not now, not after what he'd just said. She tried to put it out of her mind, but the idea persisted. So deal with it. Ask him. It was okay to ask him now.

"Liam?"

"Mm?"

"When do you have to leave?"

He lifted his head so he could look directly into her eyes. "Well," he began, "actually, I've cleared my schedule for the rest of the day."

Georgie looked up at him. "What does that mean?"

"No meetings, no calls . . . no nothing."

"You're not expected back at the office later?"

Liam shook his head, smiling down at her.

She blinked. "I don't understand."

He crooked his elbow, supporting his head on one hand. "I'm finished work for the day, for the week, as a matter of fact."

Georgie just stared at him. "What are you saying?"

He smiled again, taking hold of her hand and bringing it to his lips to kiss it. "It's Friday, I can stay . . . the night, if you want, if you'll have me."

Georgie gazed up at him. She felt flooded with happiness. "Did I tell you before that I love you?"

"Not in so many words," he replied. "You said something like you *think* you *might* have fallen in love with me. . . ."

She grinned. "I was just keeping you guessing." She pulled him close and kissed him and this time she wasn't holding back. "Do you want to slip into something more comfortable?" she murmured against his lips.

"What did you have in mind?"

"The bedroom."

Saturday

"Morning!" Georgie exclaimed as Nick opened the front door.

He looked half asleep, which was to be expected considering he was only half awake. He squinted at her. "What are you doing here so early?"

"Did I wake you?" she chirruped, walking past him into the house.

He turned around, closing the door. "You have to get up a lot earlier in the morning to earn that jersey in this household."

Georgie pranced over to where Grace was sitting in her high chair. "Hello, cotton bud," she said, kissing the top of her head, as it appeared to be the only part of her niece that wasn't smeared with soggy cereal. She slapped the newspapers down on the table. "I'll put coffee on, shall I?"

Nick was scratching the back of his head when Louise drifted down the hall in her dressing gown.

"Lulu, there's a strange woman in the kitchen pretending to be my sister, but she's not fooling me. Clearly she's an impostor." He pointed accusingly. "Make the bad lady go away," he whined.

"Hidey-ho, Louise," Georgie sang, pulling up the kitchen blind. "Have you seen what a beautiful morning it is out there?"

"Oh God," drawled Louise.

"What's up with her?" Nick scowled.

"I have a feeling she's had sex."

He screwed up his face in distaste, rushing to the high chair. "Jeez, Louise, don't say the 's' word, there's a child in the room. Not to mention Grace," he added, covering her ears.

"You got it in one, Louise," Georgie declared.

Louise crossed her arms. "Well, what do you know? He finally came through."

"That's an understatement."

"Okay, there's no need to brag."

"Oh, yes there is," said Georgie, turning on the tap to fill the kettle, "and that particular shade of green-with-envy does not become you."

Nick plonked himself on the nearest chair and dropped his head on the table. "You were a lot easier to take when you were desperate and dateless," he muttered. "The sex has gone to your head."

"Sex sex sex sex sex," chanted Grace, banging her spoon in time.

"See, now look what's happening," said Nick. "She sounds like a back-up singer for Kylie Minogue."

"Where's Molly?" asked Georgie, noticing her absence.

"Zan and Jules had her overnight," Louise explained.

"I think they're playing mummies and . . . mummies," Nick added. "Getting some practice."

Georgie frowned. "Has something happened? Are they pregnant?"

"Not as yet," Louise replied. "I think they assumed it was going to be a lot easier."

"I don't know what their problem is," said Nick. "We just hung our underwear on the same stretch of clothesline and next thing . . ."

"I let him believe that." Louise winked at Georgie, coming into the kitchen. "Then he doesn't suspect the tradesmen."

"What tradesmen?" Nick scoffed. "I'm the only tradesman around this place."

"That's debatable."

The kettle boiled and Georgie filled the coffee plunger and carried it across to the table. She started to whistle as she walked back to the fridge for the milk.

"Okay, that's it, Georgie," said Nick. "I can take chirpy, just. But not whistling, not before . . ." He peered across at the clock on the wall. "Actually not ever."

He watched her pouring the coffee. "So now that you've consummated your relationship with Mr. Big, when am I going to get to meet him?"

"Today."

"Today?" Louise and Nick chorused. "Where?" added Louise.

"Here."

"He's coming here?" said Nick.

"Yes."

"What made him finally decide to grace us with his presence?"

"Don't say it like that," Georgie chided, sitting down at the table. "Actually, our relationship turned a corner last night."

"Yes, we know, you finally had sex," Louise said bluntly, wielding a wet washcloth at Grace.

"Sex sex sex sex." Grace clapped along this time.

"Shh! No, Gracie, no sex!" said Louise, shaking her head firmly.

"That's right," said Nick. "Listen to your mother. No sex, Gracie. Sex is bad!"

"Anyway, I'm not just talking about S-E-X," Georgie resumed. "Last night, Liam told me he's in love with me," she said, unable to keep the smile off her face.

Nick folded his arms. "Well, I should hope so."

"We've only been going out a couple of months," Georgie reminded him.

"Do you love him?"

"Absolutely."

"So that's what you mean by turning a corner?" asked Louise.

"That's right. It changes everything. We're taking things to another level."

"Hold on," said Nick. "I'm getting dizzy. What are you doing, turning around or going up?"

Georgie sighed. "I don't know. Perhaps we're moving forward."

Nick rubbed his eyes. "I hope you two have got a compass."

"So where is he?" Louise asked. "Didn't he have the decency to spend the night?"

"Of course he did. He just had to go off and make some calls and . . . whatever it is he does," Georgie dismissed. "So I thought I'd give you a heads-up, see if I couldn't help out."

"Help do what exactly?" Louise frowned.

"Well, I don't know, I thought you'd give us lunch at least."

"But you can't cook," Nick reminded her.

"I know that. I'm not expecting anything fancy, it's only lunch. I can chop and slice and stuff like that."

"You just want to impress your boyfriend," said Louise. "You're going to slice a couple of tomatoes and tear up a head of lettuce and then when Liam arrives you'll take all the credit."

"I'm hurt," said Georgie. "Okay, if you don't need me in the kitchen, then I'll clean the bathroom, or polish the silver—"

"What silver?" Nick frowned.

"What makes you think our bathroom needs cleaning?" asked Louise.

"And when would you ever have noticed before?" Nick added.

"This is because of Liam," said Louise, folding her arms. "You want to polish *us*, not the silver."

"What silver?" Nick asked again.

"Louise!" Georgie declared. "It's not like that, I'm just so excited that he's coming and Nick's finally going to get to meet him. I don't care about the bathroom, you know that. Don't take offense."

"Too late," Louise said airily.

"I'm the one who should be offended," said Nick. "It's my house-keeping skills that are being brought into question here."

Georgie leaned over and put an arm around him. "No one has any reason to be offended. I just want Liam to know how wonderful and special you all are, okay?"

Nick smiled at her. "I understand."

"But you will have a shower, wash you hair, shave?"

"Okay, now I'm offended."

Mosman

Anna stepped into the hall and picked up the phone. "Hello?"

"Hi, it's me."

She'd been surprised when she woke yesterday morning to find Mac still asleep beside her. She'd left him sleeping but when she phoned later, there was no answer at home and when she tried the office she only got his voice mail. When Anna arrived home there was a note explaining that he felt fine and he'd ended up being called up to the Brisbane office. He'd be in touch tomorrow. She tried to phone him on his cell phone then, but he'd turned it off, he was either on a plane or in a meeting. She left a message, that she hoped he was alright and he should try to take it easy. That was the best she could do, but it didn't feel as though it was enough. Mac never got sick, he was always the one looking after her.

"Hi, Mac, how are you feeling?"

"I'm fine, much better . . . thank you. It must have been a twenty-four-hour bug, or maybe even a twelve-hour one, if there is such a thing."

Anna smiled. "Did you sleep alright? I tried to call."

"Yeah, thanks, I got your message this morning."

"So, is it hot?"

"I beg your pardon?"

"Remember when we were up north a few years ago at this time of the year? The sun was like a blowtorch at six in the morning. Did you get enough sleep?"

"Um, yeah . . . Look, sorry, Anna. I can't really talk now."

"Oh, of course," she said. "When do you expect you'll be home?"

"Ah, I'm not sure at this stage. Why?"

"Mum and Dad arrive Sunday."

"What?"

"They couldn't get a flight Christmas Eve. Besides, it would have been a little too rushed."

"I wish you'd told me about this, Anna."

"You knew they were coming, I only just found out the details," she protested. "What's the problem? Christmas is only a few days away anyway."

"But I have a lot of work to get through if I'm going to take any time off."

"So you are thinking about Noosa?"

"I didn't say that, Anna," he returned. "Maybe I'd like to visit my family seeing as you didn't even factor them into our plans."

"I brought it up with you over and over, Mac, and you wouldn't commit to anything," she added, annoyed. "You didn't even visit your family last time we were in Melbourne."

"All the more reason I should see them for Christmas."

"Well, what do you expect me to do about it now?"

"Nothing," he said flatly. "I'll make my own arrangements."

"Mac . . . you are going to be around for Christmas?" Anna asked warily.

"Of course I am. But don't make any decisions about afterwards."

Harbord

Georgie was sitting relaxed at the table, her arm casually linked through Liam's, overwhelmingly content. He was finally here, part of the family. He was not an illusion who had not survived reentry, or whatever snide comment Zan had made that day. He was her real, live . . . she hated the word "boyfriend," but there was no alternative. Grown adults had to call each other boyfriend and girlfriend because no one had come up with anything better. Partner sounded like you were in business together, lover was icky, there wasn't a term to describe the male and female parties of a mature, committed relationship until you became husband and wife. Maybe that's why marriage was still so popular. It solved the problem of what to call each other.

Georgie realized she'd just heard the words "insemination" and "endometriosis." Zan had arrived with Molly just as they were serving lunch, and decided to stay. She'd been spouting forth on her latest project, and Liam, bless him, had been asking all the right questions. Last time Georgie had tuned in it was all roof trusses and north-facing elevations. When had the conversation taken this detour? She sat up straight and started paying attention.

"So because Jules has all these problems, you're considering IVF?" Louise was asking. "Why don't you just have the baby, Zan?"

"Well, Liam," said Zan. "What do you think of Louise's proposal?"

"I beg your pardon?" he replied, taken aback.

"I'm asking, hypothetically of course, if men were able to have babies and your partner couldn't have a child, would you be prepared to bear the baby?"

There was a grumble of protest around the table led by Georgie. "Zan, I don't think that's an appropriate thing to be asking someone you just met."

"Oh, come on, Liam's a big boy, aren't you, Liam?" she said. "I'm simply getting the 'other partner's perspective.' So, what do you think, Liam?"

Georgie intercepted again. "You can't ask a man that. Men aren't built to have babies, they can't have babies even if they wanted to, so it's hypothetical at best. Whereas in a same-sex female couple, either partner has the equipment, so it's a completely valid question."

"Is it? I'm trying to make the point that there are certain expectations, defined roles, in any relationship, regardless of gender," Zan contended. "Just because I have the 'equipment' doesn't mean I want to give birth. Does that make me less of a parent? Half the parents in the world don't give birth, but no one disputes their role because they don't have the 'equipment.'"

"Liam?" said Molly loudly, obviously bored.

"Yes, Molly?"

"Did you know you've got a dick like my daddy?"

Everyone froze. Georgie was pretty sure no one was even breathing.

"He wishes," said Nick, breaking the silence.

"Nick!" Louise chided. "I'm sorry, Liam."

"Looks like there's going to be a shift in the gender balance with Liam around," said Nick. "You better watch out, Zan."

"I'm shaking in my boots," she replied, deadpan. "You know what they say. One man, one brain, two men, half a brain . . ."

"Three men, no brains at all," recited Molly.

"Okay, that's the last time you're staying at Auntie Zan's for the night," said Nick.

It was coming on dusk when Liam pulled up outside Georgie's flat.

"At least the ice is broken now," said Georgie.

"That's one way of putting it."

She winced. "Molly's not the most subtle child, is she?"

Liam switched off the engine. "I kept thinking, everyone's getting a mental picture, no matter how hard they're trying not to."

She laughed. "Well, it's not such a bad mental picture, let me tell you," she said as she leaned across and kissed him firmly on the lips. "So, I'll see you . . ." Suddenly she sat bolt upright. "Oh no, it's Christmas next week!"

"Yeah," he said awkwardly. "I wanted to—"

"Oh my God," she went on. "I've been meaning to talk to you about that."

"You have?"

"Now I feel bad, I should have said something sooner." She winced. "It's not like you're being excluded or anything, really, they've only just met you. And I know they liked you, if it was anything else . . ."

"Georgie, what are you talking about?"

"Well, it's just . . . we don't make a big deal about Christmas. We keep it very low-key, only immediate family."

"Oh, okay then," Liam said vaguely.

She sighed. "I have to tell you something, and it's going to sound really melodramatic. But it isn't, it's an untimely coincidence, that's all. I don't want you to feel sorry for me or anything." She paused. Liam was watching her, obviously intrigued. "You see, the accident happened on Christmas Eve."

His expression softened as he reached across and squeezed her hand.

"The police knocked on the door in the middle of the night," Georgie continued, trying to sound offhand but not doing a very convincing job of it. "We all went down to the morgue. Nick didn't want us to come, but Zan refused to stay behind. A lovely policeman drove us home in the morning, I remember. He said his kids were all grown up so he didn't mind doing the night shift on Christmas." She took a deep breath. "When we went inside, the tree lights were still on. There were a few presents underneath, but most of them were hidden away. Mum liked to keep up the magic." She stared out the windshield. "When we cleared my parents' room out a couple of months later, we found them, all the gifts, wrapped and tagged. But we couldn't bring ourselves to open them."

Liam drew her close to him.

"So I hope you're not offended," Georgie went on, her head on his shoulder, "but we usually spend Christmas quietly, together. We do the tree the night before and presents in the morning, for the girls, and then we go to the cemetery after lunch. After that, we just wait for the day to be over."

"I understand," he said, kissing her on the top of the head.

"So, you'll spend Christmas with your family?" she said after a while.

He nodded, though he didn't look too happy about it.

"What's the matter?" Georgie frowned, straightening up to face him. "You've been saying you want to spend more time with them."

"Yeah, I know I have. I just wish I could be with you."

"Oh, no you don't, we're a bit of a morbid lot. Christmas is a wonderful time and it should be a wonderful time. Go enjoy yourself and don't think about me."

"That's not going to happen, I'll be thinking about you the whole time."

She smiled at him. "So I'll see you in a week or so, I guess?"

He looked at her then, his expression tender but a little tortured at the same time. "Georgie, I know I haven't been much of a . . ." He hesitated. "Boyfriend's a stupid name for someone my age."

"Isn't it though?"

"Anyway, I'm going to make it up to you."

"You don't have anything to make up to me, Liam, you're perfect."

He shook his head. "No, I'm not, not even close," he said seriously. "And you deserve better, you deserve a lot more than I've been giving." She went to interrupt but he kept on, "I want to make you as happy as you've made me."

Georgie smiled. "Well, see, you just did." She leaned over and kissed him. "I think I'll be the judge of what makes me happy, Liam, and I'm very happy at the moment." She stroked a rogue lock of hair back off his forehead. "I waited a long time to fall in love, you know, and now I know why."

"Why?"

"Because I hadn't met you yet, and it was always going to be you."

Liam leaned closer and kissed her softly. "I love you, Georgie, so much."

"I love you too."

Sunday

Mac pulled over on a side street not far from the airport. He'd dropped Anna off at the domestic terminal so she could find her parents and collect their luggage. When they were ready, Anna would signal him by ringing once on the cell phone and then he'd pick them up directly in front of the terminal. It was more efficient, not to mention the fact it avoided the extortion of the parking station.

He didn't know how he was going to get through this week. Having Bernard and Caroline around would mean keeping up appearances, pretending everything was alright, when everything was far from alright. Mac was not sure he could keep the cracks from showing, and Bernard and Caroline were not stupid.

He hadn't told Anna yet, but he was definitely not going to Noosa. And not only that, he intended to suggest she go without him. He suspected she wouldn't take it all that well. He thought he'd try her trick and bring it up in front of Bernard and Caroline so she couldn't argue. Of course, it could backfire on him just as it had on Anna, but Mac had a feeling this would be different.

The cell phone rang once and he headed back to the domestic terminal. Anna and her parents were waiting in the passenger pickup bay and in less than two minutes their luggage was loaded into the trunk, everyone was in the car and they were on their way again. Bernard sat up front and they engaged in small talk about the flight, the traffic, the Boxing Day cricket match. Mac was feeling the strain already.

"So, what have you two decided about Noosa?" Caroline asked when they had joined the expressway that would take them north to the Bridge.

"I won't be able to get away from work, Caroline," Mac said plainly. He could feel Anna glaring at him from the backseat. "But I think Anna should still go with you. She needs a holiday."

"That's a wonderful idea," said Caroline.

"It's a pity, Mac, I'll miss my golfing partner," said Bernard. He looked over his shoulder. "Perhaps I can talk my only daughter into playing a round with her dad?"

Anna smiled weakly. "I don't know, Dad, I don't think I should go really."

"Why not?" said Caroline.

"Well, if Mac can't get away—"

"Caroline, talk her into it," said Mac. "She could use the break. We both could actually, but just because I can't go doesn't mean Anna should miss out."

"He's right," Caroline insisted. "We'll have a lovely time. You can have a proper rest."

"And I'll teach you to play golf—what more could you want?" Bernard joked.

"That was underhanded, Mac," Anna said later that night when they were getting ready for bed. "If I back out now, Mum and Dad will be offended."

"Why would you want to back out?" said Mac, sitting on the end of the bed to take off his shoes. "Why don't you go and enjoy yourself? You're not missing out on anything around here."

"No, I'm not, am I," she said flatly.

Mac looked up at her. She was standing with her arms folded, glaring at him.

"When you suggested a break from the IVF, it was more than that, wasn't it?"

He didn't say anything.

"You wanted a break from me."

Mac sighed. He dropped his head in his hands, staring down at the carpet.

"That's what you wanted, isn't it?" she persisted.

He sighed again, loudly. "No, that's not what I wanted," he said, slowly raising his head to look at her. "Quite the opposite. I wanted to re-connect with you, I told you that. I thought our problems were because of IVF." He paused. "Now I'm not so sure . . . or maybe we left it too late."

Anna felt as though she'd been punched in the stomach. "What are you saying?" she said, swallowing hard.

He thought for a moment. "Maybe we should have some time apart." He heard the words. He must have said them out loud. There was no tak-ing them back now.

Anna started pacing around the room. "A couple of weeks won't do," she retorted. "It's not nearly enough, is it, Mac?"

"I just thought—"

"I tell you what," she said, speaking over the top of him, "why don't you pack your bags and leave before I get home. Then you can have all the break you need."

"Anna . . ."

"What, Mac, what do you want to say?"

He met her gaze, but there was nothing else to say.

Anna covered her face with her hands as tears sprung out of nowhere. She felt . . . embarrassed. Out of everything she could have felt at that moment, embarrassment was possibly the most pointless emotion. But that's what she was feeling, embarrassed that she was crying, embar-rassed that she was showing her cards while Mac was being so cool. Em-barrassed that he might feel pity for her. She turned her back on him, but after a moment she felt his hands on her shoulders, turning her around again. He placed his arms around her, but he wasn't really holding her. She could sense his detachment even now.

"What are we going to do?" her voice muffled against his chest. "Mum and Dad are here, it's Christmas . . ."

"We're going to have Christmas together," he said calmly. "And we're going to make it nice for your parents. And then you'll go away for a cou-ple of weeks, okay? Let's just take it a step at a time."

The Reading Rooms

"Good morning, The Reading Rooms, Georgie speaking."

"I thought your name was Georgie Reading?"

"Liam!" Georgie couldn't hide her excitement at hearing his voice. She had never felt this way before. Despite all her fantasizing, all her ideas of a dream man, she had never imagined such a powerful connection. It was as though he'd become part of her. He hadn't been gone a week and she'd felt like she'd lost a limb. "Where are you?"

"In Sydney."

"When did you get back?" she said. "You're early, aren't you?"

"That's because you've ruined me. You're speaking to a ruined man."

"What are you talking about?"

"I reckon I can handle two days, tops, not seeing you. After that I get all miserable and bad-tempered and I'm no fun to be around at all."

"Ooh," Georgie crooned. "I missed you too. But you had a nice time with your family, didn't you?"

"Let's not talk about that right now," he said. "I have a surprise. How would you like to go away for a whole weekend, maybe even stretch it to a long weekend?"

Georgie's eyes widened. "Are you serious? When?"

"Tomorrow, and the next day, and the day after that . . ."

"Oh," she hesitated. "I'm rostered on this weekend."

"I'll pay for staff to replace you."

"You don't have to do that," said Georgie. "Listen, I'm an owner. If I can't take a few days off when I like, then what's the point?"

"That's the spirit."

"So where are we going?"

"Anywhere you like. Where do you want to go, the mountains or the sea? North or south? Upmarket or downmarket?"

"I don't care." Georgie laughed. "Not that I'm complaining, but why so sudden, why the urgency?"

"I missed you," he said seriously. "And I told you I wanted to make it up to you, start behaving like a proper boyfriend. Things are going to be different from now on, Georgie, I promise."

"But I like the way things are."

"Well, it's only going to get better," he assured her. "Starting this weekend." He took a deep breath. "I've got something important I want to discuss with you."

Georgie felt shy all of a sudden. "Okay."

"I better go. If we're leaving tomorrow, I've got a few things I need to get out of the way first."

"Will I see you later on?"

"You can't wait till tomorrow?"

"I suppose you've ruined me too"

Mosman

Mac was heading home early. He couldn't help feeling relieved that Anna had gone away, that when he walked into the house he would have it to himself. No tension, no recriminations. After last night, it would be a welcome respite.

Anna had not been able to leave yesterday with her parents as all the flights were fully booked; she'd had to wait until today. Mac wished now he had gone into work after they took Bernard and Caroline to the airport. Hindsight. It wasn't until they were home alone that he realized how awkward it was between them. Anna followed him around, making loaded comments, urging him to react. When he didn't, she started drinking, which only made her more strident. She was baiting him, she wanted a fight. Mac didn't want to get into it then, but she was relentless. And before he knew it he was shouting, and she was crying and then he was trying to calm her. And then they were having sex.

He'd lain there afterward, wide awake, Anna curled around him, sleeping soundly. He knew that one spontaneous physical act would have wiped away, if not all her fears and doubts, then a fair whack of them. And he knew for him it was only sex. He was just trying to comfort her and before he knew it . . . she was an attractive woman, beautiful, in fact, and he still loved her on some level. And he was a man, a weak, contemptible man with no self-control obviously. And lying there he knew she thought everything would be alright, while he was never more sure that it could never be right again.

But for the moment, a temporary reprieve. A chance to breathe easy, to offload the burden of the past few months, years even, and feel what it was like to be free for a while. He virtually threw open the front door. There was no maudlin music playing, no soulful, accusing face confronting him as he walked into the kitchen and took a beer from the fridge. He checked his watch. He still had some calls to make, but it was hot, he could use a shower. He leaped up the stairs, two at a time, carrying his beer. The bedroom was in darkness, the blinds still drawn. Anna would normally have opened the blinds before she left. He crossed to the window and pulled on the cord, allowing the afternoon light to spill into the room. And then he saw her. She was just sitting in an armchair in the corner.

"Anna? What are you doing still here?"

She didn't say anything, she didn't move.

"Anna," he repeated, walking toward her. "What's the matter, is everything alright?"

"No, everything's far from alright." Her voice had a peculiar tone.

"Did something happen, is it your parents?" He crouched in front of her. Her expression was blank, though her eyes were red and swollen. She was frightening him. "What is it? Tell me what's wrong."

She almost looked as if she were in a trance. "I was packing," she began, not making eye contact. "I decided I wouldn't need the largest suitcase, I'd use a smaller one and the overnight bag, the one you always take on your business trips. I took it out of the wardrobe and opened it." She was speaking very slowly, very deliberately. "You left a tie inside. It was dark, navy, you probably didn't see it in the bottom of the bag. So I checked all the pockets." She raised one clenched hand and opened it in front of his face. "And that's when I found these."

Mac stared at the small sealed packets. He stood, taking a couple of steps back.

Anna was glaring at him. Her expression wasn't blank now, her eyes were blazing. "Say something, Mac!"

"What do you want me to say?"

"I think these warrant an explanation, don't you? We haven't used contraceptives for nearly a decade. We don't need them! What the fuck are you doing with condoms?"

Her voice was echoing around the room. She sat there, breathing heavily, watching Mac. He turned and looked out the window.

"How many are there, Mac? Is there one in every city you visit on your so-called business trips, a port in every storm as they say?"

"It's not like that."

An admission. Anna felt sicker, if that was possible, than she had all day. "So what is it like, Mac? Screwing around while you tell me you're unhappy and it's all my fault—"

"I never said it was all your fault."

"Christ, Mac! You may as well have. I was obsessed with having a baby, we weren't connected. Fuck you, you cheating, lying, fucking bastard." She was shaking, her eyes filling.

"Anna—"

"Don't!" she almost shrieked. "Just tell me, how many, how often, how long you've been doing this."

"There's only one woman!" he said loudly above her ranting.

Anna looked up at him. That was worse. Far worse. She swallowed. "Who is it? Is it Stella?"

"No, it's not Stella."

"Is it someone we know?"

He shook his head. "Of course not."

"Why not? It's much more likely to be someone you know, from work, wherever."

"Well, I don't work with her. I didn't meet her at work."

"Does the slut have a name?"

"Anna, call me names if you want, but you don't even know her."

"I know she'd happily sleep with a married man."

"She doesn't know I'm married."

"Oh, come off it, of course she does!" Anna started to laugh, shaking her head. "My God, she's got you suckered, hasn't she? William Mac-Mullen, big-time corporate lawyer, duped by some little bimbo," she taunted.

"Anna, leave her out of this," he said in a low voice.

"How can we leave her out of this? She's the whole cause of it."

"Is she?" he said plainly, meeting her gaze.

Anna stood up. "Of course not, what was I thinking? She's not to blame. And neither are you. It's all my fault, isn't it, because I can't give you a child?"

"That has nothing to do with it!" he said angrily. "You were the one who wanted a child so badly. I told you I would have been happy, just the two of us."

"Ha! So that was a lie too, wasn't it?" Anna stood glaring at him. He had no comeback. "Where did you meet her?" she asked again.

Mac thrust his hands deep into his pockets, looking down at the floor. "In a shop, she owns a bookstore."

"What were you doing in a bookstore?"

He lifted his eyes to meet hers. "I went in to buy something for you."

"Oh, the irony of it," Anna said sarcastically, folding her arms. "What's her name?"

"Why do you want to know that?"

"What's her name?" she repeated.

Georgie

"This is Georgie Reading's phone. Leave a message and I'll get back to you, soon as I can. Bye!"

"Georgie, honey, it's, ah, it's Liam, honey. I'm so sorry, something's come up. I won't be able to make it this weekend. I'm really sorry . . . Georgie, I . . . you know how much I wanted to go. And you know how much I love you, don't you, honey? You need to know how much I love you. I'll, um, I'll talk to you soon, when I get this sorted out. Okay? I love you. Bye."

Georgie stared at her cell phone, sitting cross-legged on one of the couches. It was nearly closing time, in fact, if she could be bothered it probably was time to shut up shop. But that was the thing. She couldn't be bothered. She couldn't be bothered with much of anything today.

Her phone had rung as she was getting on the bus last night but she had been caught in the throng and hadn't managed to answer it in time. When she heard the message, she tried to call Liam straight back, but it went directly to his message bank. She told him to call her again, that she would be home all evening, that she didn't care about the weekend away, she was only worried about him. After she got home she tried him again, but again was diverted to his message bank. She told him that of course she knew he loved her, and she loved him, and he was freaking her out so he'd better call, no matter how late it was when he got the message.

But he didn't call. And Georgie tried every hour on the hour until midnight, and she started again this morning, first thing. She'd stopped leaving messages. It seemed pointless.

"Don't you think he sounds . . . I don't know, distressed?" she said to Louise when she got to work and replayed the message for her. "Something's happened, something bad."

"Georgie, he phoned you, he was able to speak. Think about it, he's obviously physically okay."

"Well, maybe it was something at work, something serious has gone wrong. Or something could have happened to someone he knows. Like his crazy flatmate, maybe she did something—"

"Calm down," said Louise.

"I can't calm down! I'm worried about him. Maybe he's sick, what if he's sick? Did he sound sick to you?"

Louise decided to keep it to herself that she thought he sounded like a condemned man. "Georgie, worrying won't do anyone any good. Not you or Liam. You're going to have to be patient while he sorts it out and then he'll call you, like he said he would. There's nothing else you can do."

"Hey, Les Miserables, want another hit?"

Georgie looked up vaguely.

"Last drinks," Adam called, waiting by the coffee machine.

"Might as well." She sighed. "I've drunk my body weight in caffeine already today, another few grams couldn't make much difference."

A couple of minutes later Adam carried two mugs over to where Georgie was sitting, handed her one and dropped down on the couch beside her. He noticed the cell phone on the coffee table. "He will call eventually."

Georgie sighed. Adam put his arm around her. "Come on, I can't stand it when you're like this."

"When am I ever like this?"

"Well, never, that's why I can't stand it."

She dropped her head against his shoulder. "I just can't put it out of my mind."

"Look, the guy said he loved you and he was sorry about seven hundred times in the space of a twenty-second phone message. That's more than a lot of women get in a whole relationship. Or so I'm told."

"So you don't think I have anything to worry about?"

"What's the bet something blew up at work. He's a suit, Georgie, that's going to be your biggest problem, getting him out of that suit."

She looked sideways at him.

"Okay, that didn't come out right." He frowned. "Ah, but look at that, at least I made you smile."

"You always do."

Adam smiled back at her. "We'd better help that customer, she keeps looking over at us."

"I'll go."

"You sure?"

"Yeah, you close up the register. I can't deal with figures right now."

Adam laughed. "What do you mean, 'right now'?"

Anna

Anna glanced over her shoulder again. The woman was coming toward her. Could that be her? She was pretty, Anna supposed, though a little scrawny. But the hair, the clothes . . . she looked like a refugee from a hippie commune.

Anna had sat in the café across the road for the past two hours, keeping surveillance on The Reading Rooms while she attempted to summon up the courage to actually go over there. Eventually she checked her watch and when she saw the time, she'd jumped up, dashed across the street and walked in the door before she realized what she was doing.

There was a young, good-looking man working the coffee machine. He had glanced up and smiled widely at her, greeting her with the standard, "How are you doing?" Anna had nodded and slipped between the rows of shelves, pretending to look for something. There didn't appear to be anyone else in the shop, but she noticed the man was carrying two mugs as he came around the counter. He walked toward the far corner of the room and Anna lost sight of him. She moved to the end of a row where she could get a better view, picked up a book and pretended to be scanning the back cover. She peered across surreptitiously; there was a woman sitting very close to the good-looking man. He put his arm around her after a while and she leaned her head on his shoulder. It obviously wasn't her. She certainly didn't look as though she owned the business, and besides, she was hardly Mac's type.

Anna didn't know what she was doing here. She should just leave, this was crazy. But something had compelled her. Last night had been excruciating. Painful. Hideous. She had told Mac to get out, to leave, but when she came downstairs later he was sitting in the sunroom, a beer in his hand, staring listlessly out at the back garden. They'd started to fight again. Anna wanted details, she wanted to know everything, when it had started, how it had started, how often they saw each other, when, where, everything. Mac refused at first but she was adamant. She said he owed her that much. So he began, slowly, reluctantly. The bookshop was in Dee Why, he'd wandered in by chance one day to look for something for her, as he'd said in the first place. He went back the next day for coffee, and the day after it was lunch . . . But before he could get any further Anna screamed at him to stop. She couldn't look at him. She told him he had to go. He said he wasn't going to leave her alone, the state she was in. She screamed at him more. Patronizing, condescending, arrogant arsehole. The language she'd used . . . She'd never before uttered half the words she screamed at him last night. She had lost it completely. Until late at night, when finally she'd passed out, curled up on the sofa.

When she woke in the morning there was a cotton blanket draped over her. She could hear Mac in the kitchen. When she walked in he was making coffee. He was dressed for work, but he looked dreadful. He hadn't shaved, his eyes were like sunken pits, his skin sallow. He met her eyes briefly, cowering. At least he had the decency to be wracked with guilt.

"Coffee's on," he said, his voice gravelly.

Anna didn't say anything. She walked past him to the breakfast table and sat, hunched over. Five, ten minutes must have passed. Mac carried a cup over and placed it on the table in front of her. He took a few steps back and leaned against the kitchen bench.

He cleared his voice. "I'm going into work for a while."

Anna sniggered. "If that's code for 'I'm going to see my girlfriend,' why are you bothering with the charade?"

"I'm not going to see her."

"Ever again?"

He sighed. "I don't want to fight right now."

Anna laughed. "When then? Should we make an appointment?"

Mac rubbed his forehead. "Look, I'm going to work, I'm not going to see her. You're right, what would be the point in lying to you now?"

Anna didn't say anything. She picked up her cup and took a sip. He was going to work to hide out. That was how Mac coped.

"Are you going to be alright?" he asked.

She turned slowly and fixed her eyes on him. "Just as soon as you leave."

So of course he did, and Anna ranged around the empty house, feeling lost and incredibly alone. She had no one to talk to, except maybe Doug. Yes, Doug; she could talk to him, but the practice was closed for the holidays and she was pretty sure he had mentioned going away. Besides, she wouldn't bother him at home. It occurred to Anna that she had no close friends, no girlfriends, no one she could phone up and ask to come over, no one's shoulder she could cry on. The very thought of it made her squirm. She sat and listened to people's problems all day but she had never been good at sharing her own. Not even with Mac, except if she'd been drinking, and that had never gone so well.

And so her mind wandered. She thought about the woman, the woman named Georgie who owned a bookshop. How fucking twee. Anna wondered what she looked like, what she gave Mac that Anna couldn't or didn't or wasn't even aware was lacking. What did they do when they were together? Did they just fuck, or did they talk? Last night Mac had strenuously maintained that the woman didn't know he was married, but Anna didn't believe it for a minute. Did he tell her how his wife didn't understand him, how difficult his marriage had been because they had been unable to have children? How trapped he felt? Eventually Anna thought her brain was going to explode with all these questions. Until it occurred to her she could answer at least some of them for herself. She opened the Yellow Pages. There was only one bookshop in Dee Why.

And now she was standing in the bookshop and the woman was walking toward her. This wasn't the woman, the woman called Georgie. This was an innocent shop assistant. Anna felt ridiculous.

"Hi, do you need some help?"

"I'm sorry, I shouldn't be holding you up, you must be wanting to close."

"Don't worry, I'm the boss."

Anna couldn't speak. She realized the woman was watching her, frowning.

"You manage the place?"

"No, Louise does that," the woman said with a coy tilt of her head. "She's my business partner and my sister-in-law, we own the shop together. I'm Georgie Reading."

Anna felt winded. As though all the oxygen had been sucked out of her. She didn't know if she was going to be able to breathe again. God, what if she passed out here, now, right in front of her, she couldn't . . .

"Are you okay?" The woman was looking up at her face, concerned.

"It's a little hot, isn't it?" Anna said. She could speak, she was breathing.

"Sit down, I'll get you a glass of water."

"No, really, I'm okay."

"It's no trouble. Ad? Grab us a glass of water, will you?" she called.

The woman darted over to the counter and returned with a glass, handing it to Anna.

"You're very kind," Anna said before she realized what she was saying. *Very kind to be servicing my husband for me.*

"No worries," said the woman, the woman whose name was Georgie. "It is hot, stinking, in fact. It's going to be one of those nights."

Anna just stared at her. Listening to her voice, looking at her face. Trying to imagine Mac standing next to her, his arm around her.

"Anna, this is Georgie. Georgie, Anna, my wife."

"Hi! I've heard so much about you, all of it bad!"

"So, were you looking for something in particular?" the woman asked.

"No, I've imposed enough."

"Not at all," she said. "You're here now. What were you after?"

Anna took a deep breath. She'd rehearsed this over in the coffee shop. "Well, I have a client . . . I'm a psychologist actually."

The woman nodded.

Anna watched her, not a blush, not a pause. She had hoped for a tiny glimmer of recognition, a spark igniting in her brain, revealed in her eyes. *"My lover's wife is a psychologist."*

"My client is having an affair with a married man," Anna said bluntly, scrutinizing the woman's face. No flinch, nothing.

"That must be hard," she remarked.

"For whom?"

"For you, to have to listen to her, sit on the fence, so to speak."

"It's my job."

The woman nodded again.

"Anyway, my client is having difficulty dealing with her guilt . . ."

The woman was listening, but Anna detected a "why are you telling me all this" slant in her expression. She was going to lose her.

"There was a book. I heard about it, or read about it, somewhere. It's written from the 'other woman's' perspective . . ."

"Oh." The woman appeared relieved. She did have a point after all. "So, is it fiction, autobiography?"

Anna shook her head. "No, self-help, I would imagine."

The woman smiled. "I didn't think real psychologists went in for that kind of thing."

"It has its place."

The woman walked toward the back wall. "Here's the self-help section. Do you know the name of the book?"

"No, I'm afraid I don't."

"The author?"

"Sorry, can't remember."

"Well," the woman breathed out. "That makes it a little more difficult." She started to scan the shelves. "Boy, there are some doozies. Look at this one, *Men: Why You Can't Trust Them As Far As You Can Throw Them*. There's even *A Dummies Guide to the Cheating Bastard*. There doesn't appear to be anything about the other woman. They all seem to focus on the man," she mused.

Anna came to stand beside her. "I wonder why that is?"

"It's where the buck stops, don't you think?"

"Do you?"

"Absolutely."

"But the prevailing wisdom is that an affair can't destroy a good marriage. That it's a sign there are problems."

The woman sniggered. "My parents had a wonderful marriage, until my father had an affair. Single-handedly destroyed my mother and ruined our family."

"Then perhaps part of the blame lies with the woman who lures him away? There is some evidence that certain women prey on married men, they like the challenge apparently."

She frowned. "Well, you'd have to be either crazy or a masochist to go after a married man, but that aside, I don't care if a woman hangs naked upside down in front of him, he's made a vow and he shouldn't break it."

Anna gazed unblinking at the woman. She was telling the truth. She had no idea what was about to detonate around her. For a moment, Anna almost felt sorry for her.

The woman was beginning to look uncomfortable. "Listen, why don't you give me your name? I'll ask Louise if she's heard of the book, and we can do a computer search—"

"No, honestly." Anna stirred, focusing. "I should find out more details. I'll come back."

The woman vanished almost before Georgie's eyes. She walked back over to the counter where Adam was finishing up.

"She was out of here in a hurry," he remarked. "Did you say something to scare her off?"

Georgie leaned against the counter, gazing thoughtfully toward the door. "She was a strange bird. Really intense, you know? Kept asking me questions and staring at me while I answered her. Gave me the creeps."

"What did she want?"

"Some book for one of her patients. She's a psychologist."

"Ha, that explains it—psychologists are all crazy."

Georgie laughed.

"That's better," said Adam. "At least she took your mind off your troubles for a while." He walked around the counter. "So I'm going to pick up where she left off and take you out for a drink."

"Oh, you're sweet, Ad. But I want to get home, you know, in case he calls, or comes round."

He shook his head. "You're too good to be waiting around for a guy to call."

"Ah, but you see, he's not just any guy."

"Yeah, only the luckiest one on the planet."

Georgie snorted. "Oh, you sweet-talker you," she said, nudging him. "I hope you don't try lines like that on real girls."

"Okay, get out of here," said Adam. "Go, wait by the phone."

Mac

Mac appeared in the doorway of his study as Anna opened the front door of the house. He was frowning.

"Where have you been?"

"I've been to Dee Why to visit the queen," Anna chanted.

"What?"

"I've been to see your girlfriend," she said, sailing past him down the hallway.

"What?"

Anna walked into the kitchen and opened the fridge. Mac stormed in after her, slamming the door so the fridge shuddered. He grabbed her by the shoulders.

"What did you do?"

"Settle down, Mac, I just talked to her."

"I told you she doesn't know anything!"

"I believe you may be right, she didn't seem to have a clue. Not real bright, is she?"

Mac looked as though his head was going to explode. He released Anna's shoulders and turned away. "Did you tell her?" he said, his voice grim.

"She's going to find out sometime—"

He spun around. "Anna! She hasn't done anything." His voice was breaking now. He was trembling and his eyes were glassy. "She's not to blame, there's nothing to be gained hurting her."

Anna glared at him. "I don't believe you, Mac. You're defending her to me?"

He stood there, breathing heavily, apparently unable to speak.

"I didn't say anything," Anna said eventually. "I'm not crazy."

Mac looked directly into her eyes. She could never remember seeing such disdain there.

"I'm not the crazy one, Mac. You are, if you think she's not going to get hurt. And if you think the blame lies with anyone but yourself."

He clenched his jaw. "I'm going out," he said, turning on his heel.

Anna leaned against the doorjamb as he strode up the hall into the study. He came out a moment later, clutching his keys.

"I suppose I don't have to ask where you're going?" she said.

He glared at her before turning around and walking out the front door, slamming it behind him.

Mac deliberately loosened his grip on the steering wheel. He had to calm down. He'd been speeding, he was going to get picked up at this rate. He took a few deep breaths as he watched the speedometer drop, consciously relaxing his shoulders.

He was just so anxious to get to Georgie. Anna claimed she hadn't said anything, but how the hell could he be sure? He had to talk to Georgie now anyway, he couldn't trust what Anna would do next. And this was going to be hard enough without Georgie finding out from someone else, least of all his wife.

He felt a knot in his gut the size of a football. Today had been unbearable. He'd desperately wanted to go to Georgie, but the situation was so fragile, he had to handle it the right way or the whole thing was likely to blow up in his face and he would lose her for good. He'd planned to have it all out this weekend, tell her everything, that his marriage was falling apart, that he didn't want to hide anymore. He wanted to do the right thing, settle things with his wife fairly and reasonably, and then build a life with Georgie.

That was before the shit hit the fan.

He knew Georgie would be upset, he knew this would be hard for her to hear. But he also knew she loved him. He could feel her love even when he was away from her. It was such a pure, trusting, generous love, rarely asking for anything in return. She didn't deserve to be hurt like this. He had never meant to hurt her. If he told her that, if he told her he'd been miserable in his marriage, that when he met her she was like a brilliant light and he was like a moth. . . . Oh fuck! That was pathetic. She'd laugh at him. But he didn't know how else to describe it. Georgie was all sweetness and light and warmth, she never made any demands, she didn't expect anything of him. He didn't have to do anything special, or be anything special, she just loved him.

But he knew it was wrong. He knew sleeping with another woman was wrong; no matter how many excuses he came up with, it was wrong. So he didn't sleep with her, though he could barely keep his hands off her, though thoughts of her filled his every waking moment, still he restrained himself. If they didn't actually sleep together, he wasn't actually cheating. That's what he had told himself. He'd also convinced himself that he wasn't in love with Georgie. They had a close bond, they were good for each other, he cared deeply for her, which was different from loving her. He could keep it under control. It wouldn't go any further.

But then it did, and all his resolve went out the window. He couldn't recall ever feeling like this. He adored her. No actually, that was not quite true. It was Anna he'd always adored, revered, put on a pedestal. She was the perfect accompaniment to the life he had mapped out for himself. But he hadn't realized till now that he had never been on fire for Anna. He hadn't even realized you could feel this way. He loved Georgie passionately, she pulsed through his veins, she brought him to life, and now he couldn't imagine a life without her.

Mac's heart was pounding hard and his mouth was dry. He was having trouble catching his breath. He pulled over to the side of the road and looked around. He was on Georgie's block and he didn't even recall driving onto her street. He gazed up toward her apartment. She loved him, he could do this. He opened the door and stepped out of the car.

Liam

Georgie opened the door wide a few moments after he knocked. It was so typical of her. Not for Georgie the peering through the keyhole, or from a gap in the door across a security chain. She trusted the world and everyone in it. Especially him. And so her face lit up seeing him standing there, her beautiful eyes wide with surprise as she threw herself at him. He wrapped his arms tightly around her, relieved beyond belief to be holding her. He buried his head in her neck, feeling her skin, the way she smelled like vanilla, or something sweet like that.

"Liam, where have you been? What's going on? Are you alright?"

She pulled back to look at his face. She was not demanding, not angry, her eyes were only full of love and concern. She touched his cheek and he covered her hand with his, holding it there.

"Come inside," she said, drawing him forward. She reached behind him to push the door closed.

"I'm sorry," he said, finding his voice.

"It's okay, I've just been worried." She was watching him closely, her brow all creased. "You look terrible, Liam, please tell me you're okay."

Her voice was like silk, draping around him. He felt an ache in his stomach, rising up into his chest. His throat was tight, he didn't know if he'd be able to speak. "I love you," he croaked.

She held his face in her hands, her eyes brimming with tenderness. "Oh, Liam, I love you too, so much." And then she brought her mouth to his, and he was lost. Her lips were so warm and soft. He felt her arms curl around him, her body mold into his, so he didn't know where he ended and she began. They could make love now, put this whole ugly mess off for another day. He'd lie against her beautiful velvety skin and she would wrap herself around him. They could stay that way all night. It might be his last chance for a while. . . .

"Liam," she breathed, pressing her forehead against his. "What happened? What's wrong?"

He sensed the faintest quiver in her voice. She was uneasy, he could tell. He had to face it. She loved him. She'd understand.

He took a deep breath, stood up straight and took hold of both her hands. "Come sit down."

Georgie sat sideways on the sofa with her legs folded underneath her, watching him expectantly. Her expression was full of fear. "Liam, if you're sick, just tell me. Whatever it is we'll get through it," she said, clutching his hand.

"No, honey," he reassured her. "I'm not sick."

"You promise?" She frowned. "You can tell me, I can take it."

"I know." His heart was heavy with what he had to tell her and all she was worried about was if he was alright. He kissed her hand. "I'm fine, I'm healthy, it's nothing like that. Okay?"

She nodded uncertainly.

He took a deep breath. "Georgie, you know I've said before there are things you don't know about me?"

She nodded again. He could see her chest heaving.

"The thing is, Georgie, there's no other way to say this. I just have to tell you. But first I want to make sure you know how much I love you. I've never felt this way before, never loved anyone the way I love you. Do you believe me?"

"Yes," she replied, her voice faint, her eyes fixed on him, unblinking.

He had to say it, he had to get it out. "Georgie." He swallowed. "The thing is . . . I'm married."

She just stared at him, frowning, as if she didn't understand. "You're not married," she said finally, shaking her head.

"I am, Georgie, but—"

"Are you separated?"

"Not yet . . ."

Georgie looked genuinely confused. "You're not married," she insisted.

"Honey—"

"That first day we met, I asked you if you were married and you told me you weren't."

"No, sweetheart, I never actually said I wasn't married."

"You did, I remember."

"Georgie, listen to me, you had some theory about white shirts and married men. I told you my shirt was new, which was the truth."

Georgie started to breathe in short, sharp bursts. She was shaking her head in disbelief. "You're not married," she whimpered.

"Honey—"

"Don't call me honey!" she said, jumping off the sofa. She held her head with her hands, turning away from him.

He stood up. "Georgie, are you okay?"

"Get out."

"I know this is a shock—"

"Get out!" she cried.

"Georgie," he said calmly, coming around in front of her and taking hold of her arms. But she hit him away.

"Don't touch me!" Her voice was shrill. It wasn't like Georgie's voice at all. "I said get out!"

"Georgie," he said firmly, "we have to talk about this."

"No we don't!" she shrieked. "I don't have to talk to you. I'll never be able to believe another word you say to me."

"Yes you can, I promise I won't lie to you."

"Ha! It's all been a lie. You've lied to me about everything—"

"No I haven't. I've been very careful to avoid lying to you."

"What?"

"I have tried not to lie to you, wherever possible."

"What the fuck are you talking about?" she cried. "You have lied every second of every minute of every hour we have been together. This whole thing has been a lie. Don't you get that?" Georgie paused, breathing heavily. "You think because you play around with words, that means you're not lying? Fuck, you're such a lawyer. You wouldn't know the truth if it came up and bit you on the arse."

"I know I love you."

"Don't!" she snapped, holding her hand up to stop him.

"Georgie, I wanted to tell you, I did. I went to tell you a few times, I just didn't know how. It all got out of hand. I didn't expect to fall in love with you, I've never felt like this before—"

"*Stop it!*"

He took a breath. "I was going to tell you everything this weekend."

"Get out!" She pushed past him and charged at the front door, throwing it open. "*Get out!*"

He walked over and took hold of the door to close it again. She resisted, but he was stronger. "Georgie, calm down."

"Don't tell me to calm down!" She dropped her head into her hands and sank down onto the floor, sobbing. He knelt in front of her, placing his hand gently on her shoulder. She pushed it off.

"Don't touch me, Liam!" she said grimly, not looking at him. "How many times do I have to say it?"

"Okay, I won't touch you. But please listen to me, Georgie. Let me explain—"

"There is nothing to explain," she said, hugging herself and shaking her head. "You're married. There's nothing more to explain."

"Georgie." He sighed. "I never meant for this to happen, I never meant to hurt you, or anyone."

She just stared down at the carpet, still hugging herself. She was rocking slightly, back and forth.

"Georgie?" he said gently. "You have to understand, things were . . . well, things haven't been right between my wife and me for a long time."

"Did she know?" Georgie snapped.

"What? About you and me?"

"Did she know things weren't 'right'?"

He frowned. "I'm not sure what you're getting at. . . ."

Georgie lifted her head, but she didn't make eye contact. He could see the pain in her eyes; her lashes were all wet, stuck together, her cheeks tear-stained. He wanted to hold her so badly.

"Did she know your marriage was in trouble? Was she unhappy too? Was she looking for a way out?"

He didn't know what to say. "I don't know. . . ."

Georgie groaned. "Let me put it another way. When did you decide your marriage was in so much trouble? Before or after you met me?"

This was some kind of a test and he didn't know the right answer. He could only tell the truth. It was all that was left now. "I'd been unhappy for a while, we had some . . . issues. I hadn't thought about leaving her, not really. Not until I met you."

"Oh shit!" Georgie cried. She covered her face with one hand, while clutching her stomach with the other as she doubled over.

"Georgie, what's the matter? What's wrong, are you okay?"

"How could you do this?" she sobbed. "How could you make me this person?"

"What, honey . . . Georgie, what person? What do you mean?"

"The other woman." She wiped her eyes with the back of her hand and took a deep breath, but she kept her head bowed. "You made me into the other woman. And I'll never forgive you for that, Liam. Never."

"Georgie, I know I've done the wrong thing. But I'm trying to fix that now. I want to fix it, I want to do what's right."

"Then leave."

"I am going to leave her."

"No!" Georgie exclaimed. "You can't leave her, you mustn't leave her. If you want to do the right thing then you have to go back to your wife and never see me again."

"No . . . I can't do that."

"Well, you're not going to have a choice."

"What do you mean?"

"I never want to see you again."

"Georgie, don't do this."

"Get out of my home, get out of my life. Don't ever come near me again."

"Georgie . . ." His chest was aching. He wanted to touch her, to hold her, comfort her. To tell her they would get through this, he'd make it right, she had to trust him. But she was looking at him as though she hated him, and he couldn't stand it. He hadn't realized how incensed she would be. He thought that once he explained he intended to leave Anna, that he was choosing her, she would be okay. Yes, it would be a shock, and he expected some anger. But Georgie loved him, she would forgive him, ultimately she'd want to be with him.

She was still hugging herself, rocking. He didn't want to leave her but they were getting nowhere. Perhaps if he gave her some time to get over the shock. It was probably best if he got out of her way now, stopped fueling the hatred she seemed to have developed out of nowhere. It would be impossible for her to hate him forever. He knew Georgie, she didn't have the capacity to hate.

"I'll go now," he said gently. "I don't want to upset you any more tonight. If you want to call me, it doesn't matter what time it is, even if you just want to yell at me . . ." He waited for some kind of response but she didn't move, her head was bowed, her hair shielded her face.

"So, if I don't hear from you, I'll phone you tomorrow, and we'll work out where we go from here." End on a positive. That was a strategy he'd learned in business. Talk as though the deal was done and only a few minor details had to be ironed out. Failure was not an option.

But he badly wanted to hold her. He loved her, he hated seeing her so distraught. And knowing he'd been the cause of it . . . He reached out to brush the hair from her face. But she flinched, jerking away from him. He sighed. "Okay, I'll go. I'll talk to you tomorrow."

He stood up wearily and stepped back to the door, looking down at her. She still hadn't moved. He watched her for a while, but it was no use. He opened the door and slipped out, closing it quietly behind him.

Monday

"Good morning, The Reading Rooms, Louise speaking. How can I help you?"

"Louise, hi, it's Liam MacMullen."

"Hi, Liam," Louise returned guardedly. She didn't know what had happened between him and Georgie. Georgie hadn't arrived at work yet. Normally she'd be here by now, and Louise and Adam had been wondering if she might have gone away with Liam after all.

"I don't suppose, well, I was hoping to speak to Georgie if she's around?"

"She hasn't come in yet, Liam."

Louise heard a loud sigh. "Have you spoken to her?" he asked.

"Not this morning."

"Did you talk to her or see her at all over the weekend?"

"No." Louise hesitated. "I thought maybe she was with you."

"No," he said gravely.

"You haven't seen her at all?"

"Sorry, I did see her Friday night," he explained. "I tried calling her all over the weekend, I've even been to the flat a few times but she doesn't answer." He paused. "I'm worried about her, Louise."

"What happened Friday night?"

Another sigh. "We had a fight. It was pretty bad."

"Oh," Louise murmured. This was awkward. "Did you break if off with her, Liam?"

"No, no," he assured her. "She's the one who doesn't want to see me anymore."

What the hell did he do to her? "Okay," Louise said briskly. She didn't want Liam's version, she'd wait until she talked to Georgie. "Well, one of us'll go over, we've got keys to her place."

"Could you ask her to call me?" he said. "Or could someone call me so I know she's alright?"

"Sure, Liam." He gave her his cell number and she wrote it down. "I'll talk to you later, bye." Louise hung up and speed-dialed home. "Hi, Nick, it's me," she said when he answered.

"What's up?"

"Liam just phoned. Apparently he and Georgie had a fight on Friday night and he hasn't been able to get in touch with her since, he's even gone round there and she doesn't answer."

"Okay, I'm on my way."

"Drop Grace off here, will you? I don't want her with you, in case . . ."

He swallowed. "Shit, Louise, you don't think—"

"No, no I don't. She'll be alright. I'm sure she'll be alright."

Nick realized his hand was shaking as he pushed the key into the lock of Georgie's door. He'd been gripped by an overwhelming sense of dread since Louise's call; he hadn't been able to get here fast enough. The whole time he kept telling himself she was not like their mother, she wouldn't go that far. But she was like their mother, everyone said so. Nick had kept a close eye on her when she was younger, but she seemed to cope fine. He had felt more at ease as the years passed. He had convinced himself eventually that Georgie was made of stronger stuff than Gillian. He'd only worried she might never find someone for herself, and then Liam had come along. She'd seemed so happy lately, so settled. Nick had really had the feeling this might be the one. He was not an aggressive man, but if Liam had hurt her, if he had pushed her to . . .

The door swung open and he burst through, calling her name. He quickly scanned the living area. "Georgie!" he called again, striding down the hall to her room. And then he saw her, or at least a tuft of coppery hair sticking out of the tangled mess of bedclothes. He walked over and yanked at the quilt.

"Georgie! Wake up, it's me, Nick." No response. He threw open the curtains to get some light into the room before pulling the covers away to reveal her head and shoulders, facedown. As he turned her over he registered that she was warm, thank Christ. He smoothed her hair away from her face, kneeling up on the bed beside her. "Georgie, wake up."

She groaned, but she was completely out of it. "Come on, Georgie," he said sternly. "Wake up." He gave her shoulders a gentle shake.

"Don't want to," she murmured, trying to roll back over, but Nick stopped her.

"Georgie! Wake up!" He pulled her up into a sitting position, supporting her with one arm while he held her face with his free hand. "Georgie, open your eyes."

She screwed up her face and opened her eyes, barely, squinting. "It's too bright." She moaned, closing them again.

"Georgie, have you taken anything?"

"What?"

"Listen carefully to me, Georgie. Have you taken anything? Any pills? Anything at all?"

"No, of course I haven't," she grumbled, shrugging him off. She looked around the room, still squinting, trying to adjust to the light.

Nick held her face up to his, peering into her eyes.

"Nick! What the hell are you doing?"

"I just . . ." He suddenly felt choked with relief. He gathered her up in his arms and hugged her tight, he couldn't help himself.

"Nicholas Reading, would you cut it out! You're freaking me out!"

He released her, sitting back to look at her.

"You're acting like I've come back from the dead or something."

He winced. "Don't say that."

Georgie frowned at him. "Why did you think I'd taken something?"

"Well"—he hesitated—"I was just worried. We've all been worried. No one's heard from you all weekend—"

"What?" She was shocked. "What day is it?"

"Monday."

"Shit." Georgie rubbed her eyes. "How did you know . . . ? What made you come over here?"

"Liam rang the shop. Georgie, what happened?"

Her eyes lifted to meet his, and Nick saw they were filled with tears. Her face crumpled and she started to sob. He moved closer and put his arm around her. "What's the matter, Sis, what happened?"

She said something but it was muffled against his shoulder. He looked down at her. "What did you say?"

Georgie sighed tremulously. "He's married," she repeated as her voice broke and tears streamed down her cheeks.

Nick held her while she cried and cried like a little girl. Why did it have to happen to Georgie? She couldn't hurt a living thing if her life depended on it. She was too bloody trusting. He should have paid closer attention. He should have protected her from this.

After a while she seemed calmer. She reached back for some tissues on her bedside table, wiped her face and blew her nose.

"I'd better ring Louise, let her know you're okay," said Nick.

"I didn't mean to worry anyone."

"It's alright." He picked up the phone next to her bed but there was no dial tone. "Your phone's dead, Georgie."

She sighed heavily. "It kept ringing. I pulled it out. I didn't want to talk to him. . . . I couldn't . . ."

Nick replaced the handset on its cradle and turned to look at her.

"He came over Friday night," she went on. "He looked awful, I thought he was ill." She stared across at the wall. "That's when he told me . . ."

Nick saw the tears creep back into her eyes. He put an arm around her, rubbing her shoulder. Georgie leaned her head against him. "He said he was going to leave her for me. He must think I was born yesterday. Even if he meant it, I couldn't break up a marriage. You know that, don't you? I would never have been with Liam if I'd known he was married."

"I know that."

"So I told him he had to go. After a while, I don't know how long, the phone started ringing. I pulled it out from the wall, and I turned off my cell phone as well. Then I went to bed."

"For the rest of the weekend?"

"I guess," she murmured vaguely. "I got up and watched some old movie on TV at one stage. I thought it was the middle of the night."

"Have you eaten anything?"

"I don't think so. I don't remember."

Nick sighed. "You're coming back to our place, okay? Stay with us a few days, till you feel better."

Georgie nodded. "Okay."

"You go have a shower and get ready, I'll plug in the phone and call Louise. Do you want me to make you something to eat?"

"No, I don't want to hang around any longer than I have to."

Nick smiled faintly at her. "You're going to be okay, Georgie."

She nodded, swallowing back the tears that were rising in her throat again. But once she was in the shower, she couldn't hold them back any longer. The pain was intolerable, that's why she had slept all weekend. Every time she was awake she felt the pain afresh, it hadn't eased at all.

The whole thing still felt unreal. She kept thinking Liam would turn up and tell her there had been problems at work, that's all it was. He would tell her he loved her and that he wanted to marry her. Not that he was married to someone else.

How long had he been married? Did he have kids? Those questions hadn't really crossed her mind at the time, but her few waking moments had been plagued by them. If he had children . . . Georgie couldn't bear thinking about it. She would not be the reason a family was torn apart. She was never going to see Liam again. If she saw him, she couldn't trust herself. He had hurt her in the worst possible way, yet she desperately wanted to hold him the other night, to feel his arms around her. So she wouldn't even let him touch her. And when he kept ringing, she was so tempted to pick up the phone and tell him to come back right away. Tell her all the terrible things about his wife, give her a reason to make it alright.

But nothing would make it right. Their whole relationship was founded on a lie. It was a myth, it wasn't real because not one moment had been honest. Liam had no right to fall in love with her, if he was in love with her. How could she believe anything he said now? The only thing Georgie knew for sure was that she loved him, he was the love of her life, and now she could never be with him.

Morgan Towers

"MacMullen."

"Hello, Liam?"

"Yes . . . Louise," he said, recognizing her voice. "Have you heard anything?"

"She's alright."

"Oh," he breathed. "That's a relief. Thanks for letting me know."

"She was at the flat the whole time, but she'd turned off the phones, hibernating for the weekend. Nick's taking her back to our place."

"I see." They must know. Georgie must have told them. He felt like a criminal. "Maybe, um, maybe I could try calling her later?"

Louise didn't answer right away. "I don't think that's such a good idea, Liam. Perhaps you'd better leave it a few days."

He swallowed. It would feel like a year. "Fair enough."

He sat still after she'd hung up, holding the phone, staring down at his desk without actually seeing anything on it. He couldn't work. He couldn't focus. He used to be able to work through anything, but not anymore. He pressed the intercom and Stella answered immediately. "Can I see you for a minute?" he asked.

She appeared at the door of his office. "What do you need, Mac?"

"Come inside, close the door."

She did as he asked, then came to stand at the other side of his desk, watching him expectantly.

"Take a seat."

Stella sat down. "What is it?"

He hadn't really thought this through. "Um, I was thinking about lunch."

"Oh?" She looked a little confused. "Well, you don't have any appointments."

"Good, okay." He nodded.

"Do you want me to order you something in?"

"No, no, I was thinking of going out."

"Okay."

"Do you want to come?"

"Sorry?"

"I thought you might like to come, I haven't taken you out to lunch for a while."

"You mean ever," she said drily.

"That's not true."

"You can't count lunch meetings when I come as your assistant."

Mac rubbed his forehead. It shouldn't be this hard. "Stella, would you like to join me for lunch?"

"That would be lovely, thank you."

He got to his feet. "Good. Let's go then."

She looked at her watch. "Mac, it's only eleven o'clock."

"Oh." He hesitated. "Well, so what? I'm hungry, and I'm the boss, so please," he said, holding up his hand to stop her, "let's not have a debate about it."

"Okay, I'll get my bag."

Mac told Stella to choose a place and she led him down to a restaurant at the Quay, overlooking the harbor. When they were seated, Mac ordered a beer.

"Anything for you, miss?"

"No, not yet, thanks." The waiter walked away and Stella looked at Mac. "Isn't it a little early?"

He shook his head. "Not today."

"Okay," she said warily. The waiter returned with Mac's beer and

Stella changed her mind about having a drink. Something was up and she had a feeling Mac was about to pour it all out. She ordered a champagne cocktail and the waiter left again.

"Celebrating something?" Mac asked.

"No, champagne's the only alcohol that feels legitimate before noon."

"Whatever you think." He became absorbed in the menu, so Stella did the same. When the waiter returned with her drink, Mac asked if they could order food yet. The waiter hesitated, the kitchen was probably not quite ready, there might be a slight delay. Mac assured him that wasn't a problem, and after they'd ordered, he also asked for a bottle of red to be brought with lunch.

When the waiter left, Stella picked up her glass. "What shall we drink to?"

Mac sighed. "You tell me."

She kept her eyes fixed on him until he looked up. "Okay, I can't stand this anymore. Are you going to tell me what's going on, Mac? This is not just about Anna, it's something else. Something that's weighing you down so much your knuckles drag along the ground. It's been going on for months and it's only getting worse. So get it off your chest for Chrissakes!"

Stella took a gulp of champagne and looked across at Mac. He was frowning, staring down at his beer bottle. "Was I too strong?" she winced.

He shook his head. "No, it's okay. You're right." He lifted his gaze to meet hers. "I've been seeing someone."

Stella's eyes grew wide. "You're having an affair?"

"I guess, if you have to put it like that." He shrugged. "I've always thought it was a bit of a stupid expression. What does it mean anyway?"

She seemed flustered. "You're not the kind of man who has an affair!"

"Oh? What kind of man has an affair?"

"Well . . . the kind who would have an affair with his secretary!" Stella picked up her glass and poured half of it straight down her throat.

"Stella . . . I . . . I don't know what to say."

"Don't worry about it," she dismissed, recovering. "I'm over you now. It was only an infatuation, I was barely twenty-four when you started, don't forget. You were a pretty impressive young Turk in those days. But it was obvious you were devoted to your wife—" Stella stopped midsentence.

Mac leaned forward. "I was devoted to Anna. I have always been devoted to Anna."

"You've got a funny way of showing it." Stella winced, holding her hand to her mouth. "Oh shit, Mac, this is what happens when I drink too early in the day."

"Don't worry about it, I'm not exactly in the position to get on my high horse."

"But you're my boss."

Mac couldn't help smiling. "When has that ever stopped you from telling me what you think?"

She shrugged, gulping down more of her champagne. "Can I have another one of these?"

"Sure." He motioned the waiter and as the place was almost empty, he came straight over. "Another one for the lady."

"Your meals won't be long, sir," he said, retreating.

"Why did you tell me this, Mac?" Stella asked.

"I guess I had to tell someone."

"Anna doesn't know yet?" she exclaimed in a high-pitched whisper.

"No, she does. She found out the other day."

"You didn't tell her?"

"I was planning to, very soon. But she found out before I got the chance."

The waiter returned with another champagne cocktail for Stella, and she skoalled what remained in her first glass, handing it to him.

"Go on," she prompted. "You were going to tell Anna . . ."

"But first I had to tell Georgie—"

"Hold on, back back," Stella said. "Georgie?"

"Her name's Georgie, she owns a bookshop in Dee Why."

"Readings?"

"You know it?"

"Sure, everyone knows The Reading Rooms. It has quite a reputation."

Mac smiled faintly. It made him feel proud.

"So you said you were going to tell Georgie? Tell her what?"

"That I was married."

"She didn't know?"

He shook his head.

"How on earth did you keep that from her?"

"You have to know her . . . she's a very trusting person. I hardly ever lied to her, I didn't need to."

"Hold on, back back again," Stella said, waving her hand. "What do you mean you hardly lied to her? She didn't know you were married!"

"But I never said I wasn't married—"

"Oh, please, Mac! It's a pretty glaring omission, don't you think?"

He just looked at her.

"God, you were even lying to yourself, weren't you?" Stella sighed. "So, where are things at now?"

"Well, long story short, they both know everything and it turns out the only person who despises me more than Anna is Georgie."

"Did you expect it to turn out any other way?"

Mac shrugged. He looked so . . . woebegone.

"What do you want me to say, Mac? That I feel sorry for you? Well, I do, but I don't. I don't because, my God, you made your bed, didn't you? You're married, Mac, no matter how bad things are, you don't solve them by bringing another person into the equation."

"But it's not like I planned it," he defended himself. "You were right, Stella, I'm not the kind of man who has an affair. I haven't even been with that many women in my life. There were girls at university, but I wasn't a big player. I worked too hard to be distracted by girls. I never even flirted much, I'm not like that."

"This much we have established."

He looked at her sheepishly. "I never thought I'd have an 'affair.' It never occurred to me, even when Anna and I barely had a sex life—"

Stella cleared her throat, shifting in her seat.

"Sorry, am I making you uncomfortable?"

She threw back more of her champagne. "No, it's okay, go ahead. I'll just pretend you're one of my girlfriends."

He shook his head ruefully. "You see, women can talk like this. Men can't. That's partly what drew me to Georgie."

Stella sat back in her chair, listening.

"Anna had been sad for so long, I can't remember the last time she was happy. Or even content. She was either uptight, waiting to see if the next cycle was successful, miserable, when it wasn't, or distant the rest of the time. She used to shut down. She never wanted to talk about it. It was too painful for her."

"So," said Stella, "if you never considered having an affair, how did it happen?"

Mac gazed out across the water. "I left work early one day . . . as a matter of fact, I think you made me go home."

"I did?"

He nodded. "Anna had phoned, the last cycle had failed. You canceled all my appointments and told me to go home. You said to buy her something nice."

"I remember."

"But I dreaded going home. I crossed the Bridge, but I didn't turn off at Mosman. I kept driving down to the Spit. And I kept driving. I got all the way to Dee Why. I pulled onto a side street, but then I saw a parking space so I got out, walked along looking at the shops, wondering what I could possibly get Anna that would make her happy. I realized it was a pretty hopeless cause, and I was about to go back to the car when I saw the bookshop. I went in, probably just to waste some more time. It was Georgie who came and served me." The memory brought a smile to his face. "She was dressed like a hippie, and her hair was all crazy, bits of purple or blue in it, I think. . . ."

"She doesn't exactly sound like your type."

He shrugged. "You have to meet her. You'd love her, Stella. I swear I was with her for two minutes and she had me laughing. And I didn't have much to laugh about at the time. But she smiles and her whole face lights up. And she's got these eyes . . . big green eyes . . ."

"So that's when you started seeing her?"

"Well, I didn't plan to, but I felt drawn to her. I went to the shop again the next day, it felt so good to be around her. Then I asked her out for lunch and we met down at the beach. I knew it couldn't go anywhere, that I shouldn't lead her on. I put her out of my mind and tried to talk things over with Anna. That's when I asked her if we could have a break from the treatment for a while. We fought about it. She said some things . . . I don't know, she was probably just angry. But it hurt. I ended up calling Georgie again."

"And you've been seeing her ever since?"

He nodded. "I couldn't stay away from her, I felt like a different person around her. I was happy. She was so easy to be with, so undemanding. And we could talk about everything—"

"Not quite everything," Stella suggested, raising an eyebrow.

Mac sighed. "Anyway, I kept telling myself we were just friends."

"How did you convince yourself of that?" she asked dubiously.

"Well, by not having sex with her."

"Really? At all?"

"Not at first. I thought that as long as I didn't sleep with her, I wasn't cheating on Anna."

Stella rolled her eyes. "Did you kiss her?"

"Mm," he murmured sheepishly.

"Like a friend, or like a *boy*friend?"

Mac looked embarrassed.

"And throughout all this, Georgie didn't wonder what was going on?"

"Well, yes, which is why eventually we did sleep together." He sighed. "Then everything changed. I felt torn, like I was two different people, loving Anna because I always had, but barely able to touch her anymore. And more in love with Georgie than I thought was possible, and barely able to keep my hands off her. I knew I wanted to be with Georgie, but I didn't want to hurt Anna. What kind of a man would leave a woman who can't have children?"

"Is that why—"

"Of course not! But that's what Anna's thinking."

Stella sipped her wine. "How is she taking all this?"

He sighed heavily. "She flew up to Noosa on Saturday to stay with her parents, break the news."

Anna had arranged everything by the time he got home Friday night. Of course, she hadn't expected him to be back from seeing Georgie so soon, if at all. She'd booked her flight and packed her bags. She told him she hated him for what he was about to make her put her parents through.

"She wants me out before she gets back," Mac finished.

Stella sighed. "That's pretty extreme. After how many years?"

"Fourteen."

"There's no hope for reconciliation?"

He shrugged, looking uncomfortable.

She considered him. "You don't want to reconcile with Anna, do you?"

He didn't answer.

"You want to be with Georgie?"

Mac nodded. "But she won't even answer my calls. She's devastated."

"Are you surprised?"

"I don't know, I knew she'd be sensitive about it. Her dad had an affair that really tore her mother and the whole family apart. I suppose that must affect her."

"You think?" Stella exclaimed.

"Look, I expected her to be angry, shocked definitely. But once she knew that I wanted to be with her, that I was going to leave Anna for her . . ."

"She probably doesn't believe you."

"Why shouldn't she believe me?"

"Oh, for crying out loud, Mac, it's what every married man says he's going to do. And you've been lying to her since the day you met. How could she think otherwise?"

He looked crestfallen. He picked up his beer and drank down a couple of mouthfuls. He leaned toward Stella after a while. "You said before that you do feel sorry for me."

"And that I don't."

"But could you tell me why you do?"

Stella sighed. "Because I know you're a good guy, Mac. I know you've been through a lot of shit in the last few years, and I know you've been unhappy. And you have as much right to be happy as the next person. But not like this."

"Why not?"

"Because you can't only consider yourself. You're a married man, and Anna hasn't done anything wrong, Mac. She doesn't deserve this."

"Georgie hasn't done anything wrong either."

"No, the buck comes to a screaming halt right at your feet, Mac."

"So I'm a cheating, lying bastard and there's no hope for me?"

"Of course there's hope for you. There's always hope. But you have to do the right thing."

"What's that?"

"I don't think you need me to tell you that."

Harbord

"Liam MacMullen is a fucking bastard," Georgie slurred.

Nick and Adam held up their glasses, a little wobbly.

Georgie was still staying at Nick and Louise's, and she was still miserable. So when Friday arrived, so did Adam, armed with alcohol and a determination to get Georgie's mind off her troubles. It wasn't working.

"No, worse than that," she declared. "He's a fucking . . . fuck."

"Can someone actually be a fuck?" Nick mused. "I mean, it's a verb, isn't it?"

"I've heard it used as a noun," said Adam. "On *The Sopranos* they're always calling each other fucks."

"Oh, sure," said Georgie expansively. "You can call someone a fuck. It's a very versatile word."

"It is," Adam agreed. "You can use it whether you've kicked your toe or won the lottery."

"Works just as well either way."

They all nodded sagely.

Louise walked outside onto the back deck to join them. "You know you can hear you lot all the way upstairs, and I'm not sure the children are asleep yet."

Georgie groaned. "Liam's got children."

"You don't know that, Georgie," said Louise.

"I bet he has. Two or three. Two boys and a girl. Or two girls and a boy."

"Or maybe they're twins," Adam said.

"Bastard," Nick muttered.

Adam nodded. "Poor little kids."

"They haven't got a daddy anymore," Georgie whimpered sorrowfully.

"Georgie," said Louise squarely, "he's not dead."

"He will be after I kill him."

"You couldn't kill anyone," said Adam. "I'll do it for you."

"You're sweet, Ad. But I want to do it, really. I hate him with all my heart."

"I don't think you can hate someone with your heart," said Nick. "You can only love with your heart."

"He's right," said Adam seriously. "You hate with your guts."

"No, you hate someone's guts, not *with* your guts," Nick explained.

"Well, I hate him from my guts with all my heart," Georgie declared. "And I don't want to talk about him anymore."

"Okay."

"Okay."

And the three of them clinked glasses. Louise watched Georgie drain her glass and then reach for the bottle again.

"Okay, I'm breaking this up," Louise said firmly. "I'll drive you home, Adam."

"No, it's late, you can't do that."

"Let him stay," Georgie pleaded.

"Where? You're in the spare room."

"But it's a double bed, there's plenty of room. You don't mind sleeping with me, do you, Ad?"

"Mind? I thought you'd never ask."

Louise shook her head. "Come on, Adam, I'm taking you home before you two do something you'll regret. Nick . . . *Nick!*"

"Hm?" He grunted, lifting his head sharply before it hit the table.

"Get your sister to bed, or Georgie, get your brother to bed. Whatever, work it out between you. But please do it without waking the girls."

The Morning After

"Whoever invented alcohol should be shot." Georgie moaned, negotiating her way through the furniture in the living room as though it were a minefield and one false move would blow her into the middle of next week.

"Shooting's too quick," said Nick from the kitchen. "They should be made to suffer a hangover for an entire week."

Georgie sat down gingerly at the table and cradled her head. "I don't know why you're complaining," she said, peering across at him. "You don't look too bad."

"That's because I've got an hour or so on you. I was not so pretty earlier, trust me. Here," he said, crossing to the table with a glass of fizzy liquid. "This'll make you feel better."

"Thank you." Georgie held the glass with both hands and drank down half of it. "Where's the rest of the womenfolk?"

"Louise went in to the shop—"

"Wasn't Adam supposed to be opening today?"

"Don't you remember the state he was in last night?" Nick grinned.

"Not really. I don't remember much at all from last night."

"Well, Louise said she'd cover for him today, she thought it was best for business."

"And what about the girls?"

"Ah," he said, carrying the coffee plunger and a cup around the kitchen bench. "My wonderful wife, whose largesse of heart is only surpassed by her beauty, took our tiny daughters to work with her so I could sleep it off."

"What did you do to deserve that?"

"The real question is, what will I have to do to repay it?"

Georgie attempted a smile.

"Anyway, I have to pick them up soon. She gave me a few hours' reprieve, but I'm not going to push it." He poured coffee into the mug for Georgie. "Now, do you want the toast and Vegemite remedy, or the deluxe greasy bacon and egg treatment?"

"You don't have to take care of me," she protested.

"Someone's got to."

Georgie looked plaintively at him. Nick closed his eyes and sighed. "I didn't mean anything—"

"It's okay. It's true, I can't seem to look after myself."

"Of course you can," he chided, pulling a chair closer and sitting down.

"Why didn't I see it?" said Georgie. "It's all so obvious now. The way he was hardly ever able to stay the night, the snatched moments at odd times through the day, the excuses."

"It's called hindsight, sweetheart."

Georgie stared at her cup, watching the image blur as tears filled her eyes. They toppled over her lashes and she sniffed, wiping them away with the sleeve of her robe.

"Hey, Georgie girl," Nick said tenderly, bringing his arms right around her. She leaned sideways against him.

"This is how Mum must have felt," she said with a tremor in her voice. "God, this is how his wife is feeling . . . and it's all my fault."

"Georgie, don't say that," Nick said firmly. "It's not your fault, let's not blame the victim here."

She sat up straight again, taking a deep breath in and out. "I keep thinking how lost and frightened we felt when it all came out about Dad . . . and now it's happening all over again," she said, her voice barely making it out of her throat. "I don't know if I can handle it."

"Georgie." Nick took hold of her shoulders and looked directly into her eyes. "You can, I know you can. I have absolute faith in you. Louise reckons you need closure. She thinks you should talk to him, even see him."

Georgie pulled a face. "What's that going to achieve?"

Nick shrugged. "You can find out the truth, the whole story."

"But I can't trust him to tell me the truth."

"He's already outed himself, why would he bother lying anymore?"

"To convince me to keep seeing him, that he's going to leave his wife, crap like that."

"You can ignore all that. And at least you can get some answers about the things that are upsetting you, like whether he's got kids. . . ." Nick paused. "I don't think he'll give up till he talks to you, Georgie. You're going to have to deal with him eventually."

"I could have my phone numbers changed."

"And what else, move? He knows where you live. And where you work."

Georgie groaned.

"I know it must be hard to imagine seeing him," Nick said, patting her arm consolingly. "But avoiding him like this says more about you than it does about him."

"I know." She sighed, gazing into her coffee cup.

"Okay, that's enough wallowing for a Saturday morning," said Nick, standing up. "What can I get you for breakfast?"

"Don't worry about me," Georgie said, "You better go pick up the girls before your goodwill runs out with Louise."

After Nick had left, Georgie got up and wandered into the kitchen, taking a couple of slices of bread from the wrapper and dropping them into the toaster. Staring out the window into the garden, Georgie spotted the collection of empties on the outdoor table. That would explain the persistent drubbing in her head. Perhaps she should go to the beach later, dive into the surf, wash away the cobwebs. They could take the girls, she and Nick. She shouldn't go alone and mope. She had to move on with her life.

Georgie felt tears pricking again. What life? Liam was her life, what did she have without him . . . ? No, stop it. Enough wallowing for a Saturday morning, Nick said. For any morning.

The toast popped and the phone rang simultaneously, giving her a start.

"Hello." She propped the receiver under her chin as she reached for the toast.

"Georgie, is that you?"

Her heart missed a beat. Feeling returned to her fingers telling her the toast was hot and she cried out, flinging it away as the phone dropped to the floor. She stood for a moment, staring at the handset. She could hear Liam's voice. "Georgie, are you there, are you alright . . . ? Georgie?"

Slowly she bent down to pick up the phone, her hand trembling. God, she didn't know if she'd be able to speak, her throat felt so tight she could barely catch her breath. She put the phone to her ear.

"Yes," she croaked. She cleared her throat. "Sorry about that, I just . . . dropped some toast."

"Oh, okay," he said hesitantly. "I can't believe I'm actually talking to you. I've called so many times—"

"What do you want, Liam?" Georgie interrupted, her voice clearer now.

"Um, well, I wanted to talk to you."

"Go ahead."

"Well, do you think, maybe, could I see you, so we can talk properly?"

"We can talk fine on the phone, that's what they were invented for. Don't push it, Liam."

"Okay." He breathed out heavily. "How are you?"

She felt tears welling. She hated being such a crybaby. "How do you think I am?"

"I'm sorry, Georgie, I'm so sorry. I never wanted to hurt you."

"Is that supposed to make me feel better?"

"What?"

"That you didn't want to hurt me?" said Georgie. "You'd be some kind of monster if you actually set out to hurt me. The fact that you seemed to have no idea that would happen is what astounds me."

"Georgie, I didn't . . . it just got out of hand—"

"That is so much crap, Liam. I don't even know what that means—'It got out of hand.' Are you saying it was out of your control? Every time you called me you knew exactly what you were doing."

He didn't answer straightaway. "I was going to try and make things right—"

"You can't make it right. You can never make this right," Georgie said plainly. She took a breath. "I want to know something."

"Sure, anything."

"Do you have children?

"No . . . I don't."

"How long have you been married?"

He hesitated. "Fourteen years."

"Christ, Liam," she breathed. That was a life. She'd destroyed a life.

"Georgie, listen to me, I told you we were having problems. They were all about having children—"

"I don't want to know."

"I'm not the person you think I am."

"No, you're not," she said flatly. "I have to go."

"Georgie, please. Can't we meet, just to talk this out?"

"No way, Liam. There is nothing to talk out. You have a wife, I suggest you talk it out with her."

She hung up. For a second—no, perhaps even four or five—Georgie felt empowered. She'd told him. She'd had the upper hand and she'd maintained it. She hadn't given him an inch.

And then her face crumpled, her back slid down the door of the kitchen cabinet behind her till she was sitting on the floor, hugging her knees and sobbing.

Sydney Airport

Mac decided that waiting near the luggage carousel would be less con-frontational than standing in the arrivals lounge. He wasn't sure why he was doing this. Anna wasn't expecting him, she didn't even want him in the house when she got home. Mostly he was doing this because Georgie wanted him to. Not specifically, it's not like she suggested he meet Anna at the airport. Georgie didn't know Anna's movements, she didn't know any-thing about Anna. She didn't want to know. He had phoned several more times over the weekend and actually spoken to Georgie once or twice. However, she didn't stay on long, just long enough to reiterate that there was nothing for them to sort out, the only person he had anything to sort out with was his wife.

So here he was. Doing what Georgie wanted. The logic was totally skewed, he was fully aware of that. If he sorted things out with Anna, then he couldn't see Georgie anymore. But he felt compelled. It was the only thing he could do to make Georgie happy. Yet it made no sense at all.

He spotted Anna as she approached the carousel. And then she saw him. He didn't know what to make of her expression—taken aback, an-noyed, a little surprised, mostly confused. But composure was Anna's de-fault position, especially in public. She wouldn't make a scene.

"What are you doing here?" she said levelly.

"I came to pick you up."

He thought she was about to say something else. But she didn't say anything, not until they were in the car, had left the parking station and had merged with the traffic heading north.

"I don't know what this gesture is about, Mac," she began, "but I assume you'll drop me home and be on your way."

He breathed out heavily. "We have to talk, Anna."

"There's nothing left to say."

"Fourteen years of marriage and there's nothing left to say?"

"Fourteen years of marriage and you have an affair and, no"—she paused deliberately—"there is nothing left to say."

He sighed, frustrated. "Is this the kind of advice you'd give a client?"

"I don't give my clients advice, it's not what a therapist does."

"So you're saying our marriage isn't worth saving, is that it, Anna? Because the ball appears to be in your court."

"What does that mean?" She frowned.

"I know I did the wrong thing. I know I'm the one at fault. I'll take the blame entirely. But"—he paused, taking a breath—"I'm also prepared to work at this, to try and rebuild our marriage, if that's what you want. It's up to you."

Anna shifted in her seat to look squarely at him. "Very clever, Mac."

He glanced across at her. "What?"

"Giving me the ultimatum. Repenting your sins, accepting your penance, absolving your guilt. Very Catholic of you, Mac. And now it's all up to me. You'll do whatever I want. Of course, if I say I don't want you around, then you're exonerated, your slate is clean and you can go off and be with your girlfriend with my blessing."

"Don't, Anna."

"Well, isn't that what all this is about?"

"No, it isn't. It should please you to know she doesn't want to have anything to do with me."

"Oh, I see," Anna exclaimed. "So I'm all you've got left now?"

"Christ, Anna, can you cut it out for one frigging minute?" he cried. "I get that you want to hurt me, I understand. But I'm trying to do the right thing here."

Anna laughed. It sounded hollow. "That's rich."

"I'm trying to do the right thing," he repeated firmly. "We've been married for fourteen years. I . . . ." He hesitated, swallowing. ". . . I made a mistake." Georgie wasn't a mistake, he could never think of her as a mistake. "If you can find a way to forgive me, then we can still salvage a life together."

Anna didn't say anything.

"I moved my things into the guestroom downstairs, right away from you. If that's not acceptable then I'll start looking for somewhere tomorrow."

She hesitated. "I wasn't expecting this. You can at least give me a night to sleep on it."

"Of course."

They drove on in silence. Anna stared out the window. Her parents had been shocked, dumbstruck in fact. They were devastated for Anna. But they could barely believe it of Mac. It didn't seem to be in his character at all. And Anna felt the same. She had never doubted his love, his absolute devotion to her. Through all the tales of cheating spouses she'd had to sit and listen to, she'd always consoled herself, smugly at times, that Mac would never be unfaithful.

So what was she supposed to make of this? Anna had hoped at first that it was all about sex, that there had been a number of women over a period of time. He was scratching an itch, having a midlife crisis. She knew their sex life had been less than satisfactory, a not unusual consequence of prolonged fertility treatment. They would have needed to work at it, but she believed that would have been more curable than this. As soon as he'd said it was one woman, the strongest sense of dread had engulfed her. Mac only functioned under single-minded commitment, in every area of his life. When he couldn't give that total commitment, he tended to withdraw. It was how he operated at work, it was obvious in his relationship with his family. He found it hard to revisit his childhood. He found it even harder to be around his father, to watch the way he treated his mother, to watch the way she put up with it. He couldn't do anything about it, he couldn't fix it, so he stayed away.

If Mac was having an affair with one woman, a woman who could bring tears to his eyes, then he was in love with that woman. And there was no room for Anna.

North Side Clinic

"Have you got a minute, Doug?"

He swung around in his chair. "For you, Anna, I have ten."

She stepped inside, closing the door behind her. "How was your holiday?" she asked. "You went away, didn't you?"

"That's right. We drove north, made it all the way to Cairns. It took us more than a week, but that's the way we wanted to do it, stopping along the way, taking our time. . . ." Doug paused, watching her. "What is it, Anna?"

"Nothing, go on, you were saying—"

"And you weren't listening."

She breathed out. "I apologize."

He waved that aside. "Take a seat."

Anna sat down, facing him. This was almost as bad as telling her parents. Doug would be calm and measured, of course. It was not his reaction that bothered her so much as saying it out loud. To actually say the words, "Mac is having an affair." Or should it be, "Mac was having an affair" . . . "Mac has been having an affair" . . .

"Anna?"

"Sorry." She stirred. "I need to let you know that I'm having a few problems at home."

"Are you starting a new treatment cycle?"

"Pardon?" Anna realized she hadn't thought about any of that for weeks. "No, no, it's . . ." She drifted off again for a moment. Doug sat patiently. "Mac has been having an affair."

Anna could plainly see the compassion in Doug's eyes. It was at once comforting and uncomfortable.

"When did you find out?" he asked.

"Just after Christmas." She paused. Doug was leaning forward, waiting for her to go on. "Evidently it's been going on for a couple of months at least," she added. She was not sure what else to say.

"So is it serious, or is he prepared to end it? Does he want to stay in the marriage?"

"All of the above," Anna replied glibly. "It's serious. He wouldn't have ended it, but she did, so now he wants to stay in the marriage."

Doug considered her. "How do you feel, Anna? What do you want?"

She felt her chest tighten. She didn't want to feel. It was too painful. Her parents' distress had already been enough to bear. She wished she hadn't agreed to let Mac stay. He was like a ghost, haunting the house when he wasn't at the office. He was miserable, he'd lost weight, his eyes were bloodshot from lack of sleep, or whatever. The last thing Anna needed right now was to watch her husband grieve for his mistress. She would have to tell him to go.

"Do you want your marriage to survive this, Anna?" Doug rephrased when she hadn't answered.

She shrugged. "I don't think it's up to me."

"Why do you say that?"

"He's in love with the woman."

"But you said it was finished."

"It is. That doesn't stop him from being in love with her."

"You also said he wants to stay in the marriage?"

Anna nodded. "Once again, doesn't stop him from being in love with her."

Doug took a moment to digest what she had told him so far. "Where's Mac now, where is he living?"

"At home."

"With you?"

"Well, he moved into the spare room."

"You're okay with that arrangement?"

"Not really."

"So what made you agree to it? He gave you a choice, I trust?"

"Of course he did." Anna sighed. "He asked if he could stay, he said we shouldn't be so hasty to give up after fourteen years."

"What do you think?"

"I agreed, that's why I let him stay." She shook her head. "But he doesn't want to be with me. He wants to be with her."

"It's not unusual to have feelings of—"

"Hold on, Doug. This isn't jealousy, or bruised ego or anything else, though I'm not pretending I'm immune," said Anna. "I'm stating the facts. Mac wants to be with her. Whether she wants him or not doesn't change the fact it's where he'd rather be. He's staying because he thinks it's the right thing to do, not because he wants to."

"He wouldn't be the first man, or woman, to do that," Doug remarked. "You still haven't answered my question, Anna. You're quite clear about what Mac wants, what he feels, what you believe his motivation is. But what about you?" He paused. "What do you want?"

Anna sat for a while, thinking. "I don't know," she said slowly, staring off at nothing across the room. "I want that none of this happened. That I could somehow turn back the clock. But I wouldn't know how far to go. A few months? A few years? Longer? Before I even started treatment? If we hadn't taken that road, would we be alright now? I can't help thinking he would have wanted a child eventually, that it all would have come undone in time."

"Those questions can never be answered, you know that, Anna," said Doug gently. "All that matters now is what happens next. It's not all up to Mac. You have the facts and you have choices. Do you want to continue in the marriage in the full knowledge Mac is in love with someone else but claims he is prepared to put it behind him? It'd be hard, but not impossible. There are marriages that have survived worse."

"I don't know, Doug. I don't know if I can do that." She paused. "But I'm not sure I'm ready to end it either."

He thought for a moment. "Why don't you try breaking the problem down? Are you content with the current situation? Do you want Mac in the house?"

"I'm finding it a strain," Anna admitted. "He's obviously grieving, and that's pretty hard to take."

"Well, be kind to yourself. Asking him to leave doesn't have to mean ending the marriage. It may give you both space and perspective to work things out."

Anna nodded vaguely.

"Do you need to take some time off?" Doug suggested.

"Oh, please don't ask me to do that."

"I wasn't asking you to do that, I was asking if you need to do that."

"It's the last thing I need," said Anna. "I have to work . . . I have nothing else."

Doug paused, considering her. "You do need to remain mindful of your responsibilities as a therapist, Anna, and not let your own issues cloud your judgment. But I trust your professionalism. In the meantime, you know my door is always open."

"I do. Thanks, Doug."

The Reading Rooms

Georgie froze. She was holding the Closed sign, half flipped over. The shop was neither closed nor open for that moment, as though time had frozen as well.

Liam was standing on the other side of the door, gazing directly into her eyes. If not for the glass between them, Georgie could have reached out and touched his face. And she probably would have, involuntarily, before she knew what she was doing. He looked so sad, so lost.

This was precisely why she'd refused to see him. She'd managed to be firm and assertive over the phone, but then she'd turn into a whimpering heap of jelly as soon as she hung up. So she'd stopped taking his calls, again. That was when he'd started to show up at the shop. She'd successfully avoided him so far by escaping to the storeroom or the loo. But a couple of times she'd only made it to the office and had had to hide behind Louise's desk, and once she'd dived into the reading cave and buried herself under the cushions. That was hitting rock bottom in more ways than one, and Louise had had every right to scold her afterward.

"What on God's green earth is wrong with you?" she'd demanded. "Why are you so frightened of him? He can't do anything to you, it's a public place."

"I know that. I'm not frightened of him, he wouldn't do anything."

"Then what is it?"

She wasn't going to tell Louise that she didn't trust herself around Liam. That it was bad enough she replayed his phone messages over and over just to hear his voice, let alone seeing him in the flesh. Everyone said she needed closure, she needed to see him, it would help her get over him. Georgie was not so sure.

"Georgie, Liam's been turning up every day since he realized you were back at work. Two weeks now. You can't hide from him forever. Just go and tell him to piss off. He needs to hear it from you, God knows Adam's said it to him often enough."

But she couldn't face him. Of course she felt stupid. And weak. She had lost faith in her ability to judge human nature, if she'd ever possessed such an ability in the first place.

And now the cause of her undoing was standing right in front of her, the sad eyes still locked on hers. Slowly Georgie turned the sign the rest of the way and let it swing free, bobbing gently against the glass. His gaze flickered down to the sign announcing the shop was closed. Liam raised one hand and laid his palm against the door frame. His eyes were pleading now. She couldn't refuse him. And it was too late to hide.

Georgie turned the lock and pulled the door back. Liam stepped inside tentatively. She closed the door again, focusing on locking the dead bolt, and on breathing, in and out. As she turned around to face him she felt as though she was no longer in her body. She was outside it, observing, from a distance.

"Thank you," he said, his voice thick.

"What for?"

"For agreeing to see me."

Georgie headed over to the counter. "I didn't agree, you just turned up."

"It's not the first time."

"I know that."

"And I know you usually hide when I come," he said.

She walked around inside the protective arc of the counter, the solid mass of the bench like a moat between them. He couldn't get any closer, which was exactly how Georgie wanted it. She was still watching herself from a distance as she spread her hands apart, laying them flat against the countertop. She looked confident, in control, from the outside at least.

"Why did you come here, Liam?"

"To talk to you, to try to explain—"

"At the risk of sounding like a broken record, Liam, I've told you repeatedly that there is nothing to explain."

"Of course there is!" he insisted, raising his voice. "There's so much to explain, Georgie. You don't know . . . things. You don't know about my life."

"I know that you're married," she returned coolly. "I don't really need to know anything else."

"Yes, you do . . . I am married, but it's falling apart—"

"Why am I not surprised?"

"It's been falling apart for a long time!" He was almost shouting. "We were incredibly unhappy, we both were." He took a moment to catch his breath. "And then I met you." His voice softened. "You made it so easy, you said you had no expectations—"

"Come on, Liam, I didn't know you were married."

"I know that, I was kidding myself. I wanted to believe it was okay . . . because I couldn't stay away from you."

Georgie swallowed, staring up at him.

"The only time I was happy was when I was with you. Was I supposed to give that up?"

"Yes, you were."

"Well, I couldn't," he said quietly. "I guess I'm weak, or selfish, I don't know. I didn't mean to hurt anybody, but I couldn't stop seeing you. And even if I had, I would have hurt you anyway. I didn't know what to do. It's not like I'd had any experience at it. But I was going to try and make it right."

"You couldn't make it right—"

"Georgie, would you just listen to what I'm saying?" he persisted. "I'm not perfect, I know that. I fucked up, people fuck up all the time. It's what makes us human. Haven't you ever made a mistake, Georgie?"

"Yeah, I'm looking at him," she said wryly.

She saw the flinch before he dropped his gaze, rubbing his forehead as he stared down at the counter. This wasn't her, she didn't say things like that to people, least of all people she . . .

"Sorry," she said quietly.

He looked up at her then. "Georgie, I know what I did was wrong. I was married, I went about it the wrong way. But what you and I had, there was nothing wrong with that. You're the best thing in my life. Even if you send me away, I won't stop loving you, nothing can change that."

"Don't talk like that," she muttered, turning and walking away. But he skirted around the outside of the counter and blocked her path, taking hold of her shoulders. She tried to shrug him off. "Let go of me, Liam."

"Not until you tell me something."

She looked up at him. She didn't want to be standing here, this close to him. She could see the blue-grey of his eyes, see the way his hair had fallen across his forehead. She wanted to stroke it away, like she used to. She wanted to touch his face. She wanted him to wrap his arms around her and tell her everything was going to be alright. There was no wife, it had been a bad dream, a misunderstanding. . . .

"Georgie, do you love me?"

She snapped out of it. "I'm not going to answer that," she said, pushing him out of the way.

"Why not?"

She ignored him, striding determinedly toward the office. Liam followed, grabbing her arm and turning her around again. "Please, Georgie."

"It doesn't make any difference!"

"How can you say that?"

"You have a wife!"

"Who can't stand the sight of me!" he protested. "I tried, Georgie, I did what you said. She wanted me out but I told her we had to work at it. But it didn't magically wipe away all our problems. I'm sleeping in the spare room and we barely even speak to each other."

He was staring directly into her eyes, unblinking. Georgie couldn't hold his gaze. "What are these 'problems' you keep harping about?" she muttered.

"Look, if you'll sit down and listen to me, I'll explain everything."

"I don't want to know," she said archly, continuing toward the office.

"But you just asked," he insisted, standing in her way again. "Come on, Georgie, if we're going to have any chance at all you're going to have to hear me out."

"There is no 'we'!" She elbowed him out of the way and walked into the office, but he was right behind her.

"Do you love me, Georgie?"

"Leave me alone."

"When you give me a straight answer."

She spun around. "Fine. Then no, I don't love you."

"You're not telling the truth," he said, backing her up against the stationery cabinet.

"Like you would know? You're not exactly an expert on the truth."

Liam leaned his hands against the cabinet, either side of her, closing her in. "I know you love me, Georgie."

She was breathing hard. "This is stupid, Liam, let me go."

"I can't let you go," he said tenderly, leaning in close to her. "That's the whole problem."

She was trembling as he brought his lips down onto hers. She tried to resist, she closed her fist and made a pathetic attempt at punching him on the shoulder. But his mouth was overpowering her, and she missed him so much. . . .

He stopped abruptly. Georgie opened her eyes and he was staring down at her, catching her unawares. She tried to compose herself.

"Please say it, Georgie." He cupped her face with both hands. "Tell me you love me."

Georgie gazed up at him, losing herself. "I hate you . . ." she breathed, ". . . with all my heart."

"I love you too." His mouth covered hers again and Georgie gave in, she couldn't resist him anymore, it was beyond her. She kissed him voraciously, mindlessly. She didn't want to think about what she was doing, she just wanted him. She'd never stopped wanting him. There was no wife, there wasn't anyone or anything outside this room, this moment, he was all hers. Georgie arched herself against him, bringing one leg up around his thigh. She wanted him badly, she wanted him now, inside her, nothing less would do. She tugged at his belt buckle, trembling as he gasped her name. She felt his hands skim down her body till they reached her skirt, drawing it up out of the way. He was breathing hard as his fingers curled around her thighs, lifting her up and pressing himself hard up against her. Georgie couldn't breathe, she clung to him as he slid her hips higher, propping her up against the metal cabinet. It clanked loudly behind them as she instinctively wrapped her legs around him. She was throbbing inside, aching for him. She moaned his name like it was a plea and he plunged deep inside her. He began to grind slowly in and out of her, gradually thrusting harder and faster, till the cabinet was rattling so violently she thought it would come down on top of them. But she didn't care, they couldn't stop, she never wanted him to stop. And then she was gone, overwhelmed, crying out. He buried his face in her neck, breathing hard as he leaned into her, supporting them both up against the cabinet. Her legs would never have held her up, her whole body was limp. Only her heart seemed to be working, pounding so fast against her ribs, her breath couldn't keep up.

Liam was covering her face with gentle kisses, stroking her hair, murmuring softly, "I love you so much, Georgie, honey. . . . Everything's going to be alright, I promise. . . ."

"Hello! Anyone there?"

She jumped. "Shit!"

"Who is it?" Liam whispered.

"Adam." Georgie's heart was racing as she hastily readjusted her clothing. She tousled her hair with her fingers. "Just stay here, okay?" she hissed, going to the door. "Don't come out unless I say."

He nodded and Georgie slipped through the door, closing it behind her. Adam appeared from the back of the shop. "Fuck!" he exclaimed, holding a hand to his chest when he saw her standing there.

"It's only me, Ad."

"I can see that now. I didn't think there was anyone here, I just checked out in the storeroom."

"I was in the office. What are you doing here? I thought you were going out tonight?"

"I was on my way back down to Manly when I saw the place lit up like a Christmas tree."

Bugger, she'd forgotten to turn off the main lights when Liam arrived.

"But you knew I was closing," she reminded him.

"No offense, Georgie, but you haven't exactly been with it lately." He frowned at her. "Are you okay?"

"Sure."

"You look flushed. Are you sure you're alright?"

"Yes, Adam."

He glanced around. "What's going on?"

"Nothing, why do you say that?"

"Well, what are you still doing hanging around here?"

"I was just . . . taking care of some . . . stuff."

"What stuff?"

"Just stuff," she said defensively. "Anyway, everything's under control here, so you better get on your way, you'll be late."

"How are you getting home?"

"By bus, as usual."

He nodded thoughtfully, considering her. "Are you sure you're okay?"

"Yes, Adam!" she declared, frustrated.

"Alright, alright. Don't get your knickers in a twist." Georgie hoped she wasn't blushing. "Now, you do know where the night-lights are?" he said, walking toward the office.

She dashed ahead of him, blocking the door. "Of course I do!"

Adam frowned. "What's going on, Georgie? What's in there that you don't want me to see?"

"Nobody," she said.

"I said what, not who!" He rested his hands on his hips, looking squarely at her. "Liam's in there, isn't he?"

Georgie blanched. "What makes you think that?"

Adam peered through the frosted glass of the door but the office was in darkness. "Georgie, is he bothering you?"

She grabbed Adam by the elbow and led him away from the office. "Okay, yes, Liam's here," she admitted. "He showed up at closing time. He just wanted to talk."

"And you let him in? When you're on your own?"

"Adam, it's not as if he'd harm me! And you lot are always going on about closure—"

"Not me, I said you should tell him to piss off and stay away from you."

"Well, I don't think he was going to do that."

"You can't trust him, Georgie. What's he been saying to you?"

"He's just trying to explain himself."

Adam nodded. "Telling you his marriage is on the rocks, his wife doesn't understand him . . ."

Georgie stared at him.

"I'm right, aren't I?"

"He's . . . said a lot of things," she faltered.

Adam regarded her doubtfully. "I'm taking you home."

"No, Adam," she protested. "I can look after myself."

"You let him take you home and next thing he'll be in your bed."

Georgie felt as though she'd been punched in the chest. Adam was right. Liam had just charmed her, seduced her, and screwed her up against the stationery cabinet. She was so easy, too easy.

"Okay," she said, a little dazed.

"Okay what?"

"Um, okay." She swallowed. "That'd be great, if you could take me home, Ad. I'd appreciate it. I just have to get rid of him first."

"Do you want me to handle it?"

"Don't go getting all alpha male on me." Georgie frowned. "Can you give me five minutes, or is that going to make you late?"

"Doesn't matter, it's only drinking with the boys."

Georgie nodded. "Okay, thanks." She turned and walked back to the office, taking a deep breath as she grasped the handle and opened the door. Liam got up from where he'd been sitting at the desk. She stood in the doorway, not moving, still holding the handle.

"I have to lock up, Adam's waiting to take me home."

"Georgie." He frowned, walking around the desk. "What are you doing?"

"I told you, closing up and—"

"Georgie!" She could hear the desperation in his voice. "Don't do this."

"It's for the best," she said quietly. "I can't see you anymore, Liam."

"How can you say that after what just happened?"

"Exactly because of what just happened. You still have a wife. And I've just had sex with a married man, knowingly, for the first time in my life. I'm not proud of myself, and I have no intention of letting it happen again."

"My marriage is over. I was only staying because you—"

"I don't want to hear it, Liam!" Georgie interrupted, raising her voice. "Listen to me. You can't come here anymore, you can't keep phoning, you have to stop harassing me. Tonight was a mistake—"

"No . . ."

"It was a mistake," she repeated firmly. "I'm not going to pretend I don't have feelings for you, Liam. That's why it happened. But we're never going to be together. Whether you and your wife solve your problems or not, I can't ever be with you."

"But why not, Georgie? If we separate—"

"I will not be the reason a marriage broke up!" she said loudly, her tone final.

"You're not the reason, I promise you. Let me explain—"

"No, Liam. I can't believe your explanations, or your promises or any of the crap that comes out of your mouth. Our whole relationship was built on a lie, I don't even know who you are."

"Yes, you do. You know me better than anyone."

"Listen to what you're saying!" she exclaimed wide-eyed. "If I know you better than anyone, then you're in trouble. Because I was in love with an illusion named Liam MacMullen, a single man whose greatest flaw was that he was a workaholic. That person doesn't exist."

"It's still me, Georgie."

"I don't know you," she said plainly. "You're not the man I fell in love with."

She didn't know where she was getting the strength to stand there and stare him down. His eyes gazed back at her in disbelief, round and glassy. He was visibly distraught. It would be so easy to reach out and put her arms around him. And so stupid.

"I'm glad this happened, you know, Liam," Georgie said calmly. "I've been avoiding you, even hiding, because I couldn't face you. But now that

I have, well, I know it's over, and you need to know it too. It's called clo-sure, I believe." She paused, looking at him steadily. "Now, if you don't mind, I have to close the shop as well."

He looked shattered, but Georgie didn't flinch. His shoulders dropped in defeat and he walked slowly past her, as though he was waiting for her to stop him. But she didn't. She watched him as he made his way over to the door, where he turned around to look back at her. She met his gaze, un-blinking. Finally he opened the door and walked out and she lost sight of him.

She was still standing there when Adam sidled over into her field of vision.

"Are you alright?" he asked.

She nodded. "I will be."

But when she walked inside her flat, she was not so sure she was going to be alright. It was really over. That's what she had told Liam, now she had to convince herself. She had to put him out of her mind. She wasn't going to listen to his phone messages anymore. In fact, she would erase them, the same way she had to erase Liam from her mind. She had to re-member her own words to him, that she had been in love with someone who didn't exist. He was no more real than her other fantasies.

Georgie sighed. So this was what closure felt like. Empty.

Mosman

"Mac?" Anna walked into the hall when she heard the front door. "I, er . . ." She couldn't help noticing he looked appalling, like he'd just seen an accident, or been in one. "Are you alright?"

His eyes flickered past hers. "I'm fine, Anna. Just dandy."

He wasn't fine at all. Maybe this wasn't the right time, but she couldn't put it off any longer. "I was actually hoping we could talk," she said tentatively.

She'd been working up to this all week, ever since she'd spoken to Doug. She had thought long and hard about what she wanted, or rather didn't want. And she knew now that she didn't want Mac here. Whatever valiant notion he had about saving the marriage, well, he could do it from somewhere else. She couldn't stand his mournful presence any longer, rubbing her face in it.

Mac sighed wearily. "Do we really have to do this now?"

His voice was so strained. He didn't even have the energy to sound annoyed, it was more of a plea.

"It won't take long," she persisted.

"Okay." He tossed the keys onto the hall table and rubbed his forehead. "Just don't expect anything from me. I'm not really up to it tonight."

Anna felt a twisting sensation in her chest. She didn't want to kick him when he was down, but then lately he was always down.

"Anna?" he prompted her.

"It's not working out," she said.

"What in particular?"

"This . . . arrangement." She paused. "I think it would be better if you moved out."

She watched him breathe out heavily. He didn't look at her.

"Fine," he muttered. He turned and headed down the hall.

"Mac?"

He stopped. "Is it a problem if I stay tonight?"

"No, of course not. I just thought we should talk about this—"

"Why?" he said, turning around to face her. "So you can tell me all the reasons you don't want me here? Give me a list of your grievances?"

Anna just stared at him. He really looked wretched.

"If it's all the same to you I'd rather skip all that. Let's just agree I'm a fucking worthless bastard and leave it at that. I'm going to bed. I'll find somewhere tomorrow and get out of your way as soon as possible."

Morgan Towers

"Stella, could you come into my office, please? I need you to take a let-ter."

Her voice came back over the intercom. "What do you mean, Mac?"

"What do you mean, what do I mean?"

"What does 'take a letter' mean?"

"It's an expression, Stella."

"You've been watching too many Rosalind Russell movies."

"I really haven't," he muttered. "Stella," he began again, "I need to write a letter and I'd like you to type it. Is that clear enough for you?"

"Sure, but you know, usually you either give me a draft or you tell me to write such and such to so and so, and you check it when you sign it."

"Thanks for the rundown on office procedure, Stella, but this time I'd like to dictate a letter."

"You do realize I don't do the whole shorthand thing?"

"You've been my assistant for seven years. I think I would have no-ticed if you did shorthand by now."

"Okay, so how are we going to do this?"

Mac sighed. "You could start by coming into my office."

A moment later Stella appeared at the door. "I've got an idea."

He looked at her expectantly.

She closed the door and turned around. "You dictate the letter while I sit at your computer and type it."

"Sounds like a plan," he said, standing up to give Stella his chair as she came round and sat down. Mac propped himself against the desk be-hind her.

"Who shall I address it to?" she said, opening a new document on the screen.

"Bob Jaeger, CEO, etcetera, etcetera."

Stella turned around to look up at him. "You're writing to Bob? Why don't you just go and see him? He's only down the corridor."

"Because it needs to be in writing."

She frowned, turning back to the keyboard.

"Dear Bob," he began, "I regret to advise I am tendering my resignation as of—"

"Mac!" Stella stopped typing and glared up at him. "What are you doing? Why didn't you tell me?"

"I am telling you. I only just decided myself."

"And this is how you break it to me?"

"I guess it is," he said lamely.

Stella pushed the chair away from the computer and turned right around to look at him. "What's going on, Mac?"

"How long have you got?"

"You're the boss. As long as you want."

He smiled faintly. "Want to go to lunch?"

She groaned. "Last time you took me to lunch I had a hangover for days," she reminded him. "Just sit, talk."

He dragged another chair closer and sat down. "I moved into a serviced apartment over the weekend."

"Oh," Stella murmured. "Whose idea was that?"

"Anna's. I mean, I would have moved out weeks ago, but Georgie insisted I stay and try to patch things up with Anna, but Anna decided she didn't want me there, and Georgie decided it made no difference whether Anna and I stayed together, she doesn't want me either."

Stella stared glumly at him. "So now you're between a rock . . ."

". . . and a cliché." He nodded. "I guess there's a certain kind of poetic justice to it all. The feminists would be gratified."

"The *feminists*?" Stella repeated. "You mean women such as myself?"

"Just call me bitter."

"Okay, you're bitter." She sighed, frowning at him. "I don't understand why you're resigning, Mac. Don't you think you've been through enough changes already? Shouldn't you try to keep one part of your life stable?"

He sat back, clasping his hands behind his head. "I don't even know what I'm doing here anymore, Stella, but worse, I don't care. You know that better than anyone. I told you how I was feeling before Christmas. I've completely lost interest."

"But you could get it back. Perhaps a focus is exactly what you need."

Mac shook his head. "What I need is a break. I'm going to take some time off."

"Then why resign? Take a break and see how you feel later."

"Stella, you were the one who told me to make some changes," he reminded her. "It's time to move on. Being here will only remind me of everything else I've lost."

Her face fell. "Oh, Mac, that's so sad."

"Isn't it though?" he said drolly. "But I brought it upon myself, didn't I? I made my bed and now I have to lie in it—alone, as it turns out. I have to face the music, be a man—"

"Okay, Mac!" Stella interrupted. "You're weirding me out just a little. You don't have to be so stoic about it, like it doesn't bother you."

He folded his arms across his chest. "But I don't expect sympathy. I cheated on my wife. I cheated on the woman I was cheating on my wife with. I lied to them, I dug a hole so deep for myself I had no way of getting out unless I pulled them down with me. In certain countries, I'd be flogged."

"You know, amazingly enough, you wouldn't be," said Stella. "But Georgie would probably be stoned to death."

Mac's expression became serious. "I hurt her, you know. I hurt her badly. That's the hardest part, knowing she'd have been better off if she'd never met me."

Stella watched him. "You really loved her, didn't you?"

"Still do." He took a deep breath in, composing himself. "I just can't get used to the idea that I'm not going to see her again."

"You never know. . . ." Stella shrugged.

"Oh, I know," he assured her. "You should have seen her face. The determination in her eyes. I got the feeling she wouldn't want me if I was the last man on earth."

"She's angry. . . ."

"She's over me," he said flatly. "I took advantage of her good nature. She has a sweet, generous, trusting soul and I abused it. I suspect she'll never be so trusting again, which is a great legacy I left her." Mac sat forward, leaning his elbows on his knees as he stared down at the carpet. "The most decent thing I can do for Georgie is what she asked me to do, and that's leave her alone." He sat there, rubbing his hands slowly as though warming them over a fire.

"What about Anna?" Stella asked after a while.

He looked up then. "I hurt her too, there's no excusing that. But I honestly don't believe it's what broke us up. We were already on the downward spiral."

"You don't think you would have come through it?"

"I suppose we'll never know. But I do know that after I met Georgie I realized how unhappy I'd been. I loved Anna, I probably always will. But now I feel like a burden's been lifted off me." He gazed out the window for a moment before looking back at Stella. "I spent my whole life striving to be someone better than I was, but Georgie didn't care about all that, she just loved me, and I was never better than when I was with her." He paused. "I wish I could be with her more than anything, but even without her, I'm happier now."

Stella was thoughtful. "You know there's a saying that perhaps we only get the strength to fly on the wings of somebody else."

"Yeah?" Mac lifted an eyebrow. "Pretty corny, isn't it?"

She smiled. "I'm just saying maybe you fell in love with Georgie to escape."

"I fell in love with her because I couldn't do anything else."

Stella sighed deeply, propping her chin on one hand. "So you meet the love of your life but you're not free to be with her, and I'm free but I can't even meet someone I'd like to have dinner with. Life's a bitch, isn't it?"

Mac nodded. "And then you die."

March

Zan cleared her throat, claiming the family's attention from the photos they were passing around. "You know we didn't only go for a holiday?"

"You weren't drug-running, I hope?" said Nick. "I've warned you about that."

Zan rolled her eyes. She had come alone tonight. Jules was going through the worst part of the treatment cycle, just before egg retrieval. She was taking a cocktail of hormones that left her feeling sick and bloated and tender, the last thing she was up for was a night out.

"We visited a couple of clinics while we were in the States," Zan explained.

"Fertility clinics?" asked Louise.

"Ours aren't good enough for you?" said Nick.

"Not for what we're considering. One of the reasons Jules is having so much difficulty has to do with the quality of her eggs. We could have more luck with donor eggs, but it's not a very common practice here in Australia. It's against the law to pay for eggs, so there are barely any donors, and long waiting lists. Some legislation even prevents the use of donor eggs unless there are genetic issues involved. So you can imagine a couple of lesbians are way down the eligibility list."

"But it's different in America?" Nick asked.

Zan nodded. "In the birthplace of capitalism, if you're prepared to pay the price, you can get anything you want. We're crossing our fingers for this cycle, and hopefully they'll retrieve enough eggs for at least one frozen cycle as well. But if we've had no luck after that, we'll make arrangements to go back to the U.S. later in the year."

"So let me understand this," said Louise, glancing across at her daughters who were lying on the floor in front of the television, engrossed in *The Simpsons*. For once it didn't bother her. "You're prepared to go halfway across the world and use some American woman's eggs—"

"We'll be using my eggs," Zan corrected her.

"What?" Nick and Louise said simultaneously.

"I'll be the egg donor. I'll have to go on a course of drugs similar to what Jules is taking now, up to the point where they retrieve the eggs. Then it proceeds the same as any IVF treatment—they fertilize the eggs, freeze some and implant some, but they'll implant them into Jules instead."

"Why don't you just have the baby and get it over with, Zan?" Louise declared.

"Because," Zan returned calmly, "I don't want to have a baby. We've been through this before."

"And it still doesn't make any sense," said Louise. "Why you would put yourself, let alone Jules, through that when in all likelihood you could go through a simple insemination and get pregnant straightaway?"

Zan was unfazed. "Actually, Jules and I are quite excited about the idea. I mean, think about it. We were using donor sperm and Jules's eggs and her uterus, I wasn't part of it, except in spirit. Now we'll use donor sperm to fertilize my eggs, and Jules will carry the baby and give birth to it. It'll certainly be her baby, and this way it will biologically be mine."

Louise stood up and started clearing plates noisily.

"Why does it bother you so much, Louise?"

"I'd rather not get into it," she said curtly.

"No, let's get right into it," Zan insisted. "Boots and all, Louise, just say what's on your mind."

Louise stopped stacking the plates and looked directly at her. "You really want me to tell you what I think?"

"I really do."

"You really don't," Nick muttered.

"I think some people are not meant to have babies. There I said it."

Zan was momentarily speechless.

"By that, I don't mean for a nanosecond that they don't deserve a baby like anyone else, that they wouldn't make as good a parent, if not better than the general population. That's not what I'm saying. But physically, biologically, whatever, some women are not equipped to become pregnant and deliver a healthy baby. You should look at the statistics sometime, Zan, I'm sure I've read there's more risk of complications during IVF births, and a higher incidence of birth defects in IVF babies as well."

"You don't think we've researched this, Louise? What do you take us for?" said Zan. "The higher rate of complications is almost directly related to the higher incidence of multiple births from IVF. And try as they might, they can't find conclusive evidence that IVF itself causes defects at birth. But I wonder if you read about this, Louise? They have studied attachment after the birth and IVF parents have it all over 'natural' parents."

"That's not the point. Tell me, Zan, if something happens to Jules while she's pregnant or delivering, how are you going to feel? Will it all be worth it then?"

"Jules knows what she's doing. I'm not forcing her, this is something she wants to do. It's entirely her choice."

"Fifty years ago she wouldn't have had a choice. People who couldn't have babies just got on with their lives."

"But now we do have choices, Louise."

"Simply because medical technology *can* doesn't mean we should."

Zan paused, her eyes narrowing. "Okay, so when Nick's heart gives out on him in twenty years—"

"Steady on, that only puts me in my fifties."

"You're not going to avail yourself of everything medical science has to offer?" she continued. "Of course not, you'll just say, oh well, that's his use-by date. C'est la vie."

"I'm not talking about saving lives that already exist," said Louise. "I'm talking about going to extreme and ridiculous lengths to create new lives for an already overcrowded planet."

"Oh, for crying out loud, Louise, you had no problem adding another two lives to an overcrowded planet."

"We simply replaced ourselves, that's all."

"And I'm sure if Jules was married to a man, you wouldn't have a problem with her employing all the medical know-how available to bear him a child and prop up the patriarchal order of things."

"Zan! Look who you're talking to," Louise cried, raising her arms. "Have you noticed much propping of the patriarchal order going on around here? I couldn't care less if it's a man and a woman, two men, two women, two donkeys, whatever, it's a waste of limited resources."

"IVF does not prevent poor people from receiving medical attention or children from getting vaccinations, that's not how it works. In fact, we don't get it for free, but I don't mind paying because it enables research into infertility to continue."

"Okay, I'm pulling patriarchal rank now," said Nick. "Time to change the subject."

"Good idea," Louise muttered, carrying a stack of plates over to the kitchen.

"You're quiet, George," said Zan.

"Hmm?"

"You haven't got anything to add to the debate?"

"I thought we were changing the subject?" said Georgie.

"I'm sure if you were the one having a baby, we wouldn't be changing the subject so readily."

Georgie sighed. "So now we're playing hypotheticals?"

Nick winked at her, leaning forward with the bottle of wine to top off her glass. Georgie covered it, shaking her head. "My stomach's not up to it."

"How come?" asked Zan.

"I've just had a mild bug," Georgie explained. "It's nothing."

Zan sat back in her chair, regarding her sister. "So, how are you, George, you know, generally?"

"I'm okay," she answered lightly.

"Has the dickhead been hanging around, bothering you?" Zan had taken to referring to Liam only as "the dickhead."

Georgie shook her head.

"She's been incredible," said Nick proudly. "Really moving on with her life, haven't you, Sis?"

"I don't know." Sometimes Georgie wished Nick would stop being so damned proud of her. He didn't see her moping around the flat, crying herself to sleep. But she had to keep up a brave face. It was bad enough

she'd been fooled by a liar and a cheat, if they had any idea she'd suc-
cumbed to his advances the minute she'd laid eyes on him again . . . "I'm
not so sure I'm moving on anywhere," she admitted.

"Why do you say that?" asked Zan.

Georgie shrugged. "I'm in exactly the same place as I was before. I
think I'd like to do something else with my life."

"You're not happy at the shop?" Louise frowned, rejoining them at
the table.

"Yes! Of course I am, I love the shop," she insisted. "I don't really
want another career . . . but I do want something."

"You want another bloke," said Zan. "Just make it a single one this
time."

Georgie was shaking her head. "Oh no, no, no, that ship has sailed . . .
and sunk, deep down under the ocean."

"Come on, Georgie, you're only thirty-three," Nick chided.

Georgie looked at Louise "I told you that number had bad feng shui."

"So what's the something you're talking about?" Zan persisted.

"I don't know," said Georgie. "But I feel like this has been one of
those pivotal moments in my life, a seminal moment, where nothing will
be as it was before."

"She's been raiding the self-help section at the shop," said Louise.
"You should see the tripe she's been reading: *Strong Hearts Don't Break*,
Women Who Run with the Wild Horses, *Feng Shui for the Wounded Soul*."

"Make fun if you will," said Georgie airily. "But I'm only taking on
what speaks to me."

"George, could you please stop talking like a Zen monk?" said Zan.

"Leave her alone," said Nick. "If it helps, what's wrong with that?"

"Because it's crap," Zan exclaimed. "Chanting trite couplets won't
magically improve her life. George has spent enough time in fantasy land,
she needs to face up to the real world."

"That's a bit harsh, Zan," said Nick. "I think Georgie's had a big dose
of reality lately."

"Yeah, only because her head was so far up in the clouds she didn't
even realize the dickhead was stringing her along."

"Could you talk *to* me, not about me, please?" Georgie said politely but firmly. They both looked at her. "I know I've had a tendency to go off with the pixies, Zan, you're right. I've made some poor choices based on pretty fanciful ideas at times. I told Nick what went through my head the first day Liam came into the shop—"

"What? What!" Zan and Louise chorused.

"Don't tell them," Nick warned.

"It's alright," said Georgie calmly. "The first time I saw Liam, the thought came to me from nowhere—'I'm going to spend the rest of my life with him.'"

Zan shook her head, rolling her eyes. Louise made a snorting noise in an attempt to contain her laughter.

"Go ahead, laugh, I deserve it," said Georgie. Problem was, part of her still believed it, even now. She felt so inextricably bound to Liam she wondered if she would ever get over him. "From now on you're going to hear every foolish notion that crosses my mind, and I want you to laugh loudly and tell me how stupid I am."

"You're not stupid, Georgie," Nick chided. "You're just very trusting, and there's nothing wrong with that. In fact, it's endearing."

"It may be endearing, Brother," said Zan, "but it's also got her into trouble. She needs to wise up."

"Once again, I would ask you to speak *to* me," Georgie reminded her.

"You go girl." Zan laughed, punching the air. "This is exactly what you need to do, George, get tougher, more savvy."

"There's absolutely nothing wrong with the way you are, Georgie," Nick insisted. "I don't think you need to change."

"But I have changed, Nick," Georgie said seriously. "What happened changed me, I can't pretend it never took place or that it hasn't affected me. But at least Liam did one good thing for me—I won't ever be fooled like that again."

Mosman

Anna heard the bell and walked slowly up the hall, full of misgiving.
Perhaps she shouldn't have suggested meeting here. But Mac needed to
pick up some things, and they had to decide how to divide up their belongings, or at least start the process. Anna had never imagined anything
like this would ever be necessary, it felt as though her life had turned on a
penny and she was suddenly inhabiting a parallel universe, much like the
old one but slightly off-kilter. Every day felt like that. Slightly skewed,
awry. She wondered how long it would be before things went back to
normal, or at least felt normal. She supposed things were never going to
go back.

True to his word, Mac had moved out that same weekend into a serviced apartment in the city. Anna had never been there, but she believed
him when he told her he wasn't seeing the woman, Georgie, anymore.
There was a hollowness in his eyes that was quite poignant on some level.
She was surprised to learn that he'd put his notice in at work the following
Monday, though she shouldn't have been. It fit the pattern. Mac had set a
new course and he would charge along it single-mindedly, shedding his
old life like it was so much dust under his feet. He'd used the apartment as
his base since then, traveling almost constantly to notify his clients in the
Asia-Pacific region of his pending resignation and to ease the transition
for his replacement. He arranged a post-office box where his mail could
be forwarded and he told Anna his cell phone number would remain the
same if she needed to contact him. But Anna had only called once. She
wanted to put the house on the market, she didn't see any point putting it
off any longer. He said she should do whatever she felt was appropriate.

But then she'd discovered Mac had to cosign the contract with the real-estate agent. She'd forgotten about that, or never really thought about it. As a couple they did those things together automatically; she had never thought much about the fact that both signatures were actually required on most documents.

Anna took a deep breath and opened the door. Mac had his back to her, gazing up the street, his hands thrust deep in his pockets. He turned around, smiling faintly at her. "Hi."

"Hello." His hair was longer, that was the first thing she noticed. He was wearing jeans and a T-shirt and he looked better than the last time she'd seen him, when he was misery on legs. "Come in," said Anna, standing back out of the way.

He nodded. "Thanks."

He followed her down the hall to the kitchen. Anna had laid all the papers out on the breakfast table. "Would you like a cup of coffee?" she asked.

"Thanks, if you're having one."

"Everything's on the table if you want to start looking it over."

"Alright."

When Anna brought his coffee over, Mac was already signing the contract. "It all looks pretty straightforward to me," he said, turning a page and signing again.

He ought to know, he had a law degree after all. Anna sat down as he returned his attention to the papers. Who the hell was this man sitting here, forging William MacMullen's signature? Anna didn't even know him anymore. He looked so relaxed, so self-possessed. Had they really been married for fourteen years? Anyone watching the two of them would be forgiven for thinking they were barely acquaintances. If he intended to leave here without some mention—no, more than that—some discussion about what had happened between them, well, Anna was not going to tolerate it. They needed closure. Or at least she did.

Eventually Mac laid the pen down on top of the papers. "What do you think it'll go for?" he asked.

Anna shrugged. "The agent is optimistic, but they always are."

"I wanted to mention, Anna, that you should work out how you'd like to split the difference. I know your parents helped us out—"

"They helped us with a deposit," Anna interrupted. "You've been earning more than me all our married life, Mac. You're entitled to your fair share."

"I won't be taking any more than half," he said flatly.

"And neither will I."

He picked up his cup and drank from it. As he put it down, he regarded her for a moment from across the table. "How are you, Anna?"

She wasn't prepared for that. How did he expect her to answer?

Casually? *Fine, and you?*

Guilt-inducing? *I'm desperately unhappy.*

Provocatively? *How do you think I am, you bastard?*

"I have my days." That certainly didn't let him off the hook, but she hoped it didn't sound desperate either. "How are you?"

"Good . . . not bad, you know, getting along."

"You've been away a lot?"

He nodded. "That'll all wrap up this week. I won't officially be on the payroll any longer, but I might have to do some consulting until the new guy is up to speed."

"Is that what you're going to do now, consult?"

"No way." He shook his head. "Actually, I'm going for a position with an NGO."

"What was that?"

"Sorry, an NGO, a nongovernment organization."

"I know what the acronym stands for. What's the organization, what's the job?"

"Well, the organization supports small business owners and the job involves working with members when they've been audited, or are about to be, helping them prepare submissions, representing them to the taxation office, that kind of thing."

Anna was gobsmacked. "That's a change of direction." To say the least.

He shrugged. "Thought it was maybe time I gave something back, you know?"

What was this, penance?

"The thing is, Anna, I've been following the one path all my life, since I was a kid. I never considered another direction, I barely even stopped to look at the scenery along the way." He seemed lost in thought. "Sorry, I'm rambling," he said, snapping out of it. "I want to do something useful with the skills I have. Not just make rich people richer."

Anna didn't know what to say to him. It was not so long ago that he was striving to be one of the rich getting richer.

"Guess who I caught up with in Malaysia a couple of weeks ago?" Mac was saying.

Small talk now? Anna shook her head, she had no idea.

"Sean. He's backpacking across Asia, you know, surfing, generally bumming around."

"Your little brother, Sean?" He was the youngest of the nine Mac-Mullen children and had been page boy at their wedding. He'd barely started school at the time, as Anna recalled. "Is he old enough to be traveling around like that?"

Mac smiled. "That's what I said to Mum when she first told me. But Sean's twenty-one and not exactly my 'little' brother anymore," he went on. "You should see him, big swarthy bloke, rides a surfboard, drinks beer. Nice kid, though. I don't think he knew what to make of me at first, I suspect he always thought of me more like an uncle."

"Well, you left home when he was born, didn't you?"

"Just after." He became thoughtful. "It was so great seeing him, spending some time with him." He shrugged. "Maybe it was because we were in a foreign country, I don't know, but I felt this really strong bond, that we were brothers. . . ." Mac looked across at her, sheepish. "Sorry, I'm rambling again."

Anna didn't think she could take much more of this. So Mac had abandoned his corporate career to become a crusader for the little people, and he was embracing the family he had kept at arm's distance for all these years. Did this make him a great guy all of a sudden? Did it make up for the fact that he turned to another woman when his marriage was floundering and his wife needed him the most?

"I can't do this, Mac."

"What?"

"Sit here talking about everything but the obvious. Don't we have anything else to say to each other?"

Mac took a slow breath in and out. "I don't know, you tell me, Anna."

"After fourteen years I would like to think so."

"That's why I was prepared to stay and work it out," he returned calmly. "You were the one who asked me to leave."

"Because you didn't want to be here!" she insisted. "You stayed out of some cavalier idea about right and wrong, but you didn't do anything to rebuild the relationship. You just moped about, pining for your girlfriend."

"And exactly what did you do to rebuild the relationship, Anna?" he said tightly. "This didn't start with Georgie and you know it. I was unhappy for a long time, but you wouldn't talk to me. You shut me out—"

"Because I was frightened you'd want to stop the treatment!" she cried. She paused, catching her breath. "And I was right. Quitting was the only solution you could come up with. You never coped with IVF from the beginning."

"That's not fair, Anna, I always supported you."

"Yes, you did. But you were never happy about it."

"Show me someone who is! It's not exactly a picnic."

"That's not what I meant. You couldn't stand the idea of having to seek treatment, that we couldn't have children ourselves. It was hard for you to accept that we weren't the perfect couple after all."

"That's rubbish. I was completely prepared to give up having children. You were the one who was obsessed, who started the whole thing. I hadn't even thought about kids at that stage."

"But you would have," Anna said, calmer now. "Eventually. You expected to have the perfect family, Mac, part of the perfect life you had planned. And one day you would have wanted a child, and if we had found out then and it was too late, you would have been devastated."

"Oh, for Chrissakes, Anna, this is all hypothetical. What's the point arguing about it? Besides, if I was so determined to have the perfect family, why did I suggest a break from the treatment, even giving up?"

"Because you couldn't face the failure anymore. You don't handle crises well, Mac, it's not one of your strengths. You'd rather walk away."

"Don't psychoanalyze me, Anna," he said grimly.

But she was on a roll. Ever since she'd found out about the affair, she had been tormented, trying to understand what had gone wrong between them, to make sense of it from the ruins, sifting through the debris, looking for clues like some kind of emotional archaeologist.

"You know what I think, Mac? We were perfect, maybe a little too perfect. Like some delicate piece of porcelain that's flawless but incredibly fragile. The slightest knock is all it takes to destroy it." She paused. "I don't think you and I ever had a chance of withstanding the knocks."

"Then it's just as well we never had children," he said ruefully. "You think parenthood wouldn't have knocked us around?"

Anna just looked at him.

"We had nothing but knocks for years on end, Anna. Our life together wasn't perfect, it was miserable." He sighed, leaning forward on the table. "I still don't think you have any idea how unhappy I was. It got so I didn't even know if I wanted a baby anymore, but I couldn't talk to you about it. You were so driven to keep going, no matter what. You didn't seem to care how I felt as long as I kept filling that cup."

"You keep going back to that one stupid remark."

"It wasn't just one remark, Anna, it was every day, our whole life. And I couldn't do it anymore. You gave me no choice."

She glared at him. "I beg your pardon? Are you trying to say I forced you into having an affair?"

"No, no." He shook his head. "That's not what I meant. But I didn't see how we could keep going the way we were. I was beginning to hate my life, Anna. I dreaded coming home—"

"Thanks."

"Because I couldn't stand to see you so unhappy," he tried to explain. "And I couldn't do anything to fix it. I felt useless and hopeless. I don't know how you couldn't see how miserable we both were. It wasn't a life, it was an endurance test." He paused. "The first time I met Georgie she made me laugh. And I kept going back to see her because I felt good when I was around her."

"It had nothing to do with being weak and selfish?"

"I'm not pretending it was right, I've never said otherwise. I'm just trying to get you to see how it was for me."

"Well, I'm sick of hearing how hard it was for you, Mac," she cried. "Think about it from my perspective for a change! After everything I've been through, can you imagine how it feels to be discarded like this, like I'm faulty goods—"

"That had nothing to do with it," he said loudly, standing up. "I would never have left you because you couldn't have children. And if you think for a second I could do that, then you don't know me at all." He pushed his chair in, holding the back of it. "Truth is, Anna, you didn't know me at the end. And I think what upsets you most is losing your chance to have a baby, not losing me."

North Side Clinic

Anna sat in the chair, her mind drifting; she wasn't really listening to Evelyn, the words were floating free-form past her. She hadn't been able to focus properly since the other day, the day Mac came, and left again.

"Anna?"

She stirred. "Yes, Evelyn, go on, I'm listening."

"No, you're not."

"Pardon?"

"You're not listening, you haven't been listening to anything I said. You're just like my husband, this is exactly what he does, just like I told you. . . ." Her voice began to undulate, like a radio tuning in and out, Anna was only able to catch fragments, snatches of what she was saying. "Never takes his eyes of the TV . . . doesn't matter what's on . . . just won't listen . . ."

"Then leave him!" Anna said suddenly.

Evelyn was clearly startled.

"If he's that bad, if you really can't stand him, then leave him. But you won't ever do that, will you? Because what would you have to complain about then? And who would you have to blame for how unhappy your life is? You'd only have yourself, and that wouldn't be any fun. You couldn't come here harping on endlessly . . ."

Anna froze. What was she saying? Evelyn looked exactly like some kind of tiny, furry animal caught in the headlights of a dirty, big SUV bearing down upon it. A big SUV with Anna behind the wheel. She'd put on the brakes too late she feared.

"Excuse me for a moment?" she said as she leaped from her chair and out the door. She looked around the waiting room. Empty. Good. Think, think. It's four thirty. She had no more clients today, thank God.

"Dr. A?"

Kerrie was standing behind the reception desk, watching her, frowning. "Are you alright, Dr. A?"

She took a deep, calming breath before she spoke. "Yes, thank you, Kerrie. Is he with anyone?" she asked, cocking her head toward Doug's office.

"Not till five."

"Could you . . . Would you mind seeing Mrs. Delaney out, Kerrie? Please make my apologies and tell her I'll be in touch in a day or two. Oh, and don't bill her for today."

Kerrie was clearly puzzled, but Anna knew she could count on her to do as requested and not ask any questions. Anna walked over to Doug's office and knocked lightly on his door. She heard a muffled "Come in," and slipped inside, leaning heavily back against the door as she closed it behind her. Doug swiveled around in his chair, standing immediately when he saw the expression on Anna's face.

"What is it, Anna?" he said, his voice steady but full of concern.

That was it. Anna erupted into tears, holding her hands over her face, ashamed, embarrassed, despairing. She felt Doug's arms close around her. He held her gently in the circle of his arms, but the tears kept coming, and then she started to shake. She felt like she was going to fall apart, like a car in a cartoon, parts would start springing off and she'd collapse in a heap of useless metal, hissing and steaming.

Doug stepped back to look at her, holding her firmly by the arms. "Anna, what is it?"

"I feel like I can't catch my breath," she gasped.

"Here, sit down." He led her over to a chair and she sat. "Put your head down and breathe slowly."

He patted her back rhythmically, and after a while Anna found herself breathing in time, calmer. Eventually she sat up straight. Doug poured her a glass of water from a jug on a tray on his desk and handed it to her.

"I feel ridiculous," she muttered, taking the glass from him.

"Well don't." He passed her a box of tissues and she took one, wiping her eyes and sniffing.

"I just told off Evelyn Delaney," Anna told him, shaking her head. "Abused her, insulted her. I must be going mad."

"You're not going mad, Anna, though I'd prefer it if we use a less pejorative term." He paused. "What happened with Mrs. Delaney?"

Anna was thoughtful. "I don't know. I don't know where it all came from, I didn't even realize I was saying the words until I heard them coming out of my mouth."

"Do you remember what the words were?" Doug asked.

"I told her to stop harping and leave her husband. But then I suggested she would never do that because then who would she have to blame for her problems?" Anna held her hand to her mouth. "Oh my God. How could I say that to a client, to anyone? I am going mad."

"Where is Evelyn now?"

"I asked Kerrie to take care of her, see her out, not bill her, of course."

Doug nodded. "A 'mad' woman wouldn't have had the presence of mind to organize that."

Anna looked at him. "What's the matter with me?"

"You tell me."

She shrugged. "I've been finding it hard to focus all week. . . ."

Doug watched her, waiting.

"I saw Mac," she said quietly. "He came over to sign some papers, we're putting the house on the market."

"Anna," he chided gently, "you didn't say anything."

She shook her head. "I didn't think it was a big deal. It was just the next step."

"A fairly major step, I would suggest."

"I don't know. I don't really care about the house. I'll be glad to be out of there, to be honest."

"What makes you say that?"

"It doesn't mean anything to me anymore," she tried to explain. "It's strange, to have been together for so long, and then there's nothing." Anna gazed across the room. "We had it all out. Mac said some things . . . things I didn't realize . . . He'd been unhappy for a long time." She paused. "You know, he said that I was more upset about losing the chance to have a baby than about losing him."

"How did that make you feel?"

"Terrible. I couldn't believe he thought that of me." Anna swallowed. "But then when I thought about it . . . the emptiness I felt after he left . . . The thing is, if I was ever going to have a baby, a family, it was going to be with Mac. It's too late for me to have a chance with anyone else. So maybe he's right."

Doug let a moment pass before speaking. "Anna, you are dealing with loss on many levels. And perhaps focusing on the lost opportunity to have a child is easier than dealing with feelings of abandonment or rejection."

Anna blinked at him.

"Psychologists are their own worst enemies, Anna," he went on. "We're expected to have the answers to everybody else's problems, but we're not always so adept at handling our own. You have had a very difficult time over the past few years, and I think you need some space to work through that."

"I've got plenty of space, too much in fact. All I have is space. If I don't have work . . ."

"You'll always have work, as soon as you feel ready to come back to it," Doug assured her. "But I think we both know it's not appropriate for you to see clients at the moment."

"Of course, you're absolutely right."

He checked his watch. "I'd like to get Kerrie to begin contacting your clients, with your permission, as soon as possible."

Anna nodded.

"Why don't you go back to your office?" Doug suggested. "Take your time, you might want to pack up some things. I have a client shortly, we can talk again afterward."

Just after six there was a light knock on her office door and Anna called, "Come in."

Doug entered, closing the door behind him. Anna had put away the files from the day, but that was as far as she'd got. She had been sitting there for the past hour, lost in thought.

"You know, Doug, I might come in another time to sort through all of this."

"Of course," he dismissed. "Come on, I'll walk you to your car."

Anna stood up. "Did Kerrie say anything about Evelyn Delaney?"

"You don't have to worry," Doug assured her. "She was a little bewildered apparently, but she was fine."

When they came out of the office, Kerrie was just finishing a phone call to one of Anna's clients. "Yes, that's right, we'll call you in a month to reschedule. . . . Thank you too."

"A whole month?" Anna sighed, propping an elbow on the reception desk. "What am I going to do with myself for a whole month?"

"You have a house to sell, and you have to find somewhere else to live," Doug reminded her. "You'll have plenty to keep you occupied."

"May I make a suggestion, Dr. A?" Kerrie said tentatively.

"Go ahead."

"Two words: 'folk art.' Saved my sanity when the kids started school. I didn't know what to do anymore without them running around my ankles. Then I saw a course advertised and I said to myself, I said, Kerrie, that's for you. Well, not only did I end up with some beautiful hand-crafted decorator items for the home, it gave me the confidence to take on a computer course, and one thing led to another and here I am."

Doug had been listening with some amusement. "And what would we do without you?"

"Oh, Dr. Doug," she dismissed, but she was clearly chuffed.

"Thank you, Kerrie," said Anna, "you know, for taking care of things."

Kerrie waved it aside. "Not a problem. Go and enjoy your time off. We'll see you soon."

"She has a point, you know," Doug said as they left the building.

"I'm sorry?"

"Kerrie, what she said about finding something to do."

"You think I should take up folk art?" Anna asked.

"It doesn't have to be folk art, but I think it would help you to have some other focus."

Yes, she would need another focus . . . now that she didn't have work, or a husband, or a baby. Or a hope, it seemed.

Dee Why

"Hi, Georgie?" called Louise.

"In here, in the bathroom."

Louise appeared in the doorway. "I tried knocking."

"Sorry, couldn't hear you from here." Georgie was sitting on the floor between the toilet and the shower recess, her back against the wall, resting her head against the cistern.

"You're still throwing up?"

"No, I'm thinking about taking up plumbing, so I'm acclimatizing."

Louise put her hands on her hips. "Sarcasm a side effect of the illness, is it?"

"Sorry," said Georgie, smoothing the hair back off her forehead. "I'm just in a bad mood."

"I can understand that." Louise crouched down to Georgie's level, frowning at her. "Have you got a temperature?"

"I don't think so. I only feel flushed when the nausea hits, and it comes and goes in waves. Sometimes I even feel hungry, but if I eat anything my stomach says, you've got to be kidding, I'm not having that in here. And up she blows."

Louise grimaced. "Well, I brought you some flat lemonade and arrowroot biscuits."

Georgie managed a weak smile. "That's what Mum used to give us when we were sick."

"Mine too. I think it's in the user's manual."

"There's a manual?"

25 **Dianne Blacklock**

"No, more's the pity." Louise sighed, watching her. "Why don't you come home with me?"

She shook her head. "I don't want to infect you all, especially the kids."

"Nick's going to get into a lather when he hears how crook you are."

"Then don't tell him. He's been such a mother hen lately, ever since . . ."

"Okay, but I'm going to make an appointment for you with Dr. Gupta tomorrow morning. I'll come by and pick you up."

"Oh, Louise, what good's a doctor going to do?"

"Gee, you're right, six years of medical training, a decade or more in general practice, but why don't we humor him and see what he can come up with?" said Louise drily. "I'm worried about you, chook. You don't look that good, and this has been hanging around for weeks. It's not your average, garden-variety bug."

Georgie looked wide-eyed at her. "Do you think it's something serious?"

"No," she replied firmly. "I just think it should be checked out."

"Okay, I'll go to the doctor as long as you don't tell Nick, at least till we know what it is?"

"Deal." Louise looked thoughtful. "There's no way you could be pregnant, is there?"

leave it, we'd find out soon enough. But he couldn't wait. He was like a big kid himself." She smiled faintly, thinking about it.

"I've had so many fantasies. . . . I'm guessing that doesn't surprise you," Georgie added wryly. "But I always imagined meeting my husband for dinner in our favorite restaurant, telling him in some clever, romantic way. . . ." She dropped her head, hoping Louise wouldn't notice that her face was all contorted trying to hold back the tears.

"Georgie?"

She couldn't hold back anymore. The dam burst and she began to sob violently. Louise put her arms around her, hugging her tight. Which only made her cry harder.

Eventually Georgie calmed down a little, sniffing and wiping her cheeks with the palms of her hands. "It's just," she blubbered, "it wasn't supposed to happen like this. It was supposed to be a wonderful thing, a happy thing. I've always wanted a family of my own. But this is a disaster. I can't have a baby with a man who's married to someone else. . . ." Her voice started to break and she took a deep, tremulous breath. "But what if this is my last chance? I don't know if I can give that up. But then it can't all be about me either, it has to be what's best for the child. Can I bring up a child without a father? Is it selfish to want a baby on my own?"

"Georgie, this is a huge decision," said Louise. "I don't know what to tell you, no one can tell you what's the right thing to do. But you know I'll be there for you. We all will be."

Georgie nodded.

"And in the meantime," Louise added, "you're better off not doing anything."

"What do you mean?"

"Well," she faltered, "maybe you shouldn't have the ultrasound yet."

"Why not?"

"It'll be easier to be . . . objective."

Louise watched Georgie as tears filled her eyes again. "How am I supposed to get through this?" she breathed, her voice barely making it out of her throat.

Melbourne

"Darling, your father and I both feel the very best thing would be for you to move back here to Melbourne and live with us."

Anna didn't say anything. She was traipsing along in her mother's wake as she made her very determined way around the Queen Victoria Markets. Caroline was on a mission, buying up big for the Easter Sunday luncheon she was hosting on the weekend.

She glanced at her daughter. "Now I don't want you thinking we're being clingy, Anna. Neither of us wants you wasting your life looking after us in our old age. We're not talking about forever, only until you get yourself sorted. We could help you find a place. You know that real estate here is much more affordable than Sydney."

"Mum, are you forgetting I have a job?"

"But you've just been telling me you're not even sure it's what you want to do anymore."

Anna had flown down yesterday. She couldn't stay in the house another day, especially with the procession of prospective buyers coming through at odd times. And she really didn't want to spend Easter alone. Eggs, bunnies, chocolate on tap . . . could there be anything more depressing?

"You could start afresh, Anna," her mother was saying, charging ahead into the throng. "New place, new job, new life."

Right back where she started from. How could Anna explain to her mother that it would feel like a backward step? She loved Melbourne, and she did have a stronger attachment to it than Sydney. But it wasn't that. It was the idea of moving back to the place of her childhood, to a time when she was happily married, before she was even aware that she couldn't have children of her own. She didn't see how she could move on by hiding out in the comfort zone of her past.

Caroline was waiting for her a little farther along. She was looking at Anna expectantly. "Well, what do you think?"

"Look, Mum, for the moment I just want to get through the auction and settling up with Mac—"

"I still can't bear thinking of it." Caroline sighed. "I don't understand him. He's having some kind of midlife crisis, Anna. He's going to snap out of it and wonder what on earth he's done." She lifted her eyebrows. "Is that why you don't want to leave Sydney?"

"No, Mum, it has nothing to do with him." She decided not to enter into yet another conversation about Mac's crisis, midlife or otherwise. Caroline was constantly trying to nut it out, as though understanding his motivation would prove something, or solve something, or in some way make things better. "I want to tackle one thing at a time, Mum. And I don't want to go through any more changes than I already have to right at the moment."

"But coming back here is not a change, Anna, it's your home."

"Be that as it may, Mum, I've been in Sydney for seven years and I'm not going anywhere until I've worked out what I want to do with my life."

Caroline looked at her squarely. "Well, you know you have our support whatever it is you decide."

Anna leaned over and kissed her cheek.

"Well," said Caroline, taking Anna's arm as they proceeded along, "perhaps you'll follow my footsteps this time, become an academic."

"But I only have a bachelor's degree. I'd need to do more study."

"That's right."

"I think I'm getting a bit old."

"Nonsense, Anna. We regularly had students at university who were in their sixties. And even a few older than that."

"But I don't think I want to do any more study in psychology."

"Who says you have to continue with psychology? Why don't you try something different?"

Anna shrugged. "I wouldn't know what."

"When you were young I always thought you might end up in the arts, studying literature or something along those lines."

"Why?"

"You always had your head in a book. You loved reading, and when you weren't reading you were scribbling away in one of those exercise books you were always getting me to buy for you."

Anna was frowning.

Caroline glanced at her. "Don't you remember?"

"Vaguely. How old was I?"

"The exercise books were primary school. I think you might have kept a journal in high school, and you were still a voracious reader. You always did very well in English and history. But then you became hell-bent on becoming a psychiatrist like your father and you had to focus on the science subjects. You didn't seem to read much after that."

She was right. Anna had forsaken everything else in the vain attempt to get into medicine. She'd never really returned to reading with the same enthusiasm, it seemed an adolescent indulgence to lie around and waste whole days absorbed in a book. Anna remembered the exercise books though, she wondered what had happened to them.

"Mum, you know those boxes of my stuff you brought from the house?" she asked. "They're still at the apartment?"

"Yes, dear, but don't concern yourself," Caroline replied. "I know I've been nagging you to do something about them, but that's the least of your worries at the moment."

Later that night after her parents had gone to bed, Anna carried the stepladder into the guestroom and climbed up to investigate the very top shelf of the built-in wardrobe. She remembered seeing the row of boxes, each one simply marked *ANNA*, and her mother prompting her from time to time to sort through them. She reached in and slid the first box out. It didn't feel too heavy, so she lifted it off the shelf and stepped carefully back down the ladder. She rested it on the bed and opened the lid. Anna smiled. It was packed full of stuffed animals. She'd had a bit of an obsession during her teens and even though she outgrew it eventually, she had never been able to bring herself to part with them. But Caroline had finally made her cull the collection when she was getting married. Anna had narrowed down her favorites to one box, she supposed with the idea of keeping them for her own child. She picked up a koala nestled on top and smoothed the fluffy fur on its ears. What on earth was she going to do with all these now? She replaced the koala and the lid and climbed back up the stepladder.

The next box felt heavier, so Anna only pulled it partway out and lifted the lid, peering inside. It looked like university stuff. She removed the lid completely and drew out a cardboard folder from the top. She was right, it was one of her final assignments. She decided to leave that box for the moment, doubtful she would find what she was looking for there. The next box felt heavy as well. Anna slipped her hand under the lid, feeling around inside. She drew out a book and looked at the cover. *Anne of Green Gables*. Anna was suddenly catapulted back in time, lying on her bed, tears streaming down her face as she read. She slid the box out, and though it was heavier than the first, she managed to climb back down the stepladder and dump it on the bed. As she sifted through the contents it was like her childhood flashing before her eyes. There were more books: *Black Beauty*, *The Diary of Anne Frank*, *To Kill a Mockingbird*, *Wuthering Heights*. There were school reports: "Attendance—*perfect*; Uniform—*perfect*; Conduct—*perfect*; *Anna is a model student, serious, diligent, with poise beyond her years*." There were photos from school, from formals, from her debutante ball. There was one from her graduation, all gowned up, her parents on one side and Mac on the other. He looked so young and his eyes were full of pride as he gazed down at her. It felt like another lifetime.

There were certificates and merit awards and birthday cards, but no exercise books. Anna was beginning to feel weary. Maybe she'd look through the other boxes tomorrow. She replaced the lid and carried the box over, putting it on the floor against the wall. Then she returned for the box of stuffed toys. When she picked it up she realized it felt a little heavier than it should. She gave it a shake, there was something solid in the bottom. She set it back down on the bed and opened the lid. After extracting a couple of bears, a tiger, a monkey, assorted bunnies, she finally came to a flat rag doll lining the base of the box. It was a pajama bag, Anna remembered. She picked it up, there was something inside. She turned the doll over and unzipped the back, pulling out a bundle of exercise books tied together with a green ribbon. Anna sat down on the bed, unraveling the bow. Some of the books were covered with wrapping paper, some had doodles scribbled all over them: *Private*, *Keep Out*, *This Book is the Private Property of Anna Caroline Gilchrist*. *No Peeking*. Anna kicked off her shoes and shifted up the bed till she reached the headboard, propping up the pillows and settling herself against them. She ran her hand across the cover of the first book in the bundle. It was as good a place to start as any.

At two thirty Anna rubbed her eyes and told herself she had to get some sleep. She had read almost every word through eight exercise books. She'd worked out that they must have been written throughout grades four, five and six, when she was nine up to about eleven or twelve years old. There was mention of going to high school in the future, but not of being there yet. Parts were autobiographical, like a diary, but mostly they were filled with stories and poems. The poems were often clumsy and self-conscious, though Anna was impressed by the vocabulary she had used at such a young age. The stories were sometimes bizarre fables with talking animals or fairies and goblins, or girlie tales of best friends and sleepover parties, or blatant ripoffs of books she'd obviously been reading at the time.

But throughout, to Anna's surprise, there was a great deal of anger, anger that Anna couldn't even recall feeling, let alone expressing. She was quite sure she never had, but clearly she had found a way of venting it. Some seemed to be directed toward her parents for not being around as much as she would have liked, though other people earned her ire as well—various teachers, some of the girls from school. It was strange, like looking into a mirror and seeing features she had never noticed before.

Anna was too exhausted to even change for bed. She rolled over on her side, drawing the covers around her and hugging her pillow. That night she dreamed of a little girl. At first she thought it might have been her daughter, but then she realized it was herself.

The Reading Rooms

Zan threw open the door of the shop, armed with an oversized bunch of flowers wrapped in purple tissue paper. She spotted Georgie behind the counter and charged over, thrusting the flowers at her.

"I hear congratulations are in order," she barked. "It would have been nice to have heard it from you instead of Nick. But at least somebody told me."

Needless to say, heads turned.

"Zan," Georgie said, lowering her voice in an effort to quiet her sister. "Come into the office."

"So you've decided to keep the baby," Zan began the second Georgie had closed the door behind them. "It's great, really, it is. I don't know how Jules is going to take it, but I suppose that's not your concern. I haven't even told her you're pregnant yet. You were so negative last time I spoke to you, I really didn't think you'd actually keep the baby. But you've swung right around again I see." She looked squarely at Georgie. "This is your final decision, I trust? I don't want to upset Jules for nothing."

Georgie leaned back against the desk. "Yes, Zan, it's my final decision."

"I figured it had to be," she dismissed, pacing up and down the small square of floor in front of the desk. "You couldn't disappoint Nick now anyway. You'd think it was his baby the way he's carrying on. He's certainly never been that excited about the idea of Jules and me having a baby."

Georgie sighed. "Is that what this is about, Zan? You think I'm having this baby to spite you and Jules? To show you up somehow?" She shook her head. "I didn't plan for this to happen, I didn't wish for it in my wildest dreams—well, not like this anyway. Do you have any idea how terrified I am? I don't know if I'm making the right decision, I'm just too gutless to do anything else."

Zan stopped pacing. "What do you mean?"

"I'm not strong enough to go through an abortion," Georgie explained. "I don't think I'd be able to handle it. That's what it came down to."

"And you think having a baby is going to be easy?"

"No, I don't think one thing about this is going to be easy!" she exclaimed. "I'm shit scared, Zan, which is why I'd like to have my only sister's support, rather than her envy . . . or whatever this is."

"It's not envy," Zan declared. "It's shock, frustration, mixed feelings . . . alright, maybe a little envy." Her shoulders dropped and she came over to sit on the desk beside Georgie. "I'm sorry, George. I'm just worried about Jules. The frozen cycle failed as well. So now she has to either face another drug cycle here, or we go to the States. There she is, jumping through hoops trying to get pregnant and you do it by accident. It's going to be difficult for her to come to terms with."

"Her and me both," Georgie muttered.

Zan looked at her. "Are you really that scared?"

She nodded. "Petrified. You know how hopeless I am around the house. I can't cook, I can't even keep my place in any kind of order. I don't know how I'm going to manage with a baby."

"That stuff doesn't matter, George. You'll make a fantastic mother."

Georgie looked at her.

"I mean it, you're a natural. Look at how you get on with Molly and Grace."

She shrugged. "That's only the fun stuff, playing with them and fooling around. But I'm going to be completely responsible for this little person. I'm not even responsible enough to handle my own life, let alone someone else's."

"Come on, George, you're financially independent with your own business and your own flat. You're not doing too badly."

"I'd swap all that for a supportive partner," she admitted.

Zan eyed her suspiciously. "You're not going to tell the dickhead are you?"

"I said *partner*. If I do decide to tell Liam, it won't be about us getting back together," Georgie said flatly. "Don't forget, he's still married."

"It pisses me off, you know. Women are always the ones left holding the baby, literally," said Zan. "You tell the dickhead, and then he gets to decide whether he wants to be involved, whether he wants to provide for his child, or whether he wants to stay out of it altogether. Why should he get the choice? And how will you feel if you decide to tell him and then he says, 'Sorry, not interested'?"

"Well, I have to be prepared to accept that. I ended it because I didn't want to break up a marriage, so I'm not going to do anything to threaten it now."

"Then why tell him?"

She sighed heavily. "Because, regardless of all that, he is the father."

"So? That doesn't automatically give him rights."

"Nick thinks it does."

"Because Nick's a bloke."

"Well, you have to admit that's a relevant perspective."

"Look, you can't trust the dickhead. That much is indisputable. I think you're better off preparing yourself to do this on your own." She looked at the expression on Georgie's face. "Only you won't be on your own," she added quickly. "You'll have all of us. This baby's already part of a family." She looked sideways at Georgie. "Even if the aunt is a little bullheaded."

Georgie smiled. "Just a little?"

Northern Beaches Evening College

Anna walked gingerly up the stairs and along the corridor, clutching her map. She stopped short of an open doorway and checked the number on the door. This was the room. And she was late. Well, not really late; she was on time, but only just. She had hoped to get here early so she could slip to the back of the room and check out everyone else as they arrived. Anna stood still, listening for noises from inside. She couldn't hear any talking but she could hear evidence of life—coughing, chairs scraping . . .

"Are you alright? Can I help you?"

What she hadn't heard were footsteps coming up behind her. Anna turned around to face a tall, and it had to be said, not unattractive man looking down at her. He seemed intrigued, regarding her with a curious smile.

"What room are you after?" he asked.

"This one," she said lamely.

"Well, then you found it." He had very intense green eyes, and he was young, younger than her at least. His caramel-blond hair was pulled back into a ponytail and one of those barely there goatee beards dusted his chin. He was carrying a kind of satchel on one shoulder. Anna wondered if he was doing this class as well. And he was probably wondering why she was staring at him.

"You're here for Introduction to Prose Writing?" he asked.

She nodded.

"Shall we go in then?"

Anna shrugged, hesitating. "We're a little late, maybe they've started already?"

"They haven't," he assured her.

"I mean I know it's quiet," she went on, "but they might be in the middle of a writing exercise and we might distract them if we go barging in now."

He was smiling at her, in a kindly way. Like she was an idiot, Anna imagined.

"We won't distract them, they're not in the middle of a writing exercise and the class hasn't started yet."

"How do you know?"

"Because I'm the teacher," he said, offering his hand. "Vincent Carruthers."

Anna shook his hand, dumbfounded. She was an idiot.

"And you are—"

"Going home," she said.

He smiled again. "No you're not."

She sighed. "I'm Anna, Anna Mac . . . Gilchrist."

"Anna MacGilchrist?"

"No, Gilchrist, just Gilchrist."

"Okay, Gilchrist—"

"No." She smiled despite herself. "You can call me Anna."

"Okay, Anna, let's go in and get this show on the road." He considered the doubtful expression on her face. "Come on, you made it this far. Only a few more steps to go."

"Not metaphorically speaking," she mumbled, allowing him to lead her in.

"Apologies everyone," Vincent said expansively, striding across the front of the room and dumping his bag on the desk, giving Anna the chance to slip into a chair at the side, unnoticed. "Anna and I just got caught up discussing the use of metaphor as an effective exposition of emotion."

Every head turned to look at her.

"But let's not jump ahead of ourselves," he said, regaining their attention. "My name is Vincent Carruthers and this class is Introduction to Prose Writing. We have to do some housekeeping before we get to the fun stuff, so let's get that out of the way."

During the roll call and subsequent detailing of emergency exits and procedures, Anna had the opportunity to check out her classmates. Babies, all of them. Barely in their twenties, she guessed. She had thought there would be more of an age spread.

Just then there was a commotion outside the door and a woman burst through, red-faced and panting. She was quite diminutive, dressed in purple from head to toe. She looked like an avant-garde leprechaun.

"Hello! Sorry I'm late, story of my life," she chirped.

"We haven't started yet," Vincent assured her. "I'm Vincent Carruthers—"

"I know," she said breathlessly. "I've got one of your books for you to sign."

Vincent was clearly amused. "I hope you heard that, class, there's a surefire way to get on my good side. Please take a seat, Miss . . ."

"No such luck, Vincent." She winked, wiggling her wedding ring finger at him. "I'm Deb, Deb Pellegrini."

"Nice to meet you, Deb." He was smiling as he scanned the printout to mark off her name.

Deb dropped herself onto a chair next to Anna. "Hi," she breathed out heavily. "Made it."

Anna smiled politely. She seemed a bit over the top, but at least she was closer to Anna's age.

Once Vincent got underway he was magnetic. He began by reading aloud passages from books they had never heard of, and others they had, but they'd never heard them read like this before. The class was enthralled.

"He should be an actor, not a writer," Deb murmured to Anna.

"I wonder if he has done some acting," Anna mused. "There's something familiar about him."

Vincent went on to quote from a couple of well-known writers about their difficulties putting pen to paper, and then suddenly, without warning, he ordered them to write.

Everyone looked blankly at him.

"Pick up your pens and start writing," he repeated.

"About what?" someone in the back was brave enough to ask.

"Whatever you like," he replied.

There followed some dithering and more questions and pleas for direction until Vincent finally said, "Just get on with it." Then he sat down at his desk, opened a book and apparently began to read, ignoring them all.

Anna sat there, blank as the piece of paper in front of her. She had never felt so intimidated.

Would he want to see what she'd written? Worse, would she have to read it out loud to the class while they laughed and mocked her as she fled from the room, never to show her face again? Why on earth had she decided to take this ridiculous class? She didn't need to put herself through this. What the hell had she been thinking?

She eventually noticed that everyone else was writing, or at least moving their pens across the page and leaving trails of ink. That was all she needed to do. He couldn't make her read it out loud. He couldn't demand to see what she'd written. This wasn't school, and she was never going to come back again. So fine. She picked up her pen and wrote. "I hate this."

Sometime later, Anna had no idea how long, Vincent cleared his throat and told them to finish up. Anna stared at the page in front of her, covered in writing. Then she looked up. Vincent was standing in the middle of the U formed by the desks. He was holding a wastepaper bin.

"Does anyone want to read what they've written to the class?" he asked. The terror in the room was palpable. "Anyone at all?" he paused, waiting, every pair of eyes studiously avoiding his as he scanned the group. "I didn't think so," he said finally, a wry smile playing at the corners of his mouth. "Would anyone like to tear up what they've written and throw it in the bin?"

There was a sigh of relief throughout the room, a general murmur of assent, followed by the sound of paper being released from notepads.

"Hold on a minute," Vincent interrupted. "Let's not be quite so hasty. If you genuinely feel there is not one worthwhile sentence, one reasonable phrase, even one well-chosen word, then go ahead and tear it up. But look back over what you've written, carefully, and take your time." He strolled around the room, still holding the wastepaper bin, as everyone became absorbed again in their pages. "And when you find that one word, or phrase, or sentence, mark it somehow, circle it, or underline it. Think about why you like it, why it stood out to you. I won't ask you to share it, it's for your eyes only."

Anna looked at her first line: "I hate this." If she picked up a book and it opened with that, she would have to read on. It was a teaser. It was direct. It was honest, stark, clean. She circled the line.

"Does anyone still want to throw their work out?" Vincent asked after a while. No one did. "Then I've been carrying this around for nothing." He walked back to the front of the room and put the bin down, turning to face them again. "If you managed even one word you're happy with after writing for twenty minutes, then you're doing pretty well," he continued. "Many writers will tell you they're happy with one good afternoon in a whole week of writing. It's one of the hardest things to come to terms with. I can't teach you to write. But I can tell you what it's like to write, what to expect when you're writing, what's the range of normal experiences for a writer. And most importantly this class will give you the opportunity to write. I'll give you feedback, and you'll give each other feedback. And you will start to become appropriately critical of your work so that you can discern the one good line, the one good idea, and not throw the baby out with the bathwater . . . or resort to tired clichés when you can't think of a more original way to say something."

He went on to encourage them to keep a journal, beginning with a reflection on what they had written that night. He said they should write every day, and if they thought they had nothing to write about, then write about how it really pissed them off when the toast burned. Or why it was so hard to set a toaster to get the toast exactly right. Or about the simple joys of toast. Or about how the beach looked that morning as they passed it on the way to work.

"Virginia Woolf said something interesting happens every day. Go write about it."

Anna was hooked.

Small Business Agency

Kath Oliver peered through the glasses resting halfway down the bridge of her nose as she read the résumé in front of her. She was a world-weary woman in her fifties, the grey hair and the deep furrows in her face brought about as much as by the passing of time as the manner in which she'd passed it.

"So, is it William, Will, Bill?" she murmured without looking up.

"None of the above."

Kath lifted her head, her eyebrows raised, clearly waiting for an explanation.

"William's a traditional family name," he said. "I've never really gone by that name."

"So what should we call you, Mr. MacMullen?"

He hesitated. "Ah . . . Liam. You can call me Liam."

She looked intrigued. "How'd you end up with that?"

"It's short for William." He smiled faintly. "The Irish do it back to front."

"Oh." She nodded, thinking about it. "I never realized that." She cleared her throat. "Well, apologies for the delay in setting up this interview, Liam, but this is what happens in chronically underfunded and understaffed nongovernment organizations. We desperately needed to hire someone but couldn't spare anyone to process the applications." She paused. "Am I turning you off yet?"

Liam smiled. "We've only just begun."

"Mm, I just don't want you to have any illusions from the get-go." Kath sat back, folding her arms as she considered Liam skeptically. "Are you aware of the kind of drop in income you're looking at? I figure we're offering somewhere in the vicinity of a quarter of your present salary."

"It's probably more like a fifth," he corrected her. "But I'm not actually on a salary at present. I've already left my previous position."

He had found a flat to rent only last weekend. When he hadn't heard from the Small Business Agency he was unsure about whether to stay in Sydney. He thought about traveling, going back to Melbourne, moving somewhere new altogether. The house was sold and he and Anna had divided up their belongings. There was nothing keeping him here, but something was making him stay.

And that something was probably Georgie. He missed her dreadfully. Every single day. It was so bad at first that he used to drive past the shop and try to catch a glimpse of her, but he never had. He had, however, almost managed to drive up the back of another car on one occasion. He'd felt like some kind of pathetic stalker that day, picturing the scene if he had had an accident, Georgie coming out of the shop, seeing him there.

So he stayed away, but he couldn't leave Sydney. Not yet.

"You would have been swamped with offers once it got around you were leaving Morgan Trask," Kath was saying. "I'm intrigued as to why you would choose to work for an under-resourced, decidedly unglamorous NGO for a fraction of your previous salary."

"There have been offers," he acknowledged. "But I'm not interested in that kind of work. I left Morgan Trask because I'd been feeling restless for a long time. Right now I can't see myself ever working in that kind of environment again."

"Well, I need to be sure of some level of commitment on your part," she returned. "That this isn't midlife angst and as soon as the going gets tough, you'll get going."

He was beginning to find Kath Oliver's attitude galling. If working here made you bitter and twisted, perhaps he was better off elsewhere. Or perhaps she was. He wasn't giving up that easily.

"Do you think I'd take this on lightly, on some kind of a whim?" he asked. "I've worked on some of the largest corporate mergers in the Australasian region over the past decade. It was my job to make sure I knew all there was to know about the stakeholders, the risks, the gains, everything." He paused, taking a breath. "I know you have a permanent staff of twelve, plus a fluctuating army of volunteers, primarily law and commerce students. Your funding is tied to demonstrating you have achieved stated outcomes, and you've been able to do that for sixteen years now. Predecessors in my position have typically handled a bottomless caseload and have significantly altered or reversed tax department decisions, not an easy thing to do, in an impressive percentage of those cases." He leaned forward in his chair. "I believe I have skills that could be useful to your organization, but more importantly from my perspective, I'd like to feel I was doing something worthwhile."

"Very noble," Kath remarked. "No need to get tetchy, Liam, this interview is only a formality. If I don't hire you, the committee will have my head. I'm merely interested to know what brought about your change of heart from big business to this."

Liam thought about. "Maybe I just want to be able to sleep at night."

"That's as good a reason as any," said Kath. "How soon can you start?"

Northern Beaches Evening College

*Anna walked into the room to find she was the first one there this eve-*ning. She sat on the side like last week, but a little farther back, and was occupied finding pens and paper in her bag when Deb appeared in the doorway. Anna looked up and smiled politely. Deb headed straight over.

She sat down next to Anna. "So you came back?"

"You too?"

"Wouldn't miss it for the world." Deb grinned. "Did you start a journal?"

"Yes, I did actually," she said. "Made me feel like a teenager again."

"Speaking of teenagers," Deb muttered as a group of their classmates spilled into the room, laughing and talking amongst themselves. They didn't notice that Vincent was at the tail end of the group until he broke away, veering toward the desk at the front of the room.

Deb and Anna watched him as he removed books and notes from his bag and arranged them on the desk.

"I bet he'd be great in bed," Deb murmured.

"I beg your pardon?"

"There's nothing like the brooding sexuality of the intellectual. And he's one damned sexy man."

Anna glanced at her. "Aren't you married?"

"Yeah, but I'm not blind."

Anna smiled. "He reminds me of somebody, it's been bugging me all week."

"Ooh, he's coming over," Deb hissed like a schoolgirl.

"Evening, Deb." Vincent nodded, settling himself on a desk in front of them. "You're back, and on time."

"I am." Deb smiled, chuffed that he remembered her name.

"So it wasn't too painful last week?"

"What do they say: no pain, no gain?"

He laughed lightly. "And what about you, Anna Gilchrist?"

Anna's eyes flew up to meet his. "You have a good memory."

"Yeah, considering it's been over twenty years."

"I beg your pardon?"

"You don't remember me, do you?" he said, smiling down at her.

She regarded him curiously. "To be honest, I thought you looked familiar. I was just saying to Deb that you reminded me of somebody. But I can't place you."

"You lived on Meredith Street and we lived around the corner on Carrington Parade."

Anna was listening, intrigued.

"You went to school with my sister, Bronwyn." He paused, watching her face. "Bronwyn Carruthers."

Anna's eyes grew wide and her mouth fell open. "You're not!"

Vincent smiled. "I am."

"Incey Wincey Vincey!"

He flinched. "You realize I don't go by that name these days."

"My God, you've changed!" Anna exclaimed, still barely taking it in.

"Anna, I was eleven when we moved away. I hadn't even hit puberty."

"I know. You were a tiny little fellow. And damned annoying as I remember."

Vincent laughed. "I really have changed, I promise you."

Anna still couldn't get over it. "But how on earth did you remember me?"

"Come on, Anna, I was an impressionable boy and you were a gorgeous sixteen-year-old. You were pretty hard to forget. And you've hardly changed at all," he added.

Anna felt self-conscious. Deb felt invisible.

"So how is Bronwyn?" Anna said in an attempt to shift the focus.

"Oh, she's married, three kids, you know, the usual." He nodded. "How about you?"

She breathed out. "Oh, you know, separated, no kids, the usual."

"Well," he said, unfazed, "we should have a drink after class. Catch up properly."

"Sure, we'll have to do that . . . sometime."

"Is there anything wrong with tonight?"

"Oh . . . can't. Deb and I made plans." Anna didn't know why she said that. It had been a long time since someone had asked her out, she'd forgotten how to play the game. Fortunately, Deb went along with her, nodding vaguely.

"Rain check?" Vincent said, standing up.

"Sure." Anna nodded.

People had been filing into the room and the hubbub gradually building.

"Okay, everyone," Vincent said loudly, getting their attention. "Glad to see you were all brave enough to show your faces again. Obviously I'm going to have to work harder to frighten you off."

RNS Ultrasound Department

Georgie was going to burst. This was some kind of cruel and unusual torture. Not only had she had to drink two huge glasses of water, she was expected to hold it in for an hour till her appointment at nine thirty. And foolishly she'd had every faith they would do their utmost to be on time, what with all these poor pregnant women with compromised bladder control. But no, the clinic was operating on some time scale all its own. Everyone was walking around in slow motion; forms were twice as long and took three times longer to fill out, and none of the clocks appeared to be working. Nick had tried to assure her they had only kept her waiting ten minutes past her appointed time, but she didn't believe him. He was just trying to make her feel better. That wasn't working either.

And after all that, when she finally made it into the screening room and up onto a bed, the technician squirted a big blob onto her tummy, the coldest substance Georgie had ever felt in her entire life. She wondered how many women, then and there, had simply wet themselves from the shock. The final insult was this interminable digging with the sensor thingo, poking and prodding around her bladder. Didn't this woman realize what was likely to happen? Had she never played with a balloon as a child until it burst? Georgie started to wonder if the technician even knew what she was doing.

"There, did you hear that?"

It was a heartbeat. Which made Georgie's own heart stop beating as she listened breathlessly. She didn't want to miss a second of it. She grabbed Nick's hand and held it tight.

"Where's the baby?" she asked the technician.

"I'm trying to move him around a little. He's lying low, probably having a snooze."

"It's a he?"

"Nick!" Georgie warned.

"You don't want to know the sex?" the technician asked.

"No!"

"Yes!"

"So Dad wants to know but Mum doesn't?"

"He's not the dad, he's the brother."

The woman looked in disbelief from Nick to Georgie and back again.

"No," Nick explained. "I'm *her* brother, not the baby's."

"Oh, rightio. Well, sorry, Brother, Mum always gets the final say."

"Story of my life," he told her.

"Now, so you don't read anything into what I say, Baby will be referred to as 'he,' because I really don't like calling him 'it.' Okeydokey?"

Georgie was beginning to like this woman. Maybe she'd call the baby after her if it was a girl. She glanced at her name badge. Gretchen. Or maybe not.

"So, let's see if we can't get Bub to come out and play." Gretchen maneuvered the sensor around Georgie's abdomen. "I hope that's not too uncomfortable?"

Georgie realized she wasn't feeling any discomfort at all now, she didn't even feel like going to the toilet anymore.

"There we go, that's his head, obviously, now let's move down . . . oh, look, he's waving for the camera."

There it was, right there on the screen, her baby's hand. Somewhat cartoonlike, but it was a hand. With five fingers. It was the most beautiful hand she had ever seen. And after that she saw his arms, elbows, legs and knees and feet. He was so beautiful, he had everything, just like a real baby, a real person. Georgie watched, mesmerized, tears streaming freely down her face.

"Now let's get a profile shot," said Gretchen, continuing her running commentary. "See the forehead, tapering down to the eye socket, just there, and the nose, look at that, only tiny, but perfect. And you can just make out his mouth, right about there. This is a very good-looking baby," she declared.

"Like his mother," Nick murmured.

Georgie stared at the screen through a haze of tears. "And his father," she said quietly. She turned to look at Nick. "I have to tell him, don't I?"

"You don't have to do anything, Georgie."

"But it's not fair." She looked back to the screen. "He has a right to see this, to know his baby."

She felt Nick squeeze her hand.

"Now," said Gretchen, "let's work out how old Bub is, shall we?"

"ihav2cuPlscallAsap"

Liam gazed blankly down at the letters swimming before his eyes as he came to terms with the realization that the text message that had just been sent to his cell phone had come from Georgie. He hadn't heard from her or seen her in almost four months, but still not a day went by that he didn't think about her. He'd nearly dropped his phone when he saw her name in the inbox. He sat at his desk, oblivious for once to the hubbub going on around him in the open-plan office. He was still getting used to his new work environment. Everything was so different, the atmosphere, the noise, the staff, the clientele. A woman had burst into tears at his desk the other day. He'd had clients who were about to lose multimillion dollar deals but he'd never had anyone cry before.

Worst of all, there was no Stella. She would never have allowed the printer to run out of ink or the photocopier to run out of toner, as they seemed to do around here every other day. Stella would have recorded his messages coherently, scheduled his appointments judiciously and organized his files according to established convention, alphabetically for example. And Stella would have known what to do with the crying woman.

"Bad news?"

Liam stirred, looking up. It was James, or maybe Tom . . . or Tim? Anyhow, it was one of the young student volunteers. Liam still hadn't quite wrapped his brain around all the names and faces. Stella would have helped him with that as well.

"No, ah, at least I don't think it's bad news. I don't know, I'm not sure what it says. It's in text message shorthand."

"You're in luck, I'm an expert," said Tim/Tom/James, coming around beside Liam to read off the tiny screen. " 'I have to see you, please call as soon as possible.' " He straightened up again. "Stalker?" he suggested.

Liam shook his head. "She's . . . she's an old friend."

"Well, she's hanging out to see you," he said. "Is she hot?"

Liam glanced up and Tim/Tom/James got the hint that his input was no longer required. He left Liam staring at the phone, debating his next move. "Please call." His heart was beating faster just at the thought of hearing Georgie's voice again. But what could she want after all this time? He hoped nothing was wrong. Why she would call him if there was, he had no idea, he wasn't exactly part of her life anymore. There was only one way to find out what it was. He brought up her number on the screen, pausing to take a breath before he pressed Call.

Georgie heard the familiar ringtone of her cell phone, but she couldn't remember where she'd put it. She had slipped into the storeroom to message Liam; she thought if she was alone she might be able to think more clearly. Not that that had helped last night. She had gone to do it a dozen times but kept hesitating, unsure of exactly what to say. Should she give at least some information seeing as she was contacting him out of the blue like this? But what? *Hi there. Boy, have I got some news for you!* Hardly. How about: *I think you left something behind last time*. . . . Georgie's absurdist tendencies always took over when she was anxious. In the end she decided it was best to keep it low-key and brief, nothing that could be misconstrued or misinterpreted.

Adam was coming from the back of the shop, holding up her phone. "You left it in the storeroom," he said, handing it to her.

"Thanks." She looked at the screen. "Shit!"

"Who is it?"

"Shit . . . shit!"

Adam looked at the screen. "Yeah, it's shit alright. What's he doing calling you?"

"I sent him a message asking him to."

"So why are you surprised?"

"I didn't think he'd do it straightaway."

Adam shook his head. "Do you want me to deal with him?"

"No, no. I have to talk to him."

"So answer the phone. It's going to stop ringing any second."

Georgie winced, closed her eyes and pressed Answer. She gingerly brought the phone to her ear. "Hello," she croaked.

"Hi, Georgie?"

"Yes," she breathed. "It's Georgie speaking." She remembered he used to say, "I thought it was Georgie Reading," which was pretty lame really. But it had always made her smile.

"It's Liam MacMullen, Georgie. I just got your message."

Why did he give her his surname? Did he think she knew so many Liams that she had to sort them alphabetically? No, clearly he was trying to keep it formal because he was back with his wife and everything's fine thanks and I think it's best for all concerned if you stay out of my life. *Shit!*

"How are you, Georgie?"

Well, the morning sickness seems to have passed. *Keep your wits about you, woman!* "Fine, thanks, Liam. How are you?"

"I'm okay." She heard him take a breath, waiting. "Georgie, if I'm reading your message right, you want to see me about something?"

"Yes, that's right. Um, not for long, maybe half an hour if you can spare it?"

"No problem. Should I come to the shop?"

"No!" she said. "Um, no, I thought we could meet at the Manly Wharf Hotel. Do you know it?"

"Yes, of course."

"Out on the Jetty Bar." It was probably not the time of the year to be sitting outside, but she wanted to meet somewhere noisy and busy, and the smell of cigarette smoke made her nauseous, so it had to be outside.

"Alright. What time?"

"Sorry?"

"What time do you want to meet? You are talking about tonight, aren't you?"

"No!" she said again. She'd had this all planned out. He was supposed to ring later on, maybe this evening. She was going to suggest tomorrow night at six, giving her plenty of time to prepare herself. She swallowed, her mouth kept going dry. "Is tomorrow okay? I have something on to-night." Good. That sounded cool. Her life was full, busy. He didn't have to know the only thing she had on tonight was *ER*.

"Okay. What time tomorrow?"

"I was thinking six."

"Then six it is, at the Jetty at the Wharf Hotel, tomorrow night. I'll look forward to it, Georgie."

You may not feel that way after tomorrow. "Okay, see you then."

Georgie hung up and walked over to the counter, holding the phone to her forehead, grimacing.

"What's wrong with her?" Louise asked Adam.

"Maybe the phone is stuck to her forehead and she can't get it off."

"That was Liam," said Georgie.

"Oh." Louise frowned. "Did you tell him?"

"No!" Georgie exclaimed. "As if I'd tell him over the phone!"

"I thought it was a little strange. So what's wrong?"

"He just sounded so calm, so . . . reserved, I guess. And he called himself 'Liam MacMullen.' "

"Freaky," Adam muttered.

"He was being overly formal, impersonal, you know?" Georgie explained.

"He probably felt awkward," Louise suggested. "You haven't spoken in a while."

Georgie shook her head. "It's not that. I could tell. He's obviously worked out things with his wife, his life is back in order and the last thing he wanted was to hear from me."

Louise thought about it. "Well, how did he react when you said it was you?"

"He knew it was me. He was the one who rang."

"I don't get it," said Louise. "Why did he phone you and then become all awkward as if he didn't want to speak to you?"

"I messaged him and asked him to call me." Georgie looked at her plaintively. "I really got the impression he was being polite, but keeping his distance."

"Well, what's wrong with that? It's not as if you want to get back with him."

"Of course not, but if his marriage is on track again I can't tell him about the baby. I just can't. Can you imagine the fallout?"

"Baby comes first," Adam reminded her. "He's going to have to deal with it."

"But what about his wife?"

"Well, she married the philandering prick."

"Adam! That's not fair, it's not her fault!" Georgie protested. "God, maybe I should call the whole thing off."

"What thing?" asked Louise.

"I'm supposed to meet him tomorrow. I don't think I can do it." Georgie groaned, plonking down on a stool. "How the hell am I going to get through another"—she checked her watch—"twenty-eight hours?"

Louise considered her. "Easy." She took the phone out of Georgie's hand and scrolled through the directory till she came to Liam's name. "Call him back and change it to tonight."

"No! Why? I can't! I'm not ready."

"Georgie, you've been procrastinating for two months. It's driving you crazy, and frankly, you're taking us all along for the ride." She thrust the phone at her. "Get it over with."

Georgie looked at Louise. And then Adam. They were both staring back at her, unblinking, their arms folded. Louise was right. She had to do it. Nothing was going to change magically overnight, she'd only lose more sleep. She pressed Call and waited for Liam to answer.

"Hello?"

He sounded tentative. Maybe he still had her number in his phone, which would mean he knew it was her. So of course she couldn't hang up now. And not only that, it was customary to actually speak when you were the one who'd made the call.

"Hi, Liam, it's me, Georgie, sorry to bother you again," she said breezily. This was good, she was coming across very natural, very casual.

"It's no bother, Georgie."

"Look, my plans have just changed, and . . ." Don't make it sound desperate. "I can't make it tomorrow night now. But tonight works after all, if that's still okay with you?"

She heard him clear his throat. "Sure, same arrangement?"

"Uh-huh. The Jetty Bar at six."

"I'll see you later then."

Liam hung up. He'd barely got over the first call when his phone had rung again and Georgie's name had appeared on the screen, sending his heart plummeting to somewhere around his ankles. She was calling it off. She'd decided not to go through with it after all. Probably because of the way he'd spoken to her, as if she were nothing more than a business associate, and he was . . . Well, a block of wood had more warmth. God, he even said his whole name, "Liam MacMullen," as though they barely knew each other. He'd wanted to tell her how good it was to hear her voice, how much he missed her. There were so many things he wanted to say to her but as he had no idea what this was all about, he didn't want to push it. He was relieved once he realized she was only calling the second time to change it to tonight. He wouldn't have gotten any sleep if he'd had to wait till tomorrow. It was going to be hard enough getting through the next few hours.

Liam was still mystified as to why she wanted to see him. In a wild flight of fancy he momentarily seized upon the vague hope that somehow she'd heard he and Anna had split. But that was impossible. They didn't have any mutual friends, there was no way she was likely to cross paths with anyone they knew. Though Anna had gone to the shop that time. Could she possibly have returned, told Georgie they'd separated? Now he was really getting ridiculous. Of course his estranged wife would go to the trouble of visiting his former mistress to let her know he was free now. And on her way she would see a pig flying across the sky.

It was more likely that he'd left something at Georgie's place and she wanted to return it. Because she had a new boyfriend. He felt an uncomfortable pang in his chest. Maybe the boyfriend was moving in with her, or she was moving in with him and when she was packing up she'd found an odd sock or a T-shirt, whatever. She'd considered throwing it out but then decided she should see him one more time, let him know she was engaged. They were going to marry later this year and have lots of children and live happily ever after. Liam sighed heavily, rubbing his forehead. Georgie deserved to be happy. He would tell her that. He would restrain himself and wish her all the best for her future. And he would try very hard to mean it.

Six P.M.

*Liam had planned to get there early but parking in Manly was a night-*mare and he'd ended up leaving the car miles away. He checked his watch. He was right on time as he walked along the boardwalk past the main bar to the Jetty. It was a calm night, if a little cool. Still, enough people obviously preferred the outdoors even at this time of the year, given the throng gathered already. He stood at the edge, scanning the deck.

And then he saw her. She was sitting with her back to the water, looking straight at him. She gave him a faint, polite smile, raising her hand tentatively. She looked beautiful, more beautiful than he remembered. Perhaps it was just because it was so good to see her again, but there was something else. Her hair was a little longer, the color more subdued than usual, softer. Her skin was glowing. If she was in love, it certainly agreed with her.

"Hi," he said as he made it to her table.

"Hi," she said shyly. "Sit down . . . please."

Georgie watched him take a seat opposite her. He was apparently unsure what to do with his hands. He crossed them on his lap and uncrossed them again, rested them on the bench beside him, and finally clasped them together, placing them on the table in front of him. He seemed nervous. He took a deep breath and lifted his gaze to meet hers. "It's good to see you, Georgie. You look . . . you look wonderful."

He looked . . . rumpled, she decided. At least in comparison to the way he usually looked. He'd always dressed so immaculately, nearly always in a suit, his hair just so. But today he wore casual trousers and a shirt with a sweater, not a jacket. His hair was longer and thicker, and it suited him. It felt weird sitting here now, so close. Here was the face she loved, the blue-grey eyes. It was still him, but he had a whole other life, a reality she had known nothing about. It was like falling in love with a character in a TV show. Sure, there's probably a lot of the actor's mannerisms in the character, they have the same voice, they look the same. But in all likelihood, the similarity ended there. The part of Liam Mac-Mullen had been played by an actor who shed the character every time he left Georgie to go home to his wife. So who was this man sitting opposite her? She didn't really know him. And she had to keep that in mind because it was disconcerting how much he looked like someone she was still very much in love with.

"How are you, Georgie?" Liam was asking.

"Fine, very well, thanks." She nodded. "How are you?"

"I'm okay."

"I got myself a drink while I was waiting, did you want something?"

"No, thanks, I'm alright at the moment."

He wanted to get down to business. His wife probably had dinner waiting for him at home. Georgie started to feel sick. She took a sip of her soda water. "I . . . ah . . . I won't . . . um, this won't take long."

He nodded.

"Before I start, I just wanted to ask, if you don't mind . . ." Georgie swallowed. Her heart was pounding hard in her chest. "Can I ask you a personal question?"

Liam felt the blood drain from his face. It suddenly occurred to him what this was all about. Georgie had some kind of sexually transmitted disease. It made sense, there was no other reason she would need to see him four months after they'd broken up, out of the blue, and so urgently. He hoped it wasn't serious, that she was alright.

"Go ahead," he managed to say.

"I wanted to know if you and your wife . . . well, if you worked it out, if you're okay now?"

He wasn't sure what that had to do with anything. Though she probably had to know who else he'd had contact with. "Anna and I have separated," he said plainly.

Georgie stared at him. "What? When?"

He looked down at his hands. "She asked me to leave right after the last time I saw you."

"Is it permanent . . . or, I mean, are you having counseling, are you trying to work it out?"

Liam met her eyes directly. "We're past all that, Georgie. We've sold the house, settled the property. I guess one or the other of us will file for divorce when the need arises."

Georgie held her hand to her mouth. She felt like crying. "Please tell me you didn't break up over me," she breathed, her eyes glassy.

Liam reached across the table and took hold of her hand. "Georgie, I told you we were having problems. It wasn't because of you. You were . . ." He paused. "There's something I've wanted to say to you. I never got the chance to apologize."

"Liam—"

"I wanted to say," he went on, over the top of her, "that I realize you were worse off for having known me—"

"Liam, I don't—"

"Georgie, please let me get this out."

She fell silent, trying to ignore the feel of his hand around hers.

"I know I hurt you and that I made you unhappy, and I'm not proud of myself for that. I wish I could take it all back. But I did want you to know I'm better for having known you, for having you in my life even for a short while."

The lines sounded rehearsed. Now he was playing the role of Liam MacMullen, reformed man. Maybe she wasn't being fair to him, but he had lied to her. If only he hadn't lied.

"Okay . . . thanks," she said quietly. She moved her hand and he released it. They sat for a while, not saying anything.

"What did you want to see me about?" Liam asked eventually.

Georgie cleared her throat. She had to do this. She sat up straight. "What I have to say will probably come as a shock. I've struggled over whether or not to tell you. If you and your wife had still been together, I didn't want . . . well, never mind. But regardless, I'm not telling you because I expect anything from you. I don't, not at all. And this doesn't change things between us. Well, it does. But . . ." She sighed, as though she was a little exasperated with herself.

Liam was trying to follow her but he had no idea what she was talking about.

"Liam," she resumed, calmer, "do you remember the last time we saw each other?"

He nodded.

"Do you remember what happened?"

God, it was a sexually transmitted disease. He hadn't used a condom. "Yes, I remember."

"Well, the thing is"—she took a deep breath in and out—"I'm pregnant."

His face went white, and he appeared to freeze. He didn't even look like he was breathing.

"Liam?" Still he didn't move. His eyes were glazed, she wasn't sure if he could hear her. "Liam?" she said a little louder.

"Yes," he croaked, startled.

"Are you alright?"

"You're pregnant?" he said, his voice barely making it out of his throat.

"That's what I said."

"Are you saying it's mine?"

"Of course," she retorted. "Why else would I be telling you?"

"But I don't understand, it was just that one time."

"That's all it takes."

"Once? You're sure, you're absolutely sure?"

"Yes, Liam," Georgie said through clenched teeth.

"This is unbelievable," he muttered. He ran his hands up over his face and raked his fingers through his hair, trying to snap himself out of it. "I'm sorry, this is such a shock. . . . It's . . . it's the last thing I ever imagined . . . you have no idea . . ."

"I think I do," Georgie bristled. She wasn't going to sit here and listen to this crap, that he found it "unbelievable," implying it wasn't his, carrying on as though it was the shock of his life. Zan had been right. She shouldn't have bothered telling him, but it was too late now. He'd been caught out unrehearsed and unprepared. This wasn't in the script, not in his copy anyway. And Georgie was not going to hang around and give him an audience. She moved to the end of the bench. "Look, I just thought it was the right thing to tell you, but like I said, I don't expect anything from you. You don't have to worry, I won't bother you again." She got to her feet.

Liam stared up at her. What was she doing? Where was she going?

"Georgie!" he exclaimed, almost leaping off the bench. "Georgie, don't go, please." He took hold of her shoulders. "I'm sorry, it is a shock but it's a good shock, a wonderful shock, the best shock I've ever had." And then without warning, he pulled her close to him, hugging her tight.

"Liam!"

He released her immediately. "Sorry, I just had to do that. . . . I won't touch you again, I promise. But please don't go, not yet."

His eyes were pleading with her. Who was he now? Was this real, or had he pulled himself together and got back into character? But what did he have to gain from pretending? God, she wished she could trust him.

He was gazing down at her with a kind of awe. "Look at you," he said quietly, surveying her up and down.

Georgie's hand moved instinctively to her tummy. "Yeah, it's popped a little, just lately."

"Are you okay? Is everything alright?"

She nodded. "I'm fine, the baby's fine."

The baby. There was a baby inside her, his baby. Liam still didn't think he was grasping this fully. "Won't you sit down again, please?"

There was a tone in his voice that was actually quite touching. Georgie supposed she ought to hear him out. She lowered herself back onto the bench.

"Can I get you anything?" he asked, still standing.

"No, I'm fine," she said, indicating the glass of soda water.

He nodded vaguely. "I might have a drink now, if it doesn't bother you?"

"No, not at all."

"You won't go away?" he added.

Georgie looked up at him. "No."

"You promise?"

She smiled, despite herself. "I promise."

Liam returned shortly after with some kind of spirit, maybe Scotch, in a tumbler. Georgie had never seen him drink spirits before. He slid back onto the bench opposite her, leaning toward her across the table.

"So, you're okay?" he asked again.

"Yes, I'm fine, Liam," Georgie insisted. "I had some morning sickness, but it's passed."

"I was working it out while I was waiting at the bar, you'd have to be nearly four months along, wouldn't you?"

"A little further, the way they calculate it," she explained. "The baby's due on the fourth of November."

Liam seemed dazed. "I never thought I'd hear those words. . . ." He looked across at Georgie who was frowning at him. "I have to tell you something."

"Okay." She felt a little uneasy, with good reason. The last time he had to tell her something it was that he was married. God only knew what it was this time.

He took a sip of his drink. "Anna and I were on the IVF program for seven years."

Georgie's mouth dropped open and her eyes grew wide.

"So you can see why this is a shock."

She swallowed. "You thought you couldn't—"

"No, it wasn't me," he assured her. "Anna had what they ingeniously refer to as 'unexplained infertility.' We did everything, drugs, insemination, then the full IVF treatment."

Georgie nodded vaguely. "Mm, Jules, Zan's partner, she's going through all that now."

"I remember Zan talking about it. Are they having any luck?"

"Not yet."

Liam sighed. "It's very soul-destroying. There's only about a thirty percent success rate."

"I didn't realize it was that low."

"Oh, they muck around with the statistics and have you believing your chances are better than that. But however they put it, the majority of couples don't come out of it with a baby. That's a lot of broken hearts . . . and lives." He was staring down at the table. "I think it's what destroyed our marriage."

Georgie frowned. This was the problem he was always going on about. "How exactly did it destroy your marriage?" she asked, feeling uneasy.

He looked across at her. "It took over, it was all we ever talked about, when we did talk. We couldn't make any plans in case they interfered with treatment cycles, we stopped going on holidays, we stopped seeing friends when they started having children. Anna was either sick, or depressed, or anxious—she was never happy anymore. Neither of us was happy. I wanted to stop, or at least take a break. I wasn't sure that there was anything left between us."

"So what happened?"

"She couldn't handle the thought of giving up. We were at a stalemate." He paused. He looked a little awkward. "That's around the time I met you."

Georgie's heart quickened. "Then it became about me, didn't it?"

He shook his head. "No, not really, only on the surface. Anna clung to that at first, but really, it just brought everything to a head."

Georgie didn't know what to believe. To think that all this had been going on in his life and she'd had no idea, not an inkling. She had to blend what she did know about him with what she was only just discovering. Her picture of Liam MacMullen had to expand to include a picture of his wife. It made Georgie heartsick thinking of her. She had blamed Georgie, which was hardly surprising, she probably hated her. She had been left with nothing. No baby, no husband. It was so unfair.

"Where's your wife now, is she alright?"

Liam shrugged. "She's staying in Sydney for the meantime, though I imagine she'll move back to Melbourne eventually. Her family's there as well. I know she's taken some leave from her job, but I'm not sure what her plans are."

Georgie wanted to know how she really was. This poor woman who had been through hell and back and ended up with nothing. Georgie felt almost guilty, like she was having the baby Anna should have had.

"Georgie?" said Liam, breaking her reverie.

"Mm?"

"What made you decide to tell me?"

"Not what, who," she returned. "Nick maintained from the start that you had a right to know, but what it really came down to in the end was what was best for the baby. He has a right to know his father. Not that I'm asking for anything," she added quickly.

"Georgie, I want to be part of this child's life, more than anything." He paused. "I still love you—"

"No, Liam, don't," Georgie said firmly. "Don't go there."

"Why not?"

"Because that's not what this is about. I said before that this doesn't change anything between you and me."

"It changes everything, Georgie. We're having a baby and I'm separated now—"

"Liam!" she interrupted. "We can't play happy families and pretend the past never happened. At least I can't. I don't even know who you are—"

"Yes you do."

"How can you say that? My God, Liam, you had a whole life I didn't even know existed."

"Well, now I can tell you everything. Ask me whatever you want, I promise I'll tell you the truth."

Georgie shook her head. "Don't you see, that's the problem, Liam. How can I know what's the truth with you, what's real and what's made up?" She paused. "Sometimes I think about all the excuses, the meetings and trips and conference calls. . . . It must have exhausted you keeping the deception going."

"Georgie, I told you the truth wherever possible—"

"Liam!"

"I know it sounds lame," he said, rubbing his forehead, "but I was so stressed, I didn't know what I was doing. It made sense to me then. But I have no reason to lie to you anymore, Georgie. Can't you learn to trust me again?"

Georgie was staring down at her glass. "Anna was the name of your flatmate. You turned your wife into a crazy woman you felt sorry for?"

He looked guilty. "I never said she was crazy. But the reality was that I was living with a woman who was going through a hard time, and she was emotionally unstable—"

"And she was your wife!" Georgie declared. "You left that little detail out."

He sighed. "It was wrong, I know that. But I won't lie to you again, Georgie. I promise."

"Well, that remains to be seen," said Georgie. "But regardless, anything we may have had has been spoiled, it's tainted, Liam. You're not the person I thought you were, the person I fell in love with. He doesn't exist."

But he does. He was that person, the one she had fallen in love with, and he was going to prove it to her. She was carrying his baby, she couldn't resent him forever, not Georgie. Liam was a patient man. He would wait, this was worth it.

"I understand," he said seriously. "I'll never do anything to hurt you again, Georgie, and I'll support you any way I can. Whatever you need, money—"

"I'm not asking for money," she insisted.

"I want to be fair about this. I'm not going to let you bear the whole burden."

"Look," Georgie said. He was getting her back up a little. She was going to be the one controlling how this played out. "I'll decide what I need and what I don't need. I don't know how I'm going to handle it all yet, on my own."

"You don't have to do it on your own."

"Liam," she warned.

"I'm just saying I'll only ever be a phone call away." He looked at her earnestly. "I'm so grateful you told me, I promise I won't make you regret it."

The Reading Rooms

"Hi, Georgie, it's Liam."

"Hello," she said guardedly.

"I'm calling to see how you are."

"But you only saw me yesterday."

"I know, but under the circumstances—"

"Liam, you can't phone me every day."

He paused. "Then how often can I phone you?"

"I don't know."

He could hear frustration in her voice. He didn't want to annoy her. "I think I just needed to make sure it wasn't a dream," he tried to explain.

"It's real, Liam." Her tone had softened. "Look, I'll keep in touch, I promise."

"Okay," he said, resigning himself. "You know, I think I should give you my other numbers. You only have my cell."

"That's all I had before."

"Well, it's different now."

"Hmm."

"Have you got a pen?"

"Yes, Liam."

"Really, you're not just humoring me?"

He heard her laugh. "Just get on with it."

Liam dictated his work number, his home number and his address. "So you'll keep in touch?"

"I will."

"Okay. Thanks."

"Bye, Liam."

"Bye, Georgie."

He hung up, smiling. He hadn't been able to wipe the smile off his face all day. He had something to look forward to again and it was something wonderful. He and Georgie shared this baby, nothing could change that and they would always be connected, that had to put the odds in his favor. He wanted to celebrate, to announce it to the world, but no one would really understand. It would only confuse his mother. She was still digesting the news that his marriage had broken down, how would he explain this?

Liam glanced around the office. He didn't really know anyone here well enough yet to share his news. Then it occurred to him. He picked up the phone again and dialed.

"Good morning, Evan Pratt's office."

"Stella?"

"Mac?"

"You haven't forgotten me?"

"As if I could," she chided. "How the hell are you anyway?"

"I'm bloody fantastic, Stella. I've never been happier."

"Wow, what's happened?"

"Let me take you out to lunch and I'll tell you all about it."

"Okay, but I do have to get back to the office this afternoon," she warned him.

Two Weeks Later

Anna didn't understand what all the mystery was about. Mac had rung insisting he needed to talk to her about something important. She'd told him to go ahead, but he'd said he didn't want to discuss it over the phone. Then he'd carried on about whether she wanted to meet at her place or his place or somewhere neutral, it was up to her. Anna had bristled. She knew when she was being handled. She told Mac not to be so melodramatic, there was no need to treat her with kid gloves. She had writing class at seven and Mac was in the city till five-thirty, traffic was the only wildcard. She said she'd meet him at a café, near the college where she could get a bite for dinner while she waited for him, and afterward she could go straight to class.

It was a little after six when he appeared in the doorway of the café. Anna was still waiting for her risotto, so he hadn't done too badly, she didn't know why he looked so ragged. He walked over to her table, his face pinched, his shoulders hunched. Was it such a trial to have to see her?

"Hello, Mac," she said breezily, in an attempt to lighten things. "You made good time across the Bridge then?"

He shrugged. "Not too bad. How are you, Anna?"

"I'm fine. I'm having the risotto. Are you hungry? Do you want to order something?"

"No." He shook his head.

"Are you going to sit down?"

"Yeah, sure, thanks." He pulled out the chair opposite her and sat. "Do you mind?" he asked, indicating the water jug.

"Help yourself." She watched him pour a large glass of water and gulp down half of it. He dragged his chair closer in and leaned his elbows on the table. Then he sat back again, crossing his arms in front of his chest. He was clearly very agitated. "What did you want to speak to me about, Mac?"

He breathed out heavily. "Anna, I've got something to tell you that's probably going to be upsetting. But I'm not doing this to be cruel, or to hurt you. I'm telling you because I don't want you to hear it from someone else. And because . . . well, it's something you should know."

Anna was beginning to feel uncomfortable.

"So I'm just going to say it, okay?" He took another mouthful of water. "Georgie, the woman—"

"Yes, I remember who Georgie is," Anna assured him.

"Okay." He nodded, pausing for a beat too long. "Well, she's pregnant."

Anna was confused. Why was this something she needed to know? Unless . . .

"Are you having a relationship with her?"

"No, I haven't seen her since January. Not until a couple of weeks ago, that is."

"I'm not sure I understand."

"Georgie's nearly five months pregnant, Anna. I'm the father."

"Your risotto, ma'am," said the waiter, placing a bowl in front of her. "Cracked pepper?"

He stood, pepper grinder poised, but Anna was somewhere else. On a hospital bed, her legs in stirrups, holding Mac's hand and watching the screen as the doctor implanted three embryos. At that precise moment, and for at least a short while afterward, Anna was pregnant. She only ever said it to Mac once, and he said technically she wasn't really pregnant and it was better not to think like that. So she didn't say it again, not out loud. But in her heart those embryos were her babies, and that's how she used to think of each and every one of them, even though most of them would never survive. Even though, in the end, none of them did.

"Anna?"

She looked across at Mac.

"Do you want pepper?"

For a second she wondered what the fuck he was talking about. Then she became aware of the waiter at her side. "Yes, thank you," she said calmly. He turned the grinder above the plate of risotto, showering it lightly with black pepper. "And could you bring me a glass of Riesling, please?"

"Certainly." The waiter turned to Mac. "Can I get you anything, sir?"

"No . . . thank you."

Mac looked perplexed. He was waiting for a reaction, Anna decided. Perhaps he wanted her to get angry—him and his desperate need for penance. Well, she wasn't going to give him the satisfaction.

"So," she began, picking up her fork, "are you going to marry her? Is that why you wanted to see me, you want a divorce?"

"No, that's not why . . ."

"Then why?" Anna lifted an eyebrow as she scooped a forkful of risotto into her mouth. "Mm." She swallowed. "This is fabulous, Mac, why don't you order something?"

He shook his head. "I'm not hungry."

The waiter returned with her glass of wine. "Honestly, Mac, you should at least have a drink with me, so we can make a toast." Anna raised her glass. "What's a good one? How about, 'To the victor, the spoils'? What's that from, is it Shakespeare?"

"I don't know."

"Or . . ." she mused. "I know! 'Winner takes all.' That's appropriate, don't you think, Mac?"

He sighed heavily. "Georgie and I are not back together, and she doesn't want to get back together, okay? I'm not the winner, I don't have it all."

"That's right, you said you weren't even sure you wanted a baby anymore, didn't you? So how do you feel now?"

"What do you want me to say, Anna?"

"Just be honest," she said flatly. "Don't pretend you're not glad this has happened. Come on, you were so keen for us to stop the treatment, I'm half wondering if you and Georgie weren't actually trying to fall pregnant at the time—"

"Oh, for Chrissakes, Anna!"

"What? It's a perfectly reasonable question."

"It is not reasonable and you know it. How could you think for a minute that I planned this? It just happened—"

"I seem to remember you saying the same thing about the affair. 'It just happened,' like it was all completely out of your control. You have women throwing themselves at you, bearing your babies no less, and there's not a thing you can do about it. Poor Mac."

He stood abruptly, shoving his chair back. "I'm not going to listen to this, Anna. I thought I was doing the right thing letting you know, but I can't talk to you, you're so incredibly bitter."

"Well, what do you reckon, Mac?" She glared up at him, meeting his gaze. She saw something flicker across his eyes, maybe pity? That was the last thing she wanted from him. "I'd like to finish my dinner now," she said calmly, picking up her fork and focusing on her plate. She didn't look up again, but she was aware of him walking away and leaving the café. Anna dropped her fork and picked up her glass, emptying it. The waiter came over.

"Would you like another?"

"Yes, thank you." He went to take the glass. "No, just bring the bottle," Anna told him. "And do you sell cigarettes?"

"Sorry, but this is a nonsmoking restaurant."

She smiled at him. "Of course."

"I'll get your wine."

Anna drank two more glasses while she considered her options. She could pick up another bottle and a pack of cigarettes and go home. But drinking alone sounded a big warning bell for her. It was alright here, she was technically on her own but there were people around. And it used to be acceptable when she was expecting Mac home anytime. She started to feel melancholy, remembering how he had always looked after her, staying with her even while she threw up. Did he do that for Georgie? Maybe when she had morning sickness? No, that couldn't be right. Her head was beginning to feel fuzzy but she was pretty sure he said he saw her for the first time only a couple of weeks ago. Was that when he found out? And she was five months already? Why had she waited so long to tell him? Maybe he'd found out by accident, or she'd taken that long to decide what she was going to do. Perhaps she'd even considered a termination, which would be the cruelest irony of all. Whatever, she'd obviously decided to keep it, and to involve Mac. But didn't he say they weren't back together, that she had no intention of getting back with him?

Anna's head was beginning to hurt. She probably shouldn't drive. She was only on her third glass, but it was under the hour. The thought of going home alone was more than she could bear. And then she remembered writing class, she was supposed to be going to writing class. That's exactly what she would do. And what's more, she'd go for that drink with Vincent afterward. She signaled the waiter for the bill. She felt much better. She had something to do, people to be with, and someone to drink with. She didn't have to go home alone and be pathetic.

Anna left the café and bought a pack of cigarettes in the convenience store farther up the block. She could walk to the college from here, giving her a chance to have a cigarette. It made her head spin, which she always found a strange though not altogether unpleasant sensation. By the time she arrived at the college she was feeling a little jittery, probably from the jolt of nicotine. She mounted the stairs and walked along the corridor, the heels of her boots clunking all the way. When she came through the door, there was only Deb and Vincent in the room. Anna winked at Deb as she strode determinedly over to Vincent's desk. He looked up as she approached and his face broke into a smile. Deb was right, he was damned sexy.

"Is your invitation still open?"

Vincent frowned slightly. "You mean for a drink?"

Anna leaned over the desk. "Uh-huh."

"Tonight?"

"Uh-huh."

"Absolutely."

"Alright then." She turned on her heel and walked over to sit next to Deb. "Hi, how are you?"

"Fine." Deb considered her curiously. "How are you?"

"Wonderful, couldn't be better," she chirped. "I'm going out with the teacher after class," she added in a whisper.

"You go, girl." Deb grinned. "What made you change your mind?"

"I feel like celebrating. I've just seen my ex. He and his tartlet are having a baby."

"Are you alright?"

"Of course I'm alright," she said briskly. "Why shouldn't I be alright?"

She busied herself finding paper and pens while the rest of the class sauntered in. Finally Vincent came around in front of his desk and perched on the edge.

"Okay," he said, getting everyone's attention. "We're going to leap straight into a writing exercise so that we'll have time to workshop in class tonight. What I want you to do is use as your starting point a familiar story. It may be a fairy tale, a Bible story, Shakespeare, whatever, but you're going to rewrite it. Now, I don't just want the same story in your own words. I want you to do something different with it. Write it from a minor character's perspective, or write in a new character or characters. Or play with the genre, turn *The Three Little Pigs* into science fiction, or *Little Red Riding Hood* into a murder mystery, which is not so far from the truth, when you think about it. Or write a gritty social realist piece where Cinderella discovers the prince is an elitist bore, and starts snorting coke with the servants before joining a resistance movement plotting to overthrow the aristocracy. Choose your source and your treatment and go with it. Don't falter, just try it out, and let's see what we come up with."

He looked around the class at the faces staring blankly back at him. "And we're starting now," he added, clapping his hands together. That roused a few of them and they began to rummage inside their bags. The three Barbie dolls who always sat together, dressed alike, spoke alike, thought alike, were clearly flummoxed. They were screwing up their pretty painted faces and whining amongst themselves. Vincent knew he would have to go and talk them through it. Others in the class were staring up at the ceiling, or out the window, or at blank pages, some doodling, jotting words, oiling the machinery till inspiration chugged to life. He scanned the rest of the way around the room coming finally to Anna. Only she had begun in earnest. She was writing furiously, her head bent over the desk while her hand moved at a lightning pace across the page. His gaze lingered on her awhile longer before he stood and made his way over to the Barbie aisle.

* * *

"So what made you choose that particular story?" Vincent asked Anna.
They were seated in a booth at a bar up the road from the college and
Anna was already making steady progress through a glass of wine. But she
felt exhilarated now, not depressed.

"Hmm, do you want the long or the short answer?" Anna mused.

Vincent leaned forward. "I'm not going anywhere."

She smiled. "Well, I guess the story of Abraham and Sarah strikes a
particular chord with me. You're aware of the original, I take it?"

"Sure, it's one of the first they feed you at Sunday school," he remarked.
"I always remember the part about God telling Abraham his descendants
would number the stars in the sky. It's a good image. God must be a poet."

"I think it reads more like Stephen King. When Abraham takes Isaac
off secretly to kill him, binding his hands and feet . . . ?" Anna shuddered.
"Poor boy would have been in therapy forever."

Vincent laughed mildly. "So in your version you have Abraham fret-
ting that he'll never have children and pursuing the slave girl. But in the
Bible, as I recall, Sarah was the one who panicked and arranged for Abraham to sleep with Hagar."

"A likely story," Anna scoffed. "I bet that was Abe's spin. 'Oh my wife
made me do it,' 'It just happened.' Sounds like my husband." She took out
a cigarette and lit it. "Poor Sarah, how did she put up with Abraham and his
unbearable ego, believing he had a direct line through to God and that he
was meant to be the father of his generation? These days he'd be diagnosed
as schizophrenic and put on medication." She drew deeply on her cigarette.
"Maybe I should have placed the story in a modern setting and Sarah could
have had Abe committed. He meets Hagar, a cleaner in the psych ward . . ."

"I'm detecting a recurring theme here," said Vincent. "Hey, that's
right, your dad was a psychiatrist, wasn't he?"

"And I'm a psychologist," she told him.

"No kidding?"

She shook her head.

"So you counsel people, are you that kind of psychologist?"

"As opposed to the kind that counsels animals?" she asked, frowning.

"No, as opposed to the kind that researches, or teaches."

"Oh." Anna nodded. "No, I work with real, live, dysfunctional people."

"What made you take a writing class?"

She shrugged. "I didn't want to do folk art."

"Does that have some deep meaning?"

"Not that I'm aware of." She stubbed out her cigarette. "So tell me, did you like my story or not?"

"I did. Especially the ending, Abraham languishing his life away with the now-contemptuous Hagar who doesn't love him but hasn't had any better offers, while Sarah takes over the reins and becomes the matriarch of her people. Interesting angle."

Anna smiled smugly. "I felt that Abraham needed to be pulled down a few pegs. He's the archetypal white middle-class male who gets away with murder, or at the very least adultery, and ends up with everything, yet he hasn't done a thing to deserve it."

Vincent reached over to refill Anna's glass. "So I'm guessing your husband is one of these archetypal white middle-class males?"

Anna picked up her glass, considering him. "What makes you think this has anything to do with my husband?"

"You said a minute ago that Abraham's excuses sounded just like your husband's."

"Oh, did I?" said Anna. She took out another cigarette and focused on lighting it so she didn't have to make eye contact with him. She didn't want to talk about Mac and his woman and his baby. "So what have you been doing with your life, Vincent?"

"Do you want the long or the short answer?"

Anna leaned forward. "I'm not going anywhere."

He smiled. "Well, I started high school just after we moved—"

"I think it's safe to skip ahead a little."

So he did, recounting his promising arrival on the literary stage when he received an award for his first novel, written while he was still at university. Great expectations followed, too great for the shoulders of a restless twenty-two-year-old to bear. So he took off, backpacking around Europe, living off his prize money and the advance for his next novel. Which he was supposed to be writing, he admitted sheepishly.

"But that was in the days before the Internet had taken over the world, e-mail was a brand name and cell phones were still an exception," said Vincent. "I couldn't be traced so easily, much as my publisher tried."

He came back with a wad of crumpled pages he had to peel off the bottom of his backpack. His publisher, needless to say, was not happy. He would have to pay back the advance or produce something. He had no money, so he moved back home, locked himself in a room and three months later he'd produced something. His publisher was still not happy, neither was Vincent, but it was all he was capable of. The book was published, sinking like a stone dropped into a river from a great height. Bad reviews only hastened the fall. There were no awards, no more advances, but Vincent felt free. He pulled beers in a pub until he saved enough money to go back overseas. This time he stayed away for five years, working in bars in England, on farms in France, teaching English in Japan, and eventually writing again.

He came home with a completed manuscript and began to hawk it around the publishing houses and literary agencies, wearing rejection like a badge of honor, paying his dues. Far from being demoralized, Vincent found it character-building. He knew by then that he could write and that he wanted to keep writing. He eventually found an agent who believed in him, who found him a publisher, who found him an audience.

"And now I get to surf when I'm not writing, and teach when I'm not doing either." He smiled. "Suits me."

Anna regarded him through her own increasingly bleary eyes. She'd been mesmerized listening to Vincent's story, but he had been talking for quite a while, and consequently she had drunk quite a lot of wine. She wanted to say something, but she suspected the line of command from her brain to her mouth had been severely compromised. She had to concentrate.

"I'd like . . . to . . . read . . . one of your books," she said slowly.

"You mean you haven't already?" he said with mock indignation. She went to apologize but he stopped her. "Don't worry, not many people have. I have a small but loyal readership, which is as much as a literary writer can expect." Vincent paused, considering her. "What about you? You still haven't told me what made a psychologist decide to take a writing class?"

"Yes, I did."

"The folk art defense? It doesn't really tell me anything."

Anna felt the room beginning to sway. "Well, I will tell you this much, I think I might be getting drunk."

"Are you okay?"

She nodded. "But I don't think I should drive home."

"You think I had any intention of letting you drive?" he replied. "Where do you live?"

Anna gave him a lame smile. "Mosman."

But twenty minutes later when Vincent pulled up outside the house, Anna was confounded. "Oh, no!" she cried.

"What's wrong?"

"I don't live here!"

"But this is the address you gave me."

"No, I mean, I used to live here, but I don't live here anymore."

"So where do you live?"

Anna closed her eyes as if that was going to help. "I can't remember. I haven't been there long. I only moved out a few weeks ago."

He peered out across the front lawn. "It looks empty."

"That's because there's no one living there yet, they don't move in for a couple of weeks. Legally it still belongs to me. Well, me and Mac." She paused. "And if I'm not mistaken . . ." She rummaged in her handbag and produced a single key, holding it up triumphantly. "Let's go inside!"

"Why?"

"I don't know. It'll probably be the last time I ever do."

Vincent considered her. "Okay, if that's what you want."

Anna handed him the key as she didn't have much faith in her fine motor skills at the moment. They walked up the front path and he opened the door.

"Pretty fancy digs," he remarked.

There was a full moon so the house was not so dark they couldn't make their way down the hallway, and the sunroom was luminous, with its bank of French windows facing the northern sky. Anna stood still, gazing around the room. She'd never seen it empty. She had left ahead of the movers and hired a cleaning service to go over the house afterward. It felt strange; cold and lifeless. The mullions on the doors and windows cast shadows, making distorted patterns across the parquetry floor. It looked like a set for some surreal art-house movie. Vincent walked across to the windows, his footsteps reverberating off all the bare surfaces.

"Nice garden."

"You should see it in the spring."

He turned around to look at her. "Were you happy here?"

Anna folded her arms, hugging herself. They had been so excited when they found this house. This was where they were going to raise their children, have birthday parties, Christmas, family gatherings. They had pored over paint charts and carpet and curtain samples and planned the scheme for every room, including a nursery. They made their way through the house systematically, starting with the sunroom, then the kitchen, master bedroom, bathrooms, dining room and formal living room, study. Finally they had refurbished the downstairs bedroom as a guest room, but they never made it to the other bedrooms. They were on hold.

Anna suddenly felt tears spring into her eyes as a sob leapt from her throat.

"Anna?"

She didn't want to do this. She didn't want to be crying in front of a virtual stranger. He was crossing the floor toward her. Why did she bring him inside? Why did she even suggest it? She shielded her face with one hand, and then she felt Vincent's arms draping gently around her, unexpectedly comforting.

"I'm sorry," she breathed.

"Don't be." He smoothed her hair back, tilting her head so she had to look at him. "Come on, let's get out of here."

"But where will I go?" she said in a small voice. "I don't have anywhere to go."

"Yes you do."

Morning

Anna didn't know if the sun had just happened upon her face or if it had been there for hours. But it felt warm and lovely on her skin. Her bedroom didn't get sun in the mornings, it didn't get sun anytime. It was rather dark in fact, situated as it was on the south side of the small, soulless townhouse she was renting in Neutral Bay.

That's where she lived. She remembered now. 12C Milner Place. Anna's eyes opened wide as a montage of brief scenes flitted across her mind like a trailer for a movie. In the café, sitting across a table from Mac, *Georgie's pregnant and I'm the father* . . . writing class, pan to Vincent, *Is the invitation still open?* she was asking, leaning toward him over his desk . . . sitting in a booth, smoking cigarettes, drinking too much . . . Vincent driving, pulling up at the house in Mosman . . . shadows on the parquetry floor . . . *Were you happy here?*

Anna sat up. She was on a large bed in the center of the room, still wearing the clothes she'd left home in yesterday. There was a wall of windows to her left, and trees, lots of trees outside. Through the canopy she could just catch a glimpse of the ocean and the distant line of the horizon. Inside the walls were green, the same green as the eucalyptus leaves outside the window. The room was a little messy, but in a homely, relaxed way. There were odd bits of furniture, a timber chest of drawers, an old armchair covered in faded cabbage roses, a wicker basket with clothes spilling out of it. Anna wasn't sure where she was, but she didn't feel afraid. In fact she felt strangely safe. Safe and sound. She swung her feet over the side of the bed and they met with bare floorboards. She was wearing fine cotton socks, the ones she wore with her boots, which she'd just spotted, languishing on the floor at the end of the bed. Anna sat for a moment, looking out to the horizon, thinking. This was Vincent's house, it had to be. But she had no memory of coming here, no memory of falling asleep in this bed, no memories at all after leaving the house.

She stood up and stretched. It was a beautiful room, not because of the furnishings, the colors, not anything tangible like that. It was just a lovely place to be, with the sun streaming in, the trees, the horizon. She wondered if Vincent worked from here, but there was no desk, no computer. Maybe this wasn't even his room. Perhaps he shared the house and his roommate was away at the moment. Anna hoped so anyway; it was bad enough that she had to go out and face Vincent, let alone someone she had never met. She wished she had some recollection of how she had got here. She was feeling a little seedy, but the morning after had never been a problem for Anna. The night before was a whole other thing. Whatever quirk of her constitution that saved her from hangovers was not so kind while she was still under the influence. She couldn't put it off any longer. She had to leave the room, find Vincent and apologize for whatever she had done. And thank him. For whatever he had done. And get through it all while retaining a modicum of dignity.

Anna walked over to the door, opened it quietly and stepped straight out into the living area. It was a long room, encompassing kitchen, dining and lounge areas, cluttered and busy. Shelves lined the walls, crammed to capacity with books, videos, DVDs, CDs, and what appeared to be vinyl records. None of the furniture matched; the couch was disguised by a couple of batik throws, another length of batik served as a tablecloth. It was crowded and colorful and Anna felt immediately comfortable. Just as she had in the bedroom. There was the same wall of glass with the same gorgeous vista, but here it was comprised of sliding doors leading to a deck apparently suspended in the trees. And there was Vincent, stretched out on a recliner, reading the newspaper. He looked up, probably feeling her gaze.

"Morning," he called, jumping up and tossing the paper onto the table. He came inside, sliding the glass door closed behind him. "How did you sleep?"

"Like a dead man."

He laughed. "I hope that's good?"

"I slept so soundly I didn't know where I was when I first woke up."

"That's because you've never been here before."

Anna looked at him. "Vincent, I—"

"You're not going to get all apologetic and awkward on me, are you?"

"That's what I was planning."

"Then let's fast-forward," he said as he turned toward the kitchen. "Coffee?"

"I don't want to inconvenience you any more than I already have."

"I hear what you're saying, because it's a huge inconvenience to make a pot of coffee," he said, regarding her dubiously from across the bench.

Anna gave him a faint smile and walked tentatively over toward the kitchen. "Vincent?"

He had his back to her, filling the kettle. "Hmm?"

"I want to assure you I'm not in the habit of getting drunk and going home with men I hardly know."

"You know me!" Vincent scoffed. "You've known me for more than twenty years."

"No, correction, I *knew* you twenty years ago."

"Same thing." He shrugged, plugging in the kettle and switching it on.

"No, it isn't, Vincent," Anna insisted. "Look, I'm embarrassed. I can't even remember how we got back last night. I remember being at the house, but not much after that. I didn't"—she took a breath—"I didn't throw up in your car or something horrible, did I? I have a tendency to do that when I drink too much."

"Oh, so you're a chucker." He nodded. "Don't worry, you spared me that trick." He smiled at her pained expression, leaning back against the bench. "Anna, you couldn't remember where you lived and you were falling asleep in the car. I had no choice but to bring you back here."

"But how did you get me inside?"

"I didn't have to carry you," he assured her. "No, you could still walk, with a little assistance. You were just very tired and emotional, as they say. You were snoring before I managed to get your boots off."

"Snoring!"

"Oh, it was very feminine, more of a rhythmic hum really."

Anna sighed. "Is that your room I slept in?"

"Yes, but I didn't sleep with you, if that's what you're worried about. I slept out here."

She winced. "You had to sleep on the lounge?"

"It wouldn't be the first time."

"Oh, there've been others like me?"

Vincent looked directly at her. "There haven't been any others like you."

Anna couldn't hold his gaze. She looked away, tousling her hair self-consciously. "Could I use the bathroom?"

"Sure." He pointed to the hall that led away from the living area. "If you want to have a shower—"

"No, really, I'll just freshen up a little."

"Suit yourself. It's the first door on your right."

When Anna returned, Vincent had taken the coffee out onto the deck. As she stepped outside she paused, gazing at the view, breathing in the salt air. "It's a wonderful spot." She sighed.

"How do you take your coffee?" Vincent asked.

"I'll do it," she said, reaching for the pot and a cup. "I didn't notice a computer anywhere. Do you write longhand?"

"God no. My study's up the hall, opposite the bathroom."

"But you wouldn't have a view from there?"

"Because I wouldn't get any work done if I did."

"Really, doesn't it inspire you?"

"Yeah, to go surfing," he said, smiling at her. "No, I like this setup. When I come out here, I can relax. It's completely separate from my work."

Anna sighed deeply, looking out to the ocean, sipping her coffee. She felt extraordinarily peaceful. She wouldn't have any trouble staying out here all day, not that she had any intention of doing so, she'd already imposed on Vincent enough. And he still hadn't given her the chance to explain herself properly.

"Vincent," she began, "look, I wanted to say . . . about last night—"

"You're not still going on about that, are you?"

"I haven't gone on about it at all, you won't let me get a word out."

"Because it's not a problem."

"It is for me. I don't remember much but I do remember the scene at the house—"

"I think calling it a 'scene' might be overstating things."

"It was a scene, in my book anyway. I don't behave like that. Ever. Especially not with strangers."

"I am going to get offended if you keep referring to me as a stranger, especially now that you've spent the night."

Anna smiled weakly at him. "Look, I would like to explain."

"If it'll make you feel better."

She leaned forward. "I saw my husband, or ex, or whatever I'm supposed to call him. . . . I saw him last night, before class. He had some news that was . . . a little confronting, I guess you'd say. I'm afraid I didn't handle it all that well."

Vincent considered her. "Do you want to talk about it?" he said carefully.

"Um, no, not really."

"Then let's drop it," he said, smiling kindly.

Anna smiled back. She really had to leave it alone now or he was going to think she was neurotic.

"Though I'd like to say something," he went on.

"Sure, go ahead."

"What you wrote in class last night was your best work so far," Vincent began. "Your first couple of pieces, they were good, they showed you can write."

"Really?"

He nodded. "But they felt repressed, like what you really wanted to say was being smothered under a layer of elegant words and phrases. They were quite beautiful, but they didn't feel real. And then last night's story leapt off the page. It was raw and emotional, even angry, because you were raw and emotional and angry. You obviously tapped into that."

"Are you suggesting I should stage fights with my ex-husband and then get drunk in order to write?"

"No . . . well, maybe"—he smiled—"but not necessarily." He took a mouthful of coffee. "Last night you kept palming me off when I asked you why you decided to take a writing class. You said it was because you didn't want to do folk art. What does that mean?"

Anna shrugged. "I had to take a break from work, I wasn't in the right frame of mind to be providing therapy for people in crisis," she added. "I needed something to occupy my time."

"So why writing?"

"My mother reminded me that I used to keep journals when I was a girl, and I found some of them. I guess I wondered if I could pick it up again."

"Why do you think you stopped for all those years?"

Anna held up her fingers and started counting off. "Oh, university, marriage, career . . ." Seven years of fertility treatment, but she wasn't ready to share that with Vincent yet. "Moving interstate, buying a house, renovating it . . . Life."

"And you never kept a journal again?"

"No . . ." It had been a common suggestion in the infertility books and pamphlets they had read, and from the counselors they had seen along the way, but Anna had had a hard enough time living it, let alone recording it for posterity. She had resolved to wait until she actually fell pregnant before starting a journal.

Vincent folded his arms, considering her. "Are you writing much away from class?"

"No, not much."

"Why not?"

"Do you need a note from my mother?"

He smiled. "I'm just interested."

Anna shrugged. "I guess I can't think of anything to write about."

"What?" Vincent frowned, leaning forward across the table. "I don't mean to pry, Anna, but your marriage broke up, you've obviously been through some major personal upheaval."

She pulled a face. "Oh, I don't want to write about all that. It's too depressing."

"You know what they say, better out than in."

"Pardon?"

"Get it out of you and onto the page."

"Writing as therapy?"

"I think it's a little self-indulgent to use writing as therapy, at least if you expect anyone else to read it," he added. "I do think, however, that the best writing draws on real emotion. You need to let some of that emotion bleed into what you write, Anna."

"I wouldn't know where to start."

"That's the easy part."

"Oh?"

"Just sit down and start writing."

When Anna arrived back at the townhouse later that day, she stared at it glumly through the car window. What possessed her to move into this ugly little box? She sighed. She should have donned a hair shirt and started fasting instead.

An hour later she'd showered, washed her hair, fixed herself something to eat and made a cup of tea. Now what? If she lived by the beach like Vincent she'd be quite content sitting out on the balcony, browsing the paper, periodically glancing up to take in the view. But here she looked out onto a busy road and other ugly buildings. She picked up the phone and rang her parents, but the machine answered. They were out. Her seventy-plus parents had a more exciting life than she did. Most people had a more exciting life than she did. She wandered restlessly around the stark, monastic rooms, thinking of the morning, of Vincent, of his comfortable lived-in house, of their conversation. There was only one thing to do. She went into her bedroom, sat down at the desk and opened her laptop. She looked around the room as the computer started up. No matter what Vincent said, Anna needed a more pleasant space to work in. She walked back out into the living area and found a patch of sun on the carpet. If she turned the sofa around the other way, she could fit the desk there. But was it near a power point? She looked around and spotted one.

Half an hour later she had moved the sofa and the desk, three or four times. But she was satisfied now. The desk was in a well-lit spot, perpendicular to the wall, next to a window that actually framed a little greenery outside. It was a savagely lopped, sad-looking tree, but a tree nonetheless, and through the fine slats of the venetian blind, it passed. She plugged in the laptop and started it again while she brought a small lamp out from the bedroom and placed it on the desk, moving it around a few times until it was just right, in the spot where she'd first put it down. She took out her notepad from writing class and some pens, arranging them neatly to the right of the laptop. The pens would be better in a cup or a pot of some kind, she decided. Anna went into the kitchen and searched through the cupboards till she found just the thing. A funky little ceramic vase that looked like a cactus, given to her by a client before he left to travel overseas. She sat the vase next to the computer and dropped the pens into it. Anna surveyed her new workstation. What else did she need? A cup of coffee? No, she'd had one and a half cups at Vincent's and a cup of tea when she got home. She'd wait. A glass of water perhaps? In fact, she'd fill a little jug and bring it to the desk.

Anna sighed. She was probably six steps away from the kitchen. It was not like she needed to stockpile supplies. What she did need to do was sit down and start writing. That's what Vincent had said. So that's what she did.

Small Business Agency

Liam returned to the office at one after a morning in the field. He was gradually getting the hang of his new job, even enjoying it. Though he'd been so idiotically happy since finding out about the baby he suspected nothing could bother him. Only Anna's reaction had managed to dampen his joy. He had tried to call her over the last couple of days, but all he got was her answering machine. She obviously didn't want to talk to him, it was probably best to leave her alone for now.

"What have you got there?" Kath stuck her head out of her office as he walked past, carrying an assortment of shopping tote bags.

"Oh." Liam hesitated, feeling self-conscious. "I've been out Black-town way this morning. They have one of those super mega mart places. They sell everything."

"Looks like you didn't get past the baby stuff," said Kath, cocking her head to check out the logos on the bags. "Doting uncle?"

"No . . ." He took a breath. "Doting father-to-be actually."

Kath looked up abruptly. "Since when?"

"Since a few weeks ago. At least that's when I found out."

"I thought you were divorced, or separated?"

"I am . . . separated at least."

"So your wife found out she was pregnant after—"

"No, no," Liam corrected. "It's not my wife's, um, my ex-wife's."

She frowned. "Who's having the baby?"

"A woman called Georgie, who I . . . ." He didn't quite know how to explain.

"You met since your separation?"

"During my separation might be closer to the truth."

Kath nodded. "I asked."

"You did."

"So you're happy about the baby?"

"I'm ecstatic."

"And Georgie?"

"I think she's happy."

"You think?"

"We're not actually together," Liam admitted. He may as well get this out. "We broke up and then she found out she was pregnant. Once she made the decision to keep it, she felt I should know."

"Well, that was decent of her, I suppose."

"It was. She's . . . um, she's a very decent person."

Kath lifted an eyebrow. "And you're still in love with her?"

Liam was a little taken aback. The chill had thawed between him and Kath since the interview and they were enjoying a good working relationship. But they hadn't ventured into personal territory yet.

"Sorry," she said, watching him, "it's none of my business."

"Oh no, that's okay. You're right . . . I am," he finished awkwardly.

"But she isn't?"

He sighed. "She's mad at me."

"Ha, well good luck then," Kath declared drily. "It's only gonna get worse. Still, if you can hang in there and she doesn't hate you by the time she has the baby, she might come around. Of course, you have to get through the birth first. If she's mad at you now, whoo, wait till she's in labor."

Liam blinked at her. "Well, thanks for the pep talk, Kath."

"Anytime," she said, retreating back inside her office.

Avalon

"Is that you, Anna?"

She was crouched on the step in front of Vincent's front door, and the sound of his voice made her jump. She stood up and spun around, clutching a thick manila envelope to her chest. Vincent was watching her curiously. He had a surfboard tucked under one arm and he was wearing a wetsuit. Well, almost wearing a wetsuit. He'd peeled off the top half and it was hanging open to his hips, rather precariously, it occurred to Anna.

"I was just . . ." she began. "I called earlier, but . . ." She couldn't finish what she was going to say, she couldn't even remember what she was going to say.

"I was down at the beach." Vincent nodded.

She still couldn't speak. And she couldn't look him in the eye, though she didn't know where else to look. She tried to be discreet, avert her eyes, but she couldn't help noticing his hair was loose, still damp from the surf, falling on his shoulders, shoulders that were broad and arms that were muscular. . . . She tried not to stare, but, well, he was standing right there in front of her, with his chest all smooth and brown. . . . Stop it, drop your eyes . . . to his stomach, impressively taut, a trail of caramel-blond hair disappearing under the straining zipper of the wetsuit and . . . oh Lord . . .

"Anna?"

Her head jerked up. She knew her face was red. "Sorry, I um, I tried to call," she said again, finding her voice. "To see if you were dressed . . . I mean busy, you know, if you had anything on . . . I mean, if you were doing anything." Oh, for crying out loud.

Vincent was smiling as he propped his board against the wall of the house. "Well, I'm getting cold. Come on inside."

"Oh, no," said Anna, backing away, "I won't stay. I was just going to leave a note, but I couldn't find the letterbox."

"I have a post-office box, stops the junk mail." He plucked a key from above the awning and unlocked the door, standing aside to let Anna in. But she didn't move. "Come on, you're here now, you might as well stay for a bit. And I promise I'll put some clothes on."

She blinked at him. "I don't want to impose."

"You're not imposing," he said, taking her arm and drawing her inside. "Why don't you make yourself at home while I get dressed? You know your way around."

Anna watched him walk up the hall and slip into the bedroom. Where she'd slept a few nights ago. And now he was in there, probably naked. She felt herself blush. What was she doing here? She never should have showed up like this, but when he didn't answer the phone she thought he wouldn't be home, so she decided to take a drive and leave it in his letterbox, but then he didn't have a letterbox. . . .

Vincent reappeared in the hallway, wearing loose cargo pants and a thin sweater that clung to the outline of his chest and shoulders. But in her mind's eye all Anna could see was his bare torso.

"Why are you still standing there?"

Anna hesitated. "I should go. You've probably got plans . . . you were going out, or you're having visitors. It is Sunday, after all, people do . . . things."

His lips curled into an amused smile as she prattled on. "Sorry, looks like you're stuck with me," he said, walking slowly back down the hall toward her. "The only thing I planned to do was maybe a little work this afternoon."

"You see, I'm interrupting your work—"

"You haven't interrupted anything. I haven't started yet."

"But you should, you must. You have to. And I should leave and let you get started."

"Anna." He was standing right in front of her now. "Shut up," he said in a low voice. He leaned toward her, reaching across her shoulder to push the door closed. Anna breathed in sharply. He smelled like the ocean, and like eucalyptus, and like a man. She was finding it all a bit heady.

"So what is that anyway?" he said, stepping back. Anna breathed out again. She was still clutching the envelope.

"Well . . ." She hesitated. "I followed your advice. I've been writing."

"How many pages have you got there?"

Anna winced. "Sixty . . . or so," she said meekly.

"You've written sixty pages since Thursday? That's like, twenty thousand words."

"Is it?" she said, biting her lip. "You see, I couldn't stop. Once I got going it just poured out. It was amazing, it was like I was possessed or something," she went on, her eyes wide. "I kept writing almost all night, then I'd sleep for a few hours, dreaming about it, and go straight back to it when I woke up."

Vincent was smiling at her. "And you want me to read it, I gather?"

"It's too much, isn't it?" she said, weighing up the envelope. "It's too much to ask. . . ."

"I'd love to read it," he assured her, turning up the hall toward the living room. He glanced over his shoulder at her. "Are you going to stand in the doorway the whole time?"

Anna stirred, following him. She'd stay for twenty minutes, maybe half an hour, to be polite.

"Can I get you a drink?" he asked her from the kitchen.

"Oh, no, I'm alright."

He sighed. "Relax, Anna. Have a drink, hang out. When I'm finished, we can talk about it."

"Finished what?"

"Reading," he said simply.

"Oh, you're in the middle of reading something?"

Vincent suppressed a smile, walking back around the kitchen bench. "You did say you wanted me to read that?" He indicated the envelope.

"You're going to start right away?" she said, wide-eyed.

"You don't want me to?"

"Oh, I don't know, I just didn't expect you to."

He shrugged. "I've got nothing else better to do. Besides, I'm curious."

Anna's forehead creased into an anxious frown.

"What's the matter?"

"Oh, Vincent, I feel bad showing up like this, I was only going to leave it here and you could have read it whenever it suited you."

"Suits me now."

She sighed.

"Have you got somewhere else you have to be?" Vincent asked her.

"No . . ."

"Then relax, go for a walk along the beach, read the paper, or—"

"Have you eaten?" she asked.

"Sorry?"

"I could make you lunch!" she declared.

"You don't have to do that, Anna."

"But I'd like to, and I really can cook," she assured him. "I've been told I'm a good cook, actually," she added breathlessly.

Vincent smiled. "I believe you. Now, how about that drink?"

"Why don't you let me get it?" said Anna.

"Alright, there's beer in the bottom of the fridge. And there's wine . . . somewhere, help yourself."

"No problem. Where will you be? In your study?"

"No, I think I'll sit out on the deck."

She looked concerned. "You won't be distracted?"

"Well, that depends."

"On what?"

"On how good the writing is."

"Oh." She nodded, her nervous smile morphing into another frown. "Oh."

Vincent grinned at her. "Stop worrying, Anna. You were brave enough to bring it over here. You must feel at least a little good about it."

"Oh, you know how it is. I do, then I don't. Then I do again." She paused. "Then I don't."

He laughed. "Sounds familiar."

Anna handed him the envelope, and watched as he crossed the living room, opened the sliding door and stepped through onto the deck, closing the door again. She kept her eyes on him as he repositioned one of the chairs and sat, stretching his legs out. He looked down at the first page, and Anna watched anxiously as his face creased into a frown. Why was he frowning? It couldn't be that bad from the start? Suddenly he jumped up and crossed to the door, sliding it open.

"Sunglasses," he explained as he grabbed a pair off a nearby shelf. "Bit glary out there," he added, slipping back through the door. He settled himself in the chair again and resumed reading. Anna couldn't tell anything from his expression, especially behind sunglasses. She didn't know what she was expecting to see, it wasn't as though it was full of laughs or anything. Though she had thought there was the odd bit of poignant humor. And then she saw Vincent smile, briefly, before he turned over a page and continued reading. What had made him smile? she wondered, trying to recall the first couple of pages. . . .

This was ridiculous, she couldn't stand there deciphering his every facial expression, it would drive her mad. Besides, she had to get on with lunch. Anna opened the fridge door, pleased to find he was a grown-up, with fresh vegetables and other basic supplies. She noticed the beers on the bottom shelf and grabbed one, opened it and took it out to Vincent. He seemed immersed as she approached.

"How is it so far?" she asked.

He didn't take his eyes off the page, only held up his hand to silence her. She circled behind him and placed the bottle on the table, then crept backward to the door. Vincent still didn't look up, he just kept reading. That had to be a good sign. Anna turned and went back inside, a tiny bubble of pride rising in her chest. She quietly slid the door closed again and walked across to the kitchen to start cooking.

"Anna?"

She jumped, startled. She had been stirring a pot on the stove and hadn't even heard Vincent come inside. For the past hour and a half he had barely lifted his eyes from the page. Anna had taken him snacks at regular intervals—nuts, a bowl of olives, another beer—but he didn't speak, or even acknowledge her. She hadn't expected him to read the whole thing right there and then, but when she tried to tell him that he held his hand up as before, motioning for her to be quiet. So she got on with lunch, looking over every so often to try to analyze his facial expression, his body language, anything. Eventually she gave up, she had no way of knowing what he was thinking, she only knew he couldn't put it down. But that didn't necessarily mean it was good. Maybe he always read like that, or maybe it was hard to follow, or maybe he wanted to get it over with.

Anna had found wine in a rack on top of the kitchen cupboard and put a bottle in the freezer to chill while she got started. She also found enough ingredients to put together an acceptable curry. Once it was cooking away happily, she poured herself a glass of wine, downing it too quickly. So she poured herself another. It was starting to go to her head, probably because her stomach was empty. She took another look at the curry and was wondering how long Vincent was going to be and if she should put rice on to steam, when she heard his voice behind her.

"You startled me!" she said, turning around. "I didn't hear you come in."

He was leaning back against the fridge, holding the bundle of pages to his chest, gazing at her . . . perhaps fondly? . . . though Anna was not sure what to make of his expression.

"So?" she asked when he still hadn't said anything.

"Extraordinary," he said, tapping the pages. "This is extraordinary. You are extraordinary."

Anna's face contorted into an expression that wasn't a smile and wasn't a frown, but was somewhere between the two. "You're just flattering me."

"No, I promise you, I never flatter people about their writing," Vincent said seriously. "They either have it or they don't. And you have it, Anna Gilchrist. You have something very special."

Anna swallowed, feeling flattered regardless. She also felt nervous and excited and proud and overwhelmed. "I cooked a curry," she said, turning back to stir the pot.

"If you cook as well as you write, I may have to keep you here indefinitely," he said in a low voice.

Anna glanced shyly over her shoulder. "Are you going to give me specifics? You can't just tell me it's good and not say why."

"You think I don't realize that? I'm a desperately insecure writer too, don't forget," he told her. "We'll go through it over lunch, page by page if you like."

And he did exactly that. He said her story was moving, heart wrenching at times, but never bleak, and always absorbing. And he said her writing was lyrical, and he read out lines and even whole passages to show her what he meant. The way Vincent read it, it sounded almost like poetry, and Anna could hardly believe she had written it herself.

He held up his glass to her when they had finished eating. "To beautiful words, beautiful food and a beautiful face."

Anna winced. "Oh dear."

He shook his head ruefully. "I knew as soon as that came out I was going to sound like Austin Powers."

She laughed.

"But you are a very beautiful woman, Anna," he said seriously. "That husband of yours must have rocks in his head."

Anna stared into her glass. "Ex-husband," she murmured.

"It is autobiographical, isn't it? Your story, I mean," he said carefully.

She shrugged. "More or less."

"You couldn't have children, so your husband had an affair and the other woman ended up pregnant."

"In a nutshell."

"How do you get through something like that?"

His gaze was so intense, it was unnerving.

"I've had dozens of clients who have been through worse," she dismissed. "Haven't you ever had a broken heart, Vincent?"

He smiled. "Of course I have. There was this beautiful girl I knew a long time ago. I was madly in love with her, but I was too young, and my parents took me away—"

"Cut it out," Anna chided. "Seriously, answer my question."

"Sure I've been hurt."

"What was her name?"

"There's a list."

"Oh, poor Vincent," she cooed, patting his arm. "Okay, well, if I was the first, who was the last?"

Vincent took a slow sip from his glass and placed it back on the table. "Her name was Joanne. We were going to get married."

"Oh, I'm sorry," said Anna. "Why did she leave?"

"She didn't leave," he said. "I left her."

"So how did your heart get broken?"

"You don't have to be the one who's left behind to have your heart broken."

Anna considered him. "What happened?"

He shrugged. "I couldn't make her happy anymore. I would have had to become someone else to do that."

"So you left?"

"Someone had to."

Anna stared across the room, to the windows, the trees, the ocean beyond, barely visible in the failing light. She stirred when Vincent went to refill her glass.

"No," she said, getting up. "I should go, really." She started stacking the plates.

Vincent got to his feet. "What's the hurry?"

"I've taken up enough of your time."

"Don't you think that's for me to decide?" he said, taking hold of her hands.

She was feeling flushed, and not just from the wine. It was the way Vincent was looking at her.

"You know, I can't let you drive," he was saying. "Not when you've been drinking."

"Well, you've been drinking too," she returned. "I can't let you drive either."

"So"—he smiled at her—"looks like you might have to stay."

"But I couldn't ask you to sleep on the lounge again."

He looked directly into her eyes. "Then don't."

Anna's heart was beating erratically. She didn't know if she was ready for this.

"You're right, I'd better call a taxi," she said, slipping her hands out of his and dashing over to the kitchen. She went to take the receiver off its cradle on the wall as Vincent's hand covered hers, replacing it.

"Anna," he said from behind, his voice reverberating down her spine. He kept hold of her hand and twirled her around to face him again. "If you really want to, then go ahead, call a taxi. But don't do it because you think you've taken up too much of my time. I can't think of any other way I'd rather be spending my time."

He was standing very close to her, his forearm resting on the wall by her head.

"I . . ." She swallowed. "Um, you see . . . Vincent, this is completely new territory for me," she said in a small voice.

"So, you haven't . . . since you separated?"

She shook her head. "And even before . . . we had sex in a test tube most of the time."

"Must have been cramped."

Anna smiled.

"You know, Anna," he said gently, "I don't want you to feel any pressure. I don't expect anything, just having you here is enough. It's like a fantasy."

"Vincent—"

"I'm serious. You know you really were my first love."

"You were only eleven."

"But you stayed with me. Probably because we moved away, you took on mythic proportions. Yours was the face in my head, Anna, through all my adolescent angst."

"That's an awful lot to live up to, Vincent." She sighed. "Fantasy is elusive. As soon as you realize it, it's not a fantasy anymore. It can't be. It's in our nature to yearn for things that are out of our reach, and then once we hold them in our hands, we find they're not so precious after all."

"You psychologists are too analytical for your own good." He stroked his fingers around the edge of her face. "What if you've been yearning for a very, very long time. Surely that would prolong the fantasy?"

"Perhaps," she said, breathing hard. "Or it could work inversely. The stronger the desire . . . the more disappointing the consummation."

Vincent smoothed his thumb across her bottom lip. Anna was trembling. "So," he said in a low voice, "if I could stop time at this point, where I don't think it would be possible to want you more than I do right now, this would be the peak of the fantasy, it's all downhill from here?"

"I don't know. . . ." She swallowed.

"Neither do I. Feels a bit empty. Maybe we could try just one thing, if you don't mind, that I've wanted to do . . . oh, for about twenty years."

Anna closed her eyes as his lips met hers, gently lingering against them. She wanted to go with it, to let go enough. She wondered if she was capable.

"You've waited twenty years just for that?" she breathed after he pulled away.

Vincent considered her curiously, but he was smiling. "Well, that was only a prelude," he said, drawing her away from the wall and into his arms as he slowly but very deliberately brought his mouth down onto hers. Anna was unprepared for the voracity of his kiss. She'd thrown down the gauntlet and he had risen to the challenge. With gusto. When he finally drew back from her, she felt breathless, sapped even. Vincent was gazing down at her.

"Are you still thinking about going home?" he asked.

"Are you still thinking about sleeping on the lounge?"

"I was never thinking about sleeping on the lounge."

The Reading Rooms

"Is that the phone?" Adam asked, coming from the back of the shop.

"Sorry," said Georgie vaguely, but he was already on his way. She was ensconced in one of the armchairs, looking through job applications, and she hadn't even registered that the phone was ringing. Her brain was a little slow these days. Adam would have beat her to it anyway, her body was pretty slow these days as well.

"Georgie, it's for you," he called from the door of the office. He handed her the phone after she'd struggled up out of the armchair and made her way over. "It's Liam."

"Hello?"

"Hi, Georgie, how are you?"

"Actually," she said, perching on the edge of the desk, "I'm feeling a little redundant at the moment, as a matter of fact."

"Why is that?"

"We're in the process of finding a replacement for me."

"No one could replace you."

"Liam said no one could replace me," Georgie repeated for Adam's benefit. He mimed throwing up. "You can leave now," she said to him. He smiled as he sauntered out of the office. "Sorry, Liam, what were you calling about?" she asked.

"Only to see if the parcel arrived."

"Oh, I don't know," said Georgie vaguely. "Let me check." She looked through the pile of mail waiting to be opened. "Liam, you send something almost every week. You have to stop," she said.

"Why?"

"Because . . ."

"It's my baby too," Liam persisted. "What's the problem?"

The problem was it gave him an excuse to have more contact than Georgie felt completely comfortable with. She had to call him to thank him every time; and if she didn't, he phoned to check that it had arrived. Not that Liam had done anything to upset her. He'd really been very caring. And Georgie had to admit she liked talking to him about the baby. He was more interested than anyone, even Nick. He wanted to know everything, every ache and pain, every movement the baby made, every detail from her antenatal visits. It was incredibly comforting, but she couldn't let herself get used to it.

"Here it is," she said to Liam. "Just give me a sec while I open it."

It was one of those padded envelopes, so Georgie had to use scissors to cut through it. She peered inside and slid out a soft packet, wrapped in tissue paper. She folded back the sheets to reveal a tiny white baby suit. She picked up the phone again. "It's gorgeous," she cooed.

"Do you like it?"

"I do." It was an all-in-one with tiny feet, and little bunny rabbits in palest pink and blue embroidered around the collar. Georgie had bought a number of outfits for the baby, but they still made her go all sappy and sentimental. She felt a lump rising in her throat.

"It's so small, I can't believe the baby will fit into it," Liam was saying.

Georgie sniffed. She couldn't speak. Tears filled her eyes as she gazed lovingly at the little suit.

"Georgie?"

She still couldn't say anything.

"Are you okay, Georgie?"

She sighed tremulously. "I'm hopeless. I cry at the slightest thing these days."

"I think that's normal," he said gently. "You're alright, though? There's nothing wrong?"

"I'm fine."

"You're sleeping okay?"

"Not too bad. I've heard it gets worse from here on in."

"Is there anything I can do?"

Georgie smiled. "Short of coming over and giving me a back rub in the middle of the night . . ."

"You only have to pick up the phone."

Her face crumpled. Every time she thought she could handle this whole platonic thing, Liam came out with something that sent her emotions reeling. Something sweet, something thoughtful, something that made her remember why she had fallen in love with him and forget for a moment what he had done to her. She couldn't suppress a loud sob.

"Georgie," said Liam, his voice full of concern.

She swallowed. "I have to go."

"Are you okay?"

"Yes, I'm fine. Just the hormones, you know. Talk to you later." She hung up the phone and lowered herself onto a chair, hugging the little suit to her chest.

Adam burst through the door. "Scuse me, some of us still have to work." He stopped in his tracks when he saw Georgie. "Hey, what's the matter? Why are you crying?"

"How the hell should I know?" She sighed, wiping her eyes.

He pulled a chair over beside her. "Is there anything I can do?"

Tears welled again. "Don't, that's what got me started in the first place."

"I'm not following you."

She breathed out. "It's just . . . Liam's being so nice. . . ."

Adam looked more confused. "That's good, isn't it?"

"Yes," she squeaked, her voice competing with more tears to make it out of her throat.

"Bloody women, you freak me out!" said Adam, shaking his head. "Do you have any idea how hard it is to get it right? Liam's being nice, so you're upset. I assume if he was being an arsehole you'd be upset too?"

She sniffed, nodding.

"So you do realize the poor bloke can't win?"

She took a deep, cleansing breath. "You're right, I know," she said. Adam passed her a box of tissues from the desk and she took one. "When did you suddenly become Liam's advocate?"

"I'm not Liam's advocate, I'm the baby's. And yours," he said. "And if you're going to get upset no matter what Liam does, you're going to be a blubbering mess, Georgie. You've invited him into your baby's life, so he's going to be a part of your life too. You better get used to it."

Neutral Bay

The phone rang as Anna was heading for the door. She hesitated for a moment, listening for a message, when she heard her mother's slightly harried voice. "Anna, are you there, dear? Oh, I don't understand this, you're never—"

"Mum, I'm here, just a minute," she said, after racing back to grab the phone. She pressed the button to stop the answering machine. "Can you hear me?"

"Finally, I'm speaking to you and not your machine."

"Hello, Mum," said Anna, sliding down onto the sofa. "How are you?"

"Darling, I've been trying to get you for weeks, where have you been?"

"Oh, out." In truth Anna was almost living at Vincent's these days. Whenever she spent any time at the townhouse she felt cold and lonely, and she couldn't wait to get back to Avalon. Vincent didn't seem to mind. In fact, he'd suggested she move in properly. But Anna wasn't ready for that.

"It's so hard to get ahold of you these days, Anna," Caroline was saying. "You never seem to be home. Are you back at work?"

"Not yet. I told Doug I'd be off for the rest of the year." She had added a month, then another month to her leave, and she was about to add another month when her conscience pricked and she realized she was being unfair. Doug had been so understanding, she didn't want to take advantage. And it was unfair to her clients. She knew that staying off for so long was effectively relinquishing her current client list, what was left of it. But she was becoming more convinced by the day that she was unlikely to return to clinical practice anyway.

"But what will you live on, dear?"

"I'm fine, Mum, the money from the sale of the house has come through."

"You don't want to be frittering that away—"

"I'm not frittering it away, I'm taking some time off, for the first time in my life, while I decide what I want to do with the rest of it."

There was a pause. Anna knew her mother was torn between wanting her daughter to be happy and wanting her to be responsible, and wondering why they both couldn't be achieved to everyone's satisfaction.

"So what exactly are you doing with your time?" Caroline asked tentatively.

Anna thought about it. A little writing and reading, lots of reading, on the recliner out on Vincent's deck, or curled up with him on the lounge at night. And cooking. She'd taught Vincent to cook a mean risotto, and he'd attempted to teach her to surf, with less spectacular results. And then there was the sex. Anna was indulging herself in the pure, exhilarating physicality of having sex simply for the sake of it. She realized she had stopped feeling like a sexual being. She had become instead an egg producer and incubator, albeit a temporary one, and ultimately a pretty useless one. She had lost all confidence in her body and what it could do. But Vincent was gradually turning her around.

"Did you hear me, Anna? Are you still there?"

"Sorry, Mum, I thought I heard someone at the door. You were saying?"

"I was wondering what you're doing with yourself. I thought with all this free time you might have considered spending a little of it with us."

"Of course, Mum. I have been meaning to come down." She hesitated. She hadn't mentioned Vincent to her parents yet. It was probably about time. "The thing is, I've been seeing someone."

"Oh." It wasn't an exclamation of excitement, or pleasure, or even surprise. It sounded like disappointment.

"What's the matter, Mum? I thought you'd be happy for me."

"It's a little unexpected, that's all, dear."

"What, you didn't expect I'd date again?"

There was a pause before she answered. "I suppose your father and I thought, or we hoped, the separation was only temporary."

"What?" Anna said in disbelief. "Even after we sold the house?"

"Well, we just assumed you'd both come back to Melbourne."

Anna sighed. There was something else she hadn't told her parents. "Mother, Mac is having a child with the other woman."

"Oh my goodness."

That was one way of putting it.

"How are you, dear?" Caroline asked, recovering. "I mean, how do you feel about it?"

"I try not to think about it if I can help it, Mum," said Anna. "I just want to get on with my life."

"Of course," she said. "Anything we can do . . ."

"I'm fine."

Caroline took another moment. "So this man you're seeing, what's his name?"

"You know him actually, Mum."

"I do?"

"Do you remember the Carruthers, they used to live around the corner?"

"You're testing my memory a little, darling."

"I was good friends with Bronwyn through high school until they moved."

"Oh, yes, I remember Bronwyn."

"Well, I'm seeing her brother."

"I don't remember a brother, she only had an older sister."

"Vincent's younger, Mum."

"Pardon?"

"Vincent is younger than Bronwyn . . . and me."

"Are you talking about the little fellow?"

"Yes, well, once upon a time Vincent was a little fellow, Mum," Anna returned drily. "But he's all grown up now."

"How old is he? Oh, what am I saying?" Caroline sighed. "I'm sounding like an old biddy. Of course you can go out with a man who's younger than you, what's wrong with that?"

Not a damned thing. "Look, Mum, it's not serious. I don't want to jump into another relationship so soon. We're just enjoying each other's company."

"Well, that's nice, dear."

"So I'll be down for Dad's birthday, you can count on it."

"But that's more than a month away."

"Oh, um . . ."

"Listen to me," Caroline berated herself. "I sound pitiful. We'll see you then and we'll both look forward to it."

"Okay, Mum, and I'll talk to you soon, I promise. Love to Dad."

Dee Why

"Hi, Georgie, it's Liam."

"Hi," Georgie said, surprised. She couldn't pretend she didn't like hearing his voice, especially on a quiet Sunday afternoon when she was sick of herself. So sick, in fact, that she had been considering taking herself over to Nick and Louise's, even though she had spent the entire day there yesterday and most of last weekend as well. She was likely to wear out her welcome at this rate. Georgie had decided this morning that she had to get used to being alone. She had to make herself a schedule and stick to it. Breakfast, chores, a walk . . . lunch . . . maybe a nap . . . She'd bored herself stupid just thinking about it.

"What are you up to?" Liam asked.

"Oh, nothing much."

"Me either." He paused. "Maybe we could do nothing much somewhere in the same vicinity as each other?"

Georgie smiled faintly. This was a first. He phoned often, and he'd dropped into the shop a few times, but Liam hadn't dared ask her out or visit her at home. She supposed there was nothing wrong with spending a little time together. They would obviously be seeing a lot more of each other after the birth, and they were going to have to get along for the sake of the baby. She just wished she felt more in control around him. Her emotions seemed to dip and soar like a drunken eagle. It was because of the pregnancy, her hormones were out of whack. That's all it was.

"Georgie?" Liam prompted. "What do you say?"

"Well," she began, "I have been thinking all day that I should go for a walk, but I haven't been able to get motivated."

"Would having some company motivate you?"

"Probably. We could meet out in front of my place, say in twenty minutes? We can walk down to the beach from here."

"See you then."

Georgie was sitting on the squat brick fence next to the letterboxes when Liam pulled into the street and parked across the road. She wandered over as he climbed out of the car. "Where's the Saab?" she asked.

"I terminated the lease when I left Morgan Trask," he said. "Thought it was the right time to . . . what was it you said? Downsize?"

But Georgie wasn't listening. She was staring into the back window. "What's that?"

"A baby seat," he replied, watching her. "It's top of the line, fully approved, meets all the safety standards. And I had it fitted professionally, at a licensed place."

Georgie was still staring at it, Liam couldn't work out her expression. He felt as though he was walking on eggshells whenever he was around her. He didn't mind, he'd crawl on broken glass if it would make her happy. But that was the problem: he never knew what was going to make her happy and what was going to bother her.

"I thought, because you don't drive . . ."

She nodded vaguely. "Nick and Louise said they'd put the girls' baby seat back in their car."

"Okay. I don't think there's any harm having two, but if it bothers you—"

"No." She stirred, looking up at him. "No, really, it's a good idea, Liam."

"Then what is it?"

Georgie sighed. "It's just sitting there, empty. Don't you think it might be bad luck?"

"How do you mean?"

She shrugged. "Oh, you know, like counting your chickens . . . I'm probably just being superstitious."

"I'll put it in the trunk," said Liam.

She winced. "See, now I'm having nightmares about the baby being locked in the trunk of a car."

"I'll leave it at my place when I get home," he assured her. "You won't see it again until after the baby's born."

"Thank you." She smiled up at him. And that was enough for him.

They walked the block down to the beach. It was cool, but the sky was clear and blue and Georgie decided it was a far sight better than being cooped up in her flat.

"We should do this more often," Liam suggested carefully.

Georgie looked at him, raising an eyebrow.

"I'm just saying," he went on, "we're going to be spending more time together once the baby comes, so we may as well get used to it."

She nodded slowly. "I was thinking the same thing."

"You were?"

"Uh-huh."

That was encouraging, he hadn't expected that. This was his opportunity. "So, for example," he began, "do you have any plans next weekend?"

Georgie shrugged. "I don't think so."

He cleared his throat. "Because I was thinking of visiting my family."

"So they're for real, your family?"

Liam met her eyes directly. "Everything I told you about my family is true."

"Does your mother have the same birthday as me?"

"Except for that." He sighed.

"Hard to keep track of the lies isn't it?" Georgie elbowed him. But then she noticed his pained expression. "I'm only pulling your chain," she cajoled.

He managed a weak smile as they took the set of stairs down to the sand.

"So, I was thinking," he persisted, "maybe you'd like to come?"

"Pardon?"

"To meet my family," he explained. "My mother in particular."

"You want me to come all the way to Melbourne to meet your family?"

"Well, yes . . ."

Georgie stopped walking. "Why?"

Liam took a breath. He had rehearsed this. "I know how important family is to you, Georgie. And whatever issues you have with me, you can't hold them against my family." He paused, watching her. He could see her mind ticking over. "The baby's only going to have one grand-mother, you have to meet sometime," he went on. "And my mother's dy-ing to meet you."

"Why?"

"Why do you think?"

Georgie looked at him, curious.

"Because I've told her all about you."

She put her hands on her hips. "So now you're resorting to flattery?"

"I thought it was worth a shot," he said lamely.

Georgie sighed. Part of her was intrigued. But a larger part of her was wary, very wary. It all sounded so reasonable, but she didn't trust Liam yet. "I don't know, it's a long way to go for a weekend."

"Not by plane."

"I'm not sure they even let you fly after seven months."

"That's only international flights," he said. "I checked."

She raised an eyebrow. "Oh did you just?"

He nodded. "And there's a really good hotel I always stay in when I'm in Melbourne—"

"We'd stay in a hotel?"

"Well, yes."

"I'm not going to stay in a hotel with you."

"I was going to book separate rooms."

"I'm not going to stay in a hotel with you, Liam," Georgie said flatly. The family thing was beginning to sound like a ruse. He just wanted an excuse to spend a weekend with her, and if he was using his family to . . . well, that was despicable. There was only one way to deal with it. "Why can't we stay at your mother's?"

Liam frowned. "You don't want to do that."

"This is about meeting your family, Liam, getting to know them. It's not like she wouldn't have enough room. She brought up nine kids in the place. Are any of them still living at home?"

"I'm not sure, the younger ones come and go a bit."

"There'd still be room regardless, so what's the problem?"

"You don't understand, the house is rundown—"

"Oh, Liam, surely you don't think that would bother me?" she chided. "Would your mother have a problem with us staying there?"

He hesitated, rubbing his forehead.

"The truth, Liam."

"No," he relented. "She'd love it."

"Then it's settled. I don't want your mother imagining that I think I'm too good to stay in her home."

He looked at her. "She wouldn't think that," he said quietly. He took a breath. "Okay, if that's what you want, I'll give Mum a call, I'll set it up."

Georgie nodded, satisfied. Oh, cripes, what had she got herself into?

Avalon

"Do you like jazz?" Vincent asked, walking into the kitchen, his head bent over a magazine.

"Hmm?" Anna murmured. She was sautéing some vegetables for dinner, shifting them around the pan absentmindedly.

"There's a jazz festival up the coast on the long weekend," he said, tossing the magazine onto the bench. He came up behind her, circling her waist and nuzzling her neck. "They have campsites, we could pitch a tent under the stars—"

"Don't they have hotels around there?" she asked.

"Where's your sense of adventure, woman?"

"What sense of adventure? I never said I had a sense of adventure."

"Come on, it'll be fun."

"Is that the October long weekend?" she asked over her shoulder.

"Yep," he said, releasing her and stepping back to open the fridge. "Do you want a drink?"

"Mm," she said vaguely. "I have to go down to Melbourne for my father's birthday that weekend."

Vincent turned around. "You can't go before or after?"

"I promised my mother, and besides I haven't seen them in ages," Anna explained. "I really have to go."

"Alright." He shrugged. "We'll go to Melbourne instead." He turned back to the fridge and took out a bottle of wine before closing the door again.

Anna was watching him. "You don't have to come with me."

"That's okay," he said, reaching for glasses in the cupboard above the bench. "I'll visit my folks. Hey, we could set up something so you can catch up with Bronwyn. That'd be a blast."

"Vincent, I have to spend the whole time with my parents. I owe them one lousy weekend."

He looked at her. "Okay."

"You should go to the festival, there's no reason you have to miss out just because I can't go."

"I don't mind going to Melbourne with you."

Anna went to say something, but decided against it. She turned back to the stove. Vincent put the glasses down on the bench and sighed. "I'm sorry, I didn't put that the right way. I'm happy to go to Melbourne, I want to go, there's nothing I'd rather do—"

"It's not that."

"Then what is it?"

She leaned back against the bench, folding her arms. "I just need to spend some time with my parents."

"Yeah . . . ?"

She hesitated. "It's just, well, they don't know you, Vincent."

"That's right," he said. "Because they haven't met me."

She didn't know what to say. Vincent was watching her intently.

"Right then, okay, I understand," he said calmly, tapping the counter-top. Then he breathed out heavily and walked around the bench and out of the kitchen.

Anna sighed, turning off the flame on the stove. She followed him out onto the deck. He was standing at the railing, looking out to the ocean.

"Hey," she said, coming up behind him. She pressed herself into his back, leaning her head against his shoulder and wrapping her arms around him. "Don't be cross. It's just not the right time."

Vincent took hold of her hands and eased them apart gently as he turned around to face her. "What are we doing, Anna?"

"What do you mean?"

"Are we dating, are we living together, are we going somewhere?"

"I thought we were having a good time," she said plainly.

He shook his head, he was clearly annoyed.

"Why are you getting angry?" said Anna.

"I'm not angry," he said. "Or, you know what, maybe I am, but so what? It's only a fucking emotion, Anna. Why are you so scared of emotions?"

"I'm not scared of emotions. What are you talking about?"

Vincent sighed, leaning back against the railing. "We've been together for what . . . a few months now? But I feel like I hardly know you."

Anna folded her arms across her chest defensively.

"Whatever I do know has come from your writing," he continued, "but you're not even doing that anymore. What's going on with you?"

"I'm relaxing and enjoying myself for the first time in a long while," Anna declared. "I don't want to analyze it, or to be analyzed, for that matter. Do you know all the years I had to put up with constant analysis of my flaws and defects?"

"No, I don't know about any of that, that's the thing."

"Well, I'm sorry but I can't help you. I don't want to be 'Anna, the infertile woman' anymore. I don't want that to define who I am."

"I don't give a shit about that, Anna. But that's not all there is to you. You've got an ex-husband you barely ever mention, parents you don't seem to have much contact with. You don't have a job, you're not writing, what the hell are you doing?"

"What's the matter, Vincent? Am I spoiling your fantasy? You have me up on a pedestal, exactly like Mac did. And I'm the one who takes the fall when you find out I'm not perfect."

"I don't think you're perfect, I don't expect you to be perfect, I just want you to be real. I want to connect with you."

"We do plenty of connecting, Vincent."

"Are you talking about the sex? Oh sure, we have plenty of sex, like you're trying to prove something. Yes, you're a sexual being, Anna, but you're not there. Most of the time it's like . . . well, you're just a warm body in the bed."

Anna glared at him. She felt a twisting sensation in her chest and it hurt. "I don't need this." She turned abruptly and marched back inside to the bedroom, picked up her overnight bag and tossed it on the bed.

She heard Vincent from the living room. "Anna, I'm sorry, that didn't come out right," he called, before appearing in the doorway. "What are you doing?"

She was ranging around the room, collecting up her things. "I think we need some space for a few days," she said, not looking at him.

"No," he said, coming toward her, "that's the last thing we need. What we need to do is work through this, and shout and yell if we have to, and then make up and make love—"

"But I'm just a warm body."

"I said I was sorry, Anna, I didn't mean it the way it sounded. What I was trying to say—"

"Don't bother, Vincent." She shoved the last of her things into the bag and picked it up. "Look, we obviously got our wires crossed here," she said coolly. "I was just having fun, I wasn't looking for anything serious."

"Don't say that, Anna."

"What? Don't tell you the truth? Let you keep living your fantasy?" she sniped, walking past him out of the room. She was up the hall at the front door when he called her name. She turned around.

"I didn't put you on a pedestal, Anna, you climbed up there yourself to keep out of reach. If you ever decide to come back down, you know where to find me."

She opened the door and walked out, closing it behind her.

Dee Why

"This is ungodly," said Georgie, opening the door.

"What is?" asked Liam.

"This hour of the morning."

"You better get used to it, I hear babies favor this time of day."

"Don't rub it in." She scowled, turning back into the flat.

Liam followed her. "Are you all set then?"

She nodded, bending to pick up her suitcase.

"I'll get that," he chided, grabbing the handle first. Georgie reached for her handbag, but he beat her to that as well.

"Liam, I think I can manage a handbag," she insisted.

"Look at the size of it," he said, holding it up. "And it's heavy. What have you got in here anyway?"

"A club for knocking you on the head when you annoy me. I think I need it now."

They drove to the airport in silence save for small talk about the traffic and the weather, the background of the car radio filling in any awkward gaps. Georgie had had second thoughts throughout the week. Why had she agreed to this? Yes, meeting his family was important, essential in fact. But it could have waited till after the birth, then at least the baby would be the focus. Georgie had thought she was so clever turning the tables on Liam, but now she wasn't so sure. She hadn't taken into account how much time they would be alone together.

After arriving at the airport and checking in, they had about a half hour before they could board the plane.

"Do you want something to drink? Coffee, or juice?" Liam asked her.

"No, coffee makes me sick these days." Georgie sighed. "I better not have anything, I'm worried about using the toilet on the plane."

"Why?"

"Have you seen the size of the cubicles? I keep having visions of getting wedged in and needing to be rescued."

Liam laughed. "I'm sure pregnant women have used the toilets without getting stuck. And fat people."

She pulled a face. "Thanks for that."

They boarded at first call and settled into their seats before takeoff.

"Hey there, Mum!" a chirpy steward announced, pausing in the aisle by her seat. "How long have you got to go?" he asked, crouching down to her level.

Georgie opened her mouth to answer, but Liam got in first. "Six and a half weeks."

The steward planted his hand on her stomach. "Your first?" he said rhetorically, looking from Georgie to Liam. "Do you know what you're having?"

"No," said Georgie, "I want it to be a surprise."

"Well, I'm Chad. You just sing out if you need anything, okay? Especially if you get stuck in the toilet!" He winked, standing up and continuing down the aisle.

Liam smiled faintly. "Does that bother you, complete strangers touching your stomach like that?"

Georgie shrugged. "It was a little weird at first, but I don't think people mean to be rude. It's kind of nice in a way."

Liam was contemplating the round bump of her belly.

"Go ahead," said Georgie.

He shook his head. "No, I didn't mean to put you on the spot."

"It's your baby."

"It's your body."

"Oh, for crying out loud, Liam." Georgie sighed, grabbing his hand and placing it squarely on her stomach. "I'll try to get him to kick for you," she said, prodding herself in the side.

"No, don't!" said Liam, alarmed.

"Relax, it won't hurt the baby," she assured him.

"What does it feel like?" Liam asked her.

"When he kicks?"

He nodded. "Does it hurt?"

"Not usually," said Georgie. "Occasionally he gives me a sharp one under the ribs or in the groin, that can be a bit of a shock. Louise said it gets more uncomfortable right at the end, but they usually don't kick as much then either."

"Why not?"

"There's not enough room left."

Liam shook his head, gazing down at her stomach, smoothing his hand gently over the curve. "It's amazing," he murmured.

"Mm . . ." Her eyes met his, only for a moment, but Georgie felt her heart quicken. She looked away and Liam removed his hand, settling back into his seat.

"So," he said after a while, "have you thought of any names?"

She shrugged. "I've thought of lots of names, but I haven't stuck on anything. I want to wait till I see the baby before I decide what name suits him or her."

"Fair enough."

"You ought to tell me any names you had picked out so I don't choose one of them."

Liam looked dejected. "Thanks."

"That came out wrong." Georgie winced. "The thing is, I don't think your wife would appreciate me naming the baby something you had chosen."

"I take your point," he said quietly.

Georgie looked at him. "Do you see her much?"

He shook his head. "No, I haven't seen her since . . . since I told her about the baby, actually."

"Oh, you never said, how did she take it?"

"Not so great."

"I wouldn't think so."

Liam looked out the window, but Georgie was not going to leave it at that.

"So how long ago was that?"

He glanced back at her. "A couple of weeks after you told me."

"And you haven't had any contact since?"

"I tried to call her a few times, but I only got the answering machine. I left it about a week and tried again. She obviously didn't want to talk to me."

Georgie was thinking. "Doesn't it feel weird, to be married that long, to see somebody every day of your life, and then suddenly you have no contact at all?"

"Yeah, I guess," he said vaguely.

"Do you miss her?"

"Georgie, these questions," he muttered, shaking his head.

"I just think it's odd that you could live with someone all those years and not miss their physical presence in your day-to-day life."

"But my day-to-day life has changed so radically—I'm not in the same house, the same job. Everything feels weird. It's like I'm living a whole different life."

Georgie nodded. "Tell me about her," she said suddenly.

"I'm sorry?"

"Tell me about Anna," she repeated. "How you met, when you got married, what she's like . . ."

Liam sighed. "Why do you want to know all that?"

"I'm curious."

"This is one of those situations where I can't win no matter what."

"What are you going on about?"

"If I say something nice about Anna, you're not going to like that, but if I say anything negative about her, you're not going to like that either."

"Hey, Liam," said Georgie, getting his attention. He looked at her. "Here's a concept. You could try telling the truth."

He seemed a little agitated. "I'm not the big fat liar you think I am, Georgie."

"I never said you were fat."

He frowned.

"I'm not trying to catch you out," said Georgie. "You can tell me everything, the good, the bad, the ugly. I want to understand what happened between you."

Liam considered her. He'd always wanted a chance to explain, to put his case to her. "What do you want to know?"

"You said that going through IVF ruined your marriage?" she asked. He nodded.

"Were you having problems before that? Sometimes couples think a baby's going to save their marriage."

Liam shrugged. "I wasn't aware of any problems. We were happy, we both loved our jobs, and when I was offered a promotion in Sydney, Anna was more excited than I was to make the move. We bought a great house, things were good . . . we were living the dream."

"The dream usually includes a family."

"I thought it would one day. But Anna was way ahead of me. When she didn't fall pregnant after a couple of years, she wanted to investigate, which was okay with me. But then she became driven, obsessed by the end. I think she would have done anything, you know. Even when our marriage was falling down around our ears, all she seemed to care about was getting back on the treatment." He paused. "And that's when it struck me, I didn't want to bring a baby into our lives the way things were. It wouldn't be fair—the expectations, the pressure on the poor kid would be ridiculous."

Georgie was watching him intently. He was staring ahead, almost talking to himself. She suddenly had a glimpse of the father he could be. "What was Anna like before?" she asked.

Liam groaned. "You're really pushing this, aren't you?"

"I'm just wondering if it changed her. Was she an obsessive type of person generally? Or was she more easygoing before it all happened?"

"I wouldn't say she was obsessive, but easygoing? I don't know." He shook his head doubtfully.

"How would you describe her then?" Georgie persisted. "What attracted you to her?"

Liam became thoughtful again. "She was very beautiful, she still is. And she was elegant and poised and . . . exactly what I was looking for at the time."

"What do you mean?"

"Well . . ." He hesitated. "You have to understand it was very important to me back then to move ahead, for every decision or choice I made to take me farther up the ladder," he tried to explain. "Marrying Anna moved me up quite a few rungs."

Georgie curled her lip. "You married her for her money?"

"No," he assured her, "I made my own money. But I think I married her, at least partly, because she had money, or she was brought up with it. She was used to it. She had breeding, I suppose."

"You're making her sound like a horse."

"You asked me to be honest and I'm only telling it like it is. Or was," he added. "Don't get me wrong, I did love her, of course I did. I was awestruck when we first met. And we were a good fit. We liked the same things, we enjoyed each other's company. I was content. It wasn't until . . ." He hesitated, glancing at Georgie. "It was only later that I realized there wasn't any passion. You know what they say, you can't miss something you've never had. But once you have, you find it hard to live without."

Georgie felt herself going pink. She sat back in her chair, staring fixedly ahead.

"You were the one who wanted to open the can of worms," he muttered.

"Well, let's close it again then," she said tightly, taking a magazine from the pocket in front of her and pretending to become absorbed in it. She wasn't going to listen to tired old lines about his loveless marriage, his wife not understanding him, blah, blah. He had a duty to work on his marriage, not abandon it when the going got tough. Was that the kind of father he was going to be? A fair-weather dad, happy to be around when the child was cute and compliant, nowhere to be found when he grew into a back-talking, difficult teenager . . . who would be even more trouble without a father around?

"You do realize a child's forever," Georgie said suddenly.

"I'm sorry?" said Liam, startled.

She took a breath and gathered her thoughts. "A child is forever. You can't divorce a child."

He looked at her seriously. "I know that, Georgie."

"Whatever happens."

"Whatever happens."

"Even when he's older. You know, I lost my parents when I was sixteen, and it wasn't their fault or anything, but it was hard. I still needed them."

"I realize that."

"So you have to keep that in mind, you know, when you get into any relationships in the future—"

"What?"

"Whoever she is will have to be made aware that you've got a prior commitment—"

"That's not going to happen."

"What?" Georgie looked at him.

"A relationship."

"How do you know that?"

"I know."

"What, never?"

"I'm not going to have this conversation with you."

"But—"

"Georgie, just drop it, okay?" he said firmly.

He looked back at his magazine, flipping over a page. They barely spoke for the rest of the flight.

Liam had organized a hire car, so he deposited Georgie in the passenger pickup bay and ordered her to sit there and not move or try to carry anything until he returned with the car.

"You're not wearing your seat belt," he remarked as they drove off.

"You know, technically, I don't actually have to wear a—"

"Put it on."

"It's not required by law when you're pregnant."

"Georgie, I'm going to pull over unless you put on that seat belt."

"Alright, alright, Mr. Bossy Big Boots." She frowned, sliding the belt around her. "Do you always come over all big-brother-like the closer you get to home?"

"I'm only concerned about your safety."

Georgie reclined her seat back a little, resting her hands on top of her belly and tapping her fingers. "So, am I going to get to meet all nine siblings this weekend?"

"Well, I'm one of the nine," Liam reminded her. "And my youngest brother is overseas, two of my sisters are interstate and another brother lives up in the Dandenongs."

"Will I meet the rest?"

"I don't know, I told Mum not to make a fuss. I didn't think you'd want to be inundated with my relatives."

"But I wouldn't mind checking out the gene pool, see if there's any good looks or brains in the family."

Liam looked sideways at her.

"I'd even settle for a sense of humor," she muttered.

They drove on along the drab, endless freeway, looking at drab, endless scenery. "How long is it going to take to get there?" Georgie asked after a while.

"About forty-five minutes. They live in Abbotsford, near Richmond."

"Oh."

Liam glanced over at her. "Do you know Melbourne?"

"No."

"Well, I've been meaning to warn you, my family's very working class."

"What does that mean?"

"You know, my brothers are tradesmen," he explained. "My sisters have worked in service industries mostly. I was the only one who went to university."

"So?"

"Well, I just thought I should warn you."

"There it is, you said it again." Georgie was incredulous. "You're such a boofhead sometimes, Liam."

He looked at her, alarmed. "Why, what's wrong?"

"In case you've never put two and two together, I've worked in a shop since I left school and I never went to university."

"That's only because your parents died."

"No it isn't. I wouldn't have gone to university even if they were alive."

"But you own the shop."

"Yeah, because I got an inheritance to pay for my share and my much smarter partner runs the show. I just work there."

"There's nothing wrong with that."

"Which is exactly what I'm saying!" she declared. "Don't you dare 'warn' me about your working-class family as if they're something . . . that needs warning about!"

"Georgie, I'm only trying to prepare you," he persisted. "I told you the house isn't much—"

"Liam—"

"Your father was an architect, mine's a fitter and turner—"

"Okay, stop now!"

"I'm only—"

"Not another word, Liam!" Georgie said, holding up her hand. "You're pissing me off. If you don't speak again for the rest of the trip, I might get over it by the time we get there."

"I wish you hadn't said that."

"Why?" She frowned, looking at him.

"Because there's something else I have to tell you and I know it's going to piss you off."

"Then keep it to yourself."

"I can't," he said seriously. He pulled the car over to the side of the road and cut the engine. "I'm just going to say it and then you can yell at me, okay?"

Georgie crossed her arms, listening.

"My mother thinks we're together." He paused, waiting for a response. "You and me. Together. You know—"

"I get it, Liam," Georgie interrupted. "How did she come to that conclusion? Oh, no, wait, let me work it out. Perhaps because you didn't tell her the truth? Could that be it? Honestly, Liam, you couldn't lie straight in bed."

"I didn't lie to her, she just assumed—"

"What a load of—"

"Georgie!" he said, raising his voice. She glared at him. He took a breath. "I did tell her the truth," he said firmly. "I told her that when things were going bad with Anna, I met a wonderful woman, and even though the timing was all wrong, I knew she was the love of my life. But it all blew up in my face before I had a chance to work it out, and I lost her. And maybe I deserved to."

He paused. Georgie didn't say anything. She was just staring at him, barely breathing.

"And when I told her about the baby . . . Well, she knew how I felt and she started getting her hopes up for me. So when I said we were coming to visit and you insisted on staying at the house, she jumped to the conclusion we'd worked things out. She was so thrilled, I didn't have the heart to tell her . . . she even started asking if we were going to get married—"

"You didn't tell her we were going to get married, did you?"

"No, I said we were taking it slowly, we wanted to do the right thing by the baby. That's the truth, isn't it?"

"Mm," Georgie grunted. "Liam MacMullen's own brand of the truth." She paused. "I hate this, you know how much I hate lying."

"I know."

"But I don't want to upset your poor mother either."

Liam was clenching the steering wheel, an anxious frown on his face.

"Alright, relax," Georgie relented. "I'll play your little game, just for this weekend. But no lovey-dovey crap, okay?"

"Okay . . . I promise."

"I mean, there's really no reason for us to lie outright, we just don't have to say anything."

Liam glanced warily at her.

"God, I'm starting to sound like you." Georgie groaned.

"I'm sorry for putting you in this position," he said seriously.

Georgie looked over at him. He was rubbing his forehead. He did that a lot when he was stressed. "Don't worry about it." She sighed. "Besides, there may be a positive side. At least I can boss you around for a change."

He started up the car and pulled out onto the freeway again. "We'll see about that," he muttered.

It was midmorning by the time they pulled up outside a single-fronted weatherboard cottage. It was painted a shade of green that had probably looked fresh and bright about twenty years ago, and a couple of spindly shrubs languished in the front garden. Georgie was trying to figure out how a family of eleven had all fit inside.

"It's charming," she remarked.

Liam grunted. "And you say I can't lie straight in bed." He got out of the car and walked around to the passenger side as Georgie was opening her door. She took the hand he offered as she stepped out onto the curb and stood up straight, arching to stretch her back. They heard a bang and turned to see his mother coming down the steps as the screen door she had flung open swung back into place with another loud bang. She hurried toward them, waving and singing out hello.

"Slow down, Mum," said Liam, shaking his head. "She only has two speeds, asleep and flat out."

"What's that you're saying, Liam?" she asked.

"Nothing," he said, holding his arms out to her. "How are you, Mum?"

She beamed as he drew her close into a hug. Georgie smiled, watching them. Moira MacMullen was a slightly plump woman, probably a little shorter than Georgie, with wiry grey hair that bore the remnants of a perm. She wore a simple shirtmaker dress topped with a blue pinafore-style apron. Georgie couldn't see Liam in her at all. Moira turned, smiling broadly at her.

"And this is Georgie!" she declared, reaching both hands out and grasping her tummy.

"Mum!" Liam protested.

"I'm only getting to know my grandchild," she said. "Georgie doesn't mind, do you, love?"

"Of course not." She smiled. "If Chad the flight attendant helped himself, then I certainly think Grandma's allowed."

"Nan," said Moira. "That's what the grandkids call us. Nan and Pop."

"Nan it is then."

Moira continued enthusiastically kneading Georgie's stomach.

"Mum, what are you doing?" Liam frowned.

"I'm working out the sex of the baby," she said, matter-of-factly. "It's all in the way they lie. I'm not as good as Great-Auntie Tess, remember

Auntie Tess, Liam? Picked all you lot, and all your cousins." She paused, concentrating hard on Georgie's belly. "I'd lay bets it's a boy."

"Do you think?" said Georgie, wide-eyed.

"Next we'll be lighting candles and swinging chains above her—"

"Liam, we will do the wedding ring test, just to make sure. Oh, but you haven't got a wedding ring yet," she said, looking plaintively at Georgie. Then she covered her mouth with her hand. "That was very naughty of me, I won't say another word on the subject. I'll just keep praying silently and hope for the best."

"Christ, Mum, we've been here five minutes—"

"And you're already taking the Lord's name in vain! You should know better, Liam."

"I apologize, Mum."

"And I don't want to have to tell you again," she said sternly. She turned to Georgie, her whole face a smile. "I couldn't wait to meet you, Georgie. Liam was tripping over his own tongue singing your praises to me on the phone."

Georgie glanced over at him, and he shrugged sheepishly.

"Now, how about a cup of tea?"

"Oh," Georgie swooned, "I'd kill for a cup of tea. I haven't had anything to drink all morning."

"Pregnancy bladder, eh?"

"Mum—"

"I had nightmares I'd get stuck in the toilet on the plane," Georgie confided.

Moira laughed loudly. "Oh, you're gorgeous. She's gorgeous, Liam." She linked her arm through Georgie's. "Now come and meet Liam's dad and we'll have that cup of tea."

"I'll just get the bags then," said Liam to no one as they walked off down the path. He entered the house a few minutes later, struck as always by the distinctive aroma; a blend of stale cigarette smoke, dampness, the smell of secondhand furniture and worn carpet, of never quite having enough. The redolence of his childhood. Familiar, but hardly comforting. He loved seeing his mum, but this house . . . just walking in made the hair on the back of his neck stand up.

"Liam!" Moira was calling. "Bring the bags straight in, I'm just show-ing Georgie where you'll be sleeping. I've put you in yours and Danny and Bren's old room."

Liam stepped into the hall as she threw open the door.

"It's so cramped with the double bed," she went on, "you have to leave the room to change your mind. But you'll find the bed's quite comfort-able, Georgie. I put nice clean sheets on this morning."

"Thank you."

"Do you need a lie-down now, pet? Put your feet up for a while?"

"No, I'm fine," Georgie assured her.

"Righto then." Moira smiled. "I'll put the kettle on. Liam, show her where the bathroom is. Come along to the kitchen when you're ready."

After she left them alone they stood for a while not saying anything, contemplating the bed.

"I'll sleep on the floor," said Liam eventually.

Georgie considered the narrow space around the bed. "Where?"

"Or . . ." He hesitated. "I'll sleep out on the lounge."

"What's your mother going to think?"

"Um, I'll wait till they've gone to bed, and I'll say you were uncom-fortable—"

"Oh, for heaven's sake, Liam." Georgie sighed. "This is not a fifties movie and I'm not Doris Day. Are you forgetting how I got this way in the first place?"

He looked sheepish.

"I think I can cope sharing a bed with you, there certainly won't be any sex happening."

"Understood," he said seriously. "I assure you that was never going to happen here anyway. Walls are paper thin."

"It was never going to happen, period, Liam."

"Of course." He nodded. "Come on, I'll show you the bathroom."

When they walked into the kitchen, Moira had her back to them, making the tea. His father was seated at the table with the newspaper open to the racing guide.

"Hello, Son."

Liam stirred. "Dad." He nodded, leaning across the table to shake his hand. "This is Georgie," he added awkwardly.

"Call me Bill, darl," he said, moving to get up.

"No, please," said Georgie, "don't get up." She walked around the table and shook his hand. "Well, I know who you take after, Liam. I feel like I'm looking at you in twenty years."

Bill MacMullen had lived a much harder life than his son, so perhaps it would take a little longer than twenty years, but the likeness was un-mistakable. The craggy, leathery skin and the red bulbous nose did not disguise that it was the same line of the nose, the set of the jaw, the chin, the eyes.

"Except for the baldness," Moira broke in, placing the teapot on a stand in the middle of the table. "Baldness passes down through the fe-male and my father died at eighty-eight years of age with a full head of hair. So you don't have to worry, Georgie, Liam won't be losing his hair."

Georgie grinned slyly at him as she took a seat next to his father. At least she seemed amused by all this.

"But as for your little fella," Moira went on, "his fate in the hair stakes is going to come from you, Georgie. Your father got a good head of hair?"

"Mum—"

"It's alright, Liam," said Georgie. "My father died when I was sixteen."

"Oh no," exclaimed Moira, dropping into the chair beside Georgie and taking hold of her hand. "That's awful. Your poor mother."

Georgie took a breath. "They both died actually, in a car accident."

Moira looked horrified. "Jesus, Mary and Joseph, what a tragic thing. What happened to you, pet? Did you have relatives to take care of you?"

"My brother was twenty-two so he was able to look after my sister and me."

"You have a sister and a brother as well?" Moira sighed. "You poor pets."

"So," said Georgie, attempting to move the conversation along, "that makes you this little one's only grandparents."

"Dad," Liam said stiffly, "would you mind not smoking around the baby?"

Bill stopped with a cigarette midway to his lips. "Baby's not here yet," he muttered.

"It's okay," said Georgie. "I'll just leave the room."

"No, love," Bill said, slipping the cigarette behind his ear. "I can wait."

At lunchtime Liam's brothers converged on the house along with their wives and about a half dozen kids between them. Danny and Brendan were big, burly, gregarious men who took turns smacking their brother on the back and ribbing him—"So you've finally managed to get one knocked up?" "We thought you were shooting blanks all this time!" To which Liam would wince, Moira would shake her head and order them to stop, as would their wives. And then they'd all apologize profusely to Georgie.

She hadn't taken offense so much for herself, but Georgie was mortified for Liam's sake. He must never have told his family the truth. Surely his brothers wouldn't have said anything like that if they'd known about the IVF. Georgie felt a little sorry for Liam at that moment.

After a noisy, riotous meal, a cricket game was announced and Georgie sprung up and out the door along with the rabble. It took Liam a minute to catch up with her.

"You're not playing, Georgie," he said sternly.

"Oh, let her have a hit," said Danny.

"That's exactly what I'm worried about—you getting hit with a ball. You're a little harder to miss these days."

Georgie made a face at him. "You have such a way with words, Liam," she said.

"Yeah, lay off her," Brendan jeered. "Jeez, who died and made you dictator?"

"He's always been a dick," Danny muttered.

"Shut up, you two. Liam's right," said Trudy. "You haven't seen these fools play, Georgie, you're better off keeping well out of the way."

Liam planted his arm firmly around her and marched her to the back of the house. Georgie brought her arm around his waist and felt for the flesh between his hip and ribs. "I could pinch you now and there's nothing you could do about it," she said under her breath.

"And I could kiss you now and there's nothing you could do about it," he returned. "So behave."

He deposited her on a garden bench next to his sisters-in-law and sauntered off to join the game. Moira came out the back door wiping her hands on her apron.

"World Series underway yet?" she asked, just as a couple of red-headed children ran into the yard from the side of the house, singing out to the other kids.

"Oh, Bridgie's here," exclaimed Moira, obviously delighted.

As if on cue, a woman appeared around the corner of the house, dressed in what looked like a nurse's uniform. "Declan, Caitlin," she called. "I hope you two said hello to Nan before you started playing."

The two redheads raced over and flung their arms around Moira, firing off "Hi, Nan," "Hi, Auntie Trude," "Hi, Auntie Chris," before scampering off again.

"Hey, Liam, get back here," Brendan called as Liam made his way over. "You're deserting midwicket."

"Declan can handle it," Liam called over his shoulder as his nephew passed him, high-fiving him on the way. "Hey, Bridge!" he exclaimed, clearly as pleased as his mother to see her. He gave her a warm hug and brought her over to meet Georgie.

"No, don't get up!" Bridget insisted, but Georgie was already on her feet.

"It's okay, I'm not an invalid," Georgie assured her.

"Just very pregnant!" Bridget declared, smiling widely, exactly like her mother. Georgie had an idea she was looking at Moira twenty years ago, and she had obviously once possessed a gorgeous mane of auburn hair. "I've been dying to meet you, Georgie. Liam can't stop going on about you."

"Where's Mick, love?" Moira asked.

"I told you, he had to drop the kids to me at the end of my shift so he wouldn't be late for work."

"Like ships in the night those two," Moira remarked to Georgie.

"Mick's a security guard so they both work shifts. They never see each other."

"That's probably what keeps us together, Mum," Bridget joked. "Is Dad inside?"

"He just ducked out to the OTB, love, he'll be back in a little while."

"Couldn't stay away for one afternoon," Liam muttered, shaking his head.

"Don't start, Liam," said Moira. "The man works hard, he's entitled to a couple of hours to himself. Now, Bridgie, have you eaten, love? Come and we'll put the kettle on. Chris made some kind of fancy cake— what did you call it, love?"

"It's a hummingbird cake, Moira."

"Wait till you see it, I think I put on a pound just looking at it."

At eight o'clock Georgie stood under a hot shower, almost falling asleep on her feet. The afternoon had been filled with cricket and cake and laughter, and so many cups of tea Georgie thought she'd float away in the end. Bill came back eventually, obviously sozzled, but harmless enough, sitting quietly in a corner watching the action. The families left one by one soon after, Bridget being the last to go after Liam spent the longest time out front saying goodbye to her. Moira suggested soup and toast for supper, but Georgie insisted she couldn't fit another thing in and all she wanted was a shower and bed.

Reluctantly she turned off the taps and stepped out of the recess. When she walked back into the bedroom, Liam had his bag open on the bed.

"How was the shower?" he asked.

"Glorious."

"Well, if you're finished with the bathroom . . ."

"Sure, go right ahead."

Georgie tossed her things on top of her bag and fell backward onto the bed, sighing loudly.

"Are you okay?" Liam asked, dropping his bag in the corner.

"I'm exhausted," said Georgie, "in a good way. Except for my feet, they're killing me." She groaned, levering herself up to sit.

Liam came around to her side and propped the pillows against the headboard for her. Georgie was settling herself back when, unexpectedly, he scooped up her feet and sat down, resting them on his lap.

"What are you doing?" she asked.

"I was going to give you a foot rub," he faltered. "You don't want me to?"

"Oh, no, I love having my feet rubbed. I just don't have anyone to do it."

"You do tonight," he said as he began to gently massage one foot. Georgie felt the relief almost instantly. He was good. He must have had a lot of practice.

"Did you do this for Anna?"

He grunted. "No, she hated anyone touching her feet. But I used to do it for Mum. I was only a kid, but she was always pregnant and her feet used to swell up. She liked to lie back in her recliner chair and watch the news after tea, and I'd sit at the end and rub her feet." He smiled faintly.

"Your mother's wonderful," said Georgie. "The whole family is."

He shrugged. "You fit right in, Georgie. I don't know how you do it so easily. I've never felt like I fit in."

"That's only because you put yourself above them."

Liam looked a little abashed. "I don't mean to."

"Oh, don't worry, they all love you—"

"Love to give me a hard time. Danny and Bren think I'm a wanker."

Georgie laughed lazily. The foot rub was almost putting her to sleep.

"Bridget's your favorite?"

"You worked that out?" He smiled. "Danny and Bren came straight after me, and they've always been the same, loud and wild. Bridge was the first one I could actually relate to. We've always been close." He paused. "She thinks you're great."

"Then it's mutual."

Liam turned his head to look at her and smiled. Georgie left her body for a second, seeing herself lying there, pregnant with his child, on the bed they were going to share that night, while he rubbed her feet. It felt like déjà vu. She must have dreamed this once. Tears suddenly rose up in her throat and she sighed tremulously as they spilled into her eyes.

"What's the matter?" Liam asked, concerned. He stopped massaging. "Did I hurt you?"

She shook her head, she couldn't speak. He lifted her feet off his lap and came closer, watching her with a worried frown on his face. "What's wrong, Georgie?" he said tenderly.

She wiped her eyes with the back of her hands. "Nothing, really, I told you I cry at the drop of a hat. I think I'm just exhausted."

"Come on then, lie down properly, under the covers."

"But I haven't said goodnight—"

"I'll say goodnight for you," he said, helping her into bed. He drew the covers back over her and paused for a moment, stroking her hair. "Are you sure you're alright? Do you want me to stay?"

"No, really, I'm fine," Georgie murmured, her eyes drooping.

"Okay," he said, his voice soft. "Sleep tight." He stood up and switched off the light, closing the door behind him as he left the room.

About five minutes later Georgie blinked, squinted, then closed her eyes again. The room was light, Liam must have come back from the shower. She opened her eyes again slowly and realized it was daylight. The baby was doing his morning workout, she should have realized. Liam was lying beside her, but his head was lowered so she couldn't see his face. She yawned, stretching one arm above her head, and he looked up at her. He must have already been awake.

"Hi," he said in a hushed voice, his eyes wide. "The baby's moving, can't you feel it?"

She nodded. "He's most active while I'm sleeping," she said, almost miming the words. "If I move or speak, he stops."

"So don't move or speak," Liam whispered urgently. "Will he stop if I speak?"

She shook her head.

"I was lying facing the other way this morning," he said, his voice low, "and, well, your stomach was pressed right up against my back, I guess there's not a lot of room in here. Anyway I thought you were poking me, and I kept asking you what you wanted. You didn't answer so I turned over and you were sound asleep. And then I saw the baby move, through your clothes and everything. It's amazing. . . ."

Georgie smiled. "Then get a load of this." She lifted her top up slowly, exposing her belly. The surface of her skin quivered and quaked, lumps and bumps protruding and retreating again. Liam was clearly awestruck, and watching him watching her, Georgie couldn't help feeling proud, and emotional, and a little overwhelmed. She reached for his hand and drew it over onto her stomach, right at the site of a nice, rhythmic kick. Liam looked up at her again, his eyes glassy. Georgie left her hand on his, and they lay very still, very close while their baby wriggled and jiggled around, oblivious to the outside world. And for a brief moment so were his parents.

Suddenly a knock at the door made Georgie jump. Liam removed his hand abruptly and turned over, swinging his feet off the bed as he sat up. Georgie pulled her top back down over her stomach.

"It's only me," came his mother's voice. "Are you decent?"

"Come in, Mum." Liam sighed.

The door opened and Moira poked her head in. "I thought Georgie might like a nice cup of tea."

"Thank you, Moira," said Georgie, struggling to sit up with all the aplomb of a beached whale.

"Help her, Liam!"

He turned and took hold of Georgie under the arm, hoisting her up the bed.

"That's better," said Moira. "Here you go, love," she added, handing Georgie the cup.

"What about me?" Liam asked.

"I'm sure you can find your way to the kitchen, Son." She turned back to Georgie. "How did you sleep, pet?"

"You know when you close your eyes and open them again and it's morning?"

"I'm so glad." Moira smiled. "That means there's nothing to put you off coming again."

"Mum—"

"You're still here, Liam?"

"Well, I would like to get dressed before I leave the room."

"Oh, for heaven's sake, Liam, as if your father could care less about seeing you in your pajamas."

Liam sighed, standing up. He was reluctant to leave them alone. He didn't know what his mother was going to come out with next.

Moira smiled warmly at Georgie after Liam had left the room. "It's been such a treat having you here, pet. I feel like you're part of the family already."

"You've all been so lovely and welcoming."

"Well, it's a big deal. Liam's never brought a girl home before."

Georgie was aghast. "But he was married!"

Moira shrugged. "Oh, he and Anna took us out for dinner a couple of times before the wedding, then they asked us over to their house after that . . . on occasion."

Georgie was barely able to comprehend what she was hearing. How could he never have brought Anna to the house? And what was more unsettling, why had he invited her?

"Liam's always been a little, I don't know, set apart," Moira went on. "Probably because he's so smart, he's got more brains than the rest of us put together, I reckon. Not that he didn't work hard, mind you. He was so determined to pull himself up by the bootstraps, and maybe he got a little above himself with Anna, who's to say? But see, now I'm gossiping and I didn't come in here to gossip. I just wanted you to know that it's been lovely to meet you. I have the best feeling about you two."

Georgie felt uncomfortable. Moira had been so kind, opening her home and her heart to her, and Georgie was deceiving her.

"You're probably thinking I'm a silly old thing—"

Georgie grabbed her hand. "I don't, I promise, Moira, I don't think that at all."

"Thank you, dear," said Moira, patting her hand. "I know everything's not quite right between the two of you, but I really believe you'll work it out. Liam loves you with all his heart, that much I know for sure."

* * *

"You planned all this so I'd feel obliged or something, didn't you?"

Georgie was addled by her conversation with Moira, and she brought it up with Liam the minute they were alone in the car on the way to the airport.

"What are you talking about, Georgie?"

"You could have told me what a big deal it would be," she said. "You never even took Anna home."

Liam glanced across at her. "Mum told you that?"

"Yes, she did. And I could hardly believe it."

"Look, I didn't think Anna would . . . understand them," Liam tried to explain.

"So she's as big a snob as you," Georgie said bluntly. "You've got this wonderful, big, loud, happy family. How can you be ashamed of them?"

"I'm not ashamed. But we weren't that happy."

"Look, Liam, I know you didn't have much money and your dad drank a bit. But everyone seems to have pulled through alright. Except for you with the big chip on your shoulder."

He sighed loudly. "Well, you don't know everything about everyone, so maybe you should keep your opinions to yourself until you have the facts."

Georgie just looked at him.

"Yeah, Dad used to drink 'a bit,' and he also used to hit Mum 'a bit.' She coped with it by having more and more babies, tying herself down so completely she could never get out. I suppose he seemed harmless to you, but truth is he's old and tired and I don't think he can be bothered anymore. He just drinks himself into oblivion every night, which you conveniently missed because you fell asleep. And Bridget's husband's a dickhead. He abuses her, but she won't leave him either, like mother like daughter. I've offered to give her money, set her up on her own, she won't take it. Then there's Kevin, he lives up in the mountains. He's had a drug problem since he was a kid, he's on the methadone program till the next time he flips out. He doesn't want to be helped, I've tried. Angela's in Queensland, she's had three kids to three different blokes and now she's with another one. I've offered her money too, she never has any trouble taking it. Kathleen was working in Alice Springs last anyone heard, but she tries not to have too much contact with the family, probably for good reason. Unlike Therese, my youngest sister, who shows up whenever she needs money or somewhere to stay, and manages to start a family feud every time, which stresses poor Mum no end. Finally there's Sean, who, thank Christ, seems to be pretty levelheaded. He's talking about taking some classes at university when he gets back from overseas, I told him to be sure and let me know and I'll help him out."

Georgie didn't know what to say. She felt like crying. "I'm sorry."

"It's alright," he said. "You weren't to know. But things aren't always as they seem, Georgie."

She looked across at him. "No, they're not."

They spent most of the trip caught up in their own thoughts. Georgie was tired and bewildered, but mostly sad. Her mind was churning, thinking about his mother, and Bridget, the lives they were leading. And Liam, trying to look after everybody.

She slept on the plane and felt a bit unsteady when they landed in Sydney. Liam made her sit for a while and sip orange juice while he collected their bags. She didn't argue with him. As they left the airport and headed north, he looked across at her.

"How are you feeling now?"

"I'm fine, really," she assured him.

He took a breath. "There's something I've been meaning to ask you, Georgie."

"What is it?"

"Do you have some kind of plan for when you go into labor?"

"You mean like a 'birth plan'?" she asked. "I don't know about them, I think they're one of those things that only sound good on paper. Louise drew up a birth plan when she was having Molly, but she tore it up halfway through. She was going to make Nick eat it, because he was reading it out to her at the time."

Liam smiled. He seemed more relaxed now. "I was only wondering what you had organized for getting to the hospital, that kind of thing."

"Oh, that's all fine, I'm covered. Louise is going to be my support person, I was hers when she had the girls."

"Oh, not Nick?"

"He was there, of course, he's just a bit hopeless. Can't stand to see Louise in pain. Any of us, really. He falls apart."

Liam was thoughtful. "So you'll have to phone Louise to come and get you?"

Georgie nodded.

"Isn't that a bit risky?"

"Risky? How?"

"Well, you're on your own. What if you can't get to Louise? Or what if the pain is so bad you can't even get to a phone?"

Georgie was smiling at him, shaking her head. "What do you think's going to happen? It's not like in the movies, Liam. Bang, one contraction and you're off to hospital. It's much slower than that. With Louise we were hanging around the house for hours before she got going. And then we were hanging around the hospital for even longer."

"But you might go quicker, you never know. You should have backup."

"Are you saying you want me to call you?"

He glanced across at her. "Just as a backup."

Georgie had been wondering if this was going to come up. "Truth is, Liam, I don't know how I'm going to feel when I'm in labor. I might want everyone I know with me, or I mightn't want anybody, I've never been through it before."

"I'm not talking about when you're in labor, Georgie, I wouldn't even presume to ask. I just want to make sure you get to the hospital safely. All I'm suggesting is that you put me on the list so you've got another option."

"Liam, you were always on that list."

When they got to her flat, Liam didn't have to insist on carrying her bag up the stairs, Georgie knew the drill by now. Besides, she appreciated it. She was tired. And when she opened the door, she didn't feel that welcome relief she normally did coming home from a time away. She felt lonely.

Liam walked inside and put her bag down, then picked it up again straightaway. "I'll put it in your room."

"Liam . . ."

But he was already walking into the hall. He reappeared a moment later. "So you're alright?" he asked. "Is there anything you need?"

She shook her head. "Thanks for taking me . . . for everything."

He hesitated. He was dragging his feet he knew, but he was reluctant to leave. His flat was going to feel very empty tonight, his bed even emptier.

And then Georgie came toward him and kissed him softly on the cheek, and then she hugged him. It was only brief. But it was enough.

October

Anna stood as she spotted Doug walking down the street toward the café. It was her suggestion to meet here, she didn't feel ready to go to the clinic. Though she was going to have to get over that.

"Anna." He smiled, grasping both her hands and kissing her on the cheek. "Good to see you."

"How are you, Doug?" she asked as they sat down.

"I can't complain."

"How's the practice?"

"Going along fine. Though we miss you."

Anna was glad to hear that. They spent the next few minutes checking the menu and ordering lunch. Anna was going to ask for a glass of wine, but when Doug declined she thought it best to follow his lead.

"So, to what do I owe this pleasure?" he asked after the waitress had left.

"I just wanted to see you," Anna insisted. "We used to see each other nearly every day. I wanted to catch up."

He eyed her dubiously. "So now the flattery's out of the way . . ."

"I do want to catch up, Doug, but I'll be honest, I also wanted to talk to you about coming back to work."

He frowned slightly. "It wasn't that long ago you told me you wanted the rest of the year off."

"Yes, I realize that, but things have changed. I was avoiding making any decisions at the time, I was even considering not coming back at all."

"That's what I suspected."

"But I don't know what I was thinking, Doug. I could never quit, seriously. Having had the break and some time to sort things out, I think I can return fresh now and see how I go."

Anna was not quite sure what to make of Doug's expression. She didn't think he was entirely disposed to her idea. The waitress returned with their drinks and left again. Doug took a sip of his mineral water.

"Tell me what you've been doing with yourself, Anna," he said.

She expected this, a kind of quasi-supervision session. Doug needed to work out where she was at now, if she was capable of counseling people in crisis. She had first to convince him she had made it through her own.

"Well, I sold the house and moved into a townhouse in Neutral Bay. But you already knew that. And I took your idea to heart, not folk art, but I did join a writing class."

"Did you?" He seemed intrigued. "What kind of writing class, may I ask?"

"Oh, you know, the kind people go to when they think they've got the great Australian novel in them."

"Is that what you thought?"

"No," she scoffed. Don't have him thinking you're delusional. "I went for fun."

"Why a writing class?"

"My mother reminded me that I was an avid keeper of journals as a girl. I went back and read some of them. They certainly gave me an avenue to express myself, even vent emotions I was possibly suppressing at the time." That sounded insightful but professional.

"So you thought taking up writing could bring some level of self-awareness?"

Think about it, Anna. Don't sound like a self-help manual.

"I did it for fun, Doug, first and foremost. But I do think it helped me explore some issues. I wrote a little about what happened between Mac and me, about my desire for a child."

"Did you come to any conclusions?"

Conclusions would be too neat. Too half-hour sitcom. Anna joined a writing class, found the answers to life and lived happily ever after.

"It gave me a chance to reflect, I suppose, writing it down, reading it over. I think perhaps it gave me some closure."

She noticed Doug's eyebrow lift, almost imperceptibly. Shit. Was that good or bad? She used to be able to read his body language better than this. The waiter returned, setting their plates down in front of them. Anna really wished she could have ordered a drink.

"Have you kept it up?" Doug asked. "Are you still taking the class?"

Anna paused, her fork poised above her salad. She had deliberated over what to say about Vincent, if anything, and had decided in the end that a casual relationship would signify she was moving on, opening herself up to new experiences. Not afraid of intimacy, that kind of thing. She was hoping she could pull it off now.

"Well, I had to stop the class because, as it turned out"—she paused, fixing a coy smile on her lips—"I ended up having a fling with the teacher."

Now both Doug's eyebrows lifted quite perceptibly. He seemed surprised, but perhaps that was good. Something he hadn't expected of her.

"To be frank with you, I think I had almost completely lost any sense of myself as a sexual being. Having a little affair of my own helped me to restore some of that sense. It was very affirming."

"I hope you don't mind me asking, but do the words 'affair of my own' suggest an element of getting back at Mac?"

"No, of course not," Anna denied. "Mac didn't even know I was seeing someone."

"You kept it from him?"

"No . . ." She hesitated. "It's just, we haven't spoken in a while. We don't really have a reason to."

Doug nodded. "Has he moved back to Melbourne?"

"Last I heard he was still here. I expect he'll stay."

"Why is that?"

Anna swallowed. She still found it hard to say. "He's having a child . . . with the woman . . ." Her voice trailed off.

Doug was watching her. Lunch with an old work colleague morphing into supervision morphing into counseling. It wasn't meant to go this way.

"How does that make you feel?"

Resentful. Jealous. Angry. Envious. Bitter.

"I haven't thought about it that much actually, Doug."

Wrong answer. She could see it in his eyes.

"I'd imagine news like that would be very painful, considering what you've been through."

"Oh, don't get me wrong," she assured him. "I did have a hard time of it at first. But then I worked through it. I wrote about it, processed it. And around the same time, Vincent and I started seeing each other."

"Has the baby been born yet?"

"You know, I'm not sure, Doug," she lied. Anna had lain awake at night thinking about it. She knew it had to be soon. "Maybe, I guess it can't be far off."

Doug nodded, he seemed thoughtful. Why hadn't she just been honest with him? It didn't make her incompetent because she was in pain. In fact, she was probably more capable of empathizing with clients. She should have taken a completely different tack. She should have been honest. But then she would have had to admit she wanted to come back because she had nothing else.

"You know, Anna," Doug said after a while, "work can provide a refuge during times of loss or uncertainty. But we don't have that option, not in our line of work."

She'd been found out. How could she ever have imagined otherwise?

"You know how I feel about you, Anna. I have enormous respect for you and your ability, your professionalism." He paused. "And I'm sure you realize we had to put someone on to replace you in a more permanent capacity, when you asked for the rest of the year off."

"Of course, Doug."

"So, we have to allow her the time and space to establish herself, see if we all suit one another," he added. "If you decide you're still interested, you're welcome to attend client conferences, ease your way back in over time. For now I'd suggest you keep up with the writing. I think it sounds like it might be good for you."

Doug was palming her off. She didn't blame him. He was only trying to save her embarrassment. But after she left him and went home and opened a bottle of wine, she sat in the cold, sterile little box and wondered about her cold, sterile little life.

Anna stared across at the desk and the funny little cactus vase still in the place she had put it before she'd started spending all her time at Vincent's. She had another glass of wine and resisted the impulse to ring him. Another glass of wine and she could forget about driving over there, she'd be over the limit. Just like the first night they slept together . . . when he wouldn't let her drive . . .

Anna got up and went into the kitchen. She left her glass on the bench as she rifled through the drawers looking for cigarettes. If she found any she knew they were likely to be stale. Vincent disliked her smoking. He never stopped her, he wouldn't. But he didn't like it, so she didn't smoke at his house. And she didn't miss it.

She couldn't find any cigarettes, so she picked up her glass again and went back out to the living room. She laughed at the idea of calling it a "living room." It was little more than an "existing room." Though for a brief period it had been her writing room. . . . She considered the desk again. The funny little cactus vase. Anna drifted over and placed her glass next to it. She stood for a moment longer, before she turned and walked determinedly into her bedroom, knelt down on the floor and reached underneath the bed. She slid out her laptop, zipped up in its case, coated in a thin layer of dust. She stood up and carried it back out to the writing room.

Small Business Agency

"What are you still doing here, Kath?" Liam said sternly, leaning against the doorjamb, his arms crossed, affecting a frown.

She looked at him over the top of her glasses. "Just finishing up a couple of things—"

"Everything's under control," he insisted.

"Yeah, but there's this batch of files I haven't had a chance to look at—"

"I'll see to them."

"And you know about the big meeting—"

"Kath, we've been all over this, and over, and over again. And you should have left by now. You were supposed to go home early."

"What, so I can start yelling at Norm sooner when I see everything that still has to be done before we take off on this stupid trip?"

"You need a holiday, Kath."

"Not this kind of holiday." She groaned. "A holiday is supposed to be luxurious king-size beds and views from the balcony and deep spas and bars on the edge of swimming pools and drinks with little umbrellas served by waiters who look like male models." She sighed longingly.

Liam suppressed a smile, passing her briefcase across the desk.

"Stop looking at me like that, a girl can dream, can't she?" She stood up, taking the bag from him. "In real life I'm going to be stuck with Norm in a caravan for three weeks out the back of nowhere, when we can barely tolerate each other in a house with eight rooms and doors we can close between us."

While she rattled on, Liam had come around behind her and lifted her jacket from the back of her chair, placing it around her shoulders.

"You just want to take over my office," she muttered while he gently but firmly propelled her out of the room.

"I know, it's pretty tempting," he replied. "What with that view of the back lane, and the ritzy décor."

They stopped in the doorway and surveyed the shabby, overcrowded office, its mustard walls, sagging venetian blinds, the shelves straining under the weight of bureaucracy.

"I promise it'll all be here when you get back," Liam assured her.

"And that's supposed to make me feel better?" She raised an eyebrow as she turned away and started along the corridor. "So, when's that baby of yours due?"

"Couple of weeks."

"Then it's any day now?"

"Well, no, it's still two weeks away."

"Which is any day now," she repeated.

"What do you mean?" said Liam, startled.

"Bye, Kath! Have a great holiday!" Tim/Tom/James called from the photocopier.

"Yeah, right."

"Kath, what do you mean it's 'any day now'?" Liam persisted.

"Only five percent of babies are born on the due date, Liam," she explained. "The rest are spread pretty even, two weeks either way."

"But the baby would be premature if it was born now, wouldn't it?"

Kath shook her head. "No, it might be a little undercooked, but your baby could arrive tomorrow or in a month and it'd be on time either way."

Liam checked his watch after he'd seen Kath out the door. The shop would be shut by now, not that Georgie stayed till closing these days anyway. Back at his desk he phoned her flat, but it rang out. He tried her cell phone next, but the voice mail picked it up straightaway, which meant she'd probably turned it off. As you would if you were in a hospital.

"Georgie, it's Liam. Just ringing to . . ." Check up on you? She wouldn't like that. ". . . to see how you're going. Could you call me when you get this message?"

He tried the shop but as he expected, there was no one there. He rang her flat again but there was still no answer. He wasn't sure what to do. He needed to hear her voice, make sure she was alright, let her know about this "due date" fiasco if she didn't know already. Why wasn't this common knowledge? Of course he realized babies didn't always come right on schedule, but he thought it was closer than two weeks either way. It all seemed pretty bloody inexact. How the hell was he supposed to stop worrying from here on in? He'd had himself all sorted to get through the next two weeks. With Kath away, work would be flat out, it would give him something to focus on. So much for that idea.

He was still ringing every half hour after he got home. By eight thirty he couldn't stand it anymore. He was thinking of driving over to Georgie's, but he didn't want to be dramatic. Nick and Louise were his only other hope. Louise was always polite to him when he called the shop, even pleasant. They'd understand, surely?

He tried Georgie's flat one more time, then he looked up Nick and Louise's number and dialed.

"Hello." It was a male voice, which meant it could only be Nick.

"Ah, hi, Nick? It's Liam MacMullen here."

"Gidday, Liam, how are you going?"

At least he sounded friendly.

"I'm fine, I'm a bit worried about Georgie though."

"Well—"

"I've been ringing her place all evening but there's no answer."

"That's because—"

"You know I don't like to bother her, or truth is, she doesn't like me bothering her, I guess she told you that."

"No, she—"

"But I was talking to my boss this afternoon and she pointed out that the baby could come any time now and I got worried—"

"Liam—"

"She's there in the flat on her own."

"No, she's—"

"And I've already told her I don't think that's a good idea, she should be staying with you guys or—"

"Liam! She is!"

"What?"

"She's staying here, okay?"

"Oh, why didn't you say?"

"I've been trying to for the last five minutes," he insisted. "Getting yourself a little worked up there, mate."

"Sorry."

"Don't apologize, I know how you feel. That's why I made her come and stay with us. And she didn't put up a fight, so I think she may have been anxious as well."

"Is she alright?"

"She's fine. Perfect. Right on schedule."

"Yeah, well according to my boss, that could be anytime from now."

"That's true, but she's more likely to go late with the first. Louise was ten days over with Molly. The longest ten days of my life," he said ruefully. "Anyway, I'd put her on, Liam, but she's in bed."

"This early?"

"Yeah, she's not doing much else besides sleeping at the moment."

"Is there something wrong?"

"No, it's normal. Louise slept all the time at the end, with both the girls. I think they get a bit tired carrying all that weight around."

"Fair enough," said Liam.

"But look, I'll tell her you called, and I'll get her to give you a ring tomorrow."

"I don't want to put her out."

"Don't worry about that. She should be able to manage it between naps."

"Thanks."

"And don't hesitate to call anytime, Liam."

"I don't think she'd like that."

"If you're worried, just give me a call," said Nick. "What she doesn't know . . ."

Liam smiled. "Thanks, I appreciate it."

Morning

"You should have told him, Georgie."

"Yeah, well there was a whole lot he never told me, so . . ."

Nick just looked at her. "Whatever he's done in the past, it doesn't make it okay for you to be inconsiderate."

Georgie blinked. Nick was scolding her. He never scolded.

"I didn't do it on purpose, I forgot, okay? I'm lucky to remember my own name at the moment."

"Yeah, well you should have heard the poor bloke last night, blathering away like a halfwit, he was worried sick about you."

"Look at me, Nick!" Georgie interrupted. "Picking up the phone, dialing Liam's number. You can stop lecturing me now."

Nick nodded, satisfied. Georgie put the phone to her ear.

"Good morning, Liam MacMullen."

"Liam, it's Georgie."

"Hi." His voice softened. "How are you?"

"I'm fine, Liam. I'm sorry I didn't call you—"

"It's okay."

"No, it isn't. Warden Nick is breathing down my neck till I apologize."

"Tell him it's okay, too."

"So you don't have to worry about me now. I'm here with Nick and Louise. Two drivers, no waiting."

"You can still call me . . . if you want to."

She wasn't about to tell him how often she thought of phoning him, whenever she felt lonely, or anxious, or melancholy. . . . She thought about him a lot since their trip to Melbourne. When she'd first found out he was married, her whole world had spun out of kilter. He was not who he said he was, so how could she believe anything else he said? Now she knew him better than she ever had. The loving son, the caring brother, the husband who had had his share of heartbreak. But to trust him again was a huge step, and Georgie wasn't ready to take it. She didn't know if she'd ever be ready.

"I hope you do call," Liam was saying, "when the baby's born, at least."

"Liam! Of course I'll call you when the baby's born! You're the father." She heard a sigh. "Thanks."

"Don't thank me for that. How could you think I wouldn't call you?"

He could hear the frustration in her voice. He was annoying her again. "Okay, Georgie. Well, you take care of yourself."

She hung up the phone as Louise walked into the room, dressed for work.

"What's with the face?" Louise asked her.

"Oh, I have to go to the loo again. I must have been five times this morning."

"Well, you've got seven odd pounds of baby sitting right on your bladder, par for the course, chook."

"Oh, you can be smug now," Georgie returned. "Anyway, it's not my bladder. I've been getting gastric cramps. Not that they seem to amount to anything."

Louise stopped abruptly. "How often are you getting these cramps? Are they constant, or do they come and go?"

"They come and go."

"Since what time?"

"I got up about seven, seven thirty."

"How far apart are they coming?"

Georgie frowned. "I don't know."

"And nothing much happens when you go to the toilet?"

She shook her head.

"Well, is it gastric pain, or is it more like period pain?"

"Well, of course it's not period pain, Louise, as if I'd be getting period pain. Look at me!"

Louise rolled her eyes. "But does it *feel* like period pain?"

Georgie shrugged. "I guess."

"And it comes and goes, every ten or fifteen minutes?"

"Maybe."

Louise sighed. "Sounds like you're in labor."

"What?" Nick looked up, shocked.

Louise crossed to the bench and picked up the phone. "It's probably too early to tell for sure. It might peter out. How did you sleep last night, Georgie?"

"Okay, till about five this morning. I had to keep getting up . . . with these pains . . ." She stared lamely at Louise.

"So we're actually looking at contractions ten or fifteen minutes apart since five this morning?"

"I didn't know they were contractions," Georgie said in a frightened voice.

"What do we do now?" Nick asked anxiously.

"Well, everyone gets a hold of themselves to begin with," Louise said pointedly to Nick. "I'll call the hospital but I'm sure they'll suggest to wait it out a little longer, if she's feeling comfortable. You are comfortable, Georgie?"

She nodded. "At least I was until a few minutes ago."

"Drive the girls to school and preschool, Nick, and then get back here. I'll call work so Adam can find someone to cover for me."

"And then what?"

"Then we wait."

"But I'm not ready," said Georgie, tears filling her eyes. Nick walked over and put his arm around her.

"You're going to be fine, Georgie," Louise reassured her. "Do you want me to call Liam?"

She wiped her eyes. "No, it's okay. Not yet."

"Zan wanted us to make sure that we called her," said Nick.

"Let's just wait till things heat up a little."

By three that afternoon things had heated up considerably. They had finally left for the hospital around midday and Zan met them there. Georgie had still resisted calling Liam. She felt as though she was slowly unraveling, and she wasn't sure she wanted him around when she wasn't in full control of her faculties.

"What did the doctor say?" Zan asked, coming back into the room after he left.

"Oh, he said I'm going to have the baby today," Georgie said, her voice manic. "Of course I'm friggin' having this baby today!" she exclaimed. "What does he think, I'm here for a sleepover?"

"Did he say how far dilated you are?"

"He reckons only five centimeters, but he obviously doesn't know what he's talking about. How can I have been in labor this long and only be halfway?"

Zan approached the bed cautiously. She'd never seen George like this. Then again, George had never been in labor before. "They say sometimes the first few centimeters are the hardest," she offered.

Georgie just scowled. "Where's Louise?"

"She went to pick up the girls."

"Why didn't Nick go?"

"He didn't want to leave you."

Georgie looked at her, confused.

Zan sighed loudly. "He can't bring himself to actually come in here and be with you, but he can't bear to leave you either. He's such a pussy, that man." She shook her head. "Now, can I get you anything? Do you want a drink of water, some ice, a back rub?"

Georgie was thinking. It was time. "I want you to call Liam."

"What?"

"You heard me, Zan."

"You want the dickhead here?"

"Yes, I do."

"Why?"

"I don't know why, I just do!" she boomed. "The same way people want their beanbags and rainforest CDs and fucking aromatherapy oil, even if all they do is hurl them at the wall in the end!"

"Okay, I'll call him."

"Wait a sec." She gasped, her face contorting. "Here comes another fucker."

* * *

"Suzanne Underwood for Liam MacMullen."

"This is Liam MacMullen speaking. How can I help you, Ms Underwood?"

She groaned. "It's Zan, Liam. Georgie's sister. I'm calling from the hospital, she's in labor."

"What?" Liam said urgently. "How is she?"

"How do you think? You try passing a watermelon, see how you feel."

"Would it be alright, do you think she'd mind if I—"

"For some reason passing understanding, she wants to see you, so you'd better get your arse over here, pronto. Don't keep her waiting."

Liam burst into the delivery room when Georgie was at the tail end of a contraction. She was in a crouching position, perched up on the bed with Zan and Louise flanking her, apparently supporting her. She didn't look very comfortable, but what the hell would he know? When it passed they released her and she flopped back on the bed. She looked like she'd run a marathon. Liam was dismayed. This was going to be harder than he'd ever imagined.

"Hi," he said tentatively, coming farther into the room. Louise and Zan both turned to look at him at the same time. Zan barely nodded, but Louise smiled, with what appeared to be relief. Then Georgie lifted her head and glared at him.

"Are you okay?" he asked.

"Why don't you two take a break?" she said.

"Are you sure?" Zan was frowning.

"Quite sure." She nodded. "Go. Liam'll stay."

Zan turned and walked past him. "Don't upset her," she warned.

"We won't be far, okay?" Louise said, giving his arm a quick squeeze.

When they had left the room, Georgie beckoned for him to come closer. He came to stand beside the bed. She looked tired, poor thing. And her eyes were . . . well, a little wild, really.

"How are you feeling?" he said gently.

Suddenly she swung her arm out, striking him across the chest. He gasped. It didn't hurt so much, she barely had any strength behind it, it was a shock more than anything.

"You bastard, how do you think I'm feeling?" she wailed.

"I know—"

"You don't know anything!" she cried. "You have no idea how this feels. You horny, uncontrollable bastard!" And she hit him again. "Why couldn't you have shown some restraint? You did this to me and now I'm the one who's got to go through it. Well, newsflash, you're not leaving this room until the baby comes out, I don't care if your bladder's about to burst or you're hungry or thirsty, or you're fucking dying. I can't leave, so you're not going to either. Got it?"

He met her eyes directly. "I'm not going anywhere," he said calmly.

"Unless I tell you to," she added.

"Okay. Now, what do you need, what can I do?"

Georgie looked up at him, panting, her eyes tearing up. He placed his hand gently on her forehead, and she grasped it with both her hands, holding it there. She began to sob. "I'm so scared," she said in a tiny, frightened voice.

He leaned across her, tucking his other arm around her. "You don't have to be scared. I won't leave you." She sobbed again, holding on to him. He could feel her fear, and he tried to absorb it into himself. He didn't know how the hell he thought he was doing that, but if willing it was enough . . .

"Oh shit, here comes another one."

He pulled back. "What do I have to do, Georgie?" She was flustered, disoriented. He held her face and made eye contact with her. "Georgie, look at me and focus. How do we get through this?"

She managed to speak. "What you just said."

He frowned. "What? Look at me and focus?"

She nodded, and then she winced, holding her breath.

"Okay, Georgie," he said firmly, "are you supposed to be breathing as well?"

She nodded again, releasing her breath. He took hold of both her hands. "Just look at me, honey, look at my eyes, and breathe, slowly, with me . . . that's it."

Georgie couldn't take her eyes off him, she didn't know what would happen if she did. She could feel the pain, but it was as though it was out of her body, in another room even, and if she looked at Liam's eyes and only saw him, she couldn't see the pain, and if she couldn't see it, she almost couldn't feel it. And then suddenly it was gone altogether. It was over.

"Are you alright?"

She nodded, sighing heavily.

He stroked her forehead. "You're hot." He glanced around the room. "I'll get you some ice—"

She grabbed his hand, her eyes terrified. "Don't leave me."

He brought his face close to hers. "What did I tell you? I'm not going to leave you, that's a promise."

"PUSH!"

"I'm trying," Georgie said tearfully. "I'm just so tired."

"I know you are, sweetheart," Liam soothed, stroking her hair away from her forehead. "But it's nearly over and then you'll be able to rest."

She turned on her side, curling up. "I don't think I can do this."

Liam crouched beside the bed, bringing his face level with hers. "Yes, you can. You're doing great, Georgie."

He was trying to stay calm for Georgie's sake, but he had nearly lost it watching her push and pant and strain for another fifteen minutes. He wanted to call a stop to it, tell them to take the baby by Cesarean, something, anything, to put an end to what she was going through. She was exhausted. But the staff were acting like it was all very normal. And then out of nowhere Georgie seemed to get a second wind. She focused, frowning and grunting with intense concentration, and finally the head crowned. Liam could see the head of his baby but he couldn't believe it. And then he saw his face, screwed up and red and angry with the world for evicting him from his haven. And then all at once his body slithered out. Everyone started laughing and crying.

"It's a boy!"

They laid him across Georgie's stomach, slippery and pink, and Liam looked at her face, at her eyes, and the fear was gone, completely, vanished, and she was laughing, tears rolling down her cheeks, and she looked up at him, beaming. "It's a boy," she cried, hooking her arm around his neck and bringing his face down to hers and kissing his lips.

"I love you," he said.

"I love you too."

"Get Nick," he heard someone say, "he's going to flip."

Then they were all pouring into the room, and Nick hugged him. And the little girls, and Jules. All talking at once.

"He's gorgeous."

"I want to see the baby."

"A baby boy."

"Finally! Another man in the family."

Liam drifted back, away from them all, watching the family from the corner of the room. After a while he stepped out. He walked in a daze down the corridor and through the swing doors. He took his cell phone out of his pocket and turned it on, pressing a series of buttons before he held it to his ear.

"Mum? It's Liam. I . . . we have a son."

He was quite sure the shriek down the line would have pierced his eardrum if he hadn't moved the phone away in time.

One Day Old

Louise picked up the phone next to Georgie's bed. "Hello."

"Ah, hi, Louise . . . ?"

"Liam! How are you shaping up today?"

"Oh, I'm fine. How's Georgie?"

"She's right here, I'll put her on." Louise handed the phone across.

Georgie took it gingerly, overcome by a rush of mixed feelings. He was wonderful yesterday, she was so grateful he'd been there. . . . But things were said, she remembered, at the height of emotion, and well, she didn't want him to think . . . She had to stay in control now.

"Hello?"

"Hi." Liam sounded as wary as she felt. "How are you feeling today?"

"Oh, a bit tired and sore, but I'm on such a high it doesn't really bother me."

"That's good, I guess." He paused. "How's the baby?"

"Astonishingly beautiful."

"So I'm remembering right?"

"Absolutely." There was a moment's silence. Georgie realized he was probably waiting to be asked. "So, are you coming in to see him?"

"Well, I wanted to, if that's alright?"

"Of course it is, Liam. He's your son."

"Okay, then, I'll see you soon, if that suits you."

"I'm not going anywhere."

Louise took the phone from Georgie. "He's coming in?"

"Yeah."

"Well, Uncle Nick," said Louise, "if you can tear yourself away, we should leave them to it."

Nick had been holding the baby the entire time, once he'd wrested him off Adam, who'd come and gone already this morning. He'd still be here but for Louise reminding him there was no one else to open the shop.

"You don't have to leave," Georgie protested. "It's not like there's anything special between the two of us."

Nick was gazing down at his nephew. "Oh, I think there's something very special between the two of you," he suggested.

Georgie frowned. Louise was watching her. "What is it, Georgie? Liam was fantastic yesterday. He's certainly shot up in my estimation. Even Zan was impressed, she referred to him as Liam after he left, not 'the dickhead,' did you notice that?"

"I didn't notice an awful lot on the sidelines yesterday, Louise."

"Of course."

"I just don't want Liam getting the wrong idea," Georgie continued. "I don't want any of you getting the wrong idea."

Louise and Nick both looked up at once.

"He's my baby's father. And I will respect that, but that's all our relationship is going to be about. Doing the best thing for him." She looked down at her little son. "He's my priority now."

Louise and Nick had not long gone when Liam appeared in the doorway.

"Oh my God," Georgie exclaimed. "Could you get a bigger bunch of flowers? It's like a shrub," she laughed.

He smiled sheepishly. "Sorry."

"Don't apologize! They're gorgeous. And what have you got there, is that a teddy bear?"

Now he looked embarrassed. "I know he's probably too young. I just wanted to get him something."

"No, it's sweet," she cooed. "Go put it in his crib."

Liam laid the flowers down and walked around Georgie's bed to the clear Perspex hospital crib where his son lay sleeping. His son. He still couldn't get used to it. He'd hardly slept last night thinking about him, thinking about Georgie. She was amazing yesterday, he couldn't believe how brave she was. He was so proud of her. He bent over the crib, gazing down at this tiny little person who was part of him, and part of her. And his heart felt like it might burst.

"You can pick him up if you want," said Georgie.

"Oh, no, he's sleeping."

"He doesn't really know the difference yet. You won't wake him."

"Maybe in a little while," he murmured, watching him, fascinated. He reached his hand in and touched his cheek with the back of his fingers. Liam had never felt anything so soft in all his life.

"Everyone's saying he looks like you," said Georgie.

Liam glanced at her. "Yeah? I can't see it. But he looks . . . I don't know, familiar? Does that sound stupid?"

"No." Georgie smiled. "I felt as though I recognized him as soon as I saw him."

The picture of the son he was supposed to have. And here he was, like he was always meant to be.

Liam straightened, turning his attention to Georgie. "So, how are you, Mum?" he said tenderly, coming over to the bed.

Georgie saw the look in his eyes. She was going to have to say something sooner than later. He squeezed her hand as he bent down toward her. Georgie offered her cheek and he kissed it. "Take a seat, Liam."

He sat down in a chair between the crib and the bed, watching her intently. Georgie could tell he suspected something was coming.

She cleared her throat. "I think it's best to establish some ground rules from the beginning, don't you? Start as we mean to go on."

He was frowning slightly now as he nodded, waiting for her to continue.

"Yesterday . . ." She hesitated, wanting to say it right. "Well, yesterday you were wonderful, Liam. I really appreciated your support and I'm so glad you were there. But . . . it was a very emotional day, don't you think?"

Liam nodded vaguely. "It was."

"And we all got pretty carried away. Things were said . . . and well, I don't want you to get the wrong idea." She didn't know how he was taking this, because she couldn't look at him. She focused on the flowers instead. "I have a hard time ahead of me and I need to get settled with a new baby, all on my own, and, um, I just don't want you to have expectations. . . ." Georgie looked across at him then and saw his expression had hardened.

"Are you going to let me see him?" he said grimly.

"Of course I'm going to let you see him," she insisted. "And by the way, his name's Nicholas."

"Oh . . ." He seemed a little surprised.

Georgie was watching him. "Is that okay, do you like it?"

"I do," he said quietly. "It's a good name."

"Nicholas William Reading."

"Pardon?"

"That's his full name."

"William's his second name?"

"You said it was a tradition. I wanted him to be a part of that," she explained. "And I thought your mum would like it. . . ."

Liam was staring at her, stunned.

"Look, if you have a problem with it, because of your dad—"

"No, of course not," he assured her, rousing. "I . . . I don't know what to say. Thank you."

"You don't have to thank me," said Georgie. "So, anyway, like I was saying, I'm going to need some time to settle into a routine with Nicholas. We'll have to come to an arrangement for you to see him. I definitely want you to be part of his life, a very important part of his life."

But not of mine. Liam could hear her loud and clear. But that was alright, he had been patient this far.

Melbourne

Anna was pacing back and forth across the living room carpet. She had arrived yesterday, to her parents' surprise and delight. She had done nothing but write for the past month or two; she wasn't sure how long it had been, she'd lost track of any semblance of a normal routine. She ate in the middle of the night and slept in the middle of the day. She'd leave the townhouse only when she ran out of milk or tea or her other staples. She ate tuna out of the tin, and fruit and crackers and chocolate. Whatever was easy, whatever she could eat at her desk so she could keep writing.

Then suddenly, without warning, without seeing it coming at all, she had hit a brick wall. She couldn't write anymore. She ranged restlessly around the townhouse, took walks on the beach, drove past Vincent's house a couple of times but didn't stop, phoned Mac and hung up again before it started to ring.

Gradually, a plan crystallized. She knew what she had to do. And she knew it was the right thing because she felt a strange, unfamiliar sensation. For the first time in a long time Anna had a feeling of hope again. But there were a couple of things she had to take care of first.

She told her parents last night over dinner.

"But I don't understand. Why do you have to go away, dear?" Caroline asked.

"I need some perspective, Mum, and I don't think I can get it here."

"Do you mean here in Melbourne or up in Sydney?"

"I don't think I can get it either place," Anna explained. "It's too comfortable for me here. It would be far too easy for me to hide away and avoid doing what I have to do. And up in Sydney, well, it's less comfortable for me there, but there're still a couple of places I could hide out."

Bernard was listening intently. "What is it that you have to do, Anna?"

She took a deep breath. "I have to finish my story."

They looked at her blankly.

"Just a minute." Anna jumped from the table and went to her bag. Zipping it open, she drew out a hefty bundle of pages, tied together with a length of green ribbon. She walked back over and dumped it on the table between them.

"Maybe this will explain a few things."

She hadn't expected them to start reading it there and then. But they did, at least until they were overcome with questions a few pages in. When had she started writing? Why? What was she intending to do, become a writer? Anna couldn't answer them, she didn't know what she was going to do either. Eventually she pleaded tiredness and took herself off to bed. When she woke in the morning, the apartment was quiet. Her father was always up early, so she thought perhaps he'd gone off to golf. She got up and made herself a cup of tea and sat staring out at the view across the city.

Finally her mother appeared, coming out of the hall from their bedroom.

"Oh, you're awake," said Anna. "I've been wondering when you were going to get up. Has Dad gone to golf?"

"No dear, he's still in bed."

"Is he alright?"

"He's perfectly alright. Why do you ask?"

"Well, you two don't usually sleep in."

"We're not sleeping, dear, we're reading your book."

Anna was stunned. "It's not actually a book—"

"Well, whatever you want to call it, we're reading it."

"I didn't expect you to read it this weekend, I was going to leave it with you."

"Well, neither of us can put it down," she said matter-of-factly. "We read last night until we couldn't stay awake any longer, and your father picked it up again as soon as he woke this morning. He's ahead of me now. I was just going to make us a cup of tea. I hope you can amuse yourself for a few hours?"

Anna blinked. "Oh, sure . . . um, do you want me to make the tea?"

"That would be lovely, dear," she said as she turned back up the hall.

Anna called out as she got to the bedroom. "Mum?"

"Yes, Anna?"

"Well, um, well, what do you think of it, so far?"

Caroline looked at her squarely. "Why, it's quite extraordinary, darling."

Anna duly served them tea and toast and came back later to take the tray away. They barely acknowledged her either time. Restless, she went for a walk along the Yarra. She was gone for more than an hour, but still her parents had not come out of their room when she returned. She filled in some more time, having a shower and unpacking a few things. And now she was reduced to pacing the floor.

"Anna."

She turned around and her father was walking across the room toward her, a look of bewildered pride on his face. He held his arms out to her.

"I didn't know, I never knew you had this in you," he said, hugging her.

Anna felt like a little girl. She'd done something to make her father proud.

"It's extraordinary," he said, looking down at her.

"That's what Mum said." And what Vincent had said.

"Come and sit with me," said Bernard, leading her across to the sofa. "When did you realize you could write like this, Anna?"

She shrugged. "I'm only just realizing."

He shook his head in awe. "And is it all true?"

"A lot of it is. The details about IVF obviously, the marriage breakdown, but it's still a work of fiction."

"What about the parents? Were you that angry with us?"

"You know, Dad, I don't think I ever was," said Anna. "But things come out when I'm writing . . . things I didn't know about myself. I think for so long I've been trying to be what I believed other people wanted me to be, without knowing if that's what they wanted at all. I think the anger was probably at myself more than anyone."

Her father took her hand in his. "All I've ever wanted is for you to be happy."

"I know that." She smiled. "So you really did like it?"

"I'm in awe—"

"Dad!" she chided.

"No, really, I am. I kept thinking as I was reading, 'My daughter wrote this.' I could hardly believe it." He patted her hand.

"Then I can't count on your opinion because it's clearly biased."

"Alright, if you want to hear an objective criticism, I'm not sure about the ending, it seems a bit abrupt."

"No, Dad, it doesn't have an ending yet. That's why I have to go away."

"You need to go away to write the ending? You can't write it here?"

"No, I need to go away so that I have an ending to write."

Harbord

"You could have asked Liam to come tonight," Nick called from the kitchen.

"So you keep saying . . . and keep saying." Georgie was sitting on the lounge feeding Nicholas, which was where she could be found almost any time of the day or night these past couple of weeks.

"I just think you should have asked him. It is a family dinner." Nick had invited everyone over because Georgie had made the decision she was going home tomorrow, finally. He wasn't able to talk her into "just one more night" like he had the first three times. He leaned against the kitchen bench, looking across at her. "It's not too late. Why don't you call him now?"

"Nick, you're going to have to get used to the idea that having a baby together doesn't make us a couple."

"But being the father of my nephew makes him family."

"You're like a dog with a bone, Nick." Georgie groaned.

He brought her a glass of water. "I just think maybe Liam deserves a second chance."

Georgie took it from him. "Why?"

"Because he seems like a pretty good guy, and he is the father of your baby—"

"So you think we should get together because of Nicholas, like couples who stay together for the sake of the children?"

Nick perched on the arm of the sofa. "It wouldn't be like that, Georgie."

"Why wouldn't it be? You're making a pretty big assumption here, Nick."

"What?"

"That I still have feelings for Liam."

"Well, don't you?"

Georgie hesitated. "That's beside the point. Look, even if I was prepared to forget that he hurt me, that he betrayed me and his wife at the same time, if I could put aside that I can't trust him, that I'll never be able to trust him, the thing is, it's not just about me anymore," she explained. "I have a child to think about now. I don't want Nicholas to have to go through what we went through, Nick. I want him to feel loved and secure and safe his whole life. He'll never know any different than his parents have always lived separately, and so he'll never have to go through losing his dad, or watching him leave."

"What makes you so sure Liam would leave?"

"Because that's what he does."

"It's what he did once, because he fell in love with you."

"And you don't think it's possible another woman could turn his head in a couple of years?"

"Anything's possible, Georgie. But is it likely?"

Georgie felt frustrated. Had Nick so completely forgotten what it felt like to be betrayed? "I can't take the chance, the odds aren't good enough for my son. And I don't have a great track record, Nick. I trust my own instincts less than I trust Liam."

Nick reached across the back of the sofa and squeezed her shoulder affectionately. "I just don't want you to be alone."

Georgie smiled at him. "I won't be alone, I've got Nicholas."

He watched her gazing lovingly down at the baby. "You don't have to go."

"Yes, we do, I'm getting too used to this. You bring me a glass of water every time I sit down to feed, make my meals, watch Nicholas while I have a shower. And best of all, keep me company."

"I like doing all that, and I appreciate the company too."

"But the longer I stay, the harder it's going to be to do it on my own." Georgie looked plaintively at her brother. "It's making me anxious. I don't know if I'm going to be any good at this until I try."

Nick smiled. "I still don't know if I'm any good at it."

The Next Day

Nick rushed inside, just beating the machine to answer the phone. "Hello?"

"Hi, Nick, it's Liam."

"Oh, hi, mate. You just missed her, I'm afraid."

"She went out?"

"No, she went home. Didn't she tell you?"

"No."

Nick groaned. "I'm going to whack that girl one day."

"Do you think she should be on her own?"

"No, of course I don't. But she's trying to be all independent and prove something or other." He paused. "Hey, why don't you go round there. Surprise her?"

"I don't know. Won't that just annoy her?"

"No, she may not show it, but secretly she'll like it. She's got this idea in her head she has to be able to do it on her own, she doesn't want to admit she needs help."

Liam hesitated, thinking it over. "Maybe I could take her some dinner?"

"Good idea. I'll give you the name of the Thai place she likes."

At six thirty, Liam stood outside Georgie's door, not at all sure he should have come after all. But he had a bag of hot food, and he really wanted to see her and the baby, even if it was only for a little while. He took a deep breath and knocked firmly. A few moments later the doors swung open and Georgie stood frowning at him, Nicholas slung over her shoulder like a sack of baby potatoes.

"What are you doing here?"

"Sorry, I should have called."

"Yes, you should have."

"I brought food."

She sighed, peering down at the bag in his hand. "What is it?"

"Thai, from your favorite place—"

"I can't have spicy food!" she exclaimed, turning and stomping back inside.

Well, this was going well. She'd left the door open, so Liam presumed he was allowed to enter. He closed the door behind him. Georgie was standing in the middle of the living room, jiggling Nicholas around. She looked agitated.

"Why can't you eat spicy food?" he asked.

"Because it might upset the baby."

"What do mothers in Thailand eat?"

"I don't know, but I'm not in Thailand, okay?"

"Sorry." He paused. Walking the tightrope. "I could cook you something else?"

"No."

"Why, have you eaten already?"

"No, I haven't, because I was going to make myself something as soon as I finished feeding Nicholas and got him off to sleep, except he did a big poo, didn't he? And now I have to change him, which will wake him right up and I'll have to feed him again to settle him off, so I guess I'll cook something sometime later tonight."

"I could change him while you eat."

"You don't know how to change him."

"Yes I do, I did it in the hospital, remember?"

She looked torn. She was biting her lip, resisting. He had to give her a way out. "I have to learn how to take care of Nicholas too," said Liam, "and I can't if you don't give me a chance."

Georgie sighed. "Okay," she relented, "change his nappy, if you want to that bad." She crossed the room to the hall. "Come and I'll show you where everything is."

He left the bag of food on the dining table and followed her.

"He'll be a mess, so you'll probably have to change his suit as well," she said, reaching for an all-in-one in the cupboard and handing it to Liam. "Use these wipes, and here are the nappies, and if he's a little red I like to put a dab of this pawpaw cream on him, but you know, don't worry about that, I can do it next time. And the singlets are in the first drawer, and what else . . ."

"Go and eat," said Liam, lifting Nicholas off her shoulder.

"Support his head," Georgie cautioned.

"I can take it from here," he assured her.

Georgie was biting her lip again, watching him.

"Scoot!" he insisted.

She trudged back out to the living room and saw the bag of takeaway sitting on the dining table. She went over and opened it, breathing in the delicious fragrant aroma. She was starving. She hadn't eaten since Nick left, after he'd made her a sandwich for lunch. God, she was useless, she hadn't even managed to feed herself today. She contemplated the plastic takeaway containers. "Bugger it."

When Liam came back out, Georgie looked up sheepishly, her fork poised above the tubs of food, all open, spread out before her. She swallowed.

"I tested it first, and it didn't seem too spicy," she said. "But I'm still going to blame you if he ends up with the runs or colic or something."

"Of course," he conceded, rocking gently from side to side as he cradled Nicholas in his arms.

"How'd you go?" she asked.

"Fine." Then he grimaced. "What's that smell?"

Georgie sighed, pointing to a knotted plastic bag sitting on top of the kitchen bin. "Oh, sour milk and petrified chicken, and some other things that defied identification. I forgot to clean the fridge out before I left. I nearly keeled over when I opened the door today. Nick forgot to take the bag with him."

"Well, I'll take it down to the bin later. But in the meantime," he said, stooping to pick up the bag while he supported Nicholas with one arm, "it might be a good idea to put it out on the balcony."

"Why didn't I think of that?" she muttered as she hurried ahead of him, sliding the door open to the balcony. He set it down and stepped back inside.

Georgie closed the door again. "Do you want me to take him?"

"He's okay at the moment, you finish your dinner."

"I've had enough anyway," she said, putting the lids back on the containers. "Just let me wash my hands."

"There's no hurry."

Georgie walked around to the kitchen sink. "Yeah, well, I don't want to keep you. I'm sure you've got more important things to do."

"Nothing more important than this," he said seriously.

She met his eyes across the kitchen bench, but she had to look away again. "Well, whatever, I have to get used to handling things by myself. I ought be able to look after the baby and feed myself, that's pretty basic."

"But if I'm right here—"

"You can't be here all the time."

"I can, actually."

"Liam!" she returned sharply. She came around the bench, took Nicholas from him, and then walked around the corner to sit on the sofa. Liam heard the television come on. She was annoyed now. He stacked up the containers of food and put them away in the fridge, giving Georgie a minute to cool off. When he came around the corner, she was feeding the baby, staring listlessly at the TV. She looked up at him.

"I'm sorry if I upset you," he began. "I was only trying to help."

Georgie sighed. She picked up the remote and muted the sound. "It's just that everybody keeps making me feel like I'm useless." Liam went to interrupt, but she continued, "I know you don't mean to, and Nick doesn't mean to, but when you keep insisting I need help, it feels like you don't think I can manage."

"No, Georgie, that's not it," said Liam, lowering himself to sit on the edge of the coffee table in front of her. "The thing is, why should you have to manage? I wouldn't want to do this on my own, I'm sure I couldn't do it on my own."

"Well, I don't have a choice."

He resisted the impulse to say, yes, you do.

"And I don't know how I'm going to manage," she went on. "God, do you think this is the first time I've let food go off in the refrigerator? I'm always forgetting things, I'm untidy, disorganized—"

"Georgie, those things don't matter."

"Yes they do," she insisted. "Damn," she said, glancing around her.

"What is it?"

"See, this is exactly what I'm talking about. I get thirsty when I'm feeding and I can't even remember to get a glass of water before I sit down."

"I'll get it for you," Liam said, ducking around to the kitchen. He returned a moment later and handed her a glass.

"Georgie, I know you don't like me saying it, but you don't have to do this on your own. I mean it. You can phone me anytime of the day or night. I should be the first one you call."

"I'll see." She sipped from the glass of water. Liam stood there awkwardly. He didn't want to go, but he didn't want to wear out his welcome either.

"Thanks, you know, for the food," Georgie said after a while.

She wanted him to go, so the decision was made for him.

"Is there anything else you need?" he asked.

She shook her head.

"Alright." He sighed. "Have a good night, try and get some rest."

"I will." He turned in the wrong direction. "Door's the other way, Liam," she called after him.

"Just getting the garbage," he reminded her.

"Oh."

He reappeared, marching the offending bag straight out the front door, pausing on the threshold. "Call me," he said, before closing the door behind him.

Three Days Later

"Georgie, what's the matter?" Liam croaked into the receiver, squinting at his bedside clock. "It's four in the morning."

"Yeah, well, Nicholas hasn't worked out how to tell the time yet, and he doesn't know it's four in the morning and therefore a completely inappropriate time to be wide awake and resisting all attempts to be put back to sleep." She took a breath. "You said you wanted to be involved, and you said to ring anytime, but obviously you didn't mean it, so—"

"I'm on my way."

Morning

Georgie lay flat on her back and stretched out. That was the longest block of sleep she'd had in days. Liam had arrived about twenty minutes after she'd called and taken Nicholas from her, insisting she go to bed. But still she hovered, until Liam decided to go for a drive, that way the flat would be quiet and Georgie could get some rest. It made sense. She fussed around, packing a bag of emergency supplies, and then they were gone. Which was when she realized it was the first time she'd been separated from Nicholas by any distance. Georgie panicked and was about to ring Liam's cell, but then she imagined him answering the phone while he was driving, and then she imagined him having an accident, and then she couldn't catch her breath, and finally she had the sense to recognize she was being ludicrous. So she got into the shower and let the warm water run onto her neck and shoulders while she breathed in and out slowly. Gradually she started to relax, and then she felt tired, so tired. She climbed into bed and drifted off to sleep, telling herself that Nicholas was in safe hands. He was with his father, and she knew she could trust Liam with his son, if nothing else.

And now lying here, she became aware that she couldn't hear anything, not a sound. She peered across at her bedside clock. It was almost eight, surely they were back by now. She sat up in bed. Her breasts felt full and a little tender. If Nicholas didn't need a feed, she certainly needed to feed him. She checked in his room first before walking out to the living room. And then she saw them both, curled up asleep on the floor. Nicholas was lying on his lambskin rug with a half circle of cushions around him. Why, Georgie didn't know, it wasn't as if he could fall off the floor. Liam was lying beside him, one arm protectively arched across his son. She crept over and picked up her camera off one of the bookshelves, and slowly got down on her knees, crawling closer to them. She positioned the camera, focused, and took the shot. Liam stirred as the flash went off. He rolled over onto his back, rubbing his eyes, staring up at the ceiling, probably wondering where on earth he was.

"Good morning," said Georgie.

He looked across at her. "Shh, he's sleeping," he whispered.

"It's okay," said Georgie. "He's going to have to wake up soon anyway, or else this dam's going to burst."

Liam frowned while he processed that piece of information. He levered himself up to sit, resting his back against the arm of one of the sofas. She saw him flinch as he flexed his shoulders in a circular motion.

"The floor's not exactly the most comfortable place to sleep," she remarked.

"It's okay, I'm just a little stiff."

"Why didn't you put Nicholas in his cot, or lie up on the lounge?"

Liam shrugged. "He grizzled whenever I went to put him down and I didn't want to wake you, so I brought him out here. I couldn't have slept on the lounge, I would have worried the whole time he'd roll off, or I would." He shuddered at the idea. "The floor was fine, it's only been an hour or so."

Georgie sighed. "Well, I appreciate you coming over; I shouldn't have summoned you like that."

"I'm glad you did. I told you to, anytime." He considered her for a moment. "You look like a new woman."

"I feel like one," she said, leaning back on one arm. "I had no idea it would be this hard. I mean, people tell you, but I don't think anything can prepare you for the relentlessness. There's just no time out." She paused to yawn. "It's the little things that are hardest. Like having a shower, or making a cup of tea, or even finishing one. I found three half-full cups of cold tea around the flat yesterday."

"How about I make you a cup now, so you get a chance to finish it?" said Liam, lifting himself up off the floor.

Georgie seemed to come out of a reverie. "No, I'll be right from here." She picked up the camera and got to her feet, replacing it on the shelf. "I've taken up enough of your time anyway."

"It's not a problem." Liam rubbed his forehead. Every time she started to relax around him, she'd suddenly snap out of it, like she'd been caught off guard.

"But you'll have to be getting to work, won't you?" she asked.

"Not on a Saturday, Georgie."

"Is it Saturday?"

He nodded, smiling faintly at her. "Let me make you a cup of tea. I was going to call you anyway this morning, there's something I need to talk to you about."

He didn't wait for an answer, he just walked around to the kitchen. She heard him run the tap for the kettle as she picked up Nicholas. When she held him against her he began to stir and Georgie carried him over to the sofa. She wondered uneasily what Liam wanted to talk about.

She was feeding Nicholas when he returned from the kitchen with a cup of tea and a glass of water. He set them both down on the end table closest to Georgie and took a seat on the sofa opposite. He looked a little uneasy as well, leaning forward, his elbows resting on his knees, clasping and unclasping his hands.

"What is it, Liam?" Georgie asked eventually.

"Well, yesterday," he began, before clearing his throat. "Last night it was actually, in the evening . . . anyway, Anna rang me, at home."

"Oh." Georgie paused. "How long is it since you heard from her?"

"Months and months," he replied. "Not since I told her you were pregnant."

"That's right, you said." She was wondering what this had to do with her.

Liam breathed out. "Anyway, she asked if you'd had the baby. She'd worked out that he must have been due, she was a little surprised to find out he was already nearly four weeks old."

"How did she take the news?"

"Okay, you know, there were a few awkward moments. But she congratulated me, asked after you . . ."

Georgie was waiting for the bombshell. She assumed one was coming by the way Liam was building this up so painstakingly.

"So, she said she needed to see me about one or two things. Apparently she's planning to take a trip overseas, she'll be away for a while." He paused, swallowing. "And, well, here's the thing, she asked if she could see the baby."

Georgie hadn't seen that coming.

"She said she knew it probably sounded odd, and she promised she wasn't going to do anything crazy, and it was only if you were completely comfortable with the idea." He paused, still waiting for some kind of response from Georgie. "She said she just wanted to see what he looked like, that it would give her . . . um . . . ?"

"Closure?" Georgie suggested.

"That's it, that's the word she used." Liam nodded, watching Georgie carefully. "How do you feel about it?"

"Look, it's fine with me," said Georgie. "I only hope it won't upset her too much. But I don't have a problem with it. Whatever she needs." She paused. "I think of her often, you know. I still feel bad about the way things turned out . . . so unfair," she murmured, gazing down at Nicholas. Then she looked directly at Liam. "So, when does she want to do this? She's welcome to come here if she wants."

Liam cringed slightly. "I don't know if that's such a good idea."

"Sorry, of course, she wants to see the baby, not me." Georgie grimaced. "She'd hardly want to see me. . . . I'm the villain of the piece."

"No, I assure you, Georgie, that's my part."

Dee Why Beach

Anna spotted Mac sitting on a bench near the playground, as arranged, a navy blue pram parked close beside him. Her stomach was churning, it had been all morning. She couldn't eat, she'd only managed a cup of tea. It had crossed her mind to call the meeting off, but she felt strongly that she had to do this. She couldn't even say why really. But Anna was done analyzing things. She wanted to follow her instincts for a change. And this was where they had led her, to a park bench overlooking the ocean, to meet her estranged husband and his infant son.

He looked up as she approached and got to his feet, turning to face her. "Hi, Anna," he said, his voice trying for warmth but being outdone by trepidation.

"Hello, Mac." Should she kiss him, shake his hand, what? Instead they both stood there awkwardly, neither wanting to overstep the bounds of what might be acceptable to the other. Though neither had a clue what that might be.

"You look well," said Anna. And he did, though she had expected him to look happier somehow. The proud new father, beaming at her. But perhaps he was playing it down for her sake.

"You do too, Anna." He hesitated. "Are you well?"

"I'm very well, thanks, Mac."

He was standing beside the bench, the pram behind him. Anna was glad of that. She needed a moment first.

"You said you're going away?" he asked.

"That's right. I'm leaving in a couple of weeks."

"Where are you off to?"

"First stop, London. After that I'll play it by ear."

He looked intrigued. "Well, good for you, Anna."

She reached into her handbag and drew out a buff-colored envelope. "I wanted to leave you some information I thought you may need."

He was frowning now.

"I know we settled the property, Mac. But when I was packing up this time, I found insurance policies in both our names, a bank account, a few other bits and pieces. The paperwork's all here, along with my solicitor's details. I've made arrangements with him, and he'll know how to contact me, so when you want to go ahead, you know, you can get in touch with him and he'll take it from there."

"I don't think I'm following you."

She took a breath. "Mac, one of us is going to have to file for divorce eventually. I suspect it'll be you. I wanted to assure you that whenever you're ready you'll be able to go ahead, even if I'm not in the country."

Mac looked a little dumbfounded. He didn't say anything.

Anna passed him the envelope. "Alright then?"

"Sure . . . thanks, Anna," he said, finding his voice again.

And now it was time.

"This is Nicholas, I presume?" she said, indicating the pram.

"Ah, yes." Mac stepped back and maneuvered the pram around in front of the bench, in front of Anna.

She stooped down to look at the baby, and caught her breath. He was so much like Mac. She stared at him . . . this is how her baby might have looked. The baby she had been unable to picture in her mind was lying in this pram, gazing up at her with the most familiar blue-grey eyes. She hadn't been able to picture him because he was never going to be hers. He was Mac's. And the woman called Georgie was his mother.

"He's beautiful, Mac," she said sincerely, glancing up at him.

"Do you . . . um, you can hold him if you want."

"No." That would be too much. But she reached in and stroked the skin on his cheek, unimaginably soft. He raised one tiny arm, and when Anna put her finger in the palm of his hand, he grasped it tightly. She thought her heart had stopped beating and for a moment she was frozen, crouched there beside the pram. She felt a wave rising in her chest. Was it grief? Despair? She didn't want it to be despair. She stood up again. Mac was watching her pensively. She should say something, but she didn't trust herself. And then he reached for her hand and held it between both of his. They didn't speak, but he could see the pain, regret and loss in her eyes, and she saw the sadness and remorse in his. And some remnant of affection.

"Anna," he said thickly. "I hope you know I wish you all the best."

"And I hope you know I want you to be happy, Mac." She glanced fleetingly down at the pram. "Don't ever forget how precious . . ." But the wave was cresting and she couldn't say any more. She pulled her hand away and turned around, walking briskly along the path without looking back.

Anna didn't know where she was headed. She was surprised she could even see the road in front of her through the tears that kept filling her eyes and streaming down her cheeks. She so didn't want this feeling to be despair. It was grief, natural and appropriate grief for the baby she had never had. Would never have. She was finally letting go. Letting it be. And she was feeling every bit of it. And she was driving. And then she was outside Vincent's house. Staring at the door. Feeling. Crossing the road. Walking to his door. Knocking. Open like a sore.

"Anna," Vincent exclaimed softly. She hadn't even noticed the door swing back. But now she saw his face, those intense green eyes staring down at her. "What is it, what's happened?"

She felt his hand on her elbow, gently drawing her inside. Anna collapsed against him, clinging to him as though he was saving her from drowning. She couldn't let go. She felt him push the door shut behind her and then his arms closed around her, holding her tight. She didn't realize till then that she was still crying, sobbing in fact. He stroked her hair, murmuring close to her ear to soothe her, gently rocking her in his arms. As her tears ebbed she gradually became aware of his body pressed against hers, the feel of it, the warmth of it, the ocean smell of him, remembering . . . Anna raised her head slowly, bringing one hand up to touch his cheek. She drew closer, brushing her lips against his, barely. She was scared, she couldn't handle it if he rejected her, though he had every right to. She lifted her eyes to meet his, and he was gazing down at her, breathing heavily. He held her face, wiping the tears from her cheeks, before running one thumb across her lips, parting them . . . and then he was kissing her, hard, ravenously. She wrapped her arms around his neck and he lifted her off the floor. They stumbled up the hallway in a kind of frenzied promenade, moving in circular sweeps, alternately pressing each other up against the wall, their mouths never separating while their hands pulled and tugged at sleeves and buttons and zippers, grasping at bare skin, caressing, clutching each other close. They almost fell through the door into his bedroom, and with a few steps Anna arched backward onto the bed, bringing Vincent with her. He was naked to the waist, his jeans open, sliding down his hips. She reached down and took hold of him, and he moaned. He propped his elbows on either side of her head, breathing hard as he looked down at her. "Anna . . ."

"Don't talk," she said, wrapping her legs around him and pushing her pelvis hard up against his.

"Fuck." He gasped.

"Yes." She breathed into his ear.

And then he lunged inside her and Anna cried out, pulling his mouth down onto hers again as they writhed around, thrusting wildly against each other. They didn't stop until they were both completely spent, gasping for breath. Vincent fell back on the bed beside her, panting heavily. Neither of them was able to speak.

After a while Anna felt his fingers lacing through hers as he lifted her hand to his lips. She turned to look at him, and he smiled, holding her hand against his chest.

"Hi," he said.

"Hi."

"I missed you."

Anna smiled. "I missed you too."

"How've you been?" he asked.

The wave rose up in her chest again, and she rolled over toward him, nuzzling close into his body and burying her face in his neck. She felt his arms tighten around her as he kissed the top of her head.

"Now you're really starting to freak me out, Anna. What's going on?"

She looked up at him, her eyes wet with tears. Vincent eased down the bed until he was level with her. "What is it?"

"I just saw Mac," she began in a small voice. "Mac and his new baby son."

He stroked her hair away from her face. "How did that happen?"

"I asked, I wanted to see the baby." She sniffed. "Put some ghosts to rest, I suppose. But when I saw him, he looked exactly like Mac, and it occurred to me my baby might have looked like that. . . ." Her voice failed.

Vincent pressed his lips firmly against her forehead, holding her close.

"I wasn't prepared . . . it was so intense. After I walked away, I couldn't stop crying."

"That's grief, isn't it?"

Anna looked wide-eyed at him. "Do you think so?"

"I do."

"I was so overwhelmed, and I thought, I don't want to be this sad, this heartbroken. I want to move on, not to feel like I'm missing something for the rest of my life."

"Isn't that exactly why you have to grieve?" said Vincent. "I thought that was pretty basic psychology."

She nodded faintly, shifting onto her back and staring up at the ceiling. "He really was such a dear little baby, Vincent, you wouldn't wish him away. And I don't begrudge Mac. How can I? I wanted to give him a baby for so long, it would be churlish to resent him for having one now."

Vincent leaned across her, kissing her soundly on the lips. "You are an amazing woman, Anna Gilchrist," he said.

"I don't know about that. I've got a long way to go yet . . . climbing down off that pedestal," she added quietly.

He crooked his elbow, resting his head on one hand. "Is that why you're here?"

Anna stared up at him. "Oh, Vincent, I shouldn't have come here like this," she said, struggling to sit up, pulling the sheet around herself.

"Hold on," he said, sitting up as well, "what's wrong now?"

"Vincent, I'm sorry, I didn't mean for you to think . . ."

"Think what?"

"You see, it's just . . . I'm going away," she explained.

He looked at her. "What do you mean?"

"I'm going away, overseas."

"For how long?"

"Indefinitely . . ."

A frown formed on his face as he took in what she was saying.

Anna watched him. "I shouldn't have come here, I'm sorry, Vincent. I didn't plan it, I didn't even know where I was going until I found myself walking across the street and knocking at your door." She paused. "I'm sorry—"

"Hey, stop that," he said, rousing. "You think I'm sorry that you're here?" He leaned toward her and kissed her gently on the lips.

Anna searched his eyes as he drew back. "Are you sure?"

"I'm sure."

She took a deep breath, bringing her knees up and hugging them. "I always felt safe here, Vincent. From the very first time. I don't know why." She looked at him. "That's why I had to leave. I was hiding out here. I'm sorry for the way I left, but I think it was what I needed to do."

He nodded slowly, leaning back against the headboard. "So what have you been doing with yourself?"

"I've been writing again, really writing, almost the entire time."

"Then you definitely did the right thing leaving. Are you going to let me read any of it?"

"I'd like that." She smiled. "But it doesn't have an ending yet. I can't finish it. That's why I'm going away."

He reached over and took hold of her hand. "You know, I could go with you."

"Come on, Vincent, you've been there, done that."

"So?"

"I never have. I want to live in my own skin for a while and see what it's like, see what I'm like," she tried to explain. "I've wasted so much time waiting for something to happen to make me complete." She paused. "Besides, I've decided I want a happy ending."

"You don't think we could have a happy ending?" He raised an eyebrow.

She shook her head. "You're young, Vincent, you haven't had children yet, and I can't give you any."

"Who says I want children?"

"Maybe you don't right now. But you might one day. And I don't want to be around when you realize you do."

"Anna—"

"Vincent, think about it. Can you absolutely say that one day you won't want kids, that it would never be an issue? And I don't blame you. But I can't commit to someone who hasn't thought that stuff through. It's a huge thing. I haven't come to terms with it yet myself."

He was watching her with that intense gaze of his. He pulled her closer, drawing her head onto his chest. "So when do you go?"

"Two weeks Saturday."

"Then we have two weeks."

November

Georgie heard a knock at the door. It was probably Liam. Nicholas had dropped off to sleep in her arms, so she eased herself to the edge of the seat and stood up, holding him steady. She walked slowly to the door and opened it. It was Liam.

"I'll just go and put him down," she whispered.

"Can I do it?"

"He's already asleep."

"Please?"

Georgie looked at him. He had an odd expression on his face, his eyes were almost begging. She sighed, carefully transferring Nicholas into his arms. Liam drifted across the living room toward the hall, never taking his eyes off his son. Georgie didn't know what this was all about. He'd phoned this morning, saying he needed to talk to her about something. He usually came over a couple of times on the weekend to see Nicholas anyway, take him for a walk, give her a break. But he'd sounded a bit strained on the phone, even a little grim. Whatever it was, she was obviously about to find out.

She walked out to the kitchen. The sun was white hot, streaming in through the window, reflecting off the sink so it shone like a spotlight. Georgie went out onto the balcony and she could feel it in the air. Summer had hit with a vengeance. Christmas would be here in a blink and Nicholas would be two months old by then. Time was galloping by, and Georgie was beginning to wish she could lasso it to slow it down.

"Georgie."

She turned around. Liam was standing watching her.

"Did he go down alright?" she asked.

He nodded. He looked strange, his face was drawn and if Georgie wasn't mistaken, his eyes were a little red, like he'd been . . . "Are you okay, Liam?"

"I have to talk to you. Can you come inside?"

"Sure." She stepped past him back into the flat. "Do you want to sit down?"

"Okay," he said. They sat opposite each other at the dining table. Liam leaned on his elbows, clenching his hands together. Georgie felt a little sick in the stomach. He looked . . . distraught, like something was very wrong.

He cleared his throat. "I promised you I would never lie to you again, that I'd always tell you the truth. So I'm going to be honest now."

Georgie's heart was beating fast.

"This isn't working out," he said plainly.

"Pardon?"

"This . . . this arrangement, or whatever you want to call it. It isn't working."

"I really don't know what you mean," said Georgie. "There is no arrangement, there's a relationship. You are Nicholas's father, it's as simple as that."

"It's very far from simple and you know it, Georgie. I can't be his father the way things are."

"What are you saying?"

"I hoped things would improve between us, Georgie, that when he was born, you might be able to . . ." He took a breath. "But I've come to accept that you really don't love me anymore, and not only that, it seems I make you unhappy." He paused. "The only thing I've ever wanted to do is make you happy, Georgie, and I just keep screwing it up."

She broke eye contact, looking away. "This is not about you and me, Liam—"

"I know you can separate it, Georgie, but I can't. I can't be around you, feeling the way I do, and pretend it doesn't bother me."

She swallowed. "So what are you suggesting?"

Liam took a deep breath. "I'm going away for a while—"

She looked up abruptly. "What?"

"I need to go away, just for a while."

Georgie got up from the table. "Well, this only proves what I've been saying all along."

"What's that?"

"That I can't trust you," she said, raising her arms. "That you'd as soon walk out on Nicholas as you did on your wife."

"I'm not walking out on Nicholas!" he insisted, standing up to face her. "I'm doing this so I can get over you and get on with fathering my son. I don't know any other way. By the time I get back, he should be more predictable. We'll be able to work out a schedule where I can take him for set periods of time, and you and I won't have to have so much to do with each other."

Georgie tried to ignore the cramping sensation in her chest. "Well, how nice for you," she taunted. "It's not as if I had any choice to go away and get over you. No, you left me holding the baby."

"I never left you! You turned me away," he reminded her. "And I have been there for you from the second you told me you were pregnant, Georgie."

She was breathing hard. "Well, fine, go off and find yourself, Liam, if that's what you think you have to do. But don't expect us to welcome you with open arms whenever you decide to come back."

"Georgie," he said firmly, "I'm going for a few months, that's all. I figure if I don't do it now, Nicholas will become too aware, he'll know me, and I couldn't leave him then. Right now he has barely any attachment to anyone but you."

"There's such a thing as bonding, Liam."

"I know, I'm missing out no matter what I do. But I don't think he will so much, if I do it now."

"How do you know that for sure?"

"I don't. But I'll only be away for a few months, it's a chance I have to take."

Georgie folded her arms, glaring at him. "Where are you going?"

"Melbourne first, then I'll see."

"When do you plan to leave?"

"My flight's at four."

"You're going today?" she exclaimed. "This is just great, Liam. You come round and dump this on me and leave the same day?"

"Why do you care, Georgie? You don't even want me around."

She hesitated. "I want you here for Nicholas."

"I will be here for Nicholas."

"When it suits you," she sniped.

"Just say the word, Georgie. Say you don't want me to leave and I won't go."

"Speaking for Nicholas, I'm sure—"

"I don't want you to speak for Nicholas," he interrupted. "I want you to tell me what you're feeling, that maybe you're still hurting, or you need time, whatever. But tell me there's some hope, Georgie. That'd be enough for me."

She felt flustered. "This is really unfair, Liam. I said from the start that this was not about us, that we would not be getting back together."

"And you don't think anything's changed?"

Georgie couldn't look at him.

Liam sighed, rubbing his forehead. "I am sorrier than I can put into words that I hurt you, that I lied, for what I did to Anna. But I'm not sorry I met you, I'm not sorry we had Nicholas. Have you ever thought about that, Georgie? That beautiful little boy wouldn't be here right now if we hadn't met. How can you still regret it?"

Georgie considered him calmly. "My mother used to say 'something good out of something bad.' Nicholas is something good, something wonderful, salvaged out of something that should never have happened, Liam. He doesn't make it right. Nothing can do that."

"So you'll never be able to forgive me, no matter what?"

"It's not about forgiving—"

"It's all about forgiving, Georgie."

She just stared at him.

"This is the hardest thing I've ever had to do, but I really think it's for the best," said Liam, his voice calm. "You're not happy anymore, Georgie, and you used to be so happy, so full of love—"

"Yeah, before you came into my life with your lies and—"

"Then you're better off without me," he said finally. "I'll keep you posted about where I am, and I'll send money."

"I don't need your money."

"Well, I'll be sending it anyway. And I'll always have my cell phone if you ever need to contact me."

"What good is that when you're a thousand kilometers away?"

"Then just say the word and I won't go."

Georgie crossed her arms and turned away to stare fixedly out the windows.

"Goodbye, Georgie." A moment later she heard the door open and close again. She turned around and he was gone.

Harbord

"Hey, where did you come from?" said Nick as Georgie charged through the front door carrying Nicholas in a baby sling. He peered out the window. "Did Liam drive you over?"

"No he didn't," Georgie exclaimed. "Liam's too busy pissing off."

"What?"

"He's leaving. Just like I said he would."

"Leaving, leaving where? What are you talking about?"

"Who's leaving?" asked Louise as she came through the back door carrying an empty laundry basket.

"Liam is going to Melbourne," said Georgie, striding over toward the kitchen. "I need a drink, it's so hot out there."

"Here, give him to me," said Nick. Georgie turned around, and Nick supported the baby while she undid the clips on the harness.

"How did you get here?" he asked.

"I walked."

"You walked the whole way?"

"In this heat?" Louise added.

"You should have called me to come get you." Nick had hold of Nicholas now and was proceeding to disengage him from his rigging. "How long did it take you?"

"I don't know." Georgie was at the sink, filling a glass. "I had to stop and feed Nicholas a couple of times along the way, he was so hot," she said, before gulping down the entire glass of water.

"So is he gone for good?" asked Louise.

Georgie turned around. "What?"

"Liam, has he gone to Melbourne for good?"

"He said only a few months, but who knows?" she said, refilling the glass.

"Is he going for work?" Nick asked.

"No, he's going to 'find himself,'" Georgie said, walking around the bench to the table where Nick had taken a seat, cradling his nephew on his lap.

"Liam doesn't seem the kind of bloke who would feel the need to do that."

"No, he's the kind of bloke who'll find any excuse."

Louise put the basket down, resting her hip against the table. "Georgie, you're talking but you're not saying a whole lot. Why is Liam going to Melbourne?"

She sighed loudly. "He reckons he needs some time to get over me." She rolled her eyes. "That he can't be a good father the way things are."

Louise nodded thoughtfully. "And he'll be back in a few months?"

"Apparently."

"I suppose it's the best time to do it," said Nick. "As long as he's back before Nicholas is about six months, it shouldn't matter too much. It's a shame, though."

"Poor man," Louise murmured in agreement.

"What are you two banging on about?" Georgie cried. "You can't seriously be on his side?"

"Who said anything about sides?" said Louise. "This isn't a contest, Georgie, it's just . . . an unworkable situation. He obviously loves you very much, but you can't overlook the past. And I respect that, I do. But I feel sorry for him as well."

"After everything he's done?" Georgie persisted.

Louise shrugged. "It is done, Georgie. He can't take it back, he and his wife have already split, and now you have Nicholas to think about. You have to move on and find a way to be parents together. If he needs to get over you to be able to do that, then I think that's fair enough."

"I don't get this." Georgie groaned.

"You're more compassionate than anyone I've ever known, Georgie,"

Nick said bluntly. "Don't you think it's time to show some to the father of your child?"

She just looked at him.

"This isn't like you," he added, his tone softening. "What's going on?"

Georgie could feel tears rising in her chest as she sank down into a chair. "It wasn't supposed to be like this." She sighed. "I used to dream about a white wedding, flowers, cars, the whole bit. And instead I got screwed by a married man up against the stationery cupboard and ended up pregnant."

"Thanks for loading me up with that image." Nick grimaced.

"You can still have a white wedding if it's so important to you," said Louise.

Georgie shook her head. "It's not that."

"Then what is it?"

She sniffed. "We'd never be able to tell our kids romantic stories about how we met, or celebrate the anniversary of our first date. Or even tell Nicholas how we came to have him. It's all been tainted."

"That's greeting-card crap, Georgie," said Nick. "None of that stuff matters in the end. Relationships survive because people are able to take the good with the bad and move on."

Georgie was thoughtful. "Liam said today it's all about forgiving," she said. "But how am I supposed to forgive him if I can't forget?"

"Because you're only focusing on whether you can live with what he did," said Nick, "when all you really have to decide is whether you can live without him. Whether you want to."

She looked perplexed. "You think it's that simple, that easy to forgive him?"

"Yeah, I do." He nodded. "Because everyone suffers if you don't, not just Liam, but Nicholas, and most of all, you. Can you honestly say you're happy right now?" He paused. "Think about it, wouldn't it have turned out a lot better for everyone if Mum had been able to forgive Dad?"

"You can't blame her for the way things turned out," Georgie declared. "What are you always telling me, Nick? 'Don't blame the victim'? It was Dad who had the affair. Everything was fine before that, we were happy, we had the perfect family and he destroyed it."

Nick glanced at Louise. She walked over and he handed Nicholas to her. "I'll take him out to see the girls," she said.

Georgie frowned, watching Louise walk out through the sliding door and close it behind her. They heard the squeals of Molly and Grace obviously prompted by the sight of the baby. Georgie turned and looked expectantly at Nick.

"Things were not perfect before Dad had the affair, Georgie, you had to know that. Mum was . . . she was not a well woman."

"What was wrong with her?"

He looked squarely at Georgie. "She had bipolar disorder."

"She did not, Nick. Where did you get that from?"

"She was diagnosed when you were only little. She was on medication, but she'd get slack with the meds and things would unravel. The manic phases were the worst, she used to do some crazy stuff. Surely you remember? It got so Dad couldn't leave her alone with us."

"She was just unconventional," Georgie said weakly. "Free-spirited . . ."

"Georgie, why do you think Annette came to work for us?"

"To keep house."

"She was there to keep an eye on Mum when Dad wasn't around."

"Why, because he was off having affairs?"

Nick sighed. "He worked long hours, Georgie. Mum had got them into some serious debt early on before she was diagnosed, and then work became a habit, or maybe respite. I think he really loved her, but it got too much for him in the end. Maybe the affair was a kind of respite too, I don't know. People have their reasons."

Georgie's head was hurting trying to take it all in. "Reasons or excuses, Nick? I mean, okay, Mum wasn't well, Liam's wife was infertile, so that gives them an out?"

"I'm not saying it's right, I'm just saying it happens," said Nick. "You've always had such a black-and-white view about it, Georgie. Dad was to blame for everything. But the lines are more blurred than that." He paused. "You even blamed Dad for the accident when Mum was the one driving."

"I know that. But she was distraught, it wasn't her fault."

Nick leaned forward across the table. "Remember the investigation? There were no skidmarks on the road, no evidence of mechanical failure or whatever else they look for, she just drove off the road and over the embankment. There were no witnesses either, so the police recorded it as an accident. They couldn't prove anything, she may have just fallen asleep at the wheel."

"Exactly. They couldn't prove anything," Georgie said shrilly. "Do you know what you're implying, Nick? That Mum killed herself and took Dad along with her? Come on, she may have been unwell, but—"

"She had attempted suicide before."

"What?"

"I don't know how many times. But I found her once."

"Oh, Nick . . ." Georgie's face went white.

"I came home at lunchtime one day when I was a senior. She was asleep on the lounge, I couldn't wake her. I rang Dad, he arrived the same time as the ambulance."

"I don't remember . . ."

"You were probably too young. I think neighbors looked after you and Zan that night. Mum was sick in bed for a few days afterward, but that wasn't unusual."

Georgie was staring across the table at him. "That's why you were so worried that time . . . after I found out Liam was married."

He nodded faintly. Georgie stood up in a daze and walked around the kitchen bench, gazing out the window at Nicholas. "What if I'm like her, Nick?"

"We would have known by now."

She turned to look at him.

Nick got up from the table and came over to lean against the bench. "I have kept a close eye on you, Sis. And on Zan, though she's a different kettle of fish, I never seriously worried about her. But you, at times . . ." He shook his head. "All the research says it would have manifested itself by now, Georgie. Losing Mum and Dad was probably your biggest test. I don't think you have anything to worry about."

Tears filled her eyes.

"Hey there, Georgie girl," he said gently, as he walked over and closed his arms around her.

"Do you really think she could have . . ."

"We'll never know. She might have been distracted, or had too much to drink, or they both did. I try not to dwell on it anymore."

"I remember being scared sometimes," Georgie murmured after a while, her head resting against his chest. "Not of Mum, she would never have hurt us. It was just scary when she was out of control. Dad was always so calm, I felt safe when he was around. But then he was hardly ever around. He should have been there for us, Nick."

"I know, I used to get angry with him too. I wanted him to stay home more and look after her, then maybe she would have been okay. But I suppose he was doing the best he could."

Georgie looked up at Nick. "After the accident, I was more scared than ever. I was terrified of what was going to happen to us." She paused. "I guess I blamed Dad for leaving us all alone."

Nick held her by the shoulders, looking squarely into her eyes. "It wasn't his fault. It wasn't her fault either. It was just a sad, tragic accident." He paused. "We weren't the perfect family, Georgie, I don't believe there is such a thing. Not even me and Louise are perfect."

"Please don't tell me some dark secret about you two, I couldn't take it right now."

Nick smiled. "Don't worry, we're fine, we're great. But it may surprise you to learn that I can be a real pain in the arse. And Louise isn't perfect either, but I wouldn't want her any other way. It's no big deal to love someone who's perfect, Georgie. The trick is to love someone despite the fact they're not."

Georgie swallowed back more tears. Nick was watching her closely.

"So, okay, Liam's not perfect, but sweetheart, much as I love you, neither are you. It seems that's good enough for him." He smiled. "What about you, what do you want?"

Georgie looked plaintively at Nick, biting her lip. "I don't want him to go."

"Then don't let him go."

"Can you drive me to the airport?"

"What time does his plane leave?"

"Um." Georgie frowned. "Four, I think he said."

Nick checked his watch. "It'll be tight, but let's give it a shot."

Sydney Airport

Anna was glad she'd been able to secure a window seat. It was a while since she'd been on a long-haul flight. They had stopped going abroad once she'd started treatment. Now she had a sense of anticipation, of excitement, she hadn't felt in years.

Vincent hadn't driven her to the airport. He'd wanted to but Anna wouldn't let him. She insisted she didn't want to do the big farewell scene, she wanted to think of him there in the house. So they made love in the morning, and he cooked her breakfast and they sat out on the deck overlooking the trees and the ocean. And when the taxi beeped out front, Anna hesitated, just for a moment. She told him she would never forget what he had done for her. He kissed her goodbye and made her promise to write. That was the whole idea, she reminded him.

She was among the first to board the plane, so she watched the other passengers filing in, settling themselves in for the long flight with books, personal CD players, laptop computers. Finally the seat beside her was taken by a man wearing a blue shirt and light trousers. Anna didn't get a good look at him—she had turned away discreetly once she realized he was about to sit next to her. She stared out the window as he sat down and made himself comfortable.

"Look at that sky," he said after a while.

Anna turned and smiled politely. He was a pleasant-looking man, around her own age.

"Take a good look," he said. "It's completely different on the other side of the world. The light, even the color."

She nodded slowly. "I'd forgotten about that."

"Not your first time overseas then?"

"No, but it's been a while."

He looked sheepish. "I want to assure you I'm not one of those people who'll talk your ear off the whole flight. But I'm also not one of those people who can sit next to someone for twenty-six hours and not even introduce myself."

Anna smiled. "That seems reasonable."

"Joe Lichaa," he said, offering his hand. "That's with two *a*'s."

"I beg your pardon?"

" 'Lichaa' has two *a*'s at the end. No one expects the second *a*."

"I guess they wouldn't." She shook his hand. "Well, Joe Lichaa with two *a*'s, I'm Anna, Anna Gilchrist."

"So, what does Anna Gilchrist do when she's not flying off across the world?"

She glanced out of the window again, to the wide blue expanse of a perfect sky, before turning back to look at him. "That's a good question."

Georgie dashed through the glass doors and came to a dead stop, overcome by the magnitude of the domestic terminal. She had no idea where to go. Last time she was here she'd just followed Liam around. And before that, well, it had been ages since she'd been on a plane. Nick had dropped her out front, he was going to park the car and bring Nicholas in. They both had their cell phones in case they lost each other. Georgie felt lost already. She spotted a bank of screens and rushed over, scanning through lines and columns of numbers and text. She had to filter out a lot of flotsam to get the information she needed, made worse by the fact she was in a rush, and still worse because it was all in twenty-four-hour time, which confused her at the best of times. There were no flights at 1600. Shit! There was one at 1545 and one again at 1615. She supposed Liam had had no reason to be absolutely precise when he'd mentioned the time of his flight. He couldn't have known she'd change her mind a couple of hours later and race out to the airport to try to stop him, like some kind of crazy person. Except Georgie didn't feel crazy. She felt like this was the sanest thing she'd done in a very long time.

But now she had to focus. One flight was leaving from Gate 34 and the other from Gate 32. Georgie went to run off until she realized that she didn't know which way to go to get to the frigging gates. She looked around frantically and saw the huge sign above the security checkpoint. ALL GATE LOUNGES. Thank you. She dashed over and pushed past the people, slowing down as she went through the metal detector so as not to arouse suspicion—the last thing she needed was airport security detaining her right now. Another sign above told her Gates 31 to 40 were straight ahead. She leaped down the escalators and skittered up the concourse, dodging people, luggage, trolleys.

"This is the last and final call for passengers traveling on Virgin flight DJ840 to Melbourne this afternoon. Please make your way to Gate 34 immediately."

Georgie saw Gate 32 on her left as she sped past, heading for the moving walkway. And then she sped right past Gate 34 as well. Bugger. She jumped off at the end and ran back to Gate 34. There were two men waiting to hand their boarding passes to the attendant, neither of them Liam. Georgie's heart was hammering behind her ribs as she rushed up to the counter.

"Excuse me, can you tell me if a Liam, um, William MacMullen is—"

"I'm sorry, we're not allowed to give out passenger information."

"Can't you just say yes or no?"

"I'm sorry." The young man looked genuinely regretful. Much good it did her.

"Then is it possible to get a message to someone who might be on board?" she said breathlessly.

"Might be?"

"Well, I don't know for sure, I only know he's flying to Melbourne at four but there are no actual flights right on four so I had to assume it would be the flight closest to four and . . ."

The attendant was regarding her curiously.

"So can I get a message on board?"

"Not usually, unless it's an emergency."

"This is an emergency!" she insisted.

"What kind of emergency?"

Georgie's mouth dropped open, but nothing came out.

The other attendant who had been collecting boarding passes came over behind the counter. "Fully boarded," she announced.

"Sorry," said the first attendant. "They'll be landing in Melbourne in less than an hour, you could phone ahead and have him paged when the flight lands."

Georgie didn't really take in anything he was saying. But she nodded, smiled lamely and walked away, stopping at the vast glass window to look at the plane still parked alongside Gate 34. Maybe Liam would glance out his window and see her there, maybe he would recognize her from this distance. Then at least he'd know she'd tried.

"Georgie?"

She swung around. Nick was walking toward her, holding Nicholas tummy down, lengthways along his forearm. Only men held babies like that. Liam often held Nicholas like that.

"No flight at four, eh?" he asked.

She shook her head sadly. "The three forty-five had already boarded. I don't know whether he's on it or not, they're not allowed to give out that information."

"So we'll wait for the quarter past. At least it hasn't started boarding yet. We can't miss him." Nicholas began to squirm and make a grunting noise. "Come on," said Nick, "let's find a seat, I think he might want feeding."

They walked back to the lounge at Gate 32 and found two seats together. Once Georgie had settled Nicholas on the breast, Nick stood up. He seemed restless.

"I'll just go have a look around," he said. Georgie gazed down at Nicholas and stroked his soft little head. She had a sinking feeling she'd missed his father already. And she couldn't help thinking it was fate. She'd had her chance this morning to stop him from leaving, and that's when she should have done it. She couldn't call him once he got to Melbourne. What would she say? She didn't want to tell him over the phone that she realized she loved him . . . it wasn't even that, she'd always loved him. She'd just been too afraid, too caught up with an idea of how things should have been instead of seeing things for how they were. Too afraid to follow the path to where it might lead her.

"Good afternoon, ladies and gentlemen, boys and girls, passengers traveling to Melbourne on Virgin flight DJ842 at four-fifteen this afternoon are advised this flight has now commenced boarding."

Nick wandered back, scanning the queue forming to board the plane. "Well, we can't miss him now. If he's getting on that plane, we'll see him."

Georgie nodded faintly. They both automatically stared up at the television screen. Cricket. Liam liked cricket. She wondered if they'd screen it on the plane.

The queue started to thin and people wandered up in dribs and drabs. A few who had been sitting in the lounge the whole time finally got to their feet and strolled calmly over to the attendant.

"Further boarding call for passengers flying to Melbourne this afternoon on Virgin flight DJ842 at four-fifteen, please make your way to Gate 32."

There was no one else joining the queue. There was no queue left to join. Georgie felt an uncomfortable cramping sensation in her chest. The same as when Liam had left this morning. And now she had to go through it all again.

"This is the final boarding call for passengers traveling to Melbourne on Virgin flight DJ842 at four fifteen. Your aircraft is fully boarded, please proceed immediately to Gate 32."

"They must be waiting on somebody," said Nick, standing up. He walked back to the concourse and looked toward the escalators. But Georgie knew it wouldn't be Liam. He'd never be late.

"Paging a Mr. Graeme Digby and a Mr. Les Byrne. Your aircraft is fully boarded awaiting immediate departure. Please proceed to Gate 32."

Georgie saw Nick's shoulders drop. He wandered back over to her. "Do you want to try Qantas?"

She shook her head sadly. "It's too late." The words stuck in her throat.

"It was a long shot, Georgie," said Nick. "But if he was on the first flight, he'll have touched down in Melbourne by the time we get home. You can call him then."

She shrugged. "I just wanted him to know that I tried to stop him."

"You can tell him when you talk to him."

"It won't be the same."

"I know."

She put Nicholas over her shoulder and stood up.

"Do you want me to take him?"

"No, I'm all right." Georgie held Nicholas close as they walked slowly back through the terminal. She'd never felt Liam's absence so strongly.

They drove back mostly in silence, with the radio down low. Georgie didn't feel like talking and Nick sensed it. After a while she looked over at Nicholas in the back. He was fast asleep, poor little man, being dragged from pillar to post all afternoon with barely a peep out of him.

"You know," said Nick, "I've been thinking lately."

Georgie turned around again. "That's dangerous."

He looked sideways at her. "I've been thinking we should have a proper Christmas this year."

She frowned. "What do you mean?"

"You know what I mean. Like regular people. The girls are getting older, and now we have Nicholas as well. I think we should stop mourning the past and start celebrating what we have together."

She thought about it. "Maybe you're right."

"I'll talk to Zan, see what she thinks."

They fell silent again until they crossed the Spit Bridge and headed up the hill on the other side.

"Do you want to come back to our place?"

Georgie shook her head. "I think I'd rather go home."

He glanced over at her. "Are you sure?"

"I'm sure."

Ten minutes later Nick turned onto Georgie's street and parked out front of her building. He jumped from the car to help her. Nicholas was sleeping, so rather than disturb him, he lifted the detachable seat out carefully and passed it to Georgie.

"Thanks, Nick," she said. "For everything." She picked up her backpack from the front seat and hooked it over her shoulder.

He considered her, frowning. "Do you want a hand? I'll walk you up."

"I'm fine, Nick," she insisted.

"Okay." He gave her a hug. "Bye, Georgie girl."

She watched him drive away and strolled slowly up to the entrance to her flat. The foyer was cool when she stepped inside out of the sun. She looked down at Nicholas, sleeping peacefully, cocooned in the soft liner of his car seat. He felt a lot heavier than last time she'd carried him like this. Or perhaps she was just tired. She trudged wearily up the carpeted stairs, relieved to get to the last flight. But as she looked up ahead, Georgie froze.

Liam was sitting on the floor of the landing with his back against the door to her flat, watching her. He didn't move. Georgie slowly stepped up once, and again, and once more, till their faces were at about the same level. She felt as if all the blood had drained down to her feet and she was barely breathing.

He was the first to speak. "I couldn't leave. I went to the airport and checked my luggage and waited in the lounge. But when they called my flight, I couldn't get on the plane." He was staring straight into her eyes, unblinking. "Anna told me once that I didn't cope well when I couldn't solve a problem, that I tended to walk away from it instead. Well, I can't walk away from you and Nicholas. I'll never be able to walk away."

Georgie climbed the last few steps and reached her hand out to him. Liam took hold of it, getting to his feet.

"That's good enough for me," she said.

Epilogue

"Georgie, you shouldn't be carrying that! Here, give it to me."

Margaret had been running the Tuesday morning book club for as long as they'd been hiring the room out, she was almost like a member of the staff. So Georgie relinquished the tray of tea and coffee to her.

"You don't have to fuss, really, I can manage."

"How long have you got to go?" said one of the other women.

"Four weeks," Georgie replied. "Though the doctor thinks I'll go early, like I did with Nicholas. Can't be soon enough as far as I'm concerned."

"So this'll be it for you?"

She shrugged. "I don't know, if it was up to my husband we'd have six."

That set off a sigh of "Aww" around the room.

Georgie glanced down at the coffee table. "Oh, you're reading *Perfect*?"

"Have you read it, Georgie?" Margaret asked.

"Yeah, I have actually," she murmured, picking it up.

"What did you think?"

"You know I'm not allowed to give an opinion, Louise gets mad at me."

"Come on, tell us. Do you know anything about the author?" said one of the women.

"Is it true she used to live around here somewhere, on the north side?" Margaret added.

"Do you think the story really is autobiographical?"

"We were all trying to guess the café where he met the woman he had the affair with."

"I reckon it's in Manly."

"I'm sure she would have changed specific details like that," said Georgie.

"Do you think?"

"Probably, I mean, she'd have to, wouldn't she?"

"Well, come on, tell us what you thought of the book," Margaret urged. "We won't say anything to Louise."

Georgie paused. "I think it's extraordinary. I mean, parts of the story were very sad, but ultimately it was uplifting. And I like that. I like to feel good about a book. I want to care about the characters, to like them, to feel like I know them . . . that they might even be someone in my family, or one of my friends. And I want to be sad when I'm finished, when there's no more left to read."

"Well, I loved the ending," one of the women piped up.

"Oh, yes," everyone crooned.

"Nothing worse than a miserable ending, makes you depressed for days."

"What I can't stand is those books that leave you up in the air and you don't know how it turned out for everyone."

There was a general murmur of agreement.

"What did you think of the ending, Georgie?"

She smiled. "It was wonderful. I thought the ending was perfect."